PANDORAX

THE SCREAMS OF dying men drowned out the wails of the horrors birthing into reality. The daemons were indiscriminate, caring not who they slaughtered and Mordian and Catachan died alongside Dark Angels, no pecking order being applied to the killing. Some turned upon each other, the lure of fresh souls not great enough to outweigh settling old scores or challenging those more favoured by their patrons.

Winged fiends flew overhead, engaging the Dark Talons that still flew air cover, macabre dogfights sporadically breaking out and filling the sky with bursts of explosions and low hanging vapour trails. Thunderhawks struggled to get airborne, their hulls caked with bloated and clawed horrors. Dark Angels armed with flamers bathed them in fire but they soon found themselves buried under a morass of the Neverborn, stripping away armour and tearing at the flesh beneath. Those Imperial Guardsmen not run mad by the sight of things that should not be walking among them, fought in vain, their lasrifles no match for iron-tough hide. Some had made it back to the shelter of the mine but they were merely delaying the inevitable. As soon as the daemons had massacred those who had stood and fought, their turn to die would come.

Their differences set aside for the sake of battle, Azrael and Draigo fought shoulder to shoulder, the *Titansword* and the *Sword of Secrets* rising and falling in concert, despatching daemons back to whence they came. The Supreme Grand Masters' armour was streaked with gore, and a heap of rapidly dissolving corpses lay in a ring around them.

WARHAMMER
40,000
SPACE MARINE BATTLES

WRATH OF IRON
Chris Wraight

LEGION OF THE DAMNED
Rob Sanders

THE GILDAR RIFT
Sarah Cawkwell

BATTLE OF THE FANG
Chris Wraight

THE PURGING OF KADILLUS
Gav Thorpe

HUNT FOR VOLDORIUS
Andy Hoare

• AUDIO DRAMAS •

MORTARION'S HEART
L J Goulding

MASTER OF THE HUNT
Josh Reynolds

VEIL OF DARKNESS
Nick Kyme

BLOOD IN THE MACHINE
Andy Smillie

THE ASCENSION OF BALTHASAR
C Z Dunn

THE STROMARK MASSACRE
C Z Dunn & Andy Smillie

BLOODSPIRE/DEATHWOLF
C Z Dunn & Andy Smillie

A WARHAMMER 40,000 NOVEL

PANDORAX

C Z DUNN

BLACK LIBRARY

Let's raise a glass to Pop Culture, just like it raised us.

A BLACK LIBRARY PUBLICATION

First published in Great Britain in 2013
This edition published in 2014 by
Black Library,
Games Workshop Ltd.,
Willow Road,
Nottingham, NG7 2WS, UK.

10 9 8 7 6 5 4 3 2 1

Cover illustration by Kai Lim of Imaginary Friends Studios.
Internal illustrations by Helge C. Balzer, Sam Lamont and John Michelbach.

© Games Workshop Limited 2014. All rights reserved.

Black Library, the Black Library logo, The Horus Heresy, The Horus Heresy logo, The
Horus Heresy eye device, Space Marine Battles, the Space Marine Battles logo, Warhammer
40,000, the Warhammer 40,000 logo, Games Workshop, the Games Workshop logo and
all associated brands, names, characters, illustrations and images from the Warhammer
40,000 universe are either ®, TM and/or © Games Workshop Ltd 2000-2014, variably
registered in the UK and other countries around the world.
All rights reserved.

A CIP record for this book is available from the British Library.

UK ISBN 13: 978 1 84970 767 1
US ISBN 13: 978 1 84970 756 5

No part of this publication may be reproduced, stored in a retrieval system, or transmitted
in any form or by any means, electronic, mechanical, photocopying, recording or
otherwise, without the prior permission of the publishers.

This is a work of fiction. All the characters and events portrayed in this book are fictional,
and any resemblance to real people or incidents is purely coincidental.

See Black Library on the internet at

blacklibrary.com

Find out more about Games Workshop and the world of Warhammer 40,000 at

games-workshop.com

Printed and bound by CPI Group (UK) Ltd, Croydon, CR0 4YY

It is the 41st millennium. For more than a hundred centuries the Emperor has sat immobile on the Golden Throne of Earth. He is the master of mankind by the will of the gods, and master of a million worlds by the might of his inexhaustible armies. He is a rotting carcass writhing invisibly with power from the Dark Age of Technology. He is the Carrion Lord of the Imperium for whom a thousand souls are sacrificed every day, so that he may never truly die.

Yet even in his deathless state, the Emperor continues his eternal vigilance. Mighty battlefleets cross the daemon-infested miasma of the warp, the only route between distant stars, their way lit by the Astronomican, the psychic manifestation of the Emperor's will. Vast armies give battle in His name on uncounted worlds. Greatest amongst his soldiers are the Adeptus Astartes, the Space Marines, bio-engineered super-warriors. Their comrades in arms are legion: the Astra Militarium and countless planetary defence forces, the ever-vigilant Inquisition and the tech-priests of the Adeptus Mechanicus to name only a few. But for all their multitudes, they are barely enough to hold off the ever-present threat from aliens, heretics, mutants — and worse.

To be a man in such times is to be one amongst untold billions. It is to live in the cruellest and most bloody regime imaginable. These are the tales of those times. Forget the power of technology and science, for so much has been forgotten, never to be re-learned. Forget the promise of progress and understanding, for in the grim dark future there is only war. There is no peace amongst the stars, only an eternity of carnage and slaughter, and the laughter of thirsting gods.

PRELUDE

WITH FELINE GRACE and the alertness of a hawk, Tzula Digriiz prowled through the benighted corridors of the museum. No light, save the wan orange glow of one of Fal'shia's moons seeping through a skylight, marked her way and no sound did her passing make. Step by silent step, she followed the route she had memorised on her sole previous visit to the museum, pausing only to check and recheck for motion sensors and noise detecting alarms she may have missed on her initial reconnaissance. She glided past priceless artefacts and irreplaceable masterpieces without stopping to give any a second look, her resolve focused solely on her mission. In a former life she would have stripped the place clean and come back for seconds once the dust had settled, but that life was nothing but a memory now, closed off to her ever since the day she'd finally been caught and pressed into the service of the Imperium of Mankind.

The corridor she was navigating terminated into a vast hall, the light filling the chamber with a lambent glow, not enough to see by but sufficient to denote the outlines of the exhibits and pieces. Manually adjusting the sensitivity of her night-vision goggles, she scanned her new environs for anything that could give away her presence but found nothing. Fortunately for Tzula, her erstwhile hosts practised a political system that preached fairness and equality in all things – the Greater Good, as the tau liked to call it – and as a result suffered very little in the way of crime within their society. So far she had yet to encounter any security measures she would have to evade and there were certainly no guards assigned to watch over the artworks and antiquities. She was even surprised when she turned up for her after hours visit and found the doors locked.

With a newfound surety that alarm bells were not about to ring nor was a cage about to descend from the ceiling and ensnare her, she headed for the far end of the main exhibition hall, though, ever cautious, she made certain to remain silent. It was sound practice like this that ensured she'd spent a profitable decade looting the finest riches all across Segmentum Pacificus and a good few years beyond that doing the same in the employ of her new master.

The works that lined the walls and plinths of the hall were worth the proverbial king's ransom and purloining a single one of them would set her up for a lifetime, several with all the juvenat treatments she would be able to afford, but even that was too small a price. The people she worked for were more than capable of tracking her wherever she chose to lie low and the ramifications of crossing them didn't bear thinking about. Her death would be the ultimate consequence, but the route they took her down to reach that destination would be long and gruelling. Besides, her new calling was not without benefits. Her master was teaching her all sorts of new skills and one day, when her apprenticeship was served, she would take his place.

One piece in particular caught her eye. She turned about and cautiously took a few steps towards it. It was a suit of power armour, Mark V judging by the shape of the helmet, in pristine condition with the exception of a small eye-sized hole in the breastplate where a shot from a fire warrior or gun drone had despatched its former owner. The combination of poor lighting and the green filter of the night-vision goggles meant that Tzula could not make out the colour of the livery, but the clenched fist outlined by a circle on the left pauldron suggested which Chapter was missing an irreplaceable relic. Under the mask of her bodyglove, she allowed herself the slightest smirk. No matter how enlightened or progressive a society may claim to be, give them the opportunity to brag about former victories or conquests and they won't hesitate to take it. You could not move in the Imperium for fear of stumbling over a statue or monument to some hero or other. There were entire worlds dedicated to the sole purpose of reminding the populace of dead saints and martyrs, and several alien races Tzula had encountered down the years sported trophies taken from fallen enemies on the field of battle. For all their claims of inclusivity and mutual assimilation, they had no qualms about displaying the product of their expansion for all to see.

Conscious that her master was tracking her progress through the bodyglove's sensors, she turned her attention back to the task at hand and cautiously completed her passage to the back of the hall. There, nestled between an exquisite eldar sculpture older than the tau race itself and a cylindrical device of unspecified origin that Tzula couldn't begin to guess the purpose of, sat the object she had broken into the museum to liberate: a knife. Not a fancy ceremonial dagger nor a weapon used to wage war, not even a duelling blade or the tool of some worthy figure's demise. Just a plain knife, its tarnished metal blade attached to a worn wooden handle by a tight binding of frayed leather cord.

Some Imperial scholars might have described it as 'prehistoric' but in the Imperium that term was a relative one at best. All that Tzula could be certain of was that the blade was very, very old. Perhaps this was why the tau had put it here in the museum, because they thought it a quaint example of a barbaric culture's roots? Had they the slightest understanding of the thing's true heritage and what it was capable of, it would have been under lock and key in their deepest, strongest vault being pored over by their finest minds until they ascertained how to use it, not merely left on a plinth in a museum on a world populated almost entirely by artists.

Carefully peeling off the tight-fitting glove on her right hand to reveal the dark skin underneath – experience had taught her that when performing a delicate task such as this, it was better to rely on the true sense of touch not dulled by the barrier of a second skin – she reached down and delicately grasped the hilt of the knife between her thumb and fingertips. Controlling her breathing, Tzula waited until it had slowed to the point where her lungs were barely moving and, on her next inhale, gently lifted the knife from the inconspicuous plinth upon which it rested.

The wail of alarms that followed was so loud that Tzula found it difficult to maintain her balance.

She spun on her heel, about to race back the way she had come when a wall of solid force sprang up mere centimetres in front of her. Turning back she found that she was enclosed on all four sides and above by coruscating energy, trapping her in a prison no more than two metres square. Already having a fair idea of the outcome, she threw the glove she'd removed at one of the walls and watched through her goggles as it disintegrated immediately upon contact. Through the translucent cell she saw security shutters glide into place, barring all exits from the main exhibit hall and when she looked skyward, saw the same happening to the glass in the ceiling. For the second time in her life, Tzula Digriiz, former cat burglar turned agent of the Ordo Malleus, was well and truly trapped.

'What in the name of the Throne have you gone and done this time, girl?' her master's voice crackled in her ear. 'We can hear those alarms from all the way over the other side of the city, and there are fire warrior teams converging on your position.' His displeasure dripped from every word and the very fact that he'd breached mission protocol to contact her on her vox-bead spoke volumes about how badly wrong the operation had gone.

'I just need a couple of minutes. The damn knife was on a pressure plate and it triggered an energy chamber. It looks similar to the ones the Imalthuti used on–'

'You don't have a couple of minutes. Those fire warrior teams are on the steps of the museum now.' The pause that followed was heavy with anticipation. 'Use it.'

The anxiety Tzula had been fighting hard to control fought its way to the surface. 'You know I can't do that. Even if it does work, how will you–'

'We'll find you. We have to. Now stop arguing and get out of there.'

The vox-link went dead in her ear. If the tau already knew that it was their human guests who were responsible for the break-in at the museum then her master and his cohort would have to make it off-world in a hurry. Just like she had to. She had never held a knife such as this – precious few throughout the history of mankind had – but she had been well-schooled in the theory of its application and, gripping it blade down in her fist, held it aloft as if she was making to stab thin air. Her forearm tensed as she waited for it to gain purchase but the knife sat there useless in her hands. With the noise of approaching tau growing ever louder, she lowered the blade. Closing her eyes, she raised it again, relaxing the muscles in her arm and letting the knife do the work instead. Within seconds she was rewarded and, as the first of the fire warriors reached the shuttered main entrance, the blade twitched as it came into contact with the edges of reality.

Tzula began to tear through it.

SHAS'UI BORK'AN KOP'LA, like all those of the tau race, was not one to believe in magic, superstition or the divine. When he tapped in the nine digit code to shut off the museum's security system and entered the main exhibit hall, he started to suspect that there was more to this universe than the surety of the Greater Good.

Pulse rifle raised, he ventured over to where he had expected to discover the gue'la woman trapped within the energy cage, but found only the charred remnants of what could have been a glove or gauntlet and a set of what he assumed to be eyewear. The other members of his team scanned the room for any sign of the intruder, butts of rifles rested firmly against their shoulders as the markerlights played across the walls and ceilings.

Kop'la signalled for one of them to deactivate the cage. The other fire warrior removed a small handheld pad from his belt and tapped a series of keys, causing the energy field to dissipate with a sharp hum. Kop'la retrieved the eyewear and, after removing his helmet, held them up to his eyes in the vain hope that they would reveal the alien's cloaked form. The goggles functioned similarly to his armour's night-vision system, but whereas the tau technology used complex algorithms to compensate for the lack of light and allowed the viewer to see as if they were in daylight, colours and all, the gue'la equivalent was crude but functional, delineating that shrouded by darkness solely in monochrome green. He moved his head in a circular motion, trying to take in the entirety of the chamber, but the only living souls he saw were the eleven other members of his la'rua.

He was about to discard the primitive device when something in the vicinity of where the energy cage had been caught his attention. There, suspended half a metre from the museum floor, was a glowing vertical slit of energy. As he watched, it faded away to nothing. When he stepped over to experimentally pass his hand through where he thought it had been, he caught the vaguest scent of something sulphuric on the air, but that too was gone as quickly as the glow. He broke his attention away and realised that every member of his la'rua was staring at him, this odd unhelmeted figure waving his hand through thin air while sniffing like a kroot hound.

'What are you staring at?' he barked to mask his embarrassment. 'The perimeter is secure so the gue'la thief is still in the building. Split into teams of two and do not report back in to me until you have found her.' He replaced his helmet and, pairing up with the fire warrior who had deactivated the energy cage, headed for the west wing of the museum to track down the interloper.

THE FIRE WARRIOR team scoured every square metre of the museum twice before Shas'ui Bork'an Kop'la called off the search for the gue'la female. With shame weighing heavy on his heart, he reported back to Aun Ki'lea that the woman had escaped. The ruler of Fal'shia was disappointed in Kop'la's failure to apprehend the woman, but the loss to the tau empire was insignificant. Rather than steal one of the priceless heirlooms of their fledgling race, the thief had only taken a small knife recovered from a Third Sphere colony, an artefact of no consequence at all, merely a curiosity that the artisans of Fal'shia had seen fit to display to show how little the gue'la had evolved in all their millennia rampaging across the universe.

Ki'lea's words brought him some solace, but Kop'la could not shake the feeling that somehow his inability to capture the woman had run counter to the Greater Good. That feeling would be augmented shortly after when an administrative error meant he was overlooked for the Trial by Fire and he and his la'rua were shipped off to Fi'rios to mop up the remnants of the ork forces the tau had wrestled the world from.

Though he and his fellow fire warriors fought well, the Be'gel worked their sheer weight of numbers to full advantage, slaying both tau and kroot alike at close quarters. Their fate sealed, Kop'la's la'rua fought a final, desperate stand atop a rocky outcrop on the arid world's desert plains, each of his brave fire warriors falling in turn until he was the last one left standing against a horde of the debased alien beasts. Firing wildly, he felled many of the orks but still they pressed on, clambering over their own corpses in their frenzied attempt to reach him. His weapon ran dry and, as he was about to start swinging his pulse rifle as an impromptu club, a blow to the side of his head cracked his helmet and smashed him to the hard ground.

As Kop'la felt the first greenskin blade pierce him close to the heart and looked up to see the brute making ready to deliver the killing blow, his final thought was: *where had the gue'la woman gone?*

228958.M41 / Undesignated Feral Ice-world, Segmentum Tempestus

INQUISITOR MIKHAIL DINALT had never been fond of the cold, hailing as he did from a scorched desert world, and as the heavy snow fell, he pulled his cloak tighter about his shoulders and ploughed on through the thick powder underfoot. Behind him, the six figures that made up his cohort followed in his wake, the three humans among them shivering in the sub-zero temperatures, the xenos and the two gun servitors seemingly oblivious to the adverse conditions.

'We'll freeze to death if we stay out here much longer,' said the tall, muscular male at the rear of the group. He wore several furs over his matching leather jacket and trousers, and snow had settled on the wide brim of his hat. The harsh lines and creases of his face were pale, frost had formed on the week's growth of stubble on his chin and his lips were rapidly turning an unhealthy shade of blue. 'I didn't spend all this time hunting for her just to end my days face down in the snow.'

Dinalt, as he had conditioned himself to do so over their many years together, tuned out the gunman's moaning and, ignoring him entirely, continued laboriously on. Dinvayo Chao might be one of the finest shots the inquisitor had ever encountered in almost two centuries of service to the Golden

Throne, but he was also one of the greatest whingers too. Dinalt had never seen Chao miss; either a shot with his twin bolt pistols or an opportunity to complain about the latest injustice being perpetrated upon him.

'All the intelligence points to this being the correct planet,' said the woman walking at Dinalt's shoulder. Her robe was the same deep crimson as that of her master and her voluminous blonde hair cascaded over it all the way down to her waist. 'According to my charts, the primary settlement is less than three kilometres away from where we put down. We should be there within the hour,' she added sternly.

Tryphena Brandd was a recent addition to Dinalt's band of operatives and though she and Chao clashed regularly, he often had to stay his tongue by dint of her rank of junior interrogator. He considered a retort but thought better of it, turning instead to the xenos. The short, hairy figure loping along beside him had picked up a heavy coating of snow, the white powder almost completely obscuring the orange-brown fur beneath.

'It's alright for you, K'Cee,' Chao said. 'You got your own fur coat. Chumps like me and Liall here,' he gestured to the slight figure of the astropath rigidly staggering along in front of them, 'we just got to fight back the cold with warm thoughts. Ain't that right, boy?'

The robed youth struggled on for several seconds longer muttering to himself under his breath before, by way of delayed reaction, he started as if shocked by the mention of his own name and stopped to face Chao and the jokaero.

'Stars burning brightly. The sun upon your cheeks. The balefire of eternal damnation,' Liall said in a monotone devoid of emotion. 'Thoughts. Warm thoughts,' he added before turning back and carrying on through the tundra, still muttering under his breath.

Most astropaths were eccentric in some way as a result of their soul-binding and contact with the immaterium, but Liall was something else altogether. Dinalt had once shared with Chao his belief that Liall's condition pre-dated his voyage on the Black Ship and was the likely root of his vast astropathic abilities. The boy had been able to send messages over large intergalactic distances without the aid of relay choirs and was far too talented to spend his servitude to the God Emperor stuck in an Administratum facility transmitting troop deployments or munitions shipping orders. His incorporation into Dinalt's retinue had not been without difficulties – a blind man who couldn't stand the touch of another human being the least of them – but his usefulness far outweighed the downsides.

Chao was about to say something else to the jokaero when from out of the whiteout he caught sight of a spear tip reflecting the planet's dim sun as it flew through the air.

'Down, down, down!' Chao yelled, drawing the pair of bolt pistols holstered at his hips. Dinalt and Brandd dropped to one knee, reaching for their own weapons while K'Cee bounded over on all fours to take up a position behind them. Liall simply threw himself forwards into the snow, burying himself into the wet powder and covering his head with both arms.

The first of the lumbering gun servitors reacted too slowly and the spear took it square in the forehead, sliding through its lobotomised brain before emerging through the back of its skull. For a few confused seconds it turned this way and that, synaptic signals failing to reach its twin heavy bolters, before crashing lifelessly to the ground. The other servitor manipulated the weapons slung at its side in place of arms, attempting to find a targeting solution through the white static but, just as it had succeeded in filtering out friendly forces from hostiles, another spear flashed through the air and struck it in the back of the head. It fell to its knees, confused at its plight before a third spear flew out of the blizzard and struck the servitor in the chest, killing it instantly.

'They've got us surrounded,' Dinalt said, pointing his plasma pistol at the vague outlines resolving through the falling snow. As if to acknowledge him, a dozen spear-carrying figures stepped forward, weapons pointed at the throats of the inquisitor and his companions.

'Want me to take them down, chief? We'll probably lose Liall and the monkey, but I'm pretty sure I can kill them all before they get you, me and blondie?'

The jokaero shot Chao a glance and narrowed his eyes. 'Nothing personal, little man,' he added.

The jokaero exhaled a sharp breath, flapping his ample lips. 'Stay your hand, Chao. If they'd wanted to kill us they would have done so by now,' the inquisitor ordered. 'Everybody put your weapons on the ground.' Dinalt allowed his plasma pistol to drop, its weight causing it to sink below the surface of the snow. Brandd and Chao did likewise. Liall lay there continuing to mutter to himself.

Their assailants, both men and women, were clad in thick, dirty furs. Long, unkempt hair stuck to their faces, wet from the blizzard. Totemic skulls of small animals hung from leather cords around the necks of some, while others wore larger skulls like shoulder pads adorning the animal hides. One particularly brutal looking savage, a mass of tight, corded muscle and matted black body hair, had what looked suspiciously like human skulls in place of where his kinsmen had animal remains.

It was this one who spoke, his deep guttural drawl sounding not dissimilar to the dark tongue of some cults Dinalt had previously encountered.

'Can you understand him, Brandd?'

'A little. All primitive human dialects seem to evolve along similar lines, at least during the formative stages. He asked us if we came from the sky.'

It had been little more than a year since Tryphena Brandd had become part of Dinalt's retinue, her former master having died in his attempt to wipe out an ancient Chaos cult, but in that time not only had her combat and investigative skills proved useful, but also her background in linguistics. A military orphan, Brandd had been placed in the care of the Schola Progenium while still an infant before finding herself inducted into the Order of the Fractured Cypher, a Dialogous branch of the Adepta Sororitas. Almost as soon as she had taken her final vows, she found herself part of an inquisitor's retinue, distinguishing herself to such a degree that even before she was out of her teens, her former master had taken her under his wing as an Inquisitorial apprentice. But her former master was dead, as would she be if she couldn't talk herself out of this situation.

Dropping her weapon, she slowly rose to her feet, the tips of half a dozen spears pointed at her throat as she did so. She cleared her throat and emitted a string of harsh, phlegmy syllables.

The dark-haired tribesman's eyes went wide as soon as she

had finished speaking and he issued several angry grunts, echoed by the others of his tribe. Spears jabbed forward threateningly, forcing Brandd to her knees again.

'What on Terra did you say to them to get them so enraged?' Dinalt asked, his piercing gaze locking with that of his junior interrogator.

'I told them to put down their weapons and surrender,' she said. 'We are agents of the Most Holy Ordos and our authority here is sacrosanct.'

Dinalt looked ready to castigate Brandd when Chao said, 'If you'll allow me.' He slowly got to his feet and raised both hands, palms out in supplication. 'What I think the lady was trying to say is, can you take us to whoever's running things around here?'

BRANDD'S ASSERTION THAT they were close to the primary settlement proved to be accurate and they were soon led through a massive stone archway that opened out into a snow-covered square, surrounded on all sides by buildings made from the same material as the gate. Braziers burned outside many of the structures and the smell of roasting meat and human waste hung on the thin, cold air. Their captors had treated the inquisitor and his cohort well, going so far as supplying the obviously ailing Liall with extra furs, but the spears remained constantly aimed at their hearts and throats.

They passed through the square towards a dominating structure at the far end, the town's inhabitants spilling from doorways to stare in awe at the captives. Most stood a respectful distance back, simply content to witness the coming of the strangers, but others prostrated themselves before them. One woman went so far as to run out into the street and try to place a necklace of rat skulls around Liall's neck, which led to a nervy few minutes of the youth shouting at the top of his lungs while Chao and Brandd attempted to calm him down.

As they got closer to the large building and visibility improved, Dinalt saw that it was far more ostentatious than he had first realised. The stone of its walls was smoother and of a better quality than the other dwellings, and crude statues of warriors lined the wide steps that led up to a set of well-crafted wood and steel doors. As they reached the foot of the steps, the high doors swung inwards and the tribesmen who had been keeping them prisoner gestured with their spears for them to ascend. All five of them did so, as did the dark-haired warrior who they assumed to be the leader, spear in one hand, an animal hide sack holding the prisoners' weapons in the other. A tribeswoman greeted them at the top and after a brief conversation with the armed warrior, he handed over the sack of weapons and received a jangling leather pouch in exchange. Without giving any of his former captives a second glance, he went back down the steps two at a time counting out his payment.

'Come. With me,' the woman said with an effort, as if her vocal cords were not used to making those sounds. Her furs were cut and arranged as if to form a dress and jewellery hung at her neck and earlobes.

'You speak Low Gothic?' Brandd ventured but all she got in response was a blank look followed by a sweep of the woman's arm urging them to move on.

Another set of doors opened at their approach to reveal a high-ceilinged throne room, the air greasy with the smoke from tallow candles set into recesses in the walls and a vast wooden chandelier overhead. The flickering light caught upon jewel-encrusted vases and goblets sat atop smoothly polished tables, and finely embroidered tapestries that covered immense sections of the wall. The other décor paled into insignificance when the five of them caught sight of the elaborate throne upon a raised marble dais upon which sat Tzula Digriiz, the near ebony of her skin in stark contrast to the alabaster flesh of the two handmaidens who attended her.

'I have to admit, Master Dinalt,' Tzula said, a playful smile forming on her lips, 'I was expecting you a little sooner.'

'Do you have the knife?' he responded, ignoring her quip.

'Two years I've been stuck here and all you–'

'Do you still have the knife?' he asked again, threat evident in his tone of voice.

Tzula sighed and parted the furs covering her midriff to reveal a crude wooden hilt. 'It hasn't left my side the entire time I've been here.'

'We have the knife, master. Now we should execute her for heresy and continue with our mission,' said Brandd, her face expressionless.

'We haven't even been introduced and already you're

22

threatening to kill me. I can see we're going to be the best of friends.' The playful grin disappeared from Tzula's lips. 'She's wearing the symbols of the Ordo, does that mean you've already replaced me, master?'

'Junior Interrogator Brandd was formerly under the tutelage of Inquisitor Morven until he died in the service of the Ordo. I had oathed to him to take Brandd as my charge and complete her training should anything happen to him, and he oathed likewise to watch over you should I fall in service to the God-Emperor.' Dinalt turned to give Brandd an admonishing look. 'And she won't be executing anybody for heresy. Not today at least.'

'But, master, she rules over these people like an empress. Even the throne she sits upon is golden. This sedition cannot go unpunished.' Brandd's cheeks started to flush with anger.

'I rule over these people because it was the best way to ensure the safety of the knife. When I fell from the sky – and believe me, this thing isn't accurate and I did, literally, fall from the sky – I could have tried to take on an entire world of spear-wielding savages or I could have taken the route of winning hearts and minds and make the aggressors my guardians and by default, guardians of the knife.' Tzula's smile returned. 'Seems the latter worked out pretty well not just for me but for you too. If I hadn't offered a vast reward for the safe capture of any other visitors from the sky then it would have been your corpses that Urk brought before me. Remember that, Brandd. You already owe me your life.'

The junior interrogator bristled and Tzula's smile broke into a grin.

'Chao, Liall, K'Cee. I didn't expect to see any of you again.'

K'Cee's lips pulled back and he gave a toothy grin that mirrored Tzula's. Liall stopped muttering under his breath at the mention of his name and gave Tzula a puzzled look with his dead eyes, as if he was trying to remember who the owner of the voice was.

Chao let out a booming laugh. 'Tzula Digriiz. You always did land on your feet.'

'Some of your luck must have rubbed off on me. How long have you been in the master's service now. Five? Six years?'

'Seven years and counting.'

'I,' she paused, weighing up the choice of her next words, 'I take it that the others are all dead?'

Chao nodded solemnly.

'Minerva?'

'She didn't make it off Fal'shia. Fire warrior took her head off with a pulse rifle from a hundred metres away,' Chao said.

'Berrick?'

'Taken down by the same cult that did for Inquisitor Morven. It happened during the operation to rescue the junior interrogator here.'

Tzula cast Brandd a dark look, adding another mark to her mental tally.

'Sivensen?'

'Went down fighting, but you wouldn't have expected anything less from him. Held off a pack of warp beasts while we made off with that damned book.'

'Book? What book?' Tzula said.

'There will be time to discuss all that later just as there will be time to honour those who laid down their lives in service to the blessed Ordo and the Golden Throne,' the inquisitor said. 'We have already tarried too long in our search for you, Tzula, and we must make with all haste for Pythos and pray that we are not too late.'

'Pythos? You've discovered its location?'

'The book has already given up many secrets and should give up many more on our journey. Now gather anything you need and be ready to head out for the shuttle as soon as day breaks.'

Tzula slid down from the throne and gracefully traversed the smooth stone floor to the door of her quarters. Opening it, she lingered on the threshold. 'Brandd?' she said.

The junior interrogator turned to face Tzula. Through the half-open door he could see an enormous bed covered in furs, fine jewellery suspended from ornately crafted wooden stands and other trappings of frippery.

'Yes,' Brandd replied.

'You were wrong about me.'

'Oh,' Brandd said, surprised. 'How was I wrong?'

'I'm not their empress.' Tzula's grin returned. 'I'm their *goddess*,' she added before entering her quarters and shutting the door behind her.

Brandd turned to Dinalt, her cheeks flushing an even deeper

shade of crimson. Before she could speak, Dinalt opened a channel on the vox-link on the forearm of his sleeve.

'Dinalt to *Terran Fury*. Are you receiving me, over?'

'Loud and clear, my lord,' replied a male voice.

'We have recovered our cargo and will be returning aboard imminently.'

'Very good, my lord. We shall prepare the landing bay.'

'And, captain?'

'Yes, lord.'

'As soon as the shuttle is clear of the planet's atmosphere, shower the surface with virus bombs.'

PART ONE

CHAPTER ONE

823959.M41 / The Deathglades. Twenty kilometres west of Atika, Pythos

THE BEAST OPENED its vast jaws, foul breath ripe with decay hitting the Catachan standing before it. Thick ropes of saliva descended from its top to bottom lip and the remnants of a previous meal nestled between teeth the size of a man's fist. The scaled saurian eyed the thick-set soldier before thrusting forward open-mouthed to feed. Its jaws clamped down on the proffered leaves and with a contented snort, the herbivore consumed its meal. The Catachan patted his mount on the head but before he could feed the other five arbosaurs that served as his squad's method of transport, the commander's voice diverted his attention.

'Leave them alone, Mack. If you feed them now they'll be sluggish for hours and I'd like to make it back to base before nightfall.' There was no malice in Piet Brigstone's voice, only the naked authority of a man used to commanding and being obeyed. 'And get over here. I want you to take a look at this.' Mack, discarding the armful of foliage he had collected, did as he was asked without question. The commander was knelt down examining a deep mark in the mud of the jungle floor while four slab-muscled figures in red bandanas looked on.

'What is it, chief?' Mack said coming over to join them. Though each man in the squad understood him perfectly, his syllables were clipped, making it sound as if he was speaking with his mouth covered.

'It's a track. First clear one we've been able to make out. Can you identify it?' The commander motioned with a finger, drawing along the entire half-metre length of the deep footprint. Mack scrunched his flattened features and scrutinised it intently. Few Catachans could claim intellect high enough to qualify them for a position within the Administratum or Departmento Munitorum, but Mack's development was notably arrested. Not that it mattered to Brigstone or the rest of the squad: what he lacked in one area he more than made up for in others. Not only was Mack a one-man heavy bolter team, but in the three years since they'd been stuck on Pythos he'd taught himself to identify the native fauna from just their spoor, droppings or bite pattern.

'Looks like a carovis, chief. Big one too,' Mack said after some deliberation.

'You sure?' Brigstone asked. Carovis were far from the biggest predators to roam Pythos but they usually stuck to the abundant hunting grounds deep into the Deathglades or out on the open plains of the Scorched Savannah. For one to come this close to a populated area was rare but if Mack was correct, this would be the third one in a week to get within twenty kilometres of Atika.

'Sure.'

Brigstone took him at his word. When the Catachan 183rd had found themselves stranded on Pythos en route to the Maelstrom, many had scoffed at Tank Commander Piet Brigstone's idea to retrain some of the men as beast riders. It didn't take long for them to come around to his way of thinking – almost thirty Chimeras and Sentinels lost beneath the swamps and rampaging carnivores accounting for several hundred souls will focus the mind like that – and it was at times like this that the patrols, or rather the native wildlife, were worth their weight in ration packs. Even if they didn't pacify the creature on their way back to Atika base, the perimeter guard could be doubled overnight and heavy weapons mounted in the sentry towers. The carovis wouldn't make it within two hundred metres of the city.

'C'mon. Let's get hunting!' said Kotcheff, one of the previously silent Catachans, enthusiastically. His sweat-soaked bandana was tied around his forehead and his moist, close-cropped scalp glistened in the late evening light. He was daubed from head to toe in mud, mirroring his fellow troopers, and his lasrifle hung at his side. Also mirroring the other squad members, one hand rested on the weapon's butt ready to swing it into action at the first sign of trouble.

'Alright, but let's not take any stupid risks. If it's steak for breakfast then let's all be around to enjoy it,' said Brigstone. Though the 183rd had enough rations and equipment to last for months and bulk freighters brought in fresh supplies every few weeks from nearby agri-worlds, unsurprisingly most of the Catachans preferred the taste of real meat. With no livestock able to survive on Pythos thanks to the predations of the numerous feral beasts that shared it with the ruby crystal miners and Imperium soldiery, the only time fresh meat was ever on the menu was when patrol bagged one of the creatures. If Brigstone and his men could make it back with a few slabs of carovis, none of them would have to pay for drinks for the next month.

Mounting up, the six Catachans headed back towards the planetary capital, the sun slowly sinking behind them.

LIKE MOST OF the surface of Pythos, the landward side of Atika was made up of swamps and marshes from which sprang vast thick-trunked trees, the canopies of which sat hundreds of metres above ground level, obscuring most of the planet's harsh sunlight. Despite the blessed respite from the biting heat, temperatures below the cloud cover could still reach the limits of human tolerance, and a blanket of warm steam hung ominously above the stinking black water.

Brigstone and his men were ever vigilant for the predatory fauna that could emerge from the fog at any moment and devour a man whole but the flora also posed a danger. Great tentacle-like creeper vines were a constant threat as were the bulbous pods that grew at the base of trees ready to explode in clouds of choking spores at the merest hint of movement. Even the swamp itself was deadly; if it wasn't the thick viscous mud attempting to suck the unwary to their doom, it was the chemical reaction between agents in the water and the air, turning the steam to acid and dissolving anything that came into contact with it.

As the Catachans slowly made their way back to Atika along one of the known solid paths through the swamp, that was what Brigstone was particularly alert for.

Each member of the squad had their assigned task on the patrol. Brigstone was keeping an eye out for signs of acid-steam: bark stripped from trees, bare patches of foliage. Cimino was on vine duty and every once in a while the 'rookie', as he was known to the rest of the squad for his not-quite five years of service, would be forced to loose off a shot to prevent one of the tendrils bringing down an arbosaur, much to the ire of the others who thought the shots were scaring off their quarry. Zens was on guard for any other threatening plantlife while Mack and Furie were detailed with looking out for carovis. Kotcheff brought up the rear, alert for signs of enemy activity.

Though this was ostensibly a peacetime operation, the 183rd simply waylaid and killing time until new transports could make it through the warp and relay them to their theatre of war, the words 'peace' and 'time' formed an oxymoron at the twilight of the 41st millennium. The enemies of the Emperor were all about and a moment's laxity could cost them dear. Many a Catachan rested in the dirt feeding worms after thinking that because the regiment wasn't at war, the war would pass them by. The commanding officer of the 183rd, Colonel 'Death' Strike, had survived for more than a decade in service to the Emperor from not thinking that way, and he drilled it into all of his commanders, who in turn instilled that same ethos in the men they led into battle.

A crash in the distance brought them all to attention.

At the head of their formation, Brigstone raised a hand and the other Catachans brought their beasts to a halt behind him. Those with lasrifles unslung them and raised them to their shoulders, barrels aimed into the jungle ready to shoot at the first thing to emerge from it. Mack checked the action of the heavy bolter pintle-mounted to the saddle of his arbosaur. Seconds passed before another crash, closer this time but still some distance off.

'It's coming from that direction,' Zens said in a stage-whisper, her half-ink, half-flesh arm pointing to the left of where they'd come to a halt. As one, six weapons all turned to point in the same direction. Through the swamp haze, the tops of plants swayed as something moved beneath them. Closer and closer it came.

'Hold your fire. Hold your fire…' Brigstone's order was barely audible over the oncoming noise. The shaking foliage was moving closer at speed.

Twenty metres. Fifteen metres. Ten metres.

'Now! Now! Open fire!' Brigstone's last three words were drowned out by a crescendo of gunshots. Concentrated fire poured into an area no more than a few metres wide, shredding anything unfortunate enough to come into the kill zone. As the barrage continued, several small saurians emerged from the undergrowth and darted straight past the mounted Catachans. Many of the tiny quadrupeds were wounded but a steady stream of them continued out of the jungle.

'Cease fire!' Brigstone signalled and after a few moments the message got through to the rest of his squad. They lowered their guns and looked on as the last few diminutive beasts scuttled through the legs of the arbosaurs and into the treeline behind them.

'Hatchlings,' said Cimino dismounting and moving to pick up one of the dead creatures.' They won't make much of a meal on their own but with the amount we've–'

'Wait. What were they running from?' Brigstone said, interrupting the trooper.

He didn't have to wait for an answer.

Heralded by a bellow of sheer pain, its approach masked by the noise of the hundreds of hatchlings fleeing in terror, the carovis loomed out of the swamp mist and decapitated Cimino with a brutal swipe of its massive claw. Before the unfortunate Catachan's head had hit the ground, the beast drove forwards, toppling Furie's arbosaur. The mount hit the floor with a thud, its neck snapping on impact, but Furie was thrown clear. He reached for the lasrifle that had landed in the mud beside him and swung the weapon to bear on the carovis. He squeezed the firing stud but nothing happened. Furie was about to try again when the sky above him went dark and an enormous foot, the same one that had made the print they found earlier, hovered above him poised to deliver a crushing blow.

Heavy bolter fire rang out followed by impact thuds. Furie recoiled as the carovis's foot exploded, showering him in blood and gore. The beast roared again and unsteadily turned to direct its attention on the source of its pain. Readjusting his firing angle, Mack rattled off a flurry of shots into the beast's chest, opening up rents in the thing's orange-scaled flesh and bringing it to its knees. It tried to cry out again but its scream was curtailed as Brigstone, Kotcheff and Zens concentrated their las-fire at the freshly opened wounds, internal organs cooking-off under the intense heat of their energy weapons.

Prone and helpless, the carovis's breathing was ragged but even at the edge of death, its claws were still capable of inflicting devastating damage. Manoeuvring around the beast in a wide sweep, Brigstone unsheathed the dulled blade of his combat knife and positioned its tip at the soft, fleshy area where the saurian's spine attached to its skull. The commander braced himself but, just as he was about to force the blade through muscle into brain matter, he noticed the look in the beast's eye. Where he had expected to see rage and primal fury, instead he found what could only be described as terror. Both hands on the hilt of the knife, he drove the weapon in with all of his considerable strength and the beast breathed its last.

Wary that the carovis might be one of a breeding pair or part of a larger pack, it was several minutes before any of the Catachans spoke or lowered their weapons. Once the sound of the hatchlings had trailed off into the distance, they set about tasks with a resolve as dark as their knife blades. Mack and Furie rounded up the spooked arbosaur mounts while Kotcheff and Zens set to work on the still-warm corpse of the carovis. Brigstone found Cimino's headless body and retrieved the dead man's night reaper blade. After several minutes searching, he also found his detached head and recovered the Guardsman's bandana. Tying the red strip of cloth around the hilt of the knife, Brigstone placed a foot firmly on the fallen soldier's body and with several firm movements of his leg, rolled the corpse into the undergrowth. What the jungle takes, the jungle keeps, such was the Catachan way.

'Chief. Come and take a look at this,' Zens called, standing over the dead carovis.

Brigstone slid Cimino's blade into his belt alongside his own weapon and joined the two Catachans over by the felled beast. 'What have you found?'

'Not sure. These are the wounds Mack inflicted,' Zens said

using her knife to indicate where chunks of flesh had been rent from the carovis's hide. 'And these are burns from our lasrifles. But this…' She pointed the tip of her weapon to a blackened patch of scales across the rump. Pus oozed from between cracks in the hide and the smell of decomposing flesh was amplified in the stifling jungle heat. 'I have no idea what caused this.'

Brigstone crouched down for a closer look, but the oppressive scent of decay caused the battle-hardened veteran to retch and cover his mouth and nose. 'Leave it.'

'But, chief, Cimino died bringing this thing down. It seems wrong to let it go to waste,' Kotcheff countered.

'And if we take it back and feed it to the regiment, it'll kill a lot more than just Cimino.' As if to reinforce the commander's point, maggots spilled from the necrotised area. 'Now come on. We still have a chance to make it back before nightfall.'

Mack, who by now had rounded up their arbosaur mounts, led the beasts over and the surviving Catachans mounted up and set off in the direction of Atika at pace.

Before they'd even made it out of sight, the jungle of Pythos was feasting on the corpses they had left behind.

823959.M41 / Atika Hive, Pythos

THE SUN WAS retreating behind the Olympax Mountains by the time Brigstone's squad made it back to Atika. The late-evening twilight bathed the Catachan base in a crimson aspect as thousands of jungle fighters checked weapons, sharpened blades and filled packs with rations and ammo. As they rode through the high metal gates under the watchful eyes of the sentries up in their watchtowers, a few of the Catachans stopped their activity and cast hopeful glances in their direction but, upon seeing that Brigstone and his squad were not dragging a saurian carcass behind them, carried on about their business.

Something struck Brigstone as being odd: it was almost dark and the base should have been getting ready for lockdown. Instead, it seemed the entire regiment were out of barracks and preparing to mobilise. A trooper he recognised bustled by and Brigstone hailed him.

'Goldrick. What's going on? Have we been given orders to ship out?'

The barrel-chested gunner stopped and looked up at Brigstone, elevated several metres off the ground in the saddle of his beast. 'No, sir,' Goldrick said, saluting briefly. 'A shuttle came in just before sundown. Small thing but armed to the teeth. Covered in aquilas too and some other symbols none of us recognise.' Both men looked skywards towards the spire of the hive city and the now occupied landing pad jutting awkwardly from its flank. 'A bunch of bigwigs in robes disembarked demanding to see the colonel. They've been in with him for the past few hours but Strike immediately ordered us to battle stations.'

'Robes? Were they Ecclesiarchy?' Brigstone had encountered the Ecclesiarchy before, back on Catachan when the missionaries had arrived to reinforce the will of the Emperor on what they saw as nothing more than savages. The people of Catachan were loyal servants of the Golden Throne but they did not take fondly to having any kind of will enforced upon them, and after the first few shiploads of missionaries found adapting to life on the death world difficult, Ecclesiarchy mission ships started bypassing Catachan altogether. Not all who hailed from the planet were such reluctant devotees and there were those in the 183rd – the colonel and many of his officers included – whose worship of the God-Emperor was heartfelt and unstinting.

'Don't think so. Two of them were women so I've heard, but not Battle Sisters. Rumour is there's more of them on the shuttle that haven't come out yet. Some of Batawski's squad are guarding it and swear blind they can hear people moving about in there.' The gunner looked around furtively, keen to be getting back on with his duties.

'On your way, Goldrick,' Brigstone said. 'But let me know if you hear anything else.'

The gunner scurried off in the direction of the hangars storing the regiment's tanks, leaving Brigstone and his squad to take their mounts back to the beast pens.

When they got there, somebody was waiting for the commander.

Brigstone dismounted and handed the reins of his arbosaur to Mack. The figure waiting by the entrance to the pens snapped off a quick salute which Brigstone returned.

'Commander Brigstone. The colonel has asked me to escort you to him the instant you got back in from patrol.'

Unlike Brigstone and his squad, the newcomer wore a sleeved khaki jacket with brass buttons fastened right up to the lapel over which rested an aquila symbol affixed to a chain. In place of a bandana was a red beret, a brass likeness of the Catachan regimental symbol pinned to it. His grizzled features were assuaged by the smoothness of his chin but the cuts to his cheeks suggested a man unused to shaving.

'Major Thorne. The colonel really must be receiving distinguished guests to get you dressed up in ceremonial togs. You look more like a Vostroyan than a death world veteran,' Brigstone smirked.

The older man shook his head and scowled before breaking out into a wide, toothy smile.

'You don't know the half of it, Piet,' he said, clasping the commander's hand and locking forearms together in a traditional tribal greeting. He glanced cautiously at the rest of Brigstone's squad. 'Can't say any more now. Strike will fill you in when we get up there.'

'I just need a few moments, Eckhardt.' Brigstone motioned to the extra blade tucked into his belt. Both men stopped smiling.

'Who was it this time?'

'Cimino. Carovis came out of nowhere and took his head clean off.'

Thorne nodded grimly and breathed a sigh of relief.

Back on their home world, the Catachan maintained strong tribal traditions and structures, and this carried over to the regiments drawn from the death world. Whereas the tribe would elect a headman, the regiment would elect its own captains, sergeants and other ranking officers and entire regiments could be drawn from relatively small geographical areas. The 183rd hailed almost entirely from a tiny archipelago chain in Catachan's southern hemisphere and as a result, many squads were made up of men related to each other. Cousin fought alongside cousin, brother alongside brother and quite often served under an uncle or, in exceptionally rare circumstances, a grandfather. None of the men in Brigstone's squad were blood relatives but Thorne's nephew fought under his command.

'How's he doing?' Thorne said motioning with his head in Mack's direction.

'You worry about him too much, Eckhardt. He's as strong as an ox and has the heart of one too. Show me a braver man in this regiment and I'll show you my arse.'

Thorne threw back his head and laughed, dislodging his unfamiliar beret and causing it to slip back over his bald pate.

'Go on,' he said, readjusting his headwear. 'Do what you need to do. I'll wait here for you.'

Brigstone nodded solemnly and headed for the clearing around the back of the beast pens. Hundreds of red bandanas fluttered in the warm breeze, each one tied to the hilt of a knife that had been thrust into the dry ground, constant reminders of those Catachans already claimed by Pythos. Carefully weaving his way between the memorials, Brigstone found a bare patch of earth and pulled Cimino's knife from where it had been sheathed at his belt. Kneeling, he stabbed down sharply and embedded the knife at a perfect vertical angle before returning to Thorne.

'Right, let's go and see what's got everybody so worked up,' Brigstone said, following the major to the base of the spire.

TO THE FEW souls in the Imperium who had ever heard their name uttered, the Inquisition were nothing more than a myth, a legend of a bygone era used by mothers and fathers as a bogeyman to scare wayward children or as a convincing lie by carousing drifters to work their way into another's bed. Many a child has gone to bed terrified that the Black Ships would come to claim them in the night, just as many a heart has been broken upon waking to find that the agent of the Ordos who had shared their bed and promised them so much had disappeared under the cover of darkness.

To others, those unfortunate few, the Inquisition were quite real and, as a force within the Imperium, highly destructive. Few who had dealings or even brief contact with the Ordos came away unscathed. At best, lives were left in tatters or people displaced once their usefulness to an agent of the Throne was at an end. At worst, it resulted in death, not only of individuals but of entire worlds, planetary systems and cultures.

Up until two hours ago, Colonel 'Death' Strike of the Catachan 183rd sat squarely in the camp of those who believed the Inquisition was a myth, the subject of conjecture and speculation by Imperial naval ratings with too much time and too big a drinks ration on their hands, or regimental lags who knew a trooper who once knew a trooper who was seconded by an Inquisitorial agent. In light of what was to follow, Strike would look back and wish that it had ever remained so, but for now his most pressing concern was that not one, but three of these 'myths', clad in identical crimson robes, stood in his command room and were making very real demands of him.

'It is a simple request, colonel,' said Inquisitor Mikhail Dinalt, idly pacing the room as if it were his own office, his crimson robes flowing behind him. 'I need to commandeer three of your Chimeras and their crews to take us deep into the jungles of Pythos and assist me and my team in the recovery of an…' He paused, considering what to say next. The two similarly robed women accompanying him looked on impassively. 'An object.' He let the word hang there euphemistically.

'My lord, with the greatest respect, that is a far from simple request.' Strike had faced down Catachan devils back on his home world and lived not only to tell the tale, but also to wear their teeth on a chain around his neck. Although he'd just become aware of their existence, he would not be cowed by the Inquisition.

Dinalt rose to his full height, a few centimetres taller than the taut figure of the colonel, and moved his face so close to Strike's that the Catachan could feel the inquisitor's breath upon his cheeks.

'If I so willed it, colonel, I could bring your entire regiment under my command and march every single one of them out into the jungle to find that which I seek,' said Dinalt. From under her cowl, Brandd smirked. Tzula, who had grown to despise the woman more with each passing day, cast her a disapproving glance.

Strike pulled his shoulders back and expanded his chest. What the colonel lacked in height over the inquisitor, he made up for in girth. 'And if that was your intention, you would have done it already.'

Dinalt arched an eyebrow.

'You work for an organisation so secret that until you showed up on my shuttle pad, I thought it was as real as a two-metre tall ratling, a commissar with a conscience, or a necron.'

Tzula looked as if she were about to say something then thought better of it.

'The last thing you want is ten thousand Catachans scouring the surface of Pythos for this "object" you're after,' Strike continued. 'Hell, there are men standing guard outside this command centre right now who have seen the three of you and still don't believe that the Inquisition is real, and I'm fairly confident that that's how you'd like things to stay.'

Dinalt was visibly impressed.

'I'm not being difficult over the Chimeras, I'm being prudent. I've been stuck here for three years and believe me when I tell you that all the good a personnel carrier is going to do you out in those swamps is make you a nice big coffin.'

'Why haven't you modified them for amphibious use?' Brandd scoffed. 'Surely that would have been the first thing you should have done when you became aware of your situation.'

Strike overrode his first, potentially suicidal, reaction before saying, 'That may be how you get things done in the Inquisition but the reality for the Imperial Guard is very different, my lady. Even if we did have the necessary parts to make those modifications, we don't have any tech-priests to carry them out. And if we had the means to ship them to a forge world we might as well head towards the Maelstrom, which is where we were going before we got waylaid here.'

'What happened to your tech-priests? A mechanised brigade should have had Mechanicus adepts assigned to it,' Tzula asked.

'They're dead,' Strike stated plainly.

'What, all of them?' Tzula responded.

'My lady, this is a death world on a par with Catachan and casualties among my own men have still been high. Those Imperial personnel without death world training didn't last very long. The Administratum clerks, tech-priests, even the commissars didn't make it to the end of our first year on Pythos.'

'An Imperial Guard regiment without commissars to instil discipline? Unheard of!' Brandd said incredulously.

'It's more common than you think, my lady,' Strike said, before adding quietly, 'especially with us.'

'I suppose that explains why their colonel is an insubordinate oaf,' Brandd said turning to Dinalt.

Strike had survived the barbs of a spiker; he wasn't about to be stung by one from the blonde inquisitor. 'Although our tanks have proven inoperable in the local environs, a detachment of my men have tamed some of the native saurians and are using them as mounts. Not as fast as Chimeras but adept at navigating the narrow paths through the Deathglades nonetheless.'

There was a loud rap on the door of the command centre.

'Enter,' Dinalt said before Strike could open his mouth. Thorne opened the door, saluted sharply, then stood to one side to allow Brigstone into the room. The commander entered and saluted the colonel, eyeing the three robed figures quizzically. Brigstone seemed entirely oblivious to his haggard appearance and poor personal hygiene after a day in the saddle.

Brandd gagged and put the back of her hand to her mouth and nose, eliciting a smirk from Strike. Thorne closed the door behind them.

'My lord, this is Commander Brigstone. He leads the detachment I was telling you about,' Strike said.

Brigstone was about to salute but upon hearing the word 'lord' was unsure whether he should bow instead. In the end he did nothing and simply stood there.

'This man can be trusted, yes?' Dinalt asked.

'*All* of my men can be trusted, lord,' Strike countered.

The inquisitor addressed Brigstone directly. 'These beasts you have tamed, do you have enough of them to carry the six of us?'

The tank commander was momentarily confused, but remembered what Goldrick had said about there being others still on board the shuttle.

'We have a few spare arbosaurs, my lord, but they are tricky beasts to ride, certainly for a novice,' he said to Dinalt's dismay before adding, 'They are quite large creatures, though, and it would be possible to double-saddle them and have your people ride with mine.'

Dinalt's mood, which had been sombre and business-like ever since he'd entered the command centre, lightened. 'Excellent. There's that Catachan adaptability I've heard so much about. How soon can you have the beasts ready, commander?'

'I'll make sure my men are ready for you at dawn's first light.'

Dinalt nodded his appreciation at the colonel.

'Lord inquisitor?' Strike said, causing Brigstone to grow pale at the realisation at who he had just been speaking to.

'Yes, colonel.'

'My men will do everything in their power to make sure you and your team make it back in one piece. Can I count on you to ensure the same for my men, lord?'

The inquisitor shared a look with the two women before answering. 'Naturally, colonel. I will treat your men as if they were my own.' With that he swept from the room, cape billowing behind him. The two women started to follow him out but Brandd stopped on the threshold and turned back to the colonel.

'Colonel "Death" Strike? I take it "Death" is an honorific and not your given name?' she asked.

'It is. One earned during my previous campaign against the insurgents of Burlion VIII.'

'Hmm. Amusing,' she scoffed.

'I don't understand. In what way is it amusing, my lady?'

'The native tongue of the Burlion System is a variant of an old Franbaric dialect if I'm not mistaken.'

'That's right. It's spoken on the dozen core worlds and several of the outlying moons.'

'Then your honorific does not mean what you think it means.'

Strike remained calm, unsure if the woman was trying to bait him again. 'No. What does it mean?'

'It's a portmanteau word. The "de" part means "from" or "of the", while "ath" means "dirt". Literally translated it means "from the dirt",' she said with a grin before following Dinalt out of the command centre.

Tzula followed close behind her but she too stopped and spoke to the colonel. 'I'd like to say she grows on you over time but she really doesn't.' The smile that followed was warm and genuine and she shared it with Brigstone too. 'The Ordo Malleus is grateful to you and your men for your cooperation, colonel,' she added before taking her leave.

'Piet. You and your men go and get your heads down but I want you all to report to me before first light so I can brief you before your mission,' said Strike.

'Understood, sir,' Brigstone said, saluting.

'And cut that crap out. It may impress the "Most Holy Ordo" but it does nothing for me.'

Brigstone smirked and moved his hand away from his head before nodding his farewell to Thorne and heading back down to the barracks.

'Would you like me to get the men to stand down from battle stations, sir?' the major asked once Brigstone had closed the door.

'Not yet, Thorne. Keep the regiment on full alert until I order otherwise.' Strike stared out of the viewport at the rear of the command centre to where the first of Pythos's moons was beginning to rise into the black night sky. 'They may claim that they're here on a mission of discovery but if only a fraction of the things I've heard about the Inquisition are true, trouble won't be far behind them.'

CHAPTER TWO

829959.M41 / The Deathglades. One hundred and seventeen kilometres south-east of Atika, Pythos

'I NEVER CLAIMED it would be easy to find,' Brandd said, pulling her robes tight to shield herself from the driving rain. On the saddle in front of her, Kotcheff drove the arbosaur on from beneath a waterproof poncho while the beast itself plodded on, seemingly oblivious to the torrential downpour.

Another arbosaur moved up alongside Kotcheff's, Brigstone deftly navigating the narrow walkways that threaded through the swamp but were now in danger of being washed away altogether. Seated behind him, the hooded figure of Dinalt replied. 'This jungle is vast. Even if we sought something the size of a city, we could spend a lifetime hunting for it and still find nothing. Are you certain your interpretation was correct?'

'My interpretation was flawless!' Brandd snapped. 'I'm certain my interpretation was flawless, Lord Dinalt,' she corrected in a more level tone, suddenly aware of whom she was addressing.

It had been a week since Dinalt, his cohort and the Catachans had set out from Atika and, despite their mounts, progress had been painfully slow. No more than a couple of hours would pass before some threat would be thrown up by the jungle and precious time would have to be spent dealing with it before they could move on. If it wasn't hungry saurians trying to make a meal of them, it was clouds of poisonous marsh gas or pit-trap glades barring their passage. The rain had been a new development, the skies opening after they'd broken camp that morning, but after hours of constant drenching, moods had darkened and tempers had begun to fray among the inquisitor's retinue. The Catachans, sheltered under their ponchos, seemed as unconcerned by the weather conditions as their mounts.

'If the auspex reads true, we should know if she's right in the next few hours,' Tzula said from the rear of the reptilian caravan. Unlike Brandd, Liall, Chao and Dinalt, Tzula was at the reins of her own arbosaur, her privileged upbringing on her home world meaning most of her formative years had been spent on the back of similar creatures.

It had been much to Brandd's chagrin that Tzula had taken to the beast like a natural and the blonde inquisitor's disgust at having to ride with Kotcheff was palpable. She'd barely said two words to the Catachan since they'd left Atika and the man wore a bandage around three broken fingers on his left hand. This was not as a result of the predations of the Deathglades but as a consequence of placing his hands a little too low below Brandd's waistline while helping her down from the arbosaur when they made camp on the first night.

'And besides,' Tzula said, taking her beast through the shallows of the swamp to draw alongside and then overtake Kotcheff and Brandd's mount. 'If we don't find anything we can always have her executed for incompetence.' K'Cee, his hairy arms wrapped tight around Tzula's waist, flashed a big toothy grin at the other acolyte as they passed her by. Brandd narrowed her eyes and scowled at the xenos.

'If we are going to find whatever it is you're looking for, it'll be tomorrow now,' Brigstone added. Despite a week spent in the saddle with Dinalt, Brigstone and his men still had absolutely no idea what the inquisitor sought, such was his level of secrecy. The Catachans could be trusted implicitly to get Dinalt and company through the jungle but that trust extended no further. 'Sun's going down, so we'll make camp at the next clearing we find with some degree of shelter.'

'Agreed,' Dinalt said. While Brigstone had full control of traversing the Deathglades, there was no doubt as to where command of the mission lay.

A sudden burst of heavy bolter fire from the head of the formation drew everybody to an abrupt halt.

'Creepers,' Mack yelled over his shoulder. 'Just creepers.' Behind him on the saddle, sodden robes clinging to his slight frame, Liall rocked back and forth, hands clamped firmly over his ears. Cautiously, the bulky Catachan placed his palm on the astropath's shoulder and gently shook him. To everybody's surprise, instead of freaking out Liall moved his hands away from his head.

'Has it gone? Did you get it?' Liall asked.

'I know your eyes don't work too good, Liall, but it wasn't no saurian. It was just creepers.'

'You got them though, didn't you? They're gone now?'

Mack smiled. 'I got them good.'

Though reluctant to share a saddle at first, in the days since they'd left Atika, Liall had formed a bond with the young Catachan to the point where they were almost inseparable. Conversation between the pair was sparse but they always sat together when it came time to open the ration packs and when it was Mack's turn to patrol the camp perimeter, Liall preferred to go out on patrol with him rather than sleep.

Zens's arbosaur drew alongside them. 'Sheesh, why don't you two get a tent,' said Chao, rainwater pouring off the brim of his hat and onto the back of Zens's poncho. 'I know I can't wait to make camp and get Zens here out of these wet things.' The female Catachan scoffed derisorily and tapped the arbosaur's flank with her heel, spurring the beast on.

'Come on,' Brigstone said. 'That clearing up ahead looks pretty well sheltered.' He urged his beast forward, followed by the others.

LESS THAN AN hour later, a half dozen tents stood pitched towards the edge of the modest clearing, rain spattering off their roofs causing puddles to form around the pegs and guy-ropes. With proximity alarms placed at regular intervals deep within the jungle, the Catachans sat around a small fire tucking into the roasted carcass of a small saurian they'd caught and playing cards, except for Furie who was on first patrol duty. Liall and Chao played with them, the blind astropath rubbing his thumb over each card dealt to him to identify the suit and rank. K'Cee watched their game in between stripping down and rebuilding Brigstone's lasrifle, and every once in a while would draw the ire of the assembled card players by shaking the rainwater from his fur with such vigour that he not only drenched them but almost extinguished the fire too.

Coming so close to the revelation that the Inquisition were not the mythical organisation they'd previously believed them to be, the Catachans' acceptance of the small xenos had been relatively straightforward and taken in stride. Aside from a few occasions where the owners of weapons had taken umbrage at K'Cee's 'borrowing' of them, the death worlders grew to tolerate him. Once they realised how effective his modifications were, they started treating him almost as if he was one of their own.

On the opposite side of the clearing, beneath the shelter of vast leaves high up in the jungle canopy, Dinalt, Tzula and Brandd huddled around a smaller fire studying the tome that had not left Brandd's side since the day she, Dinalt and nearly a full battalion of Cadians had battled across a daemon world to take possession of it. While Dinalt, Brandd, Chao, Liall and K'Cee escaped with both the book and their lives, the other half of their strike team and thousands of Imperial Guardsmen had not.

'I still have my doubts about your interpretation of the text, Brandd. If this is indeed the *Hellfire Tome*, then why does it tell us exactly where to find the stone? The written works of the Ruinous Powers usually come veiled in deceit and lies, not as point-by-point guides to finding unholy artefacts,' Tzula said, precipitation streaking down the sleeves of her bodyglove. Her robes hung suspended between two tree branches, drying in the warmth of the fire.

'It doesn't say "exactly" where the stone is, only where it is likely to manifest on any given occasion,' Brandd said, contemptuously. 'Based on previous appearances and using the formulae in the tome, I have a seventy-one per cent certainty that the Hellfire Stone is at those exact co-ordinates.' She pointed at the portable auspex unit strapped to Tzula's belt. 'Though for how long, I cannot be certain.'

'And you're happy to go along with this?' Tzula asked Dinalt.

'If there was only a one per cent chance of finding the stone, I still would have done everything I've done, and spent all those lives.' There was a solemnity to Dinalt's voice that neither woman had heard before. 'It will be another forty years before it manifests within the material realm again. We have the means to destroy it.' He motioned to the knife sheathed in Tzula's belt. 'If we now find ourselves with the opportunity then we must act.'

For the majority of Mikhail Dinalt's almost two centuries of service to the Golden Throne, he had been fixated with the Hellfire Stone, a debased artefact with rumoured power prodigious enough to open a portal directly to a point deep within the Eye of Terror. That its power remained only rumour was thanks in no small part to the vigilance and duty of Dinalt. As a junior interrogator, he and his then master, Thaddeus Lazarou, had infiltrated a cult bent on activating the stone and brought it down from within. Their mission was successful but Lazarou suffered grievous wounds. As the old inquisitor lay dying in his apprentice's arms, Dinalt was made to swear that he would devote his life to ridding the Imperium of the stone's threat.

Quickly rising to the rank of inquisitor, Dinalt dedicated himself to unearthing the secrets of the Hellfire Stone with a zeal befitting a far more seasoned agent of the Ordo Malleus. Where cults sprang up in veneration of the stone, Dinalt was there to put them down. Where Traitor Astartes warbands sought to harness the stone's power for themselves, Dinalt was there to counter them. And where scrolls, scriptures and tomes surfaced with even the merest mention of the Hellfire Stone, Dinalt was there to claim them.

His desire and single-mindedness paid off, and on its next manifestation on a backwater agri-world in the Segmentum Solar, he came within minutes of vanquishing it. With Chaos forces expending every effort to activate the stone, it was thanks to an eleventh hour interrogation of an Alpha Legion prisoner that Dinalt garnered the exact location of the stone's manifestation. Leading three entire Brotherhoods of Grey Knights and almost the entire Segmentum Solar Imperial battlefleet, Dinalt arrived in time to defeat the Archenemy fleets converging on the planet but was too late to destroy the Hellfire Stone, which frustratingly disappeared right before his eyes as he and the Grey Knights made planetfall.

The stone had eluded him that day, but his prisoner would provide yet more information beneficial to Dinalt's search.

He told the inquisitor of the *Hellfire Tome*, the means by which he could locate the stone, and he told him about the knife, the means by which he could destroy it. And, right before he died under interrogation, he told Dinalt where to start looking for it.

So many lives sacrificed for the pursuit of a single goal. Was it worth it? If Brandd had done her job properly they would soon find out.

'Lord Dinalt...' Tzula motioned over her shoulder, her movement exaggerated by her flickering firelight-shadow against the trees. Behind her, Brigstone and K'Cee approached, the Catachan examining his newly modified lasrifle. Brandd hastily put the book back into the leather satchel that constantly hung from her shoulder, while Tzula replaced her damp but warm robes.

'Pardon the interruption, lord and ladies, but if you want to eat I'd suggest you do so now. Inquisition or not, a Catachan's stomach respects no higher authority,' Brigstone said.

'My thanks, commander. I'll take mine in my tent,' Dinalt replied.

'As will I,' added Brandd heading briskly in the direction of her tent. Brigstone and K'Cee parted to allow her by, but as she passed them her thigh struck the xenos sending him sprawling backwards into the mud. Brandd carried on, either ignorant or inconsiderate of her action.

Brigstone offered K'Cee his hand and lifted the jokaero up onto his feet. Tzula puffed out her cheeks and pulled out her ears in imitation of Brandd's facial features, to which K'Cee smiled.

'Permission to speak freely, lady?' Brigstone asked.

'I wouldn't have it any other way, commander,' Tzula replied. K'Cee wandered off to the edge of the clearing where the rain was coming down more heavily and began to wash out the mud that now matted his fur.

'That woman has the manners of a grox. As mean as one too. If she pulled that crap back on Catachan she'd have gotten a boot right to her–'

Tzula never did find out to which part of Brandd's anatomy Brigstone would have applied his boot to, as at that moment two things happened simultaneously, both of which made the other redundant. The proximity alarms sounded and, felling trees as if they were matchsticks, the largest land creature on Pythos emerged from the jungle – a land dragon.

Abandoning their meal, the Catachans reached for their weapons, and within moments the clearing was lit up red from a sustained barrage. Tzula drew her plasma pistol and added her firepower to that of the Catachans as did Dinalt and Brandd, emerging from their tents with weapons blazing.

The land dragon roared as the shots hit its thick, leathery hide, more out of irritation than pain. Despite its mass and lack of legs, the thing moved quickly, leaving wide channels in its wake as it slithered across the muddy ground. Its gigantic head, the size of an ogryn, lashed forward and Mack pushed Liall out of the way before the snapping jaws could grab hold of him. The Catachan opened up with his heavy bolter and temporarily drove the land dragon back into the treeline, so ferocious was his assault.

'It's trying to get around the back of us!' Brigstone yelled, tracking the land dragon's movement through the treeline. 'Mack, same again when it re-emerges but concentrate your fire on its head. Everybody else do likewise.' Then he added, almost as an afterthought, 'Where's Furie?'

The question soon became moot. Springing forth from the trees, the land dragon opened its fanged maw and lunged for Brigstone. Blood smeared its enormous pointed teeth and bits of meat and scraps of camouflage clothing nestled in its rancid gums. The Catachan commander scrambled backwards, struggling for purchase in the mud, but somehow he avoided being clamped in the beast's jaws before finally toppling over backwards. The monster reared up ready to strike at Brigstone's prone form, but Mack opened up at the land dragon's head, supported by the combined plasma fire of Dinalt and Tzula. It slunk off back into the treeline, the smell of burning flesh trailing in its wake.

'Does it have any weak points?' Chao said, raising his voice to be heard above the din of battle and crash of falling trees. He was still sitting by the fireside chewing on a hunk of saurian meat.

'The base of the skull where it meets the spine,' Brigstone yelled back. 'Why? Do you feel like helping?' he added sarcastically.

Chao discarded the piece of meat and wiped his hands on

the front of his trousers. 'Sure, why not. But first,' he stood up and drew the bolt pistols from their holsters at each hip, 'let's even the odds a little.'

Charging back into the clearing, the land dragon kept its head down as it headed for the lone figure standing by the fire. With less than ten metres between Chao and the beast, he loosed off a shot from each pistol, both of which found their mark. The bulbous orbs of the land dragon's eyes exploded, showering those nearby in gore. For the first time its roar was one of pain. It thrashed wildly, narrowly avoiding crushing the panicked arbosaurs tethered to a tree, collapsing tents and extinguishing fires. The Catachans and Dinalt's retinue made for the trees.

Chao did likewise but rather than cowering behind a trunk like Liall, or using it as cover to fire from behind like everybody else, he holstered his pistols and began to climb. The sheer size of the trees caused a wide pattern to the bark, big enough for a man to place his hand or foot into, and Chao's progress upwards was rapid. Reaching the lowest set of branches – still some ten metres above the jungle floor – he clambered onto one and, hanging upside down, ventured out using both his hands and feet so that he was suspended over the clearing.

Predicting what he was attempting to do, the others took up positions so that the beast was completely surrounded and used their fire to force the blinded creature into position below Chao. With the beast directly beneath him, Chao let go of the branch and, spinning in mid-air, landed on the land dragon's neck. Ignoring the pain from where several of the barbs that ran along the beast's back had pierced his flesh, Chao hung on with one hand while drawing a bolt pistol with the other. Sensing that some parasite had attached itself, the land dragon thrashed and bucked erratically, trying to dislodge its unwanted passenger. Chao held firm to one of the barbs and, once the thrashing had abated, placed the muzzle of his weapon at the apex of the land dragon's spine and discharged three rounds into its brain. Instantly, the beast stilled, crashing to the floor of the clearing with a wet thud.

'Well, look at that,' Chao said, jumping down from the dead thing's back. He winced upon landing, obviously aggravating his numerous wounds. 'I just bagged the biggest living land predator on this whole dirtball.' The last part was aimed at Zens in a transparent attempt to impress her. She, along with the others, came out from the trees to examine Chao's trophy.

'Come back and see me when you've killed its mother or father,' she said to Chao as she turned away to see what she could salvage of the camp. 'This one was only a baby.'

830959.M41 / The Deathglades. One hundred and nineteen kilometres south-east of Atika, Pythos

THE HEAT OF the morning sun roared furnace-hot, turning the pooled rainwater into steam, which in turn formed a mist that reached right up to the jungle canopy overhead. Visibility was almost zero and so Tzula rode at the head of the pack with the other riders in tight formation behind her, the auspex guiding her where eyes could not. None of them spoke. Though they had been fortunate the land dragon had only caused one fatality, the Catachans were still smarting from the loss of one of their own. Brigstone's recovery of Furie's knife from the jungle had helped matters, but Brandd's subsequent petulance upon discovering that just two of the tents were salvageable and she would have to share was insensitive even by her standards. At one point during her outburst, Tzula was certain that if any of the Catachans had moved to strike Brandd, Dinalt wouldn't have done a thing about it.

'How much further?' Dinalt said quietly as Brigstone pulled their shared arbosaur alongside Tzula's. His whisper was more out of respect than at not wanting to be overheard.

'We should be right on top of it according to the auspex, but I think this moisture is playing havoc with our equipment,' Tzula said. Right on cue the screen of the handhold device flickered as it recalculated their position. 'If we split up we'd be able to cover more of the area.'

Dinalt looked to Brigstone.

'Splitting up's not a good idea, lady. With visibility this poor we'd be relying on our ears for signs of approaching predators and not all of them are as noisy as a land dragon,' Brigstone said. He looked up at the leaf cover high above. 'We can maybe think about splitting up in another couple of hours once this mist has burned off. Unless we've already found what you're looking for by then,' he added leadingly.

'Give it another hour, then we'll dismount and search the

area on foot,' Dinalt said ignoring both Brigstone's advice and his attempt to fish for information.

'Hey, boss?' Chao called out from somewhere in the humid fog. 'We got time for a quick stop?'

The inquisitor sighed and motioned for Brigstone to draw their mount to a halt. 'Don't be long,' Dinalt said. Behind him, Chao, and a couple of the Catachans taking advantage of the break, dismounted and headed into the trees, their feet splashing in the quagmire underfoot as they went.

Only a few seconds passed before the wet footsteps came back in the opposite direction.

'Boss,' said Chao, peeling out of the mist flanked by Zens and Kotcheff. 'I think we've found it.'

830959.M41 / Atika Hive, Pythos

COLONEL STRIKE WAS signing off on the latest batch of paperwork to cross his desk when Major Thorne entered the command centre. Instead of the formal attire he'd worn to greet the inquisitor and his retinue the previous week, Thorne now wore the more familiar olive drab vest and bright red bandana of a death world veteran. He approached the colonel without a salute.

'We've lost contact with Mauscolca Primus,' Thorne stated. 'No communications in or out for the past two days and a Valkyrie due to carry out a squad rotation is hours overdue back from there.'

'Sure it's not just the weather? Those storms last night could have knocked out comms and any Valkyrie pilot worth his stripes isn't going to try and land in that.' Strike got up from his desk and moved to the viewport, looking out over a blanket of grey mist that stretched all the way to the horizon.

'We're unable to reach Krensulca Hive either and the watch stations at Sepulture and Hollowfal haven't yet reported in this morning.'

'The storms–'

'I checked the meteorological reports and conditions were near-perfect at Sepulture and Hollowfal,' interrupted the major.

'Atmospherics? Solar activity is constantly affecting the vox-links.'

'Why is ours still operational?' Thorne gestured to the

vox-array at the opposite end of the command centre where three operators sat busily adjusting gauges and dials.

The gravity of what the major was implying was now apparent to Strike. 'You think this is deliberate? That they've been targeted?'

'Without the feeds from the long-range auspexes at Sepulture, we're blind to anything moving in-system and if Hollowfal has gone too then we have no comms with anything in orbit.' Thorne paused. 'Do you think it's greenskins, sir?' His words were tinged with excitement.

'Unlikely. If it was orks, they'd already be storming the base of the hive by now. Subterfuge and sabotage never was their thing. No, this is something different. I don't know what yet but I'll bet you a year's rations that it's got something to do with that inquisitor blowing through here.'

'What are your orders, colonel?'

Strike now addressed the personnel of the command centre, many of whom had already started listening in on his conversation with the major. 'Move the entire hive to combat readiness and have Valkyries ready to be in the air as soon as the mist lifts. Prep three dozen Leman Russes and station them around the base of the hive. Get the astropaths to raise Battlefleet Demeter and put them on standby.' Despite almost three years of inactivity, war was second nature to the colonel – as it was to all men and women of Catachan – and knowing what to do in a situation like this came as naturally as breathing to him.

'Anything else, sir?' Thorne asked, activity in the command centre already increasing.

'Pray,' he said simply. 'If this isn't the weather playing tricks on us then pray to the immortal God-Emperor for us all.'

830959.M41 / The Deathglades. One hundred and nineteen kilometres south-east of Atika, Pythos

LEAVING THE CATACHANS behind to guard the perimeter, Chao passed through the mist and out into the jungle clearing, Dinalt, Tzula and Brandd in lockstep behind him. One second they were enmeshed in the warm, clinging haze, the next visibility cleared as they stepped out into bright sunlight. Tzula looked around her at the wall of fog that terminated on the threshold of the treeline, as if the swamp vapour dare not encroach on this place, and directly up at the clear blue sky. Chao unfastened his holsters, wary of any unseen danger while Dinalt and Brandd fixated on the object in the centre of the tract.

Twice the length of the average human and half as wide, a flat, grey stone no more than half a metre in height lay rooted in the muddy ground. No weeds or vegetation grew around it and no moss coated its rough surface, but other than that, the thing looked entirely normal. If it weren't for the obviously unnatural condition of its surroundings, it could easily have been mistaken for a natural feature of the jungle floor. Brandd paced around the stone, studying it warily. Dinalt approached it slowly.

'This is it?' asked Tzula. 'I expected something, well, scarier. You know, all spikes and pustules, burning with the unholy green flame of the warp and screaming blasphemous litanies from a thousand fanged maws.'

Brandd scoffed. 'Not all tools of the Archenemy are so obvious. The works of the Dark Powers can take many forms.'

'Yes,' Dinalt replied, seemingly mesmerised. 'It's exactly how I remember it.' His gaze lingered on the stone for agonising moments before he snapped back to reality, suddenly aware of his surroundings again. 'Commander Brigstone,' he called.

'Yes, my lord?' came the reply from out of the mist.

'Tether the beasts and have your men stand ready. Liall. K'Cee. You will remain there.'

'You've found what you've been seeking, lord?' No reply was forthcoming. 'As you command,' Brigstone acknowledged.

'The knife, Tzula,' Dinalt ordered, taking his eyes off the rock for the first time since entering the clearing and turning to his apprentice.

'You don't want to study it first, master?' Tzula challenged, freeing the knife from its sheath.

'I have spent a lifetime studying the Hellfire Stone and in all that time I have learned one thing above all others – it must be destroyed at any cost. Tzula, give me the knife.'

Deftly gripping the tip of the blade between her thumb and forefinger, Tzula offered the small knife to her master, handle first. Dinalt reached out a hand to take it from her but a crash of falling trees from within the jungle distracted them both before he could take possession. Drawing their pistols, Chao and the three inquisitors stood back-to-back around the stone, peering out into the jungle for signs of the oncoming predator. Vague silhouettes of trunks tumbling to the ground were evident in the haze but, strangely, were not accompanied by the thudding footsteps of a saurian. The felling trees drew nearer.

'Over there. It's coming from that direction,' Dinalt said, aiming his plasma pistol towards the opposite end of the clearing from where they entered. From out of the mist a tree fell into the copse, its blackened dead trunk shattering as it made contact with the ground. Seconds later power armoured figures became apparent in the mist.

'Traitor Astartes!' Dinalt yelled swinging his pistol around to draw a bead on the largest of the armoured forms. Before he could squeeze the firing stud, there was a loud bang and an intense pain struck him between the shoulder blades, dropping him to his knees. Blood flowed freely from a fist-sized wound, and his breathing became ragged from where a round had passed straight through a lung.

Tzula turned, ready to shoot her master's assailant but found that Brandd had an autopistol aimed at her head. 'Give me an excuse.'

Rage boiled inside Tzula. 'I had you figured wrong, Brandd.'

'Really? How so?'

'I always thought you were just a bitch. Turns out you're a traitorous bitch,' Tzula spat.

More figures hove into view from out of the jungle, weapons aimed at Chao, Tzula and the kneeling, bleeding figure of Dinalt. At their head was a bloated figure in ill-fitting Terminator armour that struggled to contain his corpulent bulk. Necrosis had taken hold of his features, rotting flesh hung from his cheeks and his nose, bone and all, had rotted away completely. As he passed through the vegetation on the fringes of the clearing it shrivelled and died, leaving only desiccated husks in his wake. Flanking him were half a dozen equally pestilent figures each wearing standard power armour, albeit warped by the corruptions of the Plague God. Each one of them carried a bolter as ravaged as their armour.

'It seems your agent did not let us down, Morphidae,' the Terminator-armoured figure said. His voice had a thick, wet quality to it that sounded as if it was being spoken from the bottom of a swamp.

An ancient, wrinkled figure in ragged brown robes drew alongside him. Small even by human standards, the newcomer was dwarfed by the Traitor Marines he stood amongst. He carried a gnarled stick that came up to his shoulder but his movement was fluid and unhampered, suggesting that it was not to aid his walking. 'The Davinicus Lycae seldom fail our masters, Lord Corpulax.' In contrast to the Plague Marine, the old man's voice was like a dry wind blowing through a graveyard. He opened his mouth and directed a toothless smile at Brandd. 'Isn't that right, Tryphena?'

'Master, there are four Imperial Guardsmen along with an astropath and a jokaero in the jungle back there. None of them pose a threat but they should be dealt with nonetheless.' Brandd's haughtiness had amplified, emboldened by her treachery.

'Take care of it. Spare the astropath, he may be useful, but kill the rest,' said Corpulax ordering away two of the Plague Marines with a wave of an ungauntleted skeletal hand. They did as they were ordered and disappeared into the trees, swallowed up by the cloying mist. The hulking figure then turned his attention to the mortally wounded Dinalt. 'Do you know who I am, inquisitor?'

'Corp… Corpulax,' Dinalt ventured, blood flecking his lips with every syllable. 'You used to be… of the Consecrators Chapter but now you're nothing more… nothing more than an animated corpse. A shambling husk blindly carrying out the bidding of his… vile master.'

Corpulax smiled, baring his sharpened teeth. 'Very good, inquisitor. I'm pleased you know who I am, because I know who you are too, Mikhail Dinalt.'

Dinalt raised his head to look the Plague Marine directly in the face but said nothing.

'I know that you are a fool who has become overcome by his obsession to find this,' he pointed to the Hellfire Stone. 'A fool who is so blind that he would believe anything and anyone, any scrap of information that pertains to the stone. A fool who believed the dying words of an Alpha Legionnaire intentionally left behind for you to find and interrogate; who believed that an agent of the Davinicus Lycae was actually the protégé of another member of his Ordo whom he'd oathed to take under his wing upon her master's death; who believed that a simple, single book could unlock the unfathomable secrets and enigmas of an artefact blessed by the Four.'

With each new revelation, more of Dinalt's will ebbed away from him. 'No… You're lying. The *Hellfire Tome*–'

'The *Hellfire Tome* is nothing but a fake,' Brandd said, sliding the volume out of her satchel. Its spine was split from where it had been opened and read, and the artwork on the cover had faded to the point where all that could be made out was the faint remains of an illustration of a crude locomotion device and a human figure. 'Well, not so much a fake but a different book altogether and not a very good one at that.' She tossed the book to Corpulax who caught it in his skeletal hand. It instantly turned to dust which the Plague Marine allowed to be carried away on the light breeze.

'No. I've… I've studied it my entire life. The stone… It's a gateway for daemons. A bridge to a fixed point within… within the warp,' Dinalt said through sharp intakes of breath.

'You narrow-minded fool. Two hundred years of study and you haven't scratched the surface of what the Hellfire Stone is capable of, the raw power it possesses. It is all things to all men at all times. A portal into the warp is the least of its abilities. It is a prison for daemons and the means by which a man can ascend to daemonhood. It is a destroyer of worlds and a creator of life. It is a thing of such pure, unrefined beauty and an abominable horror. Right now it is a lock, one that my master would very much like opening.' Corpulax crouched down low so that his face was almost in line with Dinalt's. 'I'd wager that all those years of study never told you it could be used as a lock. Don't you still hunger for knowledge, inquisitor? Don't you want to know how to open the lock?'

Blood loss was taking its toll on Dinalt and he rocked from side to side, struggling to stay upright. 'How… how do you open it?'

Impossibly quickly, Corpulax drew a serrated blade from his belt with his non-skeletal hand and placed it at Dinalt's throat. 'A sacrifice, inquisitor. A blood sacrifice.' He drew the blade across Dinalt's neck with such force that he almost severed the head and allowed the corpse to drop sideways onto the stone, blood fountaining from the severed artery and coating the dull surface. Chao made to step forwards but decided against it when Corpulax's Plague Marine body-guards raised their bolters in his direction.

Tzula turned her head away, unwilling to witness her master's demise. 'You'll pay for this, Brandd. If it's the last thing I do, I'll watch you breathe your last,' she said through gritted teeth.

'You'd better hurry. By my estimate your lifespan can be measured in minutes at this point,' Brandd countered.

As the blood flowed into the grooves and runnels of the Hellfire Stone, it started to pulse and glow with an unnatural green ambience. Runes and characters from long dead blasphemous tongues formed upon its surface and a painful buzzing noise emanated from it. Just as the sound was about to become overwhelming, it ceased and the stone vanished. Tzula and Chao braced themselves for whatever horrors the unlocking was about to unleash, but it was all in vain as daemons did not suddenly materialise nor did hellfire rain down from the skies.

Corpulax chuckled wetly. 'The first seal is broken,' he said opening a vox-link. Relief was etched large upon Tzula's face – if there were more locks that needed opening there was still a chance to prevent Pythos's damnation.

Corpulax's next utterance rapidly turned that relief into abject terror.

'Inform Lord Abaddon he can begin landing his ground troops.'

JUST AS MACK could identify the native fauna by their spoor and footprints, three years out in the jungles of Pythos had taught Piet Brigstone to recognise the same by the noise they made as they moved through the trees. Carovis were slow, lumbering bipeds, noisy creatures that found it difficult to sneak up on prey, whereas land dragons slithered along the ground but gave their presence away by bringing down trees as they went. What both of these creatures, and indeed all Pythosian land predators, had in common was that if you stood stock still with your feet on the jungle floor, you could feel the vibration of their movement from kilometres away.

As Piet Brigstone stood stock still with his feet on the jungle floor in the mist outside the clearing he had been ordered to guard, he could hear trees coming down in the distance but felt no vibration underfoot. Zens, Mack and Kotcheff unslung their lasrifles in anticipation of dealing with yet another angry death world inhabitant but Brigstone raised his hand and shook his head. Something felt different, something felt wrong.

'Liall. You and K'Cee go wait with the arbosaurs but hide at the first sign of trouble,' he hissed quietly. 'The rest of you melt into the jungle.' Even if the mist hadn't been so low, the Catachans would still have instantly disappeared. One moment they were there, the next they were like phantoms in the green, malevolently haunting the jungle.

It did not take long for Brigstone's prudence to pay off.

Through the haze, two shapes resolved themselves, and though none of the Catachans had encountered this particular enemy previously, the *Imperial Infantryman's Primer* had taught them to recognise their outline: Chaos Space Marines.

Not wanting to call out and give away the element of surprise, and with visibility too poor for hand signals, Brigstone resorted to their old tribal hunting form of communication, bird calls. He made three squawks in imitation of the Catachan razorbill to signify 'knives only, target once the kill is certain' and received three identical responses by way of confirmation.

If the Traitor Marines were onto them, they weren't letting on. 'Split up. If you find them first, save some for me,' a voice rasped wetly from out of the mist, followed by the sound of an armoured figure moving further away. The speaker had given away his position and at that moment all four Catachan blades were poised ready to strike. Brigstone's opportunity came first.

A shadow in the mist formed only a few metres in front of him and, remembering what he'd been told by returning Catachan veterans who had faced this enemy before, he threw his knife aiming for the armour's weak spot. End over end, the Catachan fang flew until its tip made contact with the seal between helmet and body armour, sliding through the corroded material with relative ease. The figure made no sound as it fell to its knees, its voice now robbed of precious air, and as it flailed to remove the blade, a human shape detached itself from the mist and thrust another, identical blade into the Traitor Marine's throat. Gripping the hilts of both knives, Mack pulled them in opposite directions, opening the enemy's gullet and releasing a torrent of blood, pus and other vile substances. Forcing back the urge to gag, he tossed Brigstone's fang back to him and became one with the jungle again.

Confident that the other Plague Marine was not in close proximity and had not heard his comrade's murder, Brigstone addressed his squad in a whisper. 'We have to assume that the inquisitor and his team are either dead or captured.' He reached into the pack at his back and, after removing several items, set to work on the corpse of the Plague Marine. 'Here's what we're going to do...'

830959.M41 / Atika Hive, Pythos

'I WANT FRESH pit traps digging and the spikes coating with whatever noxious substances you can find. This planet's been trying to poison us for the past three years. It's about time we start using that to our advantage.' Colonel Strike shouted to be heard above the din of tanks being manoeuvred into position. Behind him, the vast edifice of Atika Hive thrust upwards high above the dwindling mist and into the clouds. Before him, the muddy plains that marked the approach to Pythos's capital buzzed with the activity of an army preparing for war.

'What about the rest of the armour, colonel?' Thorne asked, motioning for a squad of Catachans to carry out the colonel's order. 'We can position twice as many around the hive if we have to.'

'Keep the rest in reserve. Those Leman Russ are nothing more than fixed artillery platforms in these conditions and I won't risk losing any more than we have to.' His point was driven home by a tank to his right skidding into position before sinking into the quagmire halfway up its treads.

'Look. A meteorite!' called out a young recruit, breaking off from rolling out razor wire on the ground in front of the battle tanks.

'It's a shower,' said another, shielding his eyes from the fierce sun and looking skywards.

Strike gestured for a nearby officer to hand him a set of magnoculars. Without the aid of the eyeglasses, it did indeed look like one of the not infrequent meteor showers to hit the planet. With these, it was a very different story. Streaking through the sky leaving fiery contrails in their wake were drop pods. Thousands upon thousands of drop pods. Strike adjusted the zoom on the magnoculars to try and identify the markings and almost instantly regretted it. Every single one of them was daubed with a golden eight-pointed star inset with an eye motif.

'Sweet mercy...' Strike uttered.

'What is it?' Thorne asked.

Strike handed Thorne the magnoculars. 'I don't think you prayed hard enough, major.'

830959.M41 / The Deathglades. One hundred and nineteen kilometres south-east of Atika, Pythos

'PTHIRUS?' FROM BEHIND the grille of his helmet, the Plague Marine's words were garbled, and to Brigstone's ears it sounded as if he was saying 'virus'. The armoured traitor plodded on through the mire, his bulk causing him to sink further with every step forwards.

'Pthirus?' he said again, bolter swinging from side to side as he searched for his comrade. Covered by both mist and the trunks of trees, the Catachans drifted past him silently, towards their awaiting mounts and away from what was about to happen.

'Pthirus?' The Plague Marine's tone was now one of surprise, having found his former squadmate face down in the muddy jungle floor. Somewhere in the distance, a bird called. He knelt down and with a bloated, gauntleted hand rolled the corpse over.

It was only when he heard the multiple *clicks* of pins being pulled from grenades he realised what a terrible mistake he had made.

'I'LL TAKE THE knife now,' said Brandd.

Her autopistol was aimed at Tzula's head and the blonde acolyte held out her palm in expectation.

'Don't give it to her. Use it. Get away from here and–' Chao's words were abruptly cut off by the autopistol discharging. It took him a moment to realise that Tzula had not been the target and looked down to see a bloody hole where his stomach used to be, innards spilling out. 'I... I...' he said futilely, desperately trying to gather up the parts of his insides that had been displaced. He collapsed backwards into the mire. Brandd placed the still warm muzzle of her pistol to the side of Tzula's head.

'I'm dead either way.'

Tzula looked down at Chao, his eyes blinking wildly, still trying to stuff his guts back inside him.

'In fact, I'm not sure why I'm not dead already,' he said.

'The ritual,' Corpulax said. 'It is… inexact. I wasn't sure how much blood would be required and so you were useful. That usefulness is now at an end, but if you cooperate I will grant you and your friend here a swift death. Choose to be difficult and the pain he is currently experiencing will be a mere fraction of that I will inflict upon you.'

Tzula looked again to Chao. Stomach wounds were the worst. It could take a person hours to bleed out, every moment in pure agony. 'How do I know you'll keep your word?'

'Because you can watch me blow his head off right before I do the same to you,' Brandd said with a grin. 'I won't ask again. The knife.'

Hesitantly, Tzula reached down to her waist and gripped the handle of the knife. She slowly slid it out of her belt and briefly considered using it as a weapon. Remembering the gun at her head, she placed it into Brandd's still open palm. The blonde woman regarded the blade with obvious delight.

'I'll take that,' rasped Morphidae. He moved closer to Brandd, the hem of his already filthy robes dragging in the morass beneath his feet, and stretched out a withered hand. Brandd did nothing for a moment and the old man narrowed his eyes in displeasure. Eventually, reluctantly, she passed him the knife. He gave a low moan, relief tinged with ecstasy and he looked upon the weapon greedily before placing it in the folds of his robe. 'My eternal gratitude, Lord Corpulax. For nigh on ten millennia, the Davinicus Lycae have sought to recover that which was once ours and now, thanks in no small part to you, it is–'

A huge explosion from the jungle behind interrupted the cult leader followed shortly after by the ruined form of a Plague Marine hurtling into the centre of the clearing from out of the trees. Two of Corpulax's bodyguard moved out of its path but another was not quick enough and caught the corpse of his dead comrade squarely in the chest, knocking him backwards and pinning him down.

Brandd's Inquisition training subconsciously took over and she took the gun away from Tzula's head to track the projectile.

It was the opening Tzula needed.

Dropping to her knees, she stuck out a leg and swept Brandd's feet out from beneath her. The blonde woman dropped like a dead weight, her pistol discharging harmlessly into the air. At the same instant, from the same direction the Plague Marine's body had blasted out of the jungle, five saurians emerged, riders on the backs of all but one. Whooping and hollering, the Catachans atop them discharged their weapons, the element of surprise accounting quickly for two more of the Plague Marines.

'Tzula! Jump on that one,' Brigstone yelled, indicating the riderless arbosaur. Tzula rose to her feet and unceremoniously barged Morphidae to the ground with her shoulder. The arbosaur was still some distance away and she sprinted across the clearing, avoiding both enemy and friendly fire. Mack, with Liall seated behind him, laid down covering fire and her route to the beast was unimpeded, the heavy bolter sending Plague Marines diving for cover. As her mount tried to dart past her, Tzula gripped the reins hard and brought the arbosaur to heel. She had just got one foot in a stirrup when she heard a female voice from behind her.

'So close, Tzula. So close,' Brandd said. She was no more than ten metres away from her target and her autopistol was levelled at Tzula. 'I'm really going to enjoy this.'

Before she could squeeze the firing stud, a single bolt pistol shot rang out, catching Brandd's shoulder with a glancing hit and forcing her to drop the weapon.

'Go... go now,' Chao said weakly from where he was still slowly bleeding out, smoking bolt pistol in hand.

Tzula looked upon her friend for one last time and smiled sadly before throwing her other leg over the arbosaur and snapping the reins. Seeing that Tzula was safely mounted, the Catachans ceased firing and charged for the edge of the clearing and the comparative safety of the misted jungle. Brigstone and K'Cee were first to disappear into the haze, quickly followed by Kotcheff, then Mack and Liall. Zens wasn't so fortunate, her route out of the clearing taking her through a Plague Marine's line of fire. A short burst of bolter fire shredded her torso and dropped her corpse from the back of the arbosaur.

Ducking low to avoid the shots whizzing overhead, Tzula took a look back over her shoulder. Striding across the clearing, recovered pistol in hand, Brandd made her way over to the prone form of Chao. The last thing she saw before the fog enveloped her was the blonde traitor delivering one clean shot to the gunslinger's head.

With pained relief, she snapped the reins again and rode hard for Atika.

Corpulax was not quick to anger but, as he stood in the centre of the clearing looking around at the carnage wrought upon his bodyguard by a handful of mere Imperial Guardsmen, he could understand why some saw the attraction of following the Blood God. Four Plague Marines lay dead, another two needed the ministrations of a chirurgeon and the double-agent was bleeding from a shoulder wound. He thought about turning his ire upon her but, upon seeing the old man rising out of the mud with the help of his staff, knew that it would have more effect to channel his displeasure at the organ grinder rather than the monkey.

'This was supposed to have been simple, old man. Instead, four of the blessed are lost to us and one of Dinalt's acolytes has escaped. Lord Abaddon will flay your soul for this,' Corpulax said, his voice bubbling with rage.

Morphidae cleared his throat uneasily. 'The mission was a partial success. We have broken the first of the seven seals and soon the Damnation Cache will be opened. And besides,' he reached into the folds of his robe, 'after nearly ten millennia the Davinicus Lycae have reclaimed the athame… The Emerald Cave will be opened and its prisoner set…' His voice tailed off as he frantically patted his garb seeking the elusive blade. 'The knife. It was here. I had it only a moment ago!'

Brandd turned away, shaking her head in disbelief and disgust.

Corpulax advanced on the old man. 'There is one thing you must remember while in the service of Abaddon the Despoiler.' The towering Plague Marine placed his skeletal hand scant centimetres from Morphidae's head. 'You only ever fail him once,' he finished allowing the tips of his fingers to touch the old man's scalp, instantly turning him to dust.

Meanwhile, already over a kilometre away and heading back towards the planetary capital at speed, former thief turned Inquisition agent, Tzula Digriiz, checked her belt to make sure that the blade was still safely stowed there.

CHAPTER THREE

AS THE SUN broke over the horizon on the second day of the conquest of Pythos, Atika burned.

Battered by artillery and the twisted engines of war landed on the surface by the enemy, the spire blazed, a beacon in the half-light of dawn to guide the invaders. For a day and a half, Strike and the 183rd Catachan regiment had defended Atika Hive as if it were their own home world but still the enemy drove at them, forcing the beleaguered Guardsmen ever backwards. The civilian population, a little over ten thousand by Strike's reckoning, had been ordered into the vast network of tunnels that ran deep below the hive for their own safety and now, without collateral damage to worry about, the colonel found himself fighting a battle on two fronts.

The hive proper had been abandoned hours earlier as cultist and Traitor Legionary alike stormed through the hastily erected defences backed up by monolithic daemon engines and other debased servants of the Dark Gods, and so Strike had made the call to split his forces. Half of the regiment were valiantly keeping an escape route open to the Olympax Mountains ready for the inevitable retreat. The other half were desperately trying to hold the port long enough to load cargo ships – more accustomed to carrying ore – with the regiment's armour so they could be ferried off to safety, held in reserve for the long war that would inevitably follow. Foul magicks had taken out Atika's astropathic choir, driving them all mad the instant they had tried to send out a distress call.

No outside help would be coming to aid the Catachans. This would be Strike's war to prosecute. He would not have it any other way.

'Colonel, we've just heard from the garrison at Olympax. No enemy contact yet. Khan's Hold and Beluosus are reporting the same,' Thorne said, scrambling behind the same ore container the colonel was using for cover. Strike leaned around the side of the huge metal box and let off two shots from his lasrifle, each one felling an onrushing cultist. 'Still no word from Mauscolca Primus,' Thorne added.

Strike unleashed another volley and yet more cultists were swept down before they could reach the Catachan lines. Thorne added his firepower as more enemy soldiers poured into the killzone. Though they were consummate jungle fighters, all Catachans prided themselves on their cityfighting abilities. 'They're hitting the major population centres first. Once they've taken the hives, they'll move on to the smaller settlements and outlying strongholds.'

Thorne continued firing, mowing down more of the seemingly endless tide of wailing, tattooed madmen. 'How do you know that?' he asked.

'Because it's good warcraft and exactly how I would have gone about invading this planet.'

Cries went up from their right and both men turned to see cultists breaching a section of barricade formed from stacks of unrefined ore. Although nearly two metres high, the enemy fighters were using the bodies of the dead as steps to climb over it, and several had already made it over the top. Leaving Thorne to man his section of barricade, Strike drew his Catachan fang and waded in. A brute of a man, bigger even than the largest Catachan, had two men pinned underneath him and was battering them both with a makeshift club. Strike's first swipe of the blade took the cultist's hand off at the wrist, forcing him to drop his cudgel. The second opened his throat and killed him stone dead.

'Collapse the top section of the wall!' Strike roared, punching his blade through the chest of an onrushing cultist.

Lending his strength to the effort of his men, Strike clambered up the barricade and placed his shoulder against the rocks. On his signal, a dozen Catachans pushed at once, sliding the top of the wall down onto the hapless cultists below. Those who didn't die instantly under the crushing weight of the ore were quickly mopped up by Imperial fire.

'Defend this until the very last moment and then fall back to the next line of barricades,' Strike commanded. The invasion of Pythos had been swift but the Catachans had been stuck here for three years and had been far from idle. Thanks to Strike's predilection for overpreparedness, Atika was as defensible as any hive in the Imperium. He was about to retake his place alongside Thorne when the portable vox-unit clipped to his belt crackled into life.

'Colonel Strike. This is Major Rayston. Do you receive? Over,' fizzed the voice in an accent that was clearly from Catachan's northern hemisphere.

Strike put the device to his mouth and pressed the switch on the side to speak. 'Receiving you loud and clear, Rayston. Are you keeping that escape route open for us?' Rayston had fought with distinction alongside the colonel in many of the key battles on Burlion VIII and when he volunteered to oversee the retreat, Strike had no qualms whatsoever about putting him in charge of the operation.

'Affirmative, sir. That wasn't why I raised you on the vox though.'

Strike ducked back against the cargo container to avoid a volley of shots aimed at him from the enemy lines. 'Then what is this? A social call?' Even in the midst of a firefight, a Catachan's grim sense of humour very rarely deserted him.

'No, sir. It's Brigstone. He's made it back and has the astropath with him.'

832959.M41 / The East Gate. Atika Hive, Pythos

IT WAS DIFFICULT to determine who looked the most haggard as Strike leapt out of the still moving Chimera to greet Brigstone and the remnants of his jungle expeditionary team. The colonel bore the scars of battle: nicks and scratches from where he had got into close combat with the hive's attackers, scorch marks and burns to his shoulders where lasweapons had discharged in close proximity to him. Brigstone on the other hand was coated from head to toe in mud, as were the other four survivors. All of them bore chemical burns from where they'd charged incautiously through the noxious Pythosian swamps.

'I don't know what surprises me more, the enemy attack or seeing you walk out of that jungle.' Strike's words were mirthless. 'When those drop pods started falling out of the sky, I feared the worst.' He looked down at the exhausted band sitting wearily on the filthy ground. Mack sat alongside Liall, the astropath hugging his own knees and gently rocking while muttering quietly. K'Cee was slumped against an ammo crate. Large areas of fur were missing from his legs and arms from where acidic marsh gas had burned them away. Tzula sat staring out at nothing in particular, her jaw set rigid with determination. 'I take it the rest of you–'

'Didn't make it, chief.' Brigstone finished the colonel's sentence for him. He rose to his feet and the two men clasped arms in greeting. 'We lost Furie to a land dragon and Zens was killed by the enemy along with the inquisitor and the gunslinger. Kotcheff went only a couple of hours ago. Poor bastard breathed in too much swamp gas and disintegrated his lungs.'

'You've had enemy contact in the Deathglades?' If what Brigstone was saying was true, Strike's theory about the enemy hitting population centres was in doubt.

'A small force, no more than a dozen elite troops.' Brigstone paused but realised that the incredulity of what he was about to say did not hold up to many of the other events of the past week or so. 'Plague Marines. They were lying in wait for us as soon as the inquisitor found whatever it was he'd been looking for. The blonde was in on it too judging by the way she was shooting at us as we made our escape.' The flight towards Atika had been swift and desperate, pausing only for short breaks before mounting up and continuing on, even during the hours of darkness. Tzula had not yet spoken about what had transpired in the jungle clearing.

Strike soon rectified that. 'On your feet,' he commanded Tzula.

She slowly turned her head to regard him but made no other movement.

'I said, on your feet,' Strike repeated.

'I am an agent of the Most Holy Ordos, colonel. I am not yours to command,' she said, regretting it instantly when she realised how much like Brandd she sounded.

'I am de facto governor of this planet and, if you hadn't noticed already, trying to prevent it from falling into the hands of the Archenemy. I don't care if you're an agent of any Ordo, a High Lord of Terra or have verified lineage to the God-Emperor himself. Men and women under my command are dying by the thousands out there and I think it has something to do with the mission your boss was on and whatever it is he was trying to find.' He took a step closer to Tzula, invading her personal space. 'So start giving me some bloody answers and start doing it now!'

Sighing with reluctance, Tzula stood up. Her bodyglove was torn and frayed, and her once neat corn row braids had started to unravel. She took a step back and looked the colonel straight in the eyes. 'What I'm about to tell you–'

'Yeah. Top secret. Beyond classified. I get all that. Now cut the crap and start talking,' Strike snapped.

And so Tzula did. She told him why they'd come to Pythos, about her master's lifelong devotion and how they'd come here to destroy the Hellfire Stone. And she told him how, thanks to Brandd's betrayal, they had unwittingly aided the enemy. But in everything she told him, she was careful to leave out one very important detail.

'So this "seal" that they opened, there are more of them?' Brigstone asked once she had finished.

'They said seven, though the nature of the remaining six and what they hold bound are not known to me,' she said, honestly.

'And Abaddon himself is leading the assault?' said Strike. There was a very slight quiver to the colonel's voice.

His question hung there a moment.

'Yes,' she said eventually, the weight and inference of her answer evident to all.

Strike eyed her suspiciously. 'You're holding something back. What aren't you telling us?'

A man does not rise to command of an entire regiment of Catachans without being able to read people, and that was exactly what Strike was doing with Tzula. She briefly considered maintaining the deceit but carefully removed the blade from where it was safely stowed in her belt and held it out to show the two men.

'My master entrusted me with this knife and also with its secrets.'

Brigstone looked to his own blade at his hip, then at the tiny thing in Tzula's hand.

'It is not a weapon, but I have no doubt that if it was used as such its effect would be devastating. Ever since my master...' Tzula paused, before correcting herself. 'Ever since my former master took me on as his apprentice, he trained me in its operation so that when it came into his possession we could be ready to use it to its full potential.'

'"Its operation"? It's just a bloody knife and not a very big one at that,' Strike scoffed. When it came to knives, few in the Imperium could rival those of Catachan for both enthusiasm and knowledge.

'As I said, this is not a weapon. Though it is capable of tearing through flesh and armour, its true purpose is to tear through reality and act as a bridge between worlds,' Tzula said, the conviction of her words disarming the two Catachans.

'You're saying that if you were to use it you could put a hole in reality and we could step right through it back to Catachan?' Strike said after the implications of what Tzula had just said became apparent.

'If only it were that simple. I could use it and be as likely to open a portal to a world within the Eye of Terror as I would Catachan. And besides, even if I could get you and your regiment back to Catachan, you're not the kind of man to run away and abandon this world to the forces of the Archenemy.'

Strike smiled, Tzula having read him as well as he'd got the measure of her.

'What is vital,' she continued, 'is that this blade does not make it into the hands of Abaddon or any of the enemy agents. Entire cults have spent millennia studying and coveting this blade and they know far more about its power and application than either Lord Dinalt did or any other faithful servant of the Golden Throne. In their hands they may be able to harness it so that rifts may be opened directly to Catachan, Cadia or wherever they choose. Even Terra.' Strike and Brigstone noticeably flinched at the mention of their home world. 'Catachans above all others know the true value of a good blade. This one could be worth as much as the Imperium itself, and so we must defend it with our lives until reinforcements arrive to liberate Pythos.'

'There are no reinforcements,' Strike said coldly. 'The astropaths tried to get a message out as soon as the first drop pods hit but something prevented them. They went crazy and turned on themselves, ripping out each other's throats with their teeth and clawing at the walls of the choir chamber until fingers wore down to knuckles. By the time Thorne got to them, the only ones left breathing had to be put down out of mercy.'

'We're on our own then,' Tzula said.

'Not necessarily…' Strike turned to look at Liall, who was still sitting with his hands clasped around his legs.

'He's a single astropath. If an entire choir couldn't get a message through, what makes you think he can?'

'If a lone astropath was good enough for Dinalt's purposes then I'm sure he's more than capable of getting a message out to fleet command. And if we can get him to an astropathic chamber, his chances of success will be far greater.'

'Hollowfal?' Tzula said. 'It'll take weeks to reach there through the jungle.'

'Weeks we can't afford. That message has to be sent as soon as possible otherwise all any reinforcements will find on Pythos will be our corpses.' Strike looked skyward towards the smouldering spire of Atika Hive.

'You can't be serious. Even if you could fight your way up there, he'll never agree to it.' Tzula looked forlornly upon the emaciated figure of Liall, his filthy robes swaddled around him as he talked to himself and rocked.

'I have a feeling he could be persuaded,' said Brigstone. 'Mack? Come over here. There's something I need you to do for me.'

833959.M41 / The base of Atika Hive, Pythos

TZULA'S SLEEP HAD been fitful and restless and she had awoken feeling as tired as she had done before Strike had ordered her and the rest of the jungle survivors to get some sleep. No more than a few minutes would go by before the noise of another artillery barrage or missile strike would rouse her from her slumber and the continued chatter of small arms fire and distant enemy chanting from the frontlines made it an effort to get back to sleep. Not that Brigstone or Mack had the same trouble – an orbital bombardment could not wake a Catachan, or so they claimed – and K'Cee could grab some shuteye almost on command. Even Liall seemed to have little trouble entering a restful state, though his lack of eyes made it hard for Tzula to tell if he was truly sleeping or not.

Liall.

He had been part of Dinalt's retinue before Tzula had been taken under her former master's wing, and despite being less than useless – practically a liability, in fact – in a combat situation, his astropathic abilities had saved them on many occasions. Tzula was only here on Pythos because Liall had been able to signal for reinforcements, raise an evacuation or direct a precision strike so many times over she had lost count.

So why did she find it so easy to send him on his way to certain death?

Duty. Duty and revenge.

Dinalt and Chao were dead but the Lord Inquisitor's mission was incomplete. The Hellfire Stone was lost, not to appear again for decades, the knife still needed protecting and there was still the matter of the remaining seals. The fact that the sky had not turned upside down, the atmosphere had yet to become pure warp-stuff nor had the planet's population sprouted horns and cloven hooves, suggested that the enemy had not achieved that particular feat. Yet, as long as the seals remained unbroken, there was still a chance that she could stop them and gain some measure of vengeance while she was at it.

NOBODY SPOKE AS they trudged towards the makeshift entrance at the base of Atika Hive. Rayston had pulled some of his men away from keeping the escape route to the mountains clear to open up a corridor to the hive and, in between sporadic exchanges of fire with enemy zealots, to a man the Catachans all turned away from their emplacements and acknowledged Mack and the squad he was leading. They weren't sure what to make of the little man in scruffy robes at their compatriot's shoulder mumbling away to himself, but if he was brave enough to make his way deep into enemy territory with only a dozen Catachans by way of bodyguard, he was worthy of their respect. Or pity.

To everybody's surprise, Liall had not protested in the slightest when Mack had asked him if he would go to the top of the hive to send the message. All that he had asked was for Mack to go with him to which the brawny Catachan had agreed without hesitation. Strike had shown similar decisiveness when he put Mack in charge of the mission and told him to go and find volunteers, but even the colonel was surprised when almost a hundred men had put themselves forwards. For the first time since the invasion, Strike began to have doubts – was this simply heroic camaraderie, wanting to stand by one of their own, or was it something much darker, that they'd given up hope and sought a quick death?

No. These were men and women of Catachan, born unto a world that had tried to strangle the life out of them since birth and where survival itself was a badge of honour. Sons and daughters of Catachan did not barter their lives so cheaply, they exacted a toll from the enemy in blood and would keep them paying until the breath fled their lungs and their hearts beat their last.

The sombre troop stopped as they neared a wide rent in the hive wall. Unlike typical hive cities where buildings were piled atop each other until a crazed, haphazard structure thrust toward the sky, Atika had been built with a thick outer wall to protect those within from both the elements and the planet's native life forms.

'We're all proud of you, son,' said Strike, who had ceded command of defending the docks to Thorne while he helped cover Mack and his team's entrance into the hive. 'I'm proud of you, your uncle's proud of you. This whole damn regiment is proud of you.' A cheer went up from those manning the barricades, the sound incongruous against the din of las-fire and the screams of the dying.

'I won't let you down, sir,' Mack said, saluting the colonel. Strike stopped himself from admonishing the trooper and instead returned the gesture.

TZULA APPROACHED LIALL. 'Thank you, Liall. What you're about to do takes a lot of courage.'

His hollow eyes seemed to bore right through her. 'No, you

are quite wrong. Courage. The quality of mind or spirit that enables a person to face danger without fear. Courage.'

'Wrong?' Tzula said, puzzled. 'You don't think you're going to face any danger?'

Liall tilted his head sideways as if he was visually appraising the junior inquisitor. He lowered his voice so that Mack and his team could not hear. 'Oh no. The danger we will face up there is almost beyond human comprehension. The horrors that will be wrought upon our bodies cannot be given name but pale into insignificance compared to the atrocities our souls will endure. What you are wrong about is that I face that danger without fear.'

Tzula fought down the urge to throw her arms around Liall and hug him. 'You do remember that there is another message you have to send, once you've sent the message to fleet command?'

'Of course. Standard operational procedure,' he replied.

'C'mon. Time to go, Liall,' Mack said, shouldering the flamer he was using for the mission in place of his unwieldy heavy bolter. He approached the astropath and gently put a hand on Liall's elbow, guiding him towards the breech in the hive wall.

'The Emperor go with you,' Tzula said after them.

As Mack's team disappeared into the darkness, each one of them saluted Tzula and Strike. Right before Mack led Liall through the gap, the astropath turned back one last time. Tzula could have sworn he was smiling just before the darkness engulfed him.

'Care to tell me what all that business with the other message was about?' Strike asked, taking up position behind an impromptu barricade assembled from empty ammo crates.

'I'm sorry, colonel, but that's–' Tzula said, drawing her pistol and kneeling beside him.

'Classified,' Strike finished for her. Two rapid shots from his lasrifle burst open the chest of a charging cultist.

'If it's any consolation, if the message does get through you'll find out soon enough.' With catlike reflexes she rose from her position, took the head off a cultist about to put an axe through Strike's skull, before resuming her firing position all in one fluid movement.

'Provided we live that long, of course.'

* * *

833959.M41 / Interior. Atika Hive, Pythos

A QUICK BURST from Mack's flamer illuminated the darkened stairwell and showed them the route upwards. Although the Catachans had been billeted in tents and temporary constructs around the base of the hive ever since they'd arrived on Pythos, they all knew the layout of the interior as the bars, cantinas and other pleasure venues were the destinations of choice when they were granted a few hours R&R. Keen for the Catachans not to mix with the population any more than they had to, Strike had insisted that, where possible, his regiment use access tunnels and maintenance stairways to get around. Which was where Liall, Mack and the rest of the squad found themselves.

The way they moved was straight out of the Catachan basic training manual, or at least it would have been had the Catachans *had* a basic training manual rather than the oral tradition of teaching warfare that they practised. One trooper would advance up the steps to the next stairwell and, after he'd recced it and made sure it was all clear, signal for the rest of the squad to follow. That trooper would then cover their rear while another trooper moved to the next stairwell, checked it out and called up the rest of the squad. Although it was a slow process, Mack and his men had taken out three enemy guards without any Catachan casualties in the hour they had been ascending Atika Hive.

Lendpar, a young, dark-skinned trooper, all bundles of muscle and sinew, signalled for the rest of the squad to move up to the stairwell he had just checked for signs of the enemy. In single file, eleven more Catachans and a scrawny, bedraggled youth strode past him. Boniax, barely older than Lendpar but with the same toned physique, took his place at the head of the formation and was about to climb the next set of steps when he felt a meaty hand on his shoulder. It was Mack.

'Be extra careful up there. It's been a while since we had enemy contact and Liall has started getting twitchy.' He motioned with his thumb to the astropath who was shivering like he had been plunged into a vat of ice-cold water.

'Will do, chief,' Boniax said. He swung his lasrifle around onto his hip and advanced upwards, the barrel of the weapon pointing his way. Reaching the top of the flight, he put the muzzle of the weapon around the corner into the next stairwell before following it around with his head. He didn't like what he found.

'Stay back,' he stage-whispered back down to the waiting Catachans. 'They've left a corpse here. Classic booby trap.' He slowly moved forwards, uncertain whether the body was really dead or shamming, ready to spring an ambush. 'Just give me a minute to dis–'

There was a split second between Boniax feeling the tripwire against the fabric of his fatigues and the ensuing explosion. The force of the blast ripped away all extremities from his body and human shrapnel blasted back down the stairway along with the debris of collapsed masonry. The waiting Catachans, caught unawares, could only duck in reaction to the heat, dust and rockcrete fragments cascading down upon them. All of them, with the exception of Lendpar bringing up their rear, suffered burns and scratches, and several gagged and vomited through a combination of inhaling grime and the stench of charred human flesh.

Mack reacted first and, after patting down Liall's robes to put out smouldering sections that could easily have set him alight, scrambled up the remnants of the stairs to see how bad the damage was. The next flight was impassable, choked with rubble among which Boniax's scorched and still twitching torso sat grotesquely.

In that moment, Mack suddenly became aware of two things – he could feel a draught coming from somewhere and the intense ringing in his ears was giving way to another sound. Singing. Atonal, discordant singing.

Bringing his flamer up into firing position, he turned around and activated the firing stud just in time to incinerate the first of the cultists swarming through the hole blown into the wall of the maintenance stairway.

833959.M41 / The base of Atika Hive, Pythos

WHETHER IT WAS because the enemy knew what Strike was attempting or because operations were over elsewhere, the enemy forces surrounding the base of the hive had swelled significantly in the past few minutes and the fighting grew ever more intense. From behind improvised barricades and hastily dug trenches, Catachan lasrifles filled the rapidly dwindling no-man's-land between them and the forces of

Chaos with searing energy only to have their assaults returned upon them tenfold.

Tzula had stayed by Strike's side throughout the battle, her already haggard appearance made worse by the cauterised scar she now bore on her cheek as the result of not ducking quick enough to avoid a cultist's shot. Strike was bleeding too from numerous wounds where he and his blade had got up close and personal with a few frothing madmen who had made it to Imperial lines, but nothing that hampered either his ability to lead or fight.

Power pack depletion and weapon malfunction due to over-heating was becoming a real issue, and the Catachans would have had to retreat already if it wasn't for the ministrations of K'Cee running along the lines and servicing their weapons. Naturally, the jokaero had introduced some refinements of his own after getting his hands on the Catachan lasrifles and almost every shot that struck an enemy combatant was a kill shot thanks to the improved power and accuracy.

'To your right, colonel!' implored a trooper next to Strike. Instinctively, the Catachan commander turned and loosed off a rapid succession of las-shots, felling the cultist hurtling towards him. As the dying man went down, something cylindrical and metal fell from his hand and skittered towards the barricades.

'Grenade!' Strike yelled, the final syllable lost beneath the detonation. He put his arms over his head to protect himself from the mud and debris raining down on his position. Tzula did likewise.

'Thanks, trooper. That was a close one.' Strike patted the man next to him on the shoulder, but the trooper's body had gone limp. The colonel spun him around and the man's head, half of it missing as a result of the grenade blast, lolled sickeningly to one side. Taking the trooper's knife and tucking it next to his own on his belt, Strike returned his attention to penning the enemy back.

Something had changed. Instead of the sporadic fire followed by a charge upon the barricades, the enemy's fire had become more sustained, as if they were trying to pin the Catachans down so that they could not return fire. The reason for this soon became apparent.

From the rear of the enemy lines, massive shapes coalesced.

Armoured figures, their profiles broken by vicious spikes, loomed over the smaller cultists and bloodcurdling cries issued forth. Many of the Catachans stopped firing altogether, spooked by the guttural howls until Strike ordered them in no uncertain terms to keep shooting.

When he saw what leapt over the enemy lines and began charging towards them, those orders soon changed to retreat. Reports had come through during the early hours of the invasion that the enemy forces were backed up by Traitor Astartes, but it was only now that he saw them for himself for the first time.

'Berserkers! Fall back! Fall back!' Strike yelled at full volume, struggling to be heard above the unholy warcries. 'Make for the docks.'

The Catachans did not need to be told twice and, under a hail of bolter fire, a sea of green flowed out of the trenches and back towards the docks.

Covering his men until the last of them was clear, Strike aimed a shot at the nearest berserker and struck the behemoth in the knee with a clean shot. Fuelled by battle lust, the other onrushing Traitor Marines simply trampled him underfoot, so bent were they on reaching the base of the hive.

'Did we buy them enough time?' Tzula asked, plasma pistol glowing hot in her hand.

Strike took one last look up at the hive. 'Emperor willing we did,' he said before they both turned to follow the retreating Catachans.

833959.M41 / Interior. Atika Hive, Pythos

LENDPAR WAS THE first to fall, a solid round from an autoweapon taking him cleanly between the eyes and dropping him to the floor of the hab level before he even knew he was dead.

All about them, cultists screamed in rage and pain as Mack and the two other Catachans armed with flamers burned a path through the throng.

'Keep moving. Head towards the ramp,' Mack yelled, igniting another robed lunatic who dropped to the floor and rolled around in a futile effort to put out the inferno his clothes had become.

The Catachan squad had emerged from the ruined stairwell

onto one of the many hab levels of Atika Hive, straight into the line of sight of several dozen cultists. Many more had flooded out of the low rise hab buildings at the sound of gunfire. Mack found it odd that the first thing the cultists had done after taking over the hive was set up home in the vacated dwellings. When he saw that they were still wearing their crude armour and brandishing weapons, he realised that they weren't trying to live there but were looking for the people who used to live there. That was good. It meant that the enemy did not know that the civilians had been evacuated below the hive. He would have to tell the colonel this when he saw him again.

Then he remembered he was never going to see the colonel again.

Another Catachan went down beside him, a las-round hitting her in the throat and ripping it away in a spray of arterial blood.

'C'mon. We're nearly there!' Mack was using the flamer with one massive hand, his other was planted firmly on Liall's shoulder. The astropath's shivering had ceased and he seemed completely unfazed by the melee going on around him. It was almost as if he knew what hand fate had dealt him and was going to play it out with a serene grace.

Torching another two cultists who had taken up position on the ramp, Mack and Liall ascended to the next level of the hive. Ramps like these connected all of the hive levels to their vertical neighbours to allow bikes and other motored vehicles access, and with their stealth mission up the service stairs uncovered, they were going to have to fight their way up Atika Hive the hard way. The Catachan way.

The other surviving members of his squad followed Mack up shortly after, laying down a wall of flame to prevent close pursuit.

When the conflagration abated, the handful of cultists still drawing breath made it to the base of the ramp in time to hear the *plink plink* of the pair of grenades the Catachans had rolled down after them.

833959.M41 / Atika Dock, Pythos

'THORNE? ARE THOSE damned tanks loaded yet?' Strike bellowed down the vox. Night was beginning to fall again over

Atika but the quayside was lit up as bright as day, such was the volume of las-fire being exchanged.

'Still another fifty or so to be loaded. We're rolling them on as fast as we can,' Thorne replied down the crackling vox-link, his frayed temper evident in his tone. Since the Chaos forces had made planetfall, Thorne had eschewed sleep entirely to make sure all of the 183rd's armour was loaded onto the massive ore transporters, and though the man was doing his best, it still wasn't quick enough for the colonel's liking. Even assigning Brigstone to help Thorne hadn't sped things up.

'It's desperate down this end. I'm not sure how much longer we're going to be able to hold them off,' Strike said, his tone more conciliatory. 'I don't want those tanks to fall into enemy hands. Put them on the bottom of the ocean if it looks like any of your ships are going to be captured. Do you hear me, Brigstone?'

Under Strike's orders, Brigstone had been assigned to command the flotilla ferrying the tanks away from the planetary capital. The tank commander wasn't happy about it – the way he looked at things he'd already missed too much of the action tearing blindly through the jungle – but he saw the sense in Strike's thinking. Better to be deprived of Imperial armour altogether than be facing it across the other side of the battlefield.

'Understood, colonel,' Brigstone said, breaking across the vox channel. 'I'll get them out into deep water and await your orders.'

Strike cut the link and turned his attention to Tzula who was running at a low crouch across the quayside to avoid the superheated beams whizzing overhead.

'What in the Emperor's name are you doing back here? I thought I ordered you to evacuate the wounded to Olympax in that shuttle of yours?' Strike said. Almost as soon as the first drop pods had hit Atika's surface, Strike had ordered the Inquisition shuttle be moved from the landing bay and down to the docks. His original plan had been to load it on one of the container ships with the tanks but, now that Tzula had made it back out of the jungle, it had been put to better use ferrying the severely wounded out of Atika.

'I came back for you,' Tzula said, her jaw fixed as hard as it was the first time Strike had seen her after she came out of the jungle.

'You're wasting your time. I'm staying right here with my men and when I call the retreat, I'll be at their head leading them to Olympax.'

'And what good will you be to your men and the people of this world dead?' She fiddled with the gold Inquisition insignia hanging from the chain at her neck. 'I could pull rank on you, you know?'

'Yes,' Strike said, 'and I could shoot you, you know?'

The tension in the air was as real as the las-rounds passing through it. It was only broken when Tzula snorted and shook her head.

'Now stop hanging around drawing fire and get my men and that infernal knife out of here,' Strike said, sidling up to a stack of oil drums and shouldering his lasrifle.

'The Emperor protects,' she said coldly, before ducking her head and running back in the direction of the shuttle.

A few minutes later, the whine of twin engines carrying her craft aloft filled the docks as the backwash sent dust and debris kicking up from the battlefield. A few hopeful shots were aimed in its direction but they bounced harmlessly off its thick hull and before long Tzula's craft was two bright lights heading in the direction of the Olympax Mountains.

As it had done back at the base of the hive when the berzerkers had first appeared, the noise from the Chaos lines changed, and instead of chanting or warcries, the sound became a reverent whisper. All gunfire from the enemy stopped and for the briefest of moments, Strike thought that they had miraculously surrendered and laid down their arms.

He quickly realised it was the exact opposite of a miracle.

Heralded by cultist and Traitor Astartes alike prostrating themselves before him, an enormous figure, taller than the berzerkers thanks in part to the topknot he wore in his hair, strode through the chaos. The gold trim of his black armour reflected the pale light of Pythos's moon and an ancient power claw hung menacingly at his side, flexing in anticipation of the slaughter to come. Here, in all his brutish majesty, was Abaddon the Despoiler, Abaddon the Warmaster and, in that moment Strike knew, Abaddon the Conqueror of Pythos.

Strike's guts turned to ice, such was Abaddon's imposing presence even at more than a hundred metres away. All around him, men pissed themselves in fear.

The vox at his belt crackled rudely to life, desecrating the sombre hush that had descended.

'Colonel Strike? This is Major Thorne. It's the enemy, sir. They've stopped firing like they've given up. I hate to admit this but I'm not sure what to do. What are your orders, sir?'

From the other side of the battlefield, the son of Horus bared his teeth in a wicked parody of a smile. The sound of weapons beating against armour and cries venerating the Warmaster's name rushed in to fill the vacuum of silence.

'Are you receiving me, colonel? What are your orders?' This time Thorne's words registered with Strike.

'Get out of there,' Strike said, his voice catching in his throat. 'All of you, get out of there now,' he added, finally able to move legs he had thought turned to stone and followed the already fleeing Catachans to the last escape route left open to them.

833959.M41 / Interior. Atika Hive, Pythos

THE JET OF promethium passed through the blue pilot light burning at the flamer's tip, igniting the liquid and spewing forth fire which engulfed the throng of cultists who were either too slow or too stupid to move out of the weapon's arc. Sweat-soaked robes of crude manufacture became infernos and the front ranks, ablaze and panicked, ran blindly into their comrades behind them in turn, setting them alight and spreading the fire between them. For every cultist who burned, another would emerge from the level below, swinging a brutal close combat weapon and chanting vile litanies.

'One more level, Liall,' Mack said softly to his friend. 'One more level and we'll be at the astropathic chamber.' The Catachan had not relinquished his grip on the astropath since they'd been forced to enter the hab levels and Mack guided Liall backwards towards the final ramp, brief bursts of the flamer abating the advance of nearby cultists.

Four of them remained now. Twenty-seven levels of intense combat had accounted for the rest of the squad, each life laid down to ensure Liall reached his destination and relief for both regiment and planet be secured. Four soon became three.

Surrounded on all sides by enemy combatants, Olevski,

a squat, barrel-chested man from one of the islands near to Mack's own back on Catachan, depressed the firing stud of his flamer but nothing happened. Frantically he shook the weapon, coaxing out the last few drops of promethium in fear that it had run dry but upon hearing the fuel tank slosh half-full, noticed the blue ignition flame had gone out. Already feeling the first slashes across his back and arms from enemy blades, Olevski drew his knife and raised it high above his head before stabbing it down hard into the flamer's fuel tank.

The ensuing burst of flame was brief but devastating, instantly incinerating everything within a ten-metre radius and the shockwave from the explosion knocked those further away to the ground. Mack was able to keep his own footing and his tight grasp prevented Liall from falling prone. Janaczek, the only other surviving Catachan, put his back to the wall of the final ramp and laid covering fire with his lasrifle.

'Come on! Quick, while they're still down,' Janaczek yelled.

Mack practically dragged Liall the last twenty metres and up onto the top level of the hive. Janaczek followed, moving backwards so that he could pick off any cultist rising to their feet.

The bars and gambling dens were the most recognisable parts of Atika to the men and women of the 183rd, but all of them were familiar with the top level as it had served as regimental headquarters for the past three years. Rare was the Catachan who could keep his nose clean for any prolonged period of non-combat. During their time on Pythos, almost everyone in the entire regiment had at some point found themselves on a charge for brawling or drunken behaviour and been forced to appear before Strike to explain themselves. After a dressing down from the colonel, very few of them had made a repeat performance.

'Where to now?' Mack asked. The astropathic chamber's lack of food, alcohol or opportunities to either make a profit or get familiar with the locals meant that very few of the 183rd knew how to locate it.

'Atika. Standard Momus-pattern pre-fabricated hive city. Manufactured on over nine thousand Imperial planets and used primarily on temperate death worlds due to its thick outer shell and outstanding heat-dissipating qualities,' Liall said to the surprise of the Catachans. 'Sixty-three storeys high, four hundred and twelve metres in diameter at its base. Capable of comfortably accommodating six thousand inhabitants, that capacity can be increased to nine thousand if necessary. Optional modifications include a landing pad for shuttle craft on the exterior of the fifty-seventh level and a cupola-style astropathic chamber on the exterior of the top level.'

Over the few weeks that he'd known Liall, Mack had come to realise that the youth had an uncanny ability for remembering facts. He must have overheard one of the inquisitors discussing the hive and filed the information away.

'As interesting as all that is, it doesn't help us find it,' Janaczek said impatiently, the chanting of cultists rising in volume as they approached the ramp to the upper level.

'North,' Liall said as if it was the most obvious thing in the world. 'Astropathic chambers are traditionally sited on the north face of a structure.'

An eye constantly over their shoulders for pursuing cultists, the three of them raced past the command centre and other buildings commandeered for regimental business. The noise behind them grew in volume as they bolted and other, more guttural, sounds mingled with the profane chorus.

Rounding the final corner, a simple metal door greeted them, secured by a padlock and chain. Janaczek was about to swear when Mack doused the shackles in flame before slicing through the superheated metal with his fang. Both chain and lock hit the rockcrete floor with a satisfying thud.

'Go. I'll cover you here,' Janaczek yelled, his lasrifle coming to life in his hands and taking down the first of the cultists to round the bend. Mack nodded solemnly and threw open the heavy door with a slam of his shoulder. He bundled Liall through before following.

They were at the base of a narrow spiral staircase that hugged the profile of the hive's exterior and ascended gently upwards, presumably to the very pinnacle of the spire. Liall took the steps confidently as if some kind of sense memory were guiding him. Mack followed, ascending backwards to despatch any of the enemy who pursued them once Janaczek inevitably succumbed. From the sounds coming from behind the door at the bottom of the staircase, that would not be long.

Taking the final curve of the stairs, Mack was surprised to

find Liall waiting for him outside the door to the astropathic chamber.

'What's wrong? Is this door locked too?' Mack said.

'No,' Liall said serenely. 'I just wanted to say thank you.' He held out an open hand and, arm bent, presented it to Mack who reciprocated. The two men stood there, hands and forearms clasped in the Catachan style. No more words were said, none were needed, and after a few seconds Liall released his grip, opened the door and stepped into the astropathic chamber.

LIALL'S BLINDNESS WAS a boon as, deprived of sight, he could not see the mutilated corpses of the astropathic choir who until recently had practised their psychic arts here. Their wounds had been inflicted upon each other, but they were as much a result of the predations of the enemy as if they'd each been run through by a cultist's blade. Moving to the centre of the chamber, almost tripping over human detritus as he did so, Liall made ready to contact the Imperial battlefleet.

The temperature in the room dropped significantly and a cold sweat broke across Liall's forehead as, his psychic gifts amplified by the chamber, he engaged the aether. Blocking out the sound of the door at the bottom of the staircase being torn from its hinges, he sent the psychic cry for help the relatively short distance, easily circumnavigating the simple wards placed within the warp by the enemy.

Sensing that their cantrips and defences were void, enemy psykers targeted Liall directly and the strain upon his body caused him to convulse. He began to bleed from his nostrils and ears. Shutting off the sounds of the flamer discharging outside the door and the screams of the dying, Liall erected shields within his mind and ascended higher into the aether preparing to send his next message over a much greater distance. Finding the intended recipient within the sea of souls, he focused every fibre of his psychic might, expending the entirety of his talent in this one single message that must get through no matter what the cost.

The noise of chainweapons and booming warcries emanated from outside the chamber and the sound of Mack's flamer was soon joined by his screams as his defence of the chamber door ended.

Convulsing, bleeding, smoke pouring from the dead holes where his eyes once were, Liall was still sending the message as the door burst open.

PART TWO

CHAPTER FOUR

847959.M41 / Imperial Command Centre.
Olympax Mountains, Pythos

AS HE HAD done every day for a week since the shattered survivors of the assault on Atika had completed their deadly march through the Deathglades, Colonel Strike made his way through the secret tunnels of the delver stronghold, ascending ever higher to his vantage point atop the range's highest peak.

Unlike every previous occasion he had made this climb, this time he was being followed.

His head-mounted lume strip shone through the cloying darkness, illuminating the route both for him and his unseen pursuer and as he rounded the final corner and walked up the final steep slope, he switched it off as natural light began to filter in. Emerging into the red-hued dawn of Pythos, he took a deep breath and expelled the dank air of the stronghold's caverns, replacing it with the crisp thin air of the mountains.

Away in the distance, Atika Hive stood dark and silent, rising up out of the emerald jungle like a grim memorial to the Catachans' defeat and the massive loss of life endured there. Cells of his men had stayed behind to run a counter-insurgency against the invaders, but not one of them had made contact since the rest of the regiment had fled the hive, and speculation was rife as to what new horrors the enemy had inflicted upon them. Even then, they may have been the lucky ones.

Of the nearly eleven thousand Catachans who made it out of Atika, a little more than half had survived. Those who perished had not fallen to the guns and blades of the enemy but were instead claimed by the hostile wildlife of the death world's jungles. Abaddon's forces had not pursued them, and whether that was down to allowing the jungle to do the work of soldiers or other, darker reasons was the source of as much speculation as the fate of those who remained in Atika.

'Please don't tell me you come up here for the view, Colonel Strike,' said a woman's voice from the tunnel behind him. 'I'd hate to think you're becoming sentimental.'

Strike's fang was in his hand and clear of its sheath before she had even uttered his name. Fortunately for Tzula, with her newly-cropped hair, he identified her before he could inflict any damage with it.

'Are there no secrets from the likes of you?' Strike said, shaking his head but smiling. He safely stowed his blade back at his hip.

'All part of my job,' Tzula replied warmly. In the week since Strike had emerged from the Deathglades at the head of a column of his men, he'd formed an uneasy relationship with the junior inquisitor. Though he still placed the blame for the invasion squarely with Dinalt and his cohort, Tzula had already proven to be a valuable asset and, in Brigstone's absence, had begun training three dozen of his men how to tame and train some of Pythos's smaller saurians so that they could expand their patrols deeper into the jungle. Her xenos pet had proved his worth too, ensuring the few Valkyries and other flyers that had made it to Olympax stayed airworthy, allowing Strike to order rapid missions of opportunity whenever and wherever they presented themselves.

'And what of your secret? Are you ready to tell me who that second message was intended for? Can we expect salvation or were you double-crossing us like your blonde friend?'

'She was never my friend,' Tzula said coldly. 'And if you really believed that I was a traitor too that knife of yours would be between my ribs, not sheathed at your hip,' she added, warmth returning to her voice.

'True enough but if you really were sending for aid, I don't understand why you're being so clandestine about it.'

'If the message made it through, you'll understand soon enough.' A noise in the distance caught her attention and, shielding her eyes, she looked in the direction of the rising sun. 'Ah, I think *your* little secret is about to be revealed, colonel.'

Silhouetted against the pink disc slowly rising on the horizon, four Valkyries made their way towards the makeshift Imperial Command centre, engines whining in protest at the great cargo slung between them. As they struggled to keep formation, the bulky object – almost the size of the four flyers combined – swung precariously from thick chains, threatening to send the aircraft crashing through the canopy below.

'What in the name of the Throne is that?' Tzula asked.

'Why don't you come and find out?' Strike said, hitting the activation stud on his lume strip and climbing back down into the gloom of the stronghold.

THE HANGAR, MORE used to accommodating the dirigibles that transported Pythosian crystal to the spaceports at the planet's poles, was teeming with Catachans, so many that it was impossible to make out what the squad of Valkyries had delivered. Men and women, all clad in camouflage pattern fatigues, green vests and red bandanas, swarmed over the new arrival, obfuscating its outline as they clambered over it.

'Atten-hut!' Major Thorne bawled noticing that the colonel and junior inquisitor had entered the hangar. Within seconds, the green cover melted away, circling the rusted object beneath in an impromptu honour guard.

'Is that a–' Tzula began.

'It is,' said Strike as if it was the second coming of the Emperor himself. 'It's a Hellhammer.'

Coated in millennia of rust, the Baneblade variant more closely resembled a mobile fortress than a super-heavy battle tank, even in its dilapidated condition. A huge hellhammer cannon, from which the tank drew its pattern name, was mounted into its turret and a Demolisher cannon and autocannon were positioned beneath it. Along its thickly armoured hull, two sponsons sat either side, housing a lascannon and heavy flamer in each. Pintle-mounted in front of the turret was a huge heavy bolter. None of them looked as if they were in working condition and though the tank still had treads, close to half the links were missing.

'It's… it's…' Tzula struggled to find the words.

'One of the finest military machines ever to roll out of a forge-world? The most glorious relic of the Imperium you've ever cast your eyes upon? A miracle that the Emperor saw fit to bless us with by leaving it for us to find in the jungle?' Strike proffered.

'It's a wreck,' Tzula concluded. 'Why did you waste time and effort hauling this thing back here? None of the weapons systems are operational and you'll be waiting until doomsday to get the engine running.'

As if to spite her, the hangar filled with the *chug chug* of the ancient Phaeton thermic combuster attempting to turn over. This was quickly followed by the roar of it springing to life accompanied by a thick cloud of sooty black smoke pouring forth from the engine vents. A cheer louder than the sound of the tank's engine went up from the assembled Catachans and Tzula felt her cheeks flush in embarrassment at her pronouncement. A second wave of appreciation sounded out as the top hatch sprung open and an orange-furred hand sprang out of it making a thumbs-up gesture, soon followed by the rest of K'Cee.

'You were saying?' Strike said smugly.

888959.M41 / Hesodikas Stronghold. Hesodikas, Pythos

THE AGONISED SCREAMS of the dying merged with the roar of blue flame as the fire engulfed its victims, melting flesh, rending fat and scorching bone. Nine times nine was the required sacrifice, and warpfire was the method by which they were to be slaughtered. Corpulax had seen to the first requirement when he had stormed the delver-stronghold and made prisoners of the Catachans who fought in vain to defend it. Abaddon had fulfilled the second by supplying the Plague Lord with a seemingly endless stream of sorcerers, so numerous were the cabals who had rallied to his cause.

The death cries echoed around the huge subterranean chamber in which the sixth seal to the Damnation Cache was located before dying down. The sound of bubbling tallow and the unholy dirge of sorcerous chanting struck up in its place. The discordant wail reached a crescendo before, as quickly as the sapphire flame had been conjured into being, it dissipated, the only sign of it ever existing being the molten mass of human waste smoking on the expansive rocky floor.

One of the sorcerers, a tall, wiry figure whose neck was adorned with many rings giving it a bizarre, elongated appearance, stepped towards Corpulax, who had observed proceedings from the mouth of the chamber. 'It is done, Lord Corpulax. The penultimate seal is broken and we edge ever closer to reopening the Damnation Cache.' His voice was reed thin and laced with venom.

'Prepare the ritual. I will inform Lord Abaddon of our success and apprise him of our next objective,' said Corpulax.

At a signal from the sorcerer, a prisoner was brought before Corpulax and thrust unceremoniously to his knees. Whereas the sacrificial Catachans had been prime specimens, this one – a young captain of the 183rd – was bedraggled, his face and limbs bloated to unnatural proportions and had a jaundiced tone to them. Pus wept from his tear ducts and nostrils, mingling with the viscous sweat that coated his flesh.

'Please…' he rasped through lungs full of noxious fluid.

Corpulax leant forward and gently placed the forefinger of his skeletal hand to the Catachan's mouth. The captain's lips and tongue desiccated the instant they were touched, the dead flesh dropping to the floor and forming an ash-like mound at the Plague Marine's feet.

'Hush,' Corpulax said to the man who was tentatively touching his lower jaw, not sure what had just happened. 'We need your silence.'

Almost on cue, the cabal struck up their chant again, this time more rhythmically, in a harder, more guttural language than the one used to break the seal. The kneeling Catachan's flesh started to writhe as if things were moving around it subdermally, like rats or mice had got beneath the skin and were scurrying about inside him.

When it looked like his flesh was about to tear, the chanting stopped and Corpulax uttered a single word that turned the Catachan inside out.

Lungs and other internal organs burst forth from a mouth that was stretched impossibly wide followed by muscle, sinew and other, less identifiable parts of the human anatomy. As the pile of innards spilled onto the rock floor they took on new form, twisting and manipulating, tearing and reshaping. Thigh bone flattened and expanded until it resembled a spiked pauldron; deltoids separated to create the likeness of a power claw; wrist tendons rotated around each other to form a topknot.

When the simulacrum of Abaddon was complete, it spoke to Corpulax through a mouth made of repurposed appendix. 'Is the seal broken, Plague Lord, or is this yet another one of your requests for me to send you more warlocks you can burn out?' The rendering of Abaddon's body had been appropriated from somebody else's, but the voice was most definitely his own.

'It is broken, my master.' Although he was not actually in the presence of the Warmaster, Corpulax still took to one knee out of deference. 'And I have yet more good news. Our agents believe they have located the final seal.'

'If your information is accurate, the Black Legion themselves will be at your disposal to ensure it is broken.'

'It is not as simple as that, lord. There are… complications.'

The flesh-Abaddon scowled, cheeks of calf muscle tensing. 'Several thousand of the galaxy's finest warriors should be enough to resolve any complication. My warriors have spent weeks scouring the surface of this planet for the likely locations of the seals. I shall give them the purpose they were bred for.'

'My lord, the final seal is located directly below the delver-stronghold at Olympax.'

'Where the savages have established their new base? We would have eliminated them already if we hadn't been scouring the jungle for weeks. Olympax will burn, I will have their commander's head upon a stake and the final seal will be opened. Then my hunt can begin in earnest and you can turn your attention to opening the Emerald Cave.'

'With all due respect, Lord Abaddon,' Corpulax lied, 'the Olympax stronghold and the surrounding mountains are the most defensible location on the planet. The slopes approaching it are sheer and slow going. Even an airborne assault would be catastrophic as the bulk of their anti-aircraft weapons and flyers survived the initial assault.'

'And an orbital strike is out of the question as that risks destroying the seal before it can be opened.' Abaddon snorted. 'Is that why you contacted me, Plague Lord? To tell me that our only option is a risky suicide mission that may result in failure because an Imperial Guard regiment had the blind fortune to base themselves right on top of our objective?'

'There is another option. One that is less direct but offers us our greatest chance of success.'

'Subterfuge? I thought that was the preserve of our Tzeentchian brethren?'

'I am nothing if not pragmatic, lord. I believe I can get a cell into the Olympax stronghold and break the seal from within without interference from Imperial forces. It may take us longer to achieve but with the final seal broken, the cache will open and our allies will make short work of the cowering Catachans.'

The Abaddon-thing nodded in approval. 'I hope you are right, Plague Lord, because if you aren't and our mission on Pythos fails I will hunt you until the ends of eternity and personally flay your soul.' His final utterance complete, Abaddon remotely broke the spell and the simulacrum collapsed into a wet heap of offal.

Corpulax turned to the throng of cultists and sorcerers who had stood witness to his communion and addressed one in particular.

'Have your cell ready to move out within the hour,' Corpulax said. He reached down to his hip with his gauntleted hand and removed a vial of dark liquid from a pouch at his belt. He offered it to the robed cultist who accepted it with a feminine hand. 'You know what this is and you know when to use it. Do not fail me like your master did.'

The robed figure pulled back her hood to reveal stubble of freshly shaved blonde hair. 'Our success is assured,' she said, carefully placing the vial into the leather satchel hanging over her shoulder.

913959.M41 / Hangar Level, Imperial Command Centre. Olympax Mountains, Pythos

IT WAS THE sound of the sputtering Valkyrie engine in the distance that drew Major Eckhardt Thorne's attention from the other flyers undergoing repairs in the hangar. Field engineers put down their spanners and blowtorches and turned their heads toward the vast opening in the mountainside that allowed the Imperial aircraft easy access.

A trail of thick black smoke denoted the crazed route through the sky the Valkyrie had taken as the pilot struggled to keep it in the air with only one working engine. The craft jinked uneasily as it approached the Imperial base.

'Who's piloting that thing?' Thorne asked a bearded officer who had stopped what he had been doing to watch the stricken flyer. Many of the other Catachans in the hangar also sported substantial facial hair, the niceties of personal grooming set aside while at war.

'I don't know, sir,' the officer replied. 'All of our birds are accounted for.'

Thorne stroked his own thick stubble and furrowed his brow. 'The most recent contact we had from the colonel had them several hours flying away from Olympax. Even with a light load, an advance scout wouldn't have made it back this quickly.'

For the past few weeks Strike and the bulk of the Olympax contingent had been defending Khan's Hold from an enemy assault and, though the counter-attack had been a success, the colonel had stayed on there for some time afterwards, wary of a second attack wave and to mop up small guerrilla bands of cultists in the surrounding jungle.

'It could be an enemy trick. Shall we shoot it down?' the officer suggested.

Thorne thought for a moment. The noise of the malfunctioning engine was louder now and the Valkyrie would be attempting its landing within seconds. If this was some underhand ploy by the invaders, he did not have long to make the call.

'Stand down,' Thorne said at the last possible moment. 'Those markings on its hull are Devil's Brigade who were based at Hesodikas. We lost contact with them weeks ago. But, just in case...' He drew his laspistol and checked how much charge was left in its cell.

The screaming of the Valkyrie became a high-pitched whine as the pilot struggled to find the altitude to get his craft through the hangar opening. Buffeted by crosswinds it tossed from side to side, coming close to smashing against the mountainside more than once.

'He's not going to make it... He's not going to make it...' the officer beside Thorne muttered. All around the hangar, money started changing hands as the Catachans began to wager on the success or failure of the Valkyrie's landing.

With metres to spare, the pilot caught an updraught and the Valkyrie popped up into the view of those assembled in the hangar. The dark humour gave way to panic as it became apparent to everyone that the flyer wasn't going to come to a fiery end on the slopes of Mount Olympax but was instead going to crash, possibly quite spectacularly, right among them.

The sound of scraping metal rang out around the chamber as the pilot barely made it over the lip of the hangar entrance and sheared off the undercarriage. Sparks trailing in its wake, the Valkyrie skidded along the hangar floor forcing Catachans to dive out of its way. The further into the hangar it slid, the more its momentum was arrested and, after bouncing off two berthed flyers, causing only minor damage, it came to a halt scant metres from the back wall.

Nothing happened for what seemed like an age until, just as prone Catachans started raising themselves from the floor now that the threat of explosion had passed, the rear hatch of the Valkyrie opened with a hydraulic hiss. Obscured by the smoke still pluming from the ravaged engine, several figures descended the ramp.

Thorne raised his pistol in their direction. 'Stop right there. Name and rank. Now.'

The smoke parted revealing five figures all dressed in identical fatigues and vests, blood-red bandanas tied tightly around their scalps. A woman, the only one among the group, took a step forwards. Thorne lifted the pistol so that he was looking straight down the barrel at her head.

'I said stop.' Others in the hangar had drawn weapons and they too were trained on the newcomers. 'Give me your name and rank now.'

'Captain Troy, Devil's Brigade,' the woman said matter of factly. 'We're all that's left of the garrison at Hesodikas.'

Thorne looked her up and down, pistol still aimed at her head. On the surface she looked like a Catachan but there was something about the woman that didn't ring true. Her hair was too freshly shorn where it was visible at the base of her skull and her fingernails were clean. He'd also never heard of a Captain Troy, but in a regiment the size of the 183rd it was impossible to keep track of, or know the identity of, every soldier.

'Devil's Brigade, you say?' Thorne took a few steps closer to her, never lowering his weapon. 'Hesodikas sounds tough if you were the only ones to walk away. Still, I bet it was nothing compared to the Battle of Caol Ila.'

The woman looked him squarely in the eyes. 'I don't know what you mean, major. Devil's Brigade didn't fight at Caol Ila. We were engaged deep behind enemy lines at Mortlach at the time.'

Thorne grinned and lowered his laspistol. The other weapons pointed at the Hesodikas did likewise. Captain Troy had not only passed his little test, she had passed it with distinction.

'Can't be too careful, captain.' Thorne reholstered his weapon. 'Hesodikas is gone, you say?'

'It fell days ago. Total annihilation,' she said, fingers scratching underneath her bandana. 'Those of us who were left stayed behind to harry the enemy but when our numbers got so few that we were ineffective, I decided it was time for us to get out. We're more use here as part of the larger resistance effort.'

'Glad to have you, captain. Mulgrew?' he called to the bearded officer. 'Take Captain Troy and her men to Major Rayston and have him redeploy them.'

The woman saluted lazily. Thorne returned it in kind. Mulgrew was about to lead the five reinforcements out of the hangar when Thorne spoke again.

'And Mulgrew?'

'Yes, sir. What it is it?'

'Have that Valkyrie stripped down and used for spares when you get back,' Thorne said, gesturing with his thumb to the wreck at the back of the hangar.

Mulgrew nodded and continued on his way, Troy and her men in tow.

* * *

IN A SECLUDED corner of the hangar, somebody else had stopped their repair work to view the spectacle of the crashing Valkyrie and the subsequent entrance of the new arrivals. However, unlike Thorne, they knew that Captain Troy and her men were not what they claimed to be.

Removing his welding mask, K'Cee jumped down from the hull of the Hellhammer and loped off to find Tzula.

'SOUNDS LIKE HESODIKAS was a bit of bad business,' Mulgrew said as he led Troy and her men through the narrow man-made caverns of Olympax.

Before the invasion of Pythos, Olympax had been one of the main delver-strongholds on the planet, its high, easily defended location making it a haven from the predation of the jungle's inhabitants. Where once it had been home to the bulk of the world's crystal production, now it played temporary home to the bulk of its defenders.

'It was a bloodbath,' the woman in the captain's uniform replied. 'Not a single soul got out of there alive.'

'Except for you five of course, sir,' Mulgrew added cheerfully.

'No. Not even we survived. I mean, *we* did, obviously, but the former owners of these filthy rags are as dead as you.' She drew the stolen blade from her thigh and jabbed it hard into Mulgrew's throat before he could react. The Catachan sank to his knees, hands clamped around his neck, vainly trying to stem the flow of arterial blood. 'Nobody survived. Those I didn't kill myself, I watched die. Like Troy here.' She pulled at the chain around her neck to reveal a set of dog tags from beneath her vest. 'It took him an age to die under the ministrations of the interrogator acolytes of the Davinicus Lycae, but before he breathed his last, he told us all we needed to know to pass ourselves off as members of your regiment.'

She rotated the Catachan fang in her hand so that the blade pointed towards the ground and stabbed down hard, driving it through Mulgrew's temple. Then she withdrew it with a wet pop and, removing the red bandana from her head, wiped the knife clean before scabbarding it.

Throwing the bloodied rag to the ground next to the corpse of the Catachan officer, Tryphena Brandd led her infiltration team deeper into the stronghold.

* * *

913959.M41 / East Entrance, Imperial Command Centre. Olympax Mountains, Pythos

'BE READY TO head out again at first light,' Tzula Digriiz ordered as she swung her legs from the saddle and dismounted the arbosaur. 'Just because the enemy have left us alone until now doesn't mean it'll stay that way forever.'

She received nods from the half a dozen Catachans who'd accompanied her on patrol as they stretched and twisted, trying to work out the knots of hours in the saddle. Though not a Catachan herself, Tzula had proven a capable tutor when it came to taming and riding the beasts, and those under her command had grudgingly accepted her once she had proven her worth.

Handing the reins of her mount to one of the Catachans who would lead the beast away to the pens, she removed her bandana and wiped the sweat from her forehead. With her bodyglove ruined in the battle for Atika, she had taken to dressing in a similar fashion to the death worlders, and her fatigues and green vest matched those of the 183rd perfectly. What she didn't copy, for fear of causing offence, was the red bandanas they wore, instead choosing a black square of cloth that she wore wrapped like a headband. Regardless, she'd still look like a Catachan to the enemy rather than a servant of the Ordos which was precisely the way she wanted it if they were, as she suspected, hunting for the knife.

She was about to remove the rest of her outfit and hit the makeshift showers just inside the cave mouth of the east entrance when K'Cee emerged from the base. He looked excited or agitated, and bounded over to Tzula before grabbing her arm and tugging on it.

'What is it, K'Cee? Have you finished working on Strike's tank and want to show me?' She gripped the bottom of her vest in preparation to pull it off over her head. 'Give me a while to shower and I'll be right with you.'

K'Cee shook his head vigorously, his ample cheeks flapping. He tugged on Tzula's arm again.

She stopped trying to undress and began to take him seriously. 'I don't understand.'

The jokaero released his tight grip on her arm and placed one hand on each of his ears. He pulled them so that they stuck out and blew hard with his mouth closed to inflate his cheeks. With his impersonation finished, he jabbed out a finger and pointed upwards into the base.

Suddenly understanding, Tzula drew her plasma pistol. 'Show me. Now,' she said, following the diminutive xenos back into the caves of Olympax.

CHAPTER FIVE

913959.M41 / The Tunnel System, Imperial Command Centre. Olympax Mountains, Pythos

TZULA DIDN'T NEED to know the route Brandd was taking as the trail of bodies told her which direction to head in. A map of mortality pointing ever deeper into Olympax.

Just as Strike had found his way through the warren of tunnels to the peak of the delver-stronghold, Brandd was heading in the opposite direction. In pursuit of what goal, Tzula could only speculate but she had a pretty good idea what it was the traitor sought: the seals. One had been opened for certain but how many others still remained closed? How many seals were there to begin with? Tzula came to the sudden realisation that for all her Inquisitorial training, for all her years of experience in service to the Ordo and as a thief before that, she was utterly helpless in all this, a mere bystander to the events that were unfolding around her on Pythos. That would all change if Liall had succeeded in getting his second message out. *Liall.* Another mark on Brandd's tally sheet as far as Tzula was concerned.

'More bodies, sir,' one of the Catachans said, illuminating the roughly hewn steps with the lume strip taped to the side of his lasrifle. Once K'Cee had shown Tzula where Brandd had crash-landed in the Valkyrie and, between her and Thorne, managed to piece things together, the major had assigned her a squad to pursue the traitor.

Tzula counted three corpses in all, each one lying face down with multiple stab wounds to their backs and shoulders. Their weapons were still slung over their shoulders and no scorch marks blackened the coarse stone walls. With vox-communication impossible in the confines of the base's tunnels, Thorne had been unable to broadcast a warning that there were traitors in their midst.

Without any prompting, the two lead Catachans carefully searched the corpses for signs of traps. The squad hadn't exercised such caution with the first body they'd come across and of the ten Catachans who had begun the descent with Tzula, seven now remained. Each time they had to stop, valuable time was wasted and Brandd gained a bigger advantage over them.

'Clear,' one of them called after a couple of minutes. The brawny Catachan retrieved the blades from his dead comrades' belts and took his place at the rear of the formation as Tzula and the rest of his squad filed down the steeply descending tunnel.

FURTHER AHEAD DOWN the maze of stone corridors and out of earshot of their pursuers, Brandd and her team had reached their goal, though, at first glance, it was not immediately apparent.

She had halted in a wide vestibule in the tunnel and was facing a sheer rock surface that terminated so high above them that it seemed to go on forever. It appeared to be of the same material as the rest of the mountain, but its crafting marks were cleaner, more refined than those of the tunnel and the rest of the delver-stronghold. She placed her palm against the smooth rock. It was warm to the touch.

'The cabal's scrying was accurate. This is the place. I can feel the power coursing through the very rock itself.' She pulled her hand away from the heated rock and drew her knife.

'Ajanipol. Come here, it is time to fulfil your service,' she said. One of the fake Catachans eagerly approached her. He too had removed his bandana but instead of revealing a smooth scalp, two small protrusions sat just above his forehead, the earliest blossoming of vestigial horns.

He looked as if he was about to deliver a speech, profound last words before expending his duty but before he could say anything, Brandd's blade, already slick with blood, ran him through. With both hands, she tore upwards, parting the flesh to open up his insides.

Ajanipol moaned in pleasure-pain and placed his hands inside his wound. Moments later he removed them, covered in dripping crimson gore, and began to daub haphazardly upon the wall of the vestibule. His bloody smears formed crude sigils, blasphemous icons that were painful to look upon, and when he had made three identical marks in a triangular pattern he took his finger and drew a bloody trail to link them.

The instant the final sigil was connected to the others, the mountain itself started to shake and the already warm surface of the wall radiated an intense heat. Brandd and the other cultists retreated back to the far wall of the cavern but Ajanipol, struck dumb by loss of blood and awe at what he had set in motion, remained still, his flesh blackening as it fried. The tremors within the mountain grew more intense and a deafening noise, like two tectonic plates scraping against each other, forced the four lucid figures in the chamber to clamp their hands tightly to the side of their heads in defence of their eardrums. With one last violent shudder, a wide crack, the girth of two men, formed in the base of the smooth wall and raced up the inside of the mountain, chasing itself up towards the peak.

As quickly as the tremors and the cacophony had begun, they ceased.

'Lord Corpulax gives you both his blessing and his thanks, Ajanipol,' Brandd said, stepping over the smoking body of the cultist and into the crack.

913959.M41 / Hangar Level, Imperial Command Centre. Olympax Mountains, Pythos

THORNE WAS STILL cursing himself for allowing the traitor to get the better of him when parts of the hangar roof came showering down.

The floor began to rock and, avoiding chunks of stone that were dropping from above, he sought sanctuary in the open hatch of a Valkyrie undergoing repairs. Others too had the same idea, and for the duration of the quake Thorne was confined to the enclosed space with almost a score of sweating

Catachans, unable to cover his mouth and nose as the noise from debris hitting the hull forced him to cover his ears. For what seemed like far longer, but was in reality only a matter of seconds, the Valkyrie swayed from side to side, battering its occupants against the walls and each other.

As quickly as the tremors and the cacophony had begun, they ceased.

Emerging from the grounded craft into a billow of rock dust, Thorne took stock of the situation. All of the Valkyries within sight had sustained damage but, apart from those that had suffered damage or malfunction prior to the quake, looked airworthy. Something told him they were going to need them soon.

'What the hell was that?' asked a slab-muscled woman rubbing her shoulder from where she'd taken an impact.

'I don't know, but I'll wager any of you a year's rations it's something to do with that traitor inquisitor,' said Thorne, wiping rock dust from his eyes. 'Come on. Let's get this place cleaned up and start assessing the damage.'

'Sir. Over here. You need to see this,' called a bearded officer from the lip of the hangar entrance. Thorne strode over to join him, unable to see what the sergeant was trying to point out until he was practically alongside the man, such was the volume of dust choking the hangar.

Away in the distance, at the very limit of unaugmented human vision, the sky was full of tiny black dots, a hundred at least by Thorne's reckoning.

'Is that Colonel Strike, sir?' the sergeant asked.

'I hope so,' said Thorne gesturing to another sergeant to bring him a set of magnoculars. 'For all of our sakes, I damn well hope so.'

913959.M41 / The Tunnel System, Imperial Command Centre. Olympax Mountains, Pythos

Feeling the first vibrations, Tzula threw herself flat against the tunnel wall. Her home world was criss-crossed by multiple faultlines and the practice drilled into her as a child returned instinctively. If there had been a table or desk to duck under or a doorway to stand beneath, she would have used that as cover but, exposed as she was in the tunnel, pressing her back against the wall was the most protection she could afford herself.

The Catachans followed Tzula's lead and spread out along the rockface. A couple were too slow and in amongst the fist-sized chunks of stone that were pouring down, a weighty slab of rock crashed amongst them, pulverising bone and meat and pinning their corpses to the tunnel floor. The others could only watch on helplessly as the tremors intensified and the mountain threw more of itself down.

As quickly as the tremors and the cacophony had begun, they ceased.

With the noise of the rockfall still echoing along the tunnel, Tzula knelt down to check the bodies of the two Catachans pressed beneath the slab and, after confirming what she already knew, retrieved their knives. Handing them over to one of the surviving death worlders, she began to pick her way through the carpet of debris to continue her pursuit of Brandd.

She hoped she was not too late.

IN HER TIME as a servant of the Davinicus Lycae and while posing as the apprentice to not just one, but two inquisitors, Tryphena Brandd had witnessed many things, both wondrous and abhorrent. As she stepped inside the vast subterranean cavern opened after untold millennia by dark ritual, she wasn't sure which category to mentally file this one under.

A flickering blue glow bathed the entire area, rising in a column through the gloom. It illuminated the recesses of the vaulted ceiling high above and highlighted immense sta-lactites descending from the roof like giant fangs. The effect was spectacular but it was the source of the light that both repulsed and enthralled her.

Upon a raised dais in the centre of the cavern, a stasis field hummed and crackled gently, pulsing rhythmically in a strobe-like manner. Beneath the protective canopy of energy, thirteen robed figures, emaciated to the point of skeletism, moved in grotesque slow motion, like a pict feed slowed down to a single frame every few seconds. The attire they wore was threadbare and rotted in places, exposing cadaver-ous frames entirely bereft of muscle or fat. Limp skin hung from their limbs, giving the impression that they wore a sec-ond set of robes beneath the top layer. Their mouths moved in a fashion that was painful to observe, taut skin slowly stretching and cracking as their jaws opened and closed over a lengthy cycle. Other than the almost imperceptible movements, the only other sign that the occupants of the chamber were still alive was the puffs of breath that condensed in the freezing air of the stasis cocoon. If they were aware of the newcomers to their home, they were showing no outward signs.

'Psykers,' Brandd spat. 'Thirteen bound psykers left to watch over the final seal. All that remains now is to slay them, and after ten thousand years the Damnation Cache will be open once more. Our masters will soon walk this realm again as lords of all!'

Unprompted, one of her companions drew a crude autopistol and pointed it at the dais.

'Stop!' yelled Brandd, a moment too late.

The cultist pulled the trigger and the bullet sped inexorably towards the dome of blue energy. It hit the stasis field and bounced off, ricocheting crazily off the walls of the cavern, given new impetus by its deflection.

'The field doesn't just keep them alive, you fool. It protects them too. Killing them is going to take-'

She was interrupted by the changing sound of the rogue bullet. Instead of bouncing off the cavern walls, it had hit something metallic before dropping to the floor and rolling towards her feet from out of a benighted recess.

'What was that?' she asked.

Activating a lume strip, the shooter lit up the alcove. What they saw there gave them a moment's pause.

Covered from helmet to boots in verdigris, moss and fungal mould the form of a Terminator-armoured Space Marine stood sentinel in the alcove. Halberd in one hand, the helmeted figure was a near-perfect representation of the superhuman elite of the Imperium's armies, right down to the bolt pistol holstered at its hip and the numerous purity seals applied to its pauldrons and breastplate. A glint of silver reflected the light of the lume strip where the bullet had grazed a knee guard and removed the detritus of the ages.

Even a representation of the mighty Adeptus Astartes was enough to instil awe and it was several moments before anybody spoke.

'It's a statue,' said the cultist holding up the light. 'How typical of the Emperor's curs to leave a mere statue to keep guard over–'

A creak emanated from the recess. As one, the cultists' guns came up and aimed at the monument.

'It moved! The statue just moved,' the cultist said, shining the lume strip up and down to find the source of the noise. The statue remained immobile.

'Don't be ridiculous,' Brandd scoffed. 'It was probably just a rat.' She lowered her weapon to emphasise her point, as did the other cultists.

'That was no rat. This thing–'

He never got to finish his sentence.

'I can assure you, traitor,' said the statue drawing and firing its bolt pistol in one swift movement, turning the cultist's head to a cloud of crimson mist, 'I am far more than a "mere statue",' it added before opening fire on the remaining cultists.

913959.M41 / Hangar Level, Imperial Command Centre. Olympax Mountains, Pythos

THE VALKYRIES WERE so close now that Thorne could make out the colour schemes and markings of the individual craft. All of them were gunships that had set out from Olympax weeks earlier, and none of them were showing obvious signs of hostile intent.

But neither had the traitor inquisitor when she flew straight in and passed herself off as a Catachan captain. How did the old saying go? *Fool me once, shame on you. Fool me twice, shame on me.*

'Chief, we still can't raise the incoming Valkyries,' called a vox-operator from the back of the hangar. 'The quake knocked out the comms tower. It'll be hours before it's operational again.'

'What do you think, major? Is this another ploy by the enemy?' asked the sergeant beside Thorne.

The major put the magnoculars back to his eyes. The full glare of Pythos's sun reflected back off the cockpit canopies making it impossible to see who was piloting the craft. Would that make a difference anyway? The enemy had already tried to pass themselves off as soldiers of the 183rd, and the jungles and delver-strongholds were rife with dead Catachans from which to pilfer uniforms.

'They're about to come into range of the anti-aircraft batteries, chief. If we hit them now we should be able to down most of them before they have a chance to return fire. Do you want me to give the order to fire?' The sergeant gestured for a runner to be ready to deliver the order to the flak gun crews.

Thorne ran a hand across his bearded jaw, deep in contemplation.

'We're going to lose our chance,' the sergeant urged. 'You need to make the call now, major.'

913959.M41 / The Tunnel System, Imperial Command Centre. Olympax Mountains, Pythos

THE LAST SOUND Tzula Digriiz expected to hear as she picked her way through the rock-strewn tunnels of the depths of Mount Olympax was the report of a bolt pistol echoing up from below. When she raced through the vast crevice that had opened up in the heart of the mountain, plasma pistol already in hand, the source of the firing was the last thing she had expected to see.

Halberd in one hand blazing with blue energy, a Terminator-armoured Space Marine was exchanging fire with Brandd and her cronies. The cultists were using the stasis field as cover, circling around it and taking shots at the armoured goliath, but the mixture of solid autopistol shot and las-fire did nothing more than reveal more of the silver armour beneath the conglomeration of lichen and filth.

Sensing the presence of others in the chamber, the Space Marine aimed his pistol at the entrance but stopped short of firing it when he saw that Tzula and the soldiers accompanying her were also attacking his targets.

The air filled with the heated discharge of las and plasma fire, punctuated by the staccato of bolt shells. The Space Marine dealt with one flank while the Catachans and Tzula drove up the other, cutting off the cultists' means of escape and pinning them down under a steady barrage.

Over Tzula's shoulder, a Catachan went down hard, a well-placed volley taking off the left side of his face. Tzula avenged his death instantly by doing likewise to the cultist who had made the shot.

A scream rang out from the other side of the chamber as a bolt shell evaporated the shoulder, arm and most of the chest of a cultist. Using his corpse as a shield, another rattled off a string of las-bolts, all of which missed the onrushing Space Marine. In response, the giant fired a single shot into the cultist whose life he had just ended, the round passing straight through him and exploding the torso of his comrade behind.

That only left Brandd.

Out of options, she reached into her satchel and pulled out the vial of dark liquid given to her weeks ago by Corpulax. She held it above her head, using her other hand to alternately point her weapon at Tzula and the Space Marine.

'Do you know what this is?' Brandd said.

'Hold your fire,' Tzula ordered the Catachans behind her. 'It's a vial of Life Eater, the same thing that's used in virus bombs. Not nearly enough to threaten the planet or even the base but more than enough to kill everyone in this chamber.'

'Very good, Tzula. I knew Dinalt didn't just keep you around for your looks.' Cornered like a dog, Brandd's tone was still one of superiority. 'Do you know what else it's good for?'

Tzula said nothing.

'It's an airborne pathogen which makes it excellent at breaching stasis fields. Unfortunately, those psyker slaves in there don't have their own air supply which means the protective dome, while sufficient to prevent solid objects from passing in and out, is porous enough to allow gas and liquids through.' She emphasised this point by spitting through the field, a wad of phlegm landing on the hem of an oblivious psyker's robes. She shook her pistol at the Space Marine. 'Even he can't save you now.'

+Be ready to move when I do.+

The shock of psychic intrusion registered briefly on Tzula's face but if Brandd noticed, she did not react. Though he wore no psychic hood of the Librarius, the Space Marine was a psyker. +Do not let the vial hit the ground.+

+Understood.+ She replied in the manner her former master had taught her.

Impossibly quickly, more so because of his armoured bulk, the Space Marine slashed down with his halberd, a blur of sapphire energy crackling through the stale air of the cavern. It made contact with Brandd and sheared through bone, removing her forearm at the elbow. Moving not nearly as quickly as the genhanced warrior, but still fast by human standards, Tzula dived forwards and grasped the wrist of the severed arm, stopping the vial from smashing scant centimetres from the hard floor.

She breathed out in audible relief. Lying next to her on the dais, Brandd screamed and clutched at her cauterised stump. Strangely, her screams soon gave way to choked laughter.

'It's too late,' she rasped through gritted teeth. 'It was on a timer.'

Looking in horror at the limb she still clasped in her own hand, Tzula heard the hiss of a valve releasing as the liquid within the vial began to seep out and expand. She dropped the arm, container and all, to the ground and scrambled away from it. As the vial shattered, a tiny droplet splashed her on the back of her hand.

+Move. Now,+ the Space Marine said directly into her mind. When Tzula didn't react, instead sitting there trying to wipe the noxious substance from her hand, the Space Marine picked her up and bundled her under his arm, sprinting towards the entrance.

The black ooze spread and multiplied like liquid cancer, consuming all in its path. Brandd's severed arm dissolved at its touch, as did the still laughing traitor when the dark substance spread over her body and engulfed her. It seeped in through the stasis field and climbed over the husks of the psykers, rising over them before disappearing inside them through their slowly opening and closing mouths.

The Catachans did not need the same warning nor aid that Tzula had and were heading back towards the entrance under their own power. Chased all the way by the proliferating Life Eater virus, one of them tripped and was instantly engulfed by the blackness, all traces of him drowning beneath it. The others continued running for their lives but their efforts were too futile. Not having the speed of the augmented Space Marine, the remaining Catachans could only look on helplessly as he disappeared through the crack, Tzula under his arm, while they became the next victims of the creeping death.

'My arm,' Tzula said as the Space Marine set her down in the vestibule, confident that the virus was contained to the chamber. 'It's… it's spreading,' she said, panic rising in her voice.

The tiny splash that had landed on her hand had expanded

across her fingers and up to her wrist in the short space of time it had taken for the Space Marine to outrun the Life Eater. Tendrils were slowly creeping up her forearm and her digits were starting to dissolve.

'This is going to hurt.' The Space Marine's voice was dry and he over-enunciated each syllable as if he were speaking High Gothic for the first time.

'What? What's going to hurt?' She was only half-concentrating on his words, sickeningly fascinated by the change her body was undergoing.

'This,' the Space Marine said, slashing down with his force halberd at precisely the same spot where he had separated Brandd's arm from the rest of her body. Tzula cried out in pain and looked down at the stump expecting to be greeted by a fountain of blood but instead found the wound was smooth and cauterised. Her severed forearm and hand dissolved into nothingness at her feet.

'It was the only way,' the Space Marine said unapologetically.

Tzula stared a little longer at the space where the rest of her left arm used to be, experimentally flexing her shoulder and bicep. She closed her eyes and slowed her breathing which had become irregular and sharp. 'At least it wasn't my shooting arm,' she said eventually, wincing through the pain.

'Good. I think you'll be needing that soon,' said the Space Marine. He helped her uneasily to her feet. 'Can you walk unaided?'

'Yes. The trauma should soon pass and you took it off clean so blood loss won't be an issue,' she replied before pausing. 'Who are you anyway? I wasn't aware of any Chapter operating on Pythos. Where are the rest of you?' Tzula had fought alongside several Chapters of the Adeptus Astartes during her career, but was struck by how odd it was to find a Space Marine operating alone. The livery and markings of his armour were unfamiliar, but there was rumoured to be over a thousand Chapters scattered across the Imperium and, even as an agent of the Inquisition, she could barely name or identify a hundred of them.

The Space Marine did not answer, instead looking the junior inquisitor up and down.

'My name is Tzula. Tzula Digriiz, junior inquisitor of the Ordo Malleus and agent of the Golden Throne.'

'Zoo-ler,' the Space Marine repeated uneasily.

'It's Tzula. T. Z. U. L. A. The "t" is silent,' she paused again expectantly. 'And you are?'

'I am…' He seemed to be considering his answer. 'I am Epimetheus of the Grey Knights, Sentinel of Pythos and Keeper of the Seventh Seal.'

'A Grey Knight?' Tzula asked, surprised. 'A Brotherhood is already here on Pythos. Thank the Emperor. I thought–'

'As far as I'm aware, I am the sole Grey Knight on this planet.' He halted, the crackling of his force halberd breaking the silence. 'I do not sense the psychic spoor of any of my brethren on this world, just the presence of the Archenemy. With the final seal broken, it is only a matter of time before the Damnation Cache bursts open. Come, junior inquisitor. We have work to do.'

'I don't understand. How can you be here on your own? And your armour? How did it get into such poor condition.'

'The time for answers will come later,' Epimetheus said, starting off along the stone corridor at pace. 'For now, we have a world to save.'

913959.M41 / Hangar Level, Imperial Command Centre. Olympax Mountains, Pythos

'WHAT THE HELL happened here?' Strike bellowed to be heard above the sound of engines spooling down as he strode along the exit ramp of the Valkyrie. The floor of the hangar level was carpeted in fallen rocks and dust, and otherwise airworthy craft were dented and scratched, cockpit windows crazed and shattered. Men and women frantically dashed about attempting to clear landing spaces for the Valkyries hovering in a holding pattern at the hangar entrance.

'There was an… incident, chief,' Thorne answered sheepishly before explaining the events of recent hours.

'And the girl, the traitor, she's still in the base?' Strike asked after hearing Thorne out. He knew that the major would be giving himself a hard enough time about being duped by Brandd; admonishing him about it would serve no purpose now.

'I think so, yes. The other inquisitor, the loyal one I mean, Tzula. She took a squad after her.'

'The tremors? Was that the final seal being broken?'

'I have no idea. If it was, we probably would have known about it by now, don't you think?'

A commotion from the hangar bay opening drew both men's attention. Recently landed pilots and disembarked troops alike were staring and pointing into the distance towards Atika. Strike and the major jogged over to see what was happening for themselves.

'It's the hive, chief. It's on fire,' a pilot, still dressed in full flying gear, told him.

Unnatural smoke billowed up into the sky and over the jungle canopies, vast plumes of blackness spiralling sharply in all directions growing ever greater in volume.

'Pass me your magnoculars, Thorne,' Strike asked. The major lifted the cord attached to the eyeglasses over his head and passed them to Strike. The colonel looked through them in the direction of the planetary capital. When he removed them a few moments later, the colour had drained from his face.

'That's not smoke,' he said, fighting to keep the emotion from impinging on his voice. 'It's daemons.'

CHAPTER SIX

913959.M41 / Imperial Command Centre.
Olympax Mountains, Pythos

THE XERXES SUPPORT craft unleashed a volley from its rocket pod, each missile unerringly finding its target and blasting the daemon out of the air. The thing's serpentine body ruptured and its leathery brown wings tore and holed, sending the beast spinning towards the ground. Another Xerxes altered course in a gravity taunting motion and finished it off with a single shot from its multi-laser, gore streaking the flyer's hull as it flew through the space vacated by the now dissipating warp entity.

'Good shooting, Green Wing,' Thorne enthused over the vox from the co-pilot's chair of a nearby Valkyrie. Only a handful of the gunships returning from Khan's Hold had actually made it into the hangar at Olympax before the daemonic assault had been launched, and many of the near hundred Valkyries had simply turned around to engage this new enemy, still overloaded with troops from their previous engagement. The quake-damaged craft had also been scrambled and with their numbers added to the Valkyries already airborne, over one hundred and fifty craft of varying patterns now filled the skies above the Olympax mountain range.

'What are we dealing with here, Thorne? How many of them are there?' Strike's voice fizzed over the vox. With the comms tower out at Olympax, the colonel had boarded his newly refitted Hellhammer, currently perched on the lip of the hangar entrance, and was using it as a mobile base of operations.

The major looked out through a cracked section of cockpit. Less than a kilometre in front of the gunship formation, an angry black cloud roiled in the sky, flashes of warp energy and balefire picking out the spiteful teeth and claws of its constituent parts.

'Impossible to say, chief.' Another of the serpentine beasts forming the daemonic vanguard darted between a phalanx of Valkyries only to die screaming as door gunners ripped it to pieces with heavy bolter rounds. 'All we're encountering at the moment are the advance scouts.'

'I'm getting everybody in the base out through the east entrance, but that's going to take time. Keep them occupied for as long as you can, then split your formation to the four corners of the planet. Tell those pilots to head for any delver-stronghold that still remains in our hands and establish contact with other Catachan cells as soon as they can.'

'We're giving them Olympax?' said Thorne, sceptically rather than dissenting.

'They had Olympax the instant the sky turned black with daemons. If those seals were holding back a tide of warp-fiends we have to melt back into the jungle and keep them occupied until somebody, anybody, arrives to reinforce us.'

'But we don't even know whether the astropath was able to contact the battlefleet, and Brigstone and the armour have probably been lost at sea. Help might not be on its way.' The chatter of heavy bolter fire echoed from further back inside the Valkyrie. The door gunners had sheared a wing from one of the daemons and it flipped erratically end over end. Reaching out with a claw as it dropped, it raked the side of another gunship at lower altitude. The craft rocked precariously and, sensing easy prey, two more of the winged horrors pounced upon it before the gunners could react, tearing through armour plating like paper and casting the occupants violently down onto the mountains below before sending their craft down after them in a ball of fire.

'We can't think like that. We have to keep fighting and keep hope alive until there's not a single Catachan left to draw breath on Pythos. And even then, if our sacrifice is so total that not a single soldier of the 183rd will be around to witness it, we have to believe that Pythos will be saved.'

The sky outside lit up as the front ranks of the aerial daemon army came into range and the Catachan craft commenced their assault.

'I only hope I'm around to be proven wrong,' Thorne said launching one of the Valkyrie's hellstrike missiles in the direction of a host of flat, blue daemons that had separated from the main pack and were heading directly for him.

913959.M41 / The Tunnel System, Imperial Command Centre. Olympax Mountains, Pythos

'YOUR ARM?' EPIMETHEUS had stopped higher up the stone stairs and was waiting for Tzula to catch up with him. 'Is it troubling you?'

'Not really,' she replied. 'The opposite in fact. It feels like my forearm and hand are still there. Right now I have the sensation that I'm flexing my fingers and twisting my wrist, but that's impossible of course.'

'You'd be surprised. Brothers of mine who have lost limbs in battle claim that they've been able to feel the presence of a phantom limb even after they've had an augmetic replacement fitted.'

'And where are they?'

'What?' Epimetheus said non-plussed. 'The phantom limbs?'

'No,' said Tzula finally catching up to him. 'Your brothers.'

'I've told you, this conversation can wait. If the final seal has been broken and the cache is once again open, this entire planet is in peril.' He turned to continue his ascent.

'And I've told you that I am an agent of the Most Holy Ordos of the Emperor's Inquisition. I demand some answers.'

The Grey Knight stopped once again. +And who are you to demand anything of me?+ He did not bother to turn and face Tzula.

+I thought I just made that abundantly clear. I serve the Ordo Malleus, as do you.+

He turned to face her again. 'Then you are either deluded, a very convincing liar or a lot has changed since I have been down here.'

'What do you mean?' she asked.

'I have never heard of this Ordo Malleus of which you speak. Nor am I aware of it having any ties to the Grey Knights or the Inquisition.'

It was Tzula's turn to be non-plussed. 'How long have you been down here?'

'I'm... unsure. My implants were keeping me in a state of suspended animation. It was only the psychic wards I left in place that alerted me to the traitors' presence in the seal chamber and roused me.' His speech was becoming more normalised now, as if it was improving with practice. 'What year is it?'

Tzula was taken aback slightly. 'It is the nine hundred and fifty-ninth year of the forty-first millennium,' she answered hesitantly. She did not need to be a psyker herself to sense that this information unsettled Epimetheus.

'In that case, Tzula Digriiz of the Most Holy Ordos of the Emperor's Inquisition,' he said, climbing upwards again at speed. 'I have been down here almost ten thousand years.'

913959.M41 / Imperial Command Centre. Olympax Mountains, Pythos

BLUE FLAME ENGULFED the Valkyrie flying above Thorne's in the formation, exploding it in a shower of twisted metal and human wreckage. It rained down on the craft below, unbalancing them as they prepared to unleash their weapons into the oncoming wave of daemons. The darkening sky filled with energy beams from over a hundred multilasers accompanied by the contrails of missiles launched from the gunships supporting the troop carriers. The front rank of daemons peeled off and broke, leaving the Catachan weapons to hit those arrayed behind them. In a roar of explosions and otherworldly screaming, nigh on a thousand daemons succumbed in the space of seconds.

It was nowhere near enough.

Those that had broken under the initial assault now regrouped and engaged the Catachan craft, reinforced by swift, spindly daemons who seemed to have no discernible way of keeping aloft other than dark pacts sworn to even darker deities. Some breathed warpfire, burning plasteel hulls as if they were made of dried wood and cooking off missiles from pregnant pods. Others launched wicked barbs from their mouths and other orifices, spears of solid flesh and iron-hard bone that impaled pilots and clogged engine rotors. Those with no means of ranged attack simply flew directly at the Valkyries and barged bodily against them, crashing them into others in the tight formation or diverting them into mountain faces. A pair of the flat, blue daemons wailed monstrously as they synchronised their assault on one of the Xerxes gunships, each one tearing off a turbojet as they launched themselves under its wings at speed. The craft hung ponderously in the sky for a second before dropping like a stone onto the mountain peak below.

And still the daemons came.

Like an industrial chimney spitting out toxic pollutant into the Pythosian dusk, the flow of daemons from Atika Hive was ceaseless – a morass of newly spawned malevolence ready to claim dominion over the material world.

As the Imperial Navy pilot at the helm of Thorne's Valkyrie struggled valiantly to avoid the onrushing daemons, the major noticed a change in the pattern of the column spewing forth from the planetary capital. Where it had previously appeared to be a single mass, it had now broken up, daemons suddenly flying off like a shoal of fish dispersing once a predator got amongst them. Two vast shadows broke away from the silhouette of the hive city, massive compared to the daemons the Catachans were already battling, and faster with it. A palpable wave of panic spread through the enemy ranks. They scattered as if their very existence was under threat allowing Thorne and his men time to regroup.

'Something's happening, chief,' Thorne voxed. 'New targets have presented themselves. Big targets.'

'I see them too, major. How long can you buy us?' Strike responded. The vox-feed had grown choppy and distorted the colonel's voice in a macabre fashion.

'As much as you need.' Thorne switched to the general channel. 'All wings. New priority targets. Let's take those big bastards down.'

Taking shots of opportunity at the fleeing minor daemons, the Valkyries resumed formation and gunned their engines towards the new threats. By the time Thorne realised his mistake, it was already too late.

Moving preternaturally quickly for something with wings, the first shape collided with the lead Valkyries before any of the others could react. One moment, three gunships were taking point, the next a crimson blur barrelled through them turning them to scrap, a trio of fireballs the only evidence of them ever existing. Once the flames had cleared, the Catachans got a clear look at what had wreaked such bloody havoc.

The colour of darkest blood, the behemoth hovered in front of the Imperial position goading them to attack, every beat of its powerful leathery wings generating turbulence that swung the stationary Valkyries roughly from side to side. In one hand it wielded a double-bladed axe, thick with fresh ichor from where it had carved a path through its weaker cousins. In its other, it gripped the handle of a long, barbed whip, the thong of which seemed to be made from the same material as its wings. Curved horns sprouted wickedly from its forehead and plates of thick brass armour etched with heretical symbols that stung human eyes to gaze upon them hung over its shoulders, chest and thighs.

'Skullrender,' Thorne said down the secure line to Strike, his voice a frightened whisper. It was rare for any veterans of the Catachan regiments to return to their home world, rarer still to be breathing when they did come home. Some of those veterans, the ones whose psyche was frayed a little too much and whose anecdotes fell just the wrong side of fanciful, would speak in hushed, feared tones of an entity so bloodthirsty that entire battalions had committed suicide in their barracks rather than face one. Others in the Imperium had different names for this particular classification of warp entity but those who knew of such matters – scholars of the forbidden and the esoteric – called them Bloodthirsters.

'Emperor preserve us,' Strike replied. 'Do what you can, Thorne, we only need a few more minutes.'

'Understood, chief,' Thorne said, regaining some of his composure. He switched back to the open channel before bellowing, 'Concentrate fire!' Over a hundred weapons answered his call, enough firepower to level a small city in the blink of an eye, all trained on one target. Except their target was no longer there.

Thrusting upwards, the Bloodthirster flew in a wide, vertical arc, tucking in its wings at the apex and diving down upon the Catachans packed so tightly below. As it hit their formation, it lashed out with whip and axe simultaneously, slicing one of the Valkyries in twain while spinning another into the side of an identical craft. Three more blazing wrecks cascaded down upon the thickly forested valleys below.

In the weeks since Abaddon's invasion of Pythos, Major Eckhardt Thorne of the Catachan 183rd had seen many strange and diabolical sights, but what he witnessed next was the most bizarre of all.

Despite being almost the same size as the Bloodthirster, the second dark shape had ended up in the midst of the Valkyrie formation without anybody seeming to notice. Looming large through the cockpit window, Thorne could quite clearly make out the spindly, purple form of a feathered, bird-headed daemon. Its frame was the equivalent of its counterpart but the bulk it wore upon it was barely half that of the Bloodthirster. Instead of armour it wore robes of fine cloth that constantly changed colour and texture in a mildly hypnotic way. In place of a whip or axe it carried a staff of ornate crafting that terminated in a crescent moon shape inset with a living, blinking eye.

It opened its mouth to speak, revealing numerous sets of tiny fangs within its beaked mouth and uttered a single word that made Thorne's ears bleed to hear it. Without any physical interference or act of violence being perpetrated upon it, the Valkyrie alongside Thorne's simply fell apart, reduced to its constituent parts in mid-air and exposing its occupants to the effects of gravity.

The daemon smiled and turned its attention to Thorne's craft.

It had just opened its mouth to speak when a sonic boom sounded from somewhere back in the mountains. The thing's eyes widened in horror right before the shot from the hellhammer cannon struck it, knocking it back in the direction from which it came.

'I thought you could do with some help,' said Strike over the vox.

'But how–'

'The inquisitor's monkey made some modifications when he repaired the tank.' Thorne could hear K'Cee protesting noisily in the background.

'Got quite a range on it now.'

A purple shape whizzed over the cockpit canopy, only avoiding collision thanks to the pilot's quick reflexes. Despite the daemon's frail construction, the hellhammer shell had done little, if nothing, to impede it.

'Looks like you're about to have company, chief.'

'Don't worry about me. I'll keep our feathered friend busy, you keep that Skullrender off our backs.' The vox abruptly went dead.

'Chief? Chief?' No response. Thorne tried the open channel. 'All wings. Is anybody receiving?'

A string of affirmatives followed.

'The other daemon has breached Olympax. We can't let the Skullrender make it through as well. Break formation. Attack from all angles.'

Engines screaming as Valkyries banked and rose, heavy bolter fire joined the multilaser and missile fire as the flyers presented their flanks to let the door gunners join the attack. Surrounded on all sides as well as above and below, the Bloodthirster was penned in and took dozens of hits, flame wreathing it as explosions blossomed across its armour and hide. It roared in pain but did not succumb.

Cornered like a beast, it lashed out at the closest targets and, despite the best efforts of the pilots to dodge its wild swings, the daemon accounted for two more of the Valkyries. A third lost its tail to the axe's backswing and spun to the ground trailing smoke in its wake.

The Catachans poured on the fire, but the Bloodthirster soaked it up and returned it in kind. Having learned from the mistakes of their now dead comrades, the pilots were staying well out of the range of the daemon's axe. It lashed out instead with its whip, raking the barbs across a dozen cockpits, collapsing them and showering those inside with lethal fragments of plastiglas.

Thorne looked on helplessly as more of the flyers simply dropped from the sky, pilots dead at the controls or instruments wrecked. Every one of these pilots would fight to the death to ensure that Strike and the remaining Catachans had enough time to evacuate the base, and it was looking increasingly like that was what it was going to take to cover their retreat: the death of every one of them. Thorne made a decision.

'All wings. Get out of here. Spread out across the planet and make for the outlying strongholds. We go underground, harry the enemy at every opportunity and wait for reinforcements. The Emperor protects!' The vox channel swelled with affirmatives and repeated blessings.

Through the crazed apertures of the cockpit, Thorne saw the remaining Valkyries peel off and speed away in all directions. The Bloodthirster hung suspended, momentarily confused and unsure which targets to pursue. The pilot by Thorne's side made to pull back on the control stick and send the craft higher into the atmosphere, but the major's hand stopped him.

'Not us, son,' Thorne said solemnly. 'We have to cover *their* escape.' He looked back down the interior and received nods of confirmation from the two door gunners.

The pilot nodded in understanding and swung the Valkyrie sharply around, its weapons systems all trained on the daemon's rear. The beast was about to beat its heavy wings in pursuit of a cluster of gunships when Thorne gave the order to fire. Las-rounds and solid shot impacted against the thing, followed by a direct hit between its shoulder blades from a hellstrike missile, the detonation briefly obscuring the daemon from view.

When the smoke and flame cleared, the wounded Bloodthirster turned and bellowed in rage, its powerful breath violently shaking the craft and forcing the pilot to lower altitude to avoid the wave of turbulence. Sensing its opportunity, the daemon cracked its massive whip, wrapping it around the hull of the impertinent flyer and yanked back hard, veins the thickness of a man's arm bulging in its bicep. The Valkyrie barrel-rolled, tossed like driftwood in a tsunami and the door gunners were thrown clear, their bodies smashed as they hit the rocks below. Righting itself, the Valkyrie hovered vulnerably before the thing from the warp.

'What do we have left?' Thorne asked the pilot. Receiving no response, he turned to see the slumped form of the Navy man, face caved-in from where it had impacted against the control facia. Quickly unstrapping the man from his seat, Thorne unceremoniously dumped his corpse on the cockpit floor and assumed the pilot's seat. As part of their training, all Catachan officers were given simple instruction in operating

Imperial Guard vehicles and though it had been almost a decade since he'd been at the controls of a Valkyrie, he'd spent enough time in the co-pilot's seat these past three years to relearn the basics.

The Bloodthirster lashed out again. Instinctively, Thorne pushed forwards on the control stick, entering into a steep dive that he barely pulled out of before making contact with a mountain. Now, facing away from the daemon, he spun the craft around in a one-hundred and eighty degree turn and squeezed the firing stud for the hull-mounted multi-laser, hitting the beast in the chest and scorching the brass of its breastplate. Unfazed, the Bloodthirster lowered its head and dived towards Thorne.

The major looked all around him to see dozens of craft disappearing into the distance, tiny pinpricks of light in the Pythosian dusk. Over the Bloodthirster's shoulder, the lesser daemons were getting braver, swarming to launch a new assault. He had done enough to allow the Valkyrie wings to get to safety, but he could still buy Strike and the rest of the regiment more time. Priming the last of the hellstrike missiles in its launch pod, Thorne pulled back hard on the throttle and drove upwards towards the onrushing daemon.

Thirteen tonnes of forge-world manufactured aerial troop carrier hit almost a thousand kilometres per hour as it flew inexorably towards a warpborn fiend of almost the same weight, flying at a near-identical speed. When they hit the point where neither could pull out, Thorne launched the hellstrike. The Bloodthirster's eyes grew wide with realisation.

'I'll be with you soon, Mack,' Thorne whispered as the flames and shockwave hit.

FROM THE COMMAND compartment of the Hellhammer, Strike watched his friend die.

The orange bloom of an explosion filled the greying sky, followed shortly by the sound of metal rending through flesh and muscle. The Valkyrie had embedded itself in the Bloodthirster's abdomen and they hung suspended in the sky, before dropping towards the ground in a fiery morass. The daemon howled as it fell, its grip on the material realm slipping rapidly, and by the time Thorne's craft hit the jungle floor, all trace of the daemon-beast had passed from reality.

Strike made a fist and slammed it down on the armrest of the Hellhammer's command seat. The time for mourning would come later, not just for Thorne but all those of the 183rd who'd laid down their lives this day. Right now though, the colonel had bigger problems.

Tucking its wings back, the feathered daemon landed in the hangar bay and turned to look back at the last faint traces of the explosion in the sky. It moved uneasily on its crooked legs as if unused to its own body. When it spoke, it did so with a thousand tiny voices.

'Ah, Bellanoth. Ever the capricious beast. A shame really as I'm certain you would have revelled in the slaughter yet to come.' Its beaked head darted this way and that, giving the impression that the beast had an acute nervous tic. Tendrils of ethereal smoke clung to it like ink suspended in water. 'But where have all my toys gone? I was so looking forward to playing my little games.'

In response, the Hellhammer's main weapon came to life, a mighty boom echoing around the hangar bay as it spat one of its heavy siege cannon shells towards the bird-like monstrosity. Unperturbed, the daemon merely lifted its hand, stopping the shell mid-flight only centimetres from its palm and holding it in place. It tottered awkwardly around the immobile projectile, peering at it and tapping it with its macabre staff.

'Such an ugly thing. Artless and utterly without grace. I imagine it is effective though.' With a flick of its wrist, the daemon turned the shell on its axis and sent it flying back towards the Hellhammer. Missing the tank by some distance, it instead exploded against the wall of the hangar, collapsing part of the ceiling and turning to scrap the partly damaged Valkyries that had been awaiting repair. Chunks of Olympax thudded against the tank's hull, tearing off an armour plate mounted over the engine housing, much to K'Cee's consternation.

'Back us up! Back us up!' Strike ordered. The driver slammed the Hellhammer into reverse and coaxed the war machine backwards, crushing debris under its enormous chassis. The brief shock and revulsion the crew had felt at being so close to a warp entity had soon passed, as if the hull of the tank was protecting their souls as well as their bodies.

'No, no, no,' the daemon said in its choir of tongues. 'This game is far from over.' It tapped the butt of its staff on the floor of the hangar three times and the Hellhammer came to an abrupt halt, its super-charged engine revving frantically, but its tracks locked as if frozen.

'She won't shift, chief,' called the driver.

'Are the weapons still operable?' Strike asked the gunners. Each response was in the negative. K'Cee started banging instrument panels in frustration.

A tapping noise sounded from on the top of the hull, the arrhythmic plodding of hooves over metal.

'Come out, come out, wherever you are...' the daemon said mockingly, strutting over the motionless tank. 'Don't make me come in there and get you,' it added in a far more sinister tone, as if its thousand voices were all crying out in pain. It raised the staff above its head ready to smash open the Hellhammer's turret.

A single shot rang out, striking the daemon on the wrist and sending the gnarled rod skidding away across the hangar floor. It rubbed its wrist where it stung from the impact and arced its neck to ascertain the source of the gunfire.

WITHIN THE TANK, a ripple of confusion passed over the Catachans.

'The rest of the lads should have evacuated. Somebody must have come back,' suggested one of the gunners.

'That was a bolter round. Must be one of the Valkyries coming back to evacuate more personnel,' said another.

'If it was one of the flyboys, he must have glided in because we didn't hear any engine noise,' added the driver, Tamzarian.

Jumping down from the commander's seat, Strike clambered up the ladder to the top hatch and slid back the cover of one of the spy slits. What he saw through it made his heart sing.

'SO, A NEW player enters the game and a Space Marine at that.' The daemon's beak peeled back in a smile and it rubbed a serpentine tongue over rows of razor-sharp teeth. 'Hmmm, such sport, just like Abaddon promised.'

'Abaddon?' Epimetheus exclaimed. 'He's behind reopening the cache?'

'The Warmaster granted us our freedom in return for our fealty the next time he leads forth a crusade. A small price to pay, all things considered.' The daemon waved a hand and its discarded staff flew back into its grip. Casting it in a wide arc, a wave of boiling warp energy crackled towards the Grey Knight. Epimetheus moved out of its path, spun, and came around with his halberd in both hands. He jabbed it in the direction of the winged beast and unleashed his psychic fury in a concentrated blast, but it met a hastily erected kine shield and fizzled out harmlessly against it.

'Your mindshields are strong, Space Marine, but I do not need to read your thoughts to know that you are not of this era.' The daemon circled Epimetheus, sizing his opponent up like a pugilist looking for an opening. 'You are from the time of the Great Awakening, when your brothers cast off the shackles of the Imperium and forged a new destiny as servants of the true gods.'

'And you are a Lord of Change. Every word you utter is an untruth, every statement a trick.' Epimetheus unleashed another blast of psychic energy but this too washed harmlessly over the daemon's defences. 'The time of which you speak was not one of awakening, it was one of death and dishonour, of treachery and heresy.'

'Ah, the rich tapestry of history, ever to be woven by the victor except in cases where there was no clear victor.' It tried a different prong of attack, darting forward almost imperceptibly quickly and striking out at the Grey Knight with its staff. Epimetheus parried with his halberd, sickeningly coloured sparks and the reek of sulphur emanating from where his psychic conduit came into contact with the raw stuff of the warp. 'Of course, with the Damnation Cache open again, we draw ever closer to the final battle in the war we started ten millennia ago,' the daemon added, pulling his staff away and drawing Epimetheus forwards under his own momentum. The Lord of Change swung again but connected with thin air as the Space Marine ducked under the daemon's weapon, countering with his own thrust.

'And what do you know of the Great Heresy? I expect you were cowering behind the veil, lurking in the warp and waiting to see which side won rather than taking to the field of battle. Your kind always do.' He brought the force halberd around in a blue blur, narrowly missing the daemon's head.

The Lord of Change bristled visibly, its feathers ruffling at the slight. Its voices took on a higher pitch. 'I was far from idle, Space Marine. I helped bring half a Legion under the sway of the Four True Gods and took part in the destruction of their home world when their faith was found wanting. I looked on while a primarch died, content in the knowledge that I played a part in his downfall.'

'Yet somehow you still ended up imprisoned within the Damnation Cache. If you are so powerful, so clever that you could cause a schism among an entire Space Marine Legion, how did you come to be penned up among the ranks of lesser daemons? Does your patron no longer favour you?'

Anger took hold of the daemon. It lashed out erratically, putting Epimetheus on the back foot. 'Pythos! It was to be our foothold in the material realm, the beachhead from which we could launch our assaults on the shattered Imperium and finish what we'd started while our enemy was still weakened. Bellanoth and I leading hordes of the damned against the remnants of mankind, worlds cowering in our shadow until… until…' Its bubble of anger burst giving way to chilling laughter. 'But you already know all this don't you, just as I know who you are? Your armour may be the wrong colour through years of wear and neglect but I know who you are, Epimetheus of the Grey Knights, and your soul will belong to me.'

THE SWEATY FORMS of Catachan tank crew peered out of every available aperture, watching in awe as the Space Marine duelled with the daemon. For over a minute they sat transfixed, watching one of the Imperium's finest do battle with a thing that defied possibility, each evenly matched in the arena of psychic warfare.

It was Strike who broke their collective trance.

'Do we have control of the steering and weapons?' he barked, his voice echoing uncomfortably around the confines of the crew compartment.

Reluctantly pulling themselves away from the spectacle occurring outside, the driver and gunners retook their positions and tested their systems. The Hellhammer lurched backwards and the turret and weapons sponsons rotated as evidence of the daemon's ensorcellment having come to an end. A series of affirmatives rang out through the tank.

'Do we target the warpspawn, chief?' asked one of the gunners.

'Negative,' Strike replied, looking out through a spy slit. 'Just as likely to hit our green saviour.'

The melee outside was taking place at breakneck speed, each cut, thrust and parry happening at a pace far outstripping that of any mortal being.

'We bugging out, chief?' ventured Tamzarian.

'Affirmative, trooper. Let's get her down to the east entrance and head for Khan's Hold.' He looked through the aperture again. The Space Marine struck the daemon a wicked blow that sliced the tip from one of its wings. It retaliated with a cannonade of blue flame which the armoured figure evaded. 'I think our friend is more than capable of handling himself.'

Manipulating the ancient control levers, the driver manoeuvred the super-heavy tank, turning it around so that they could descend the exit ramp and take the transit tunnel that ran deep within the mountain's belly. Before they had moved more than a few metres, a banging sound issued forth from the roof.

'What in the name of Terra is that?' asked one of the gunners, the noise of the daemon stalking over the hull obviously still fresh in his mind.

Strike looked out to where the daemon was locked in combat with the Space Marine. Off in the distance, beyond the hangar opening, the ominous black cloud of lesser daemons was drawing ever nearer, but none had yet breached the Imperial base. Switching to the other side of the turret, Strike pulled back an aperture cover to witness a dark-skinned woman's hand bashing a rock against the armour plating.

'Halt!' he called to the driver. Still lurching forwards under the effect of braking, Strike popped open the turret hatch with a hiss of releasing pressure and the artificial light from the hangar bled into the poorly illuminated troop compartment. Moments later, Tzula Digriiz followed the light in. Still woozy from the trauma of losing her lower arm and almost at the point of exhaustion from following the Space Marine up through the warren of tunnels, she half-climbed, half-fell down the ladder.

'What happened to your arm?' Strike asked, lifting her from the cold floor of the Hellhammer and propping her up in one of the numerous unoccupied crew positions.

'A Space Marine did it.' Even in her diminished state, Tzula was careful not to use Epimetheus's name or give away his Chapter affiliation. Strike looked at her sceptically, hand reaching unconsciously for his fang. 'No, nothing like that. Brandd had a vial of contagion which she used to open the seal. I got some on my arm. He only did what was necessary.'

'Looks like you made it back just in time. We're the last ride out of here.' Strike signalled to the driver to get moving again but Tzula stopped him.

'No. We can't leave without him. Didn't you hear what I just said? He saved my life. I owe it to him.'

'And I owe it to my men and the people of this planet to prosecute this war until support arrives to reconquer it. If your friend outside is any indication, those reinforcements are already on their way. His Chapter will–'

'His Chapter will do nothing because they're not here yet. He's alone,' Tzula snapped. 'He's been here longer than anybody. Longer than you, longer than the miners, longer even than the first settlers. He helped put the seals in place and, until the cavalry arrive, he's the only chance we've got at containing the warp breach.'

Strike rubbed the several weeks of growth on his chin contemplatively.

'Right now there's an entire army of daemons headed for this place and he isn't going to be able to handle them on his own,' she continued. 'Please, Strike. Don't leave him to face them alone.'

'So YOUR BROTHERS abandoned you, did they? Left you behind to keep watch over the Damnation Cache while they went around the galaxy seeking true glory.' The Lord of Change swatted aside a riposte from the Grey Knight's halberd. 'That must rankle you, Epimetheus. To know that they chose you to remain here because you were the least of them.'

'I am immune to your words, filth,' Epimetheus spat, channelling his rage but not allowing it to overtake him. He swung low and wide with the force weapon, attempting to unbalance the daemon. It lifted one foot in time to avoid the blow, but its back foot didn't move quite as swiftly and it fell backwards, wings crumpling beneath it. Instantaneously,

Epimetheus was standing over it, halberd held aloft in both hands and poised to land the killing blow.

'That's right, Epimetheus. End me. End me so that you might at last emerge from Janus's shadow,' the daemon taunted.

The force halberd crackled with lambent psychic energy but before Epimetheus could drive it down, a dark form flew in from his blindside and bowled him over, causing him to lose hold of the weapon. Long fangs, more akin to claws, snapped at his armour, trying to chew through the aged ceramite. Gripping the serpentine thing by the neck, Epimetheus got back to his feet and tore its head from its body, showering his armour in gore. More of the detritus that coated his armour dissolved away, revealing further patches of silver beneath. He stooped to recover his halberd but when he turned back to the spot where he'd left the prone daemon, the Lord of Change was no longer there.

'Janus would have landed that blow. Khyron too.' The daemon had taken to the air now, flanked by more of the serpentine daemons and blue horrors that had earlier assailed the Catachan Valkyries. Heralded by the loud roar of engines, the Hellhammer opened up with all of its weapons, tearing over the rubble coating the hangar floor, taking out any target that presented itself. Daemons either side of the Lord of Change disintegrated as autocannon fire stitched through them. The greater daemon raised his kine shield just in time to prevent the rounds causing it damage too.

'A truly wonderful toy,' the daemon said as the Hellhammer scorched a cadre of blue horrors with its flamers. 'Come, Epimetheus, let me kill you quickly so that I can play with it.' The Lord of Change swooped down on its massive wings and struck the Grey Knight a glancing blow with its staff. Epimetheus slashed upwards but, seeing his foe unbalanced, the daemon performed a turn in mid-air that ran contrary to all known laws of physics and knocked him to the ground. Before he could react, the winged monstrosity was upon him, pinning him down with twisted, clawed hands.

'Such a waste really, to spend ten thousand years waiting for something only to find that the something you were waiting for was your own death.' Thick strands of spittle drooled from its beak, spilling over Epimetheus's helmet.

'I am nothing if not patient,' the Space Marine said, straining to break the daemon's grip. 'For centuries I dwelt on Titan while the Sigillite kept us hidden from reality, training my mind and arming myself with the knowledge I would need to go forth and eradicate the daemonic from the material realm. I had hundreds of years to not only armour my mind from psychic assault but also to turn it into the sharpest blade with which to sever my enemies' links with the corporeal. But that was not the greatest weapon I armed myself with.'

'Wasn't it? Please illuminate me, Grey Knight,' the Lord of Change said in amusement, its myriad voices raised over the din of the Hellhammer's slaughter. 'But make it quick. I can already sense the entities gathering in the warp waiting for a taste of your soul.'

'Knowledge. Knowledge is the most powerful threat I wield. I had hundreds of years to prepare to do battle with monsters like you and entire libraries at my disposal filled with books that listed the rituals of banishment, the rites of warding and, most important of all, the true names of daemons.'

The daemon sneered. 'True names are worthless if you don't know who they belong to. Come now, I am bored of your prattling. Time to die.' It raised a clawed hand ready to tear through the Grey Knight's armour.

'But I *do* know which true name belongs to you, daemon. I knew it even before you let slip that you turned half a Legion.'

The Lord of Change's expression became one of puzzlement and doubt.

'I know who you are, daemon, because I *recognised* you.' The Grey Knight lowered a portion of his psychic defences, not enough to allow the daemon full access to his mind, but enough to share the information he needed to.

The Lord of Change relinquished its grip on Epimetheus and backed away. 'No! It cannot be. You! The one who defied me, who very nearly unravelled everything. You're not supposed to be in this place. You're not even supposed to be in this *time*.'

Reaching for his weapon, Epimetheus rose to his feet and advanced upon the daemon, both Grey Knight and Lord of Change seemingly oblivious to the weapons fire exploding all around them.

'This was not foreseen. A different path was laid out for you, yet you do not walk it. How can that be?' There was genuine fear in the daemon's voices.

'Somebody switched places with me. That is now his path to walk,' Epimetheus said before crying out the daemon's true name, the one that granted him power over it.

The Lord of Change froze on the spot, its body convulsing as weird energies consumed it. Epimetheus continued to advance upon it.

'Please,' it said meekly. 'I have waited so long to be set free.'

The Grey Knight ignored the plea and, without ceremony, thrust the force halberd into the daemon's chest. It disappeared in the blink of an eye, the sound of air rushing into the space it had vacated its only fanfare.

'Not as long as I have,' Epimetheus said.

Daemons poured in through the hangar opening at a prodigious rate and, despite the best efforts of Strike and his crew, the numbers were becoming overwhelming. Drawing his bolt pistol, Epimetheus sprinted over to where the Hellhammer had drawn to a halt, downing daemons as he went. When he reached the rear of the tank, the hatch hissed open with an outpouring of pneumatic pressure to reveal Tzula, K'Cee and the skeleton crew within.

'Get on board,' Tzula called. 'We're retreating.'

The Grey Knight said nothing and ascended the ramp, ducking to get his massive Space Marine frame through the man-sized opening, to be greeted by a group of awestruck Catachans who looked like the Emperor himself had just stepped aboard their tank.

With the hatch still closing, the Hellhammer sped for the exit ramp, abandoning Olympax to its new daemonic occupiers.

INTERLUDE

343960.M41 / The Chapel of Eternal Repose.
Grey Knights Fortress-monastery, Titan

THE HALL WAS cold and silent, the tapping of the sculptors' tools having fallen silent to allow Kaldor Draigo his moment of grief. Clad in full Terminator armour, he knelt before the corpse of Lexek Hasimir, until only a few days ago Grand Master of the Fifth Brotherhood of the Grey Knights, and bowed his head low. In the days to come, the body would be transferred to the Dead Fields where it would rest for all eternity, the half-finished statue beside him placed atop as everlasting memorial, but for now he lay in state awaiting the procession of former brothers who wished to pay their respects. The noble deeds of Lexek Hasimir were numerous and, despite most of the Chapter being deployed on operations, already a lengthy queue of Grey Knights had formed at the gates of the hall, patiently waiting to mark a hero's passing.

As Supreme Grand Master, Draigo had no privilege of rank when it came to honouring a fallen brother, as no hierarchy of grief existed among the Grey Knights order. Captains, justicars, Grand Masters, all were equals in the Chapter's death rites, so the fact that Draigo had been the first in line when the gates of the hall swung open was not by dint of his station, but of the overwhelming desire to mourn for a brother he felt he owed his life to.

Draigo stood and placed his hand on Hasimir's cuirass, running his hand over the claw marks that ran deep through the ceramite breastplate. He pulled his hand away, dried blood coating the tips of his gauntlets, then ran his fingers over the shoulder pad of his own armour, finding three similar, yet not so severe rents.

The source of the gouges had been the same, but whereas Hasimir had reacted in time to prevent the servant of the Pleasure God from slaying the Supreme Grand Master, Draigo had been unable to return the favour, watching helplessly as the Keeper of Secrets had sliced open the leader of the Fifth Brotherhood. In response, the daemon had been banished and his acolytes purged from the surface of the planet they had turned into a world of debauched pleasure, but that seemed scant reward for the loss of a Chapter hero. In time, a conclave would be called so that Draigo and the Grand Masters could appoint a new commander of the Fifth, but for now ceremonies of a different kind were in order.

Uttering a prayer of gratitude to his dead brother and making a sign of warding over the corpse, Draigo took one of the unlit candles surrounding the altar and ignited it using a small psiflame he conjured forth from his fingertips. Carefully placing the taper next to Hasimir's unhelmeted head, Draigo bowed again.

'A light to guide you in dark places, brother. May your slumber grant you the peace that eludes us all in life,' Draigo said before turning to make the long walk back to the gates of the hall and allow the next mourner to take his place by the deceased Grand Master's side.

He hadn't gone three paces when the tingling started in the front of his skull, alerting him to psychic activity within the chamber. The temperature dropped rapidly, hoarfrost forming on his armour. The candle flame guttered and died, as did the braziers ensconced in the chapel walls, extinguished by an unnatural breeze that formed out of nowhere. Crackles of blue energy licked over the surface of Hasimir's torn armour, forming a corona around his head, a halo for a dead angel. Draigo's hand reached for the hilt of the *Titansword*.

With the creak of Terminator armour straining to move without a power source, Lexek Hasimir sat bolt upright and slowly turned his head to look Draigo dead in the eye.

'The Damnation Cache is open once more. You must lead the Chapter back to Pythos,' the dead man said through mortised lips. His eyeballs rolled back in their sockets and he crashed back to the altar, cracking the stone in two as his deadweight impacted against it.

Stopping neither to check the condition of the body nor relight the candle, Grand Master Kaldor Draigo raced from the Hall of Repose, not in fear at his former battle-brother's reanimation but because of the urgency of the message the corpse had conveyed.

PART THREE

CHAPTER SEVEN

766960.M41 / The Bridge. Revenge, Pythos blockade, Pandorax System

LORD ADMIRAL ORSON Kranswar was not having a good war.

From the instant the battlefleet at his command had entered the Pandorax System and lost two destroyers, *Hand of Macharius* and *Avatar of Woe*, to a surprise attack from Chaos raiders waiting in ambush, the portents had been ill for a successful campaign. Every time it appeared that the Imperial Navy were gaining the upper hand and driving Abaddon's vessels further towards Pythos, some new complication would arise to put Battlefleet Demeter on the back foot again. At the Third Battle of Sunward Gap, his ships were about to put the enemy to rout, Abaddon's general having committed his entire fleet to counter Kranswar's superior numbers, when the armada of Huron Blackheart arrived in-system at the eleventh hour, inflicting heavy casualties on the Imperium and depriving it forever of almost a dozen ancient vessels. Using the asteroids of the Adamantium Fields as a temporary refuge, the battlefleet regrouped in preparation for a counter-assault but the Fourth Battle of Sunward Gap was an even greater disaster than the Third.

With force disposition on each side now evenly balanced, the Imperial fleet emerged from the asteroid belt – in reality a graveyard for the countless vessels that had succumbed to the space-bound predators, both human and xenos, that plagued the Demeter subsector – only to find the combined forces of Abaddon and Huron lying in wait for them. With the enemy harassing them every parsec of the way, Kranswar ordered all ships back to the base they'd established at Gaea on the edge of the Pandorax System. Presenting their backs to the enemy, the Chaos forces showed them no mercy, decimating the Imperial fleet as it fled. The selfless actions of the men piloting the fast attack craft ensured casualties were not heavier and that Kranswar's ships were able to make it back to Gaea to regroup at all.

In the days that followed, whispers spread throughout the fleet drawing the Lord Admiral's ability to command into question. It was nothing he hadn't heard before, as far back as his early days in the academy at Bakka. *Plays it by the book. No innovation or flair. Too predictable.* And so, as he had done ever since his time as a cadet, he ignored them. Just as he was ignoring the pleas of an ensign on the bridge of his flagship, *Revenge*.

'But, sir, his men haven't been fed properly for almost a week and his tanks are of no use in a void battle. All he's asking is for his regiment to be allowed passage down to Gaea to resupply and recuperate while the fleet opens the route to Pythos,' the ensign said, trying to hand the Lord Admiral the written request. 'He has over three hundred tanks sitting in the holds and at least ten times that number of personnel. It would free up resources for the crew.'

Once Battlefleet HQ had received the distress call from Pythos, the reserve fleet and all Imperial ground forces in the vicinity were scrambled. Not even waiting for troop transports to arrive from other subsectors, entire Imperial Guard divisions and regiments were crammed into the battleships, cruisers and frigates of Kranswar's fleet, such was the import of liberating the conquered world.

'It's cowardice, pure and simple,' Kranswar snapped. 'What is he? A bloody Vostroyan?' The Lord Admiral was of early middle age, but the severe lines carved into his face and the rapidly developing widow's peak brought on by the strain of command made him look significantly older.

The ensign checked the piece of paper he had been trying to pass to Kranswar. 'Yes, sir. Brigadier Montague Gethsemane

Heinrick-Hague XXVII of the Vostroyan 116th Armoured regiment according to his signature.'

'Lazy bluebloods. All he wants to do is take his men down to the planet and lord it over the population. Probably stock up on a few fine wines, horses and properties while they're down there. The man needs to show some backbone. Don't hear those two Attilan regiments begging to be let off their ship, do you?' The admiral's raised voice was carrying across the bridge causing some of the crew to look up nervously in his direction.

The ensign swallowed. 'With the greatest respect, sir, both Attilan regiments were billeted on the *Avatar of Woe*.'

The Lord Admiral's cheeks went red but he did not immediately give voice to his rage. Awkward moments passed before he snatched the piece of paper from the ensign and tore it in half. 'Request denied,' he said with a flourish before stamping off to return to the other high-ranking officers of the fleet around the stone-wrought strategy table laid out in the centre of the bridge.

The *Revenge* was an ancient vessel, having made its first voyage through the warp while the Space Marine Legions were still being divided, and though its exterior resembled every other ship of its marque, the interior finish was a baroque marvel from another age. Above decks, its floors were made of the finest polished marble and the bulkheads of the bridge and vital operations stations were carved from finest basalt and slate, as were the quarters of every officer above the rank of lieutenant. Brass filigree and fluting livened up every otherwise bare surface or space, and every door was constructed from the highest grade timbers from trees extinct for millennia. Even the throne sitting before the vast occulus on the bridge was worthy of that name, cast from a single piece of silver and finished with elaborate precious stones and the engraved names of every man and woman who'd ever sat in it.

Acknowledging the salutes of the dozen or so admirals, captains and commodores standing to attention over a huge parchment map of the Pandorax System, Kranswar took his place alongside them at the table.

'Gentlemen, though the losses inflicted upon the fleet during our flight from the Adamantium Fields were grave, I believe that those losses ultimately proved worthwhile as it has finally provided me with the key to unlock their defences.' None of the officers said anything but several exchanged bemused looks. 'By using our assault squadrons to cover our defence, we exposed the Chaos forces' soft underbelly. Our fighter-interceptors were able to get in close and strike with impunity, too fast for both their defence batteries and the enemy's interceptors.'

A younger, heavy-set man with a thick red beard cleared his throat to get the Lord Admiral's attention.

'Yes, Admiral Blaise?' Kranswar said, annoyed at not being able to continue with his grand plan. Blaise wore the same pristine white naval uniform as the Lord Admiral, minus the blue tabard that denoted the higher rank. He had the bridge of the *Stalwart* and as such was the second-in-command of the fleet.

'That's not strictly accurate, sir,' Blaise said, his voice heavily accented. 'The enemy interceptors are all stationed on craft that held back and didn't pursue us to Gaea.'

Kranswar ploughed on regardless. 'Irrelevant, admiral. Intelligence suggests that our fast attack craft outnumber theirs at least twofold. Should we encounter any aerial resistance, we can split our number in two, half carrying out strafing runs, half providing cover.'

Audible murmuring rippled around the table which, like so many other things, the Lord Admiral ignored.

'Our strategy is this: the bulk of the fleet will move forward as a screen and engage the larger enemy vessels within the Adamantium Fields. The *Revenge* and *Stalwart* will stay within Gaea's orbit and launch successive waves of attack craft, refuelling and rearming each wing as it returns, ready to be sent straight back out to battle.'

The murmur became louder and some of the officers gesticulated with each other.

'Does anybody have a problem with that?' the Lord Admiral said coldly.

Blaise was the first to speak up. 'The *Revenge* and *Stalwart* are the most heavily armed ships in the fleet. They need to be at the forefront taking the battle to the enemy, not kept in reserve as mobile launch platforms.'

'You'll be leaving the capital ships vulnerable, not to

mention putting another world in peril. What if the attack fails? The path to Gaea would be left wide open,' added Commodore Yarl of the *Banshee*. Younger than either Kranswar or Blaise, he was an ambitious officer who hailed from the Pandorax System.

'Having *Revenge* and *Stalwart* in the heart of the battle means the attack squadrons won't have so far to return to resupply,' said Ibzen, a tall, gaunt man who commanded *Inviolate*, one of the fleet's Sword-class frigates.

Kranswar's cheeks flushed red again. 'This is not a committee!' he raged. 'Those are your orders. Now return to your ships and be ready to carry them out.'

Still discussing amongst themselves the wisdom of the Lord Admiral's tactics, the officers took their leave of the bridge, returning to the shuttles waiting to ferry them back to their own vessels. As they exited through the high set of elaborate mahogany doors, a young ensign squeezed past them, handwritten note clutched in his hands. He briskly strode over to Kranswar and snapped off a sharp salute.

'Begging your pardon, sir, but I have a message from a Commander Keene of the Mordian Fifth. He has asked if he and his men could take shuttles down to–'

The retort that followed could have stripped flesh from bone.

766960.M41 / Merciless Death, Adamantium Fields, Pandorax System

MALGAR IRONGRASP, WARLORD of Abaddon's fleet, navigated the corridors of *Merciless Death* with the confidence of a man assured that victory was close at hand. His ancient suit of black power armour, once the bleached ivory of a White Consul, hissed and clanked as he moved, and footsteps rang out as heavy boots met iron floor. Though many Chaos vessels developed characteristics and modifications akin to the patron god of those who crewed it, the forces of the Black Legion were pragmatic in their worship and, as such, Abaddon's ship remained relatively untouched by the pervasive influence of the warp.

One such enhancement, however, was the door that Irongrasp now approached, resembling more a curtain of woven flesh than any conventional aperture. When he halted on the threshold, a globular eyeball detached itself from the organic sheet and leered out at the Chaos warlord on a stalk constructed of twisted sinew. Unblinking, the amber sac looked him up and down before rapidly retreating back into the folds of skin with a wet sucking sound. The flesh peeled back to allow him access to the chamber within.

Two robed acolytes turned to see who this newcomer was and, upon reaching the realisation that it was the commander of the fleet, bowed in supplication before quickly taking their leave. The doors closed behind them with the sound of bloody meat hitting an abattoir floor.

The chamber was small but packed from floor to ceiling with all manner of esoteric artefacts and ephemera, both mechanical and organic. Jars of assorted liquids sat upon shelves, their contents casting an unnatural multi-coloured glow over everything around them. Brass syringes and bizarre callipers and vices of all shapes and sizes sat alongside rotting wooden trays of desiccated organs and skeletal remains of small alien creatures. Scanning the tightly packed shelves, Malgar found what he sought.

Submerged within a glass barrel filled with viscous green liquid was a human head, dreadlocked hair matted to the sides of its face, features barely visible through the opaque fluid. As soon as Malgar espied it, the head's sightless eyes opened yet its face remained entirely devoid of expression. Taking the container down from the high shelf, he placed it on a small rusted table at the edge of the chamber and unscrewed the lid. With a hiss of escaping pressure and a stench comparable to that of the grave, Malgar plunged his hand into the barrel and pulled the head out by its hair, planting it on the table alongside its former housing. Its eyes remained open, staring blankly ahead.

'I wish to commune with Lord Abaddon,' said Malgar Irongrasp, wiping some of the excess green ooze from the severed head's face. Its milky orbs rolled in their sockets and its mouth moved in a wordless incantation, the stump where its tongue used to be flapping every time it moved its jaws. Slowly, in the space before the disembodied psyker's head on the table, the flickering, diminutive form of Abaddon coalesced. The psi-image was washed out and distorted as if it was being viewed through water. Malgar was about to address it when another, similar image gradually faded into reality beside that of his master. Crimson armour washed out to pink by the projection process, Huron Blackheart leered as his features realised.

'Why is *he* present for our communion, lord?' Malgar asked, trying to retain some respect in his tone. Blackheart's intervention in the Third Battle of Sunward Gap had neither been sought nor welcomed by Irongrasp, and the brief vox-communications they had exchanged since the Red Corsairs fleet arrived in-system had been terse and confrontational.

'You should count yourself fortunate that *you* are present at this communion, Irongrasp.' Abaddon's words resonated with power and a malign dignity. 'If it wasn't for the centuries of flawless service you have given my Black Legion prior to this campaign, another would already have taken your place at the head of the fleet.'

'A role I would have accepted only too gratefully, Lord Abaddon,' Huron said, his lips peeled back in a vicious grin.

'There are a thousand men under my command who would lead my fleet before you entered into my consideration, Blackheart.' Even as a small psycholithic projection, the expression Abaddon wore on his face could have razed cities. 'Until you take to your knee before me, you will not so much as set foot on one of my ships, let alone command one. Are you prepared to do that, pirate? Here and now. Bend your knee and bow before me to pledge your allegiance and that of your band of renegades to the Black Legion? Willingly, and without query or reward, make a gift to me of your spacecraft and engines of war?'

The watery image of Huron Blackheart said nothing. His bared teeth remained on show.

'Of course not, for you are nothing more than an aspiring usurper. One eye constantly on my mantle of Warmaster, the other on your back lest you find a blade sticking in it,' Abaddon said once it was clear that Huron wasn't rising to the bait. 'For the time being, you are useful, Blackheart. The instant that situation changes, our arrangement will be at an end and you will be considered an enemy once more.'

'Understood, Abaddon.' Huron's lack of honorific was entirely intentional. 'Though I have a feeling I will be of more use to you during the coming campaign than even you yet realise,' he added cryptically.

Ignoring the Red Corsair's attempt to draw him, Abaddon addressed Irongrasp once again.

'The Imperial fleet should be nothing more than drifting wrecks by now, Irongrasp. With the Cache open, Corpulax and our daemonic allies are keen to spread their influence away from Pythos and into the Pandorax System and beyond.' He cast Huron a sideways glance. 'Besides, if I find that which I seek, I'd prefer to keep knowledge of it from those beyond the veil.'

Huron feigned a dismissive expression.

'Our forces are too evenly matched, lord, and their admiral follows Imperial naval doctrine to the letter. His every manoeuvre and feint is straight out of the academy textbooks and his execution has been flawless.' Malgar leant his head forward slightly as he spoke.

'So you have finally been outclassed. Perhaps it is time for fresh blood to assume command of the fleet.' There was no anger in Abaddon's words, only cold logic.

'Far from it, my lord,' Irongrasp asserted. 'During our last encounter I allowed him to believe that we were weak in certain areas and that his fast attack craft held the greatest threat to us. I also know exactly what his tactics will be during the next battle.'

'And how do you know that?' sneered Huron. 'Have your psykers read his mind? Do you have a spy on his bridge?'

'Neither. The fool is so predictable, so wed to Imperial naval dogma, that when he next assaults us he will do so with his small fighter craft backed up by frigates and destroyers. Instead of committing his two capital ships to close quarters fighting within the Adamantium Fields, he will keep them both back as launch platforms before moving them into position once our larger craft have been destroyed.'

'And what are you going to do to prevent your craft being destroyed? He has a numerical advantage in terms of fighters and if the battle is to be fought at close quarters, bringing them down is likely to cause as much damage to your own vessels as theirs.' As both a loyal servant of the Imperium and a renegade warlord, Huron Blackheart had fought countless space battles and was the consummate tactician.

'He believes that we will remain in the cover of the asteroid field and so his entire strategy rests on that. Once his first wave of fighters and their escorts have reached the point of no return, we shall burst forth from the ships' graveyard and engage them head-on, nullifying any advantage they would have gained from engaging us among the wrecks. Without having to worry about getting swarmed by fighters, my ships can smash through the escorts and take the battle directly to his capital ships held in reserve.'

Abaddon nodded in approval. Even Blackheart's impressed expression seemed genuine.

'A sound stratagem, Irongrasp,' said Abaddon. 'But still not entirely without risk. What if I were to supply you with the means to guarantee victory and ensure the utter annihilation of the Imperial fleet?'

'Lord Abaddon, any boon you could grant me would be a welcome one,' Irongrasp said with relish. 'Are you going to unleash the Legion for boarding assaults?'

'Resistance is stronger down here than anticipated. It seems an entire Imperial Guard regiment found themselves stranded on Pythos by the capricious whims of fate. Jungle fighters too so they're able to make the most of the terrain.' Abaddon's image began to diminish. 'I will spare you several hundred of the Legion, no more. Blackheart will also lend his aid to the fleet. I'm sure you will find his strategy an... interesting one.' The Warmaster disappeared altogether, his last words disembodied. Huron's image lingered, still wearing a feral grin.

'Tell me, Irongrasp,' he said. 'What do you know about asteroids?'

766960.M41 / Primary Flight Deck. Revenge, Pythos blockade, Pandorax System

SHIRA HAGEN STOOD upon the boarding ladder of her Kestrel-class fighter-interceptor, desperately resisting the urge to leap down and pummel into a bloody mess the flight officer who was disrupting her launch preparations.

'Didn't you hear me, pilot?' the officer said, pitching his voice so it carried over the bustle of the flight deck preparing to launch three entire wings of attack craft. 'I said your headgear isn't regulation issue.'

In annoyance, she broke off from her pre-flight check and slid down the ladder propped against the void-capable Thunderbolt variant. Removing her helmet to reveal shoulder-length black hair, she placed it under the crook of her arm and stared the officer, several years her senior, dead in the eyes.

'Would you rather I miss my launch slot and go and requisition another? Or should I forgo the mission entirely and repaint it.' She tilted her head towards the helmet. Instead of the standard grey-green headgear that her fellow pilots wore, Shira had modified hers so that the visage was that of a great bird of prey. Majestic white feathers were individually depicted along the ceramite shell and perfectly rendered eyes stared out from either side. The visor too had been customised so that it resembled a hooked beak. Finding the material necessary to personalise it had not come cheaply, but on a ship the size of the *Revenge*, anything could be had. For a price.

The flight officer cleared his throat. 'Imperial Navy statute gamma epsilon twelve niner quite clearly states that no personnel are to make modification, adjustment or adornment to...' His voice tailed off. Shira had replaced her helmet and was leisurely clambering back towards the cockpit. 'Do not ignore me. I am your superior and you will look at me while I am addressing you.'

She halted her ascent and turned back to face him, her head in line with the almost two score depictions of talons rendered in white against the drab grey hull of the Kestrel. Kill markings. Each one confirmed, each one hard won. 'I'll listen to you once something sensible comes out of that puckered hole you call a mouth. Until then, either throw me in the brig or let me get my bird ready for take-off.' Perched atop the ladder, she looked every inch the predator she imitated.

'I'll have you on a charge the instant you return to this ship, flight lieutenant...' He consulted the data-slate that he had unconsciously raised into a defensive shield before him. 'Hagen. Enjoy your mission. It'll be the last one you fly for a while.' He turned on his heel and walked off at pace back to the launch control booth. Shira made a single-digit gesture by way of send-off, much to the delight of her fellow pilots who were similarly engaged in readying their craft.

'You and that mouth of yours, Hagen. Always getting you in trouble,' a man's voice crackled through her helmet vox. 'Why don't you let your flying do the talking for a change?'

'I thought you'd be happy to see me sit this one out, boss,' she voxed back, looking over to the other side of the hangar and the source of the voice. Already strapped into his cockpit, Wing Commander Barabas Hyke sat shaking his head. Like all of the pilots of Red Wing, his hull sported kill markings in double figures, but only his tally came anywhere close to Shira's. 'It'd give everybody else a chance to catch up with me.'

'Hey, Shira. Your mouth can get me in trouble any time you like,' said another voice over the vox.

'Hey, Forczek,' Shira replied. 'Can you count backwards from five?'

'Huh? I don't get it,' the other pilot responded looking towards Shira. Forczek's Kestrel was at an advanced stage of preparation and the cockpit was already closed.

Shira held her hand up, fingers outstretched. 'Five. Four. Three. Two…' Each time she said a number, she dropped a finger until only one remained extended which she used to salute Forczek, the same way she had the flight officer.

'Cut the crap, both of you,' Hyke admonished. 'There'll be time for fun and games later. Right now we have a job to do.'

The ship-wide address system, which had been nothing but background noise until now, rose in volume. The Lord Admiral's voice boomed out, the closing stages of a no doubt rousing speech by which to inspire and rally the men and women under his command.

'…to the heart of the Archenemy and liberate the brave and loyal people of Pythos,' Kranswar intoned in his slightly nasal timbre. 'Our actions this day will determine if our names will live on in triumph or be eternally despised. Launch all attack squadrons and prepare to engage the enemy! Let us win glory!'

'You heard the Lord Admiral,' Hyke voxed, pulling down his canopy and locking it in place. 'We have a war to get back to.'

AHEAD OF HER, Forczek's afterburners became tiny red pinpricks as Shira sat at the entrance to the launch tunnel awaiting her slot. The other nine pilots who formed Red Wing were already clear of the *Revenge* and racing to catch up with their slower moving escorts, who were nearing the Adamantium Fields. Shira didn't hold much belief in superstition – she didn't believe in much other than her abilities as a combat pilot – but, as she had done for every single sortie since the Pandorax campaign started, she would be the last of her wing to launch. Last one out and, provided her Kestrel didn't let her down or she didn't do anything stupid in the heat of battle, last one back in.

'Red Six you are cleared for take-off. Commence launch procedure when ready.' Shira recognised the voice in her headset and turned to peer out of her cockpit into the launch control booth. There, hunched over a bank of instruments, the lights of which cast a pale blue glow over his strict features, was the flight officer from earlier.

'Acknowledged, launch control,' she replied. The flight officer seemed to freeze momentarily. From behind the plastiglass shield, he looked up as understanding took hold of him. Shira inclined her head, regarding him with the eagle's eyes painted on her helmet.

The officer spoke again but even through Shira's helmet vox his words were swallowed by the noise of her engines spooling up to full power. This ran entirely contrary to Imperial Navy statutes, fighter pilots were not allowed to engage full thrust until they hit the red line halfway down the launch tube, but Shira suspected that the flight officer already knew this. As the whine of her engines grew louder, he abandoned all attempts to communicate with her verbally and instead gesticulated wildly. Shira smiled, and in that instant the flight officer realised her intent. He dived to the floor of the launch booth and wrapped his arms around his head.

Shira's power gauge reached its limit and, using one hand to engage forward thrust, the other to disengage the ground brakes, her Kestrel shot forwards like a mass reactive shell from a bolter, massive G-force pinning her back in the pilot's seat. The sonic boom it generated shattered the window of the launch booth into thousands of tiny shards, but by the time the first of them hit the floor and showered the hapless officer in glass, she had already cleared the launch tube and was in the cold embrace of the void.

She didn't need the power of premonition or a reading from the tarot to know that her immediate future contained a multiple-week stay in the brig, but that was of no concern to her. Every moment spent on board the *Revenge* felt like incarceration to Shira and it was only when she was at the controls of her own craft that she felt truly free.

Picking up their returns on her auspex, Shira silently cut through the blackness towards the rest of Red Wing and their escorts, determined to make the most of every second of her liberation.

766960.M41 / The Bridge. Revenge, Pythos blockade, Pandorax System

As with any Imperial naval vessel on the precipice of battle, the bridge of the *Revenge* buzzed with suppressed urgency. Ensigns and strategicians moved from console to console, officer to officer, not running but at a pace brisker than walking. Real space navigators tapped away at arrays of buttons, their keystrokes running at a fraction more per minute under combat conditions, while beside them calculus logi ran through thousands of flight vectors per second, feeding the optimum results to their human counterparts only after every possibility had been processed.

Kranswar sat upon his command throne staring contemplatively through the occulus. To the starboard side, *Stalwart* hung motionless in space, the afterburners of her last launched wave of interceptors disappearing into the distance, while dead ahead of them lay their objective. The largest of the asteroids were constantly visible at this distance, but the Adamantium Fields sparkled periodically as the light of Pandorax's sun caught the hull of one of the wrecked Imperial vessels drifting dead among the celestial rock.

'Even the stars are taunting me,' muttered Kranswar under his breath.

'Sir?' came the confused response from the immaculately attired lieutenant beside him.

'Nothing, Faisal.' He turned his attention from the cosmos back to what was happening on the bridge. 'Report. Are all attack waves deployed and running alongside their escorts?'

'Affirmative,' replied a young woman sitting before a vast screen, streams of seemingly indecipherable letters and numbers scrolling rapidly before her augmented eyes. 'Primary and secondary flight decks are reporting that only three interceptors failed to launch.'

'*Stalwart* are reporting the same,' added a vox officer, one cup of his headset held to his ear, the other hanging loose so he could hear the activity on the bridge. 'All birds released, no failures to launch.'

The Lord Admiral smirked ruefully. Something else for that smug bastard Blaise to hold over him. 'Time until contact?' he asked nobody in particular.

'Seven minutes, Terran standard,' said one of the strategicians, reading from a sheet of parchment one of the calculus logi had just produced from its portable cogitator unit.

Kranswar was about to deliver fresh orders when activity flared over by the auspex array, followed by an excited buzz of chatter.

'Lord Admiral. We're picking up multiple contacts on the edge of the asteroid belt,' an ensign called from the far end of the bridge.

Kranswar turned his throne away from the occulus to face the bridge crew. 'Scout vessels. The enemy commander isn't stupid. He knows that his instruments are useless while he cowers behind the asteroid belts and drifting wrecks. He's running reconnaissance, for all the good that'll do him now.' He started to turn back to the occulus, but the ensign spoke again.

'There are too many contacts for scout vessels. Two, three hundred craft at least, sir.' The ensign kept looking back to his auspex as he spoke. 'They must have known we were coming for them. The entire Chaos fleet is moving to engage our assault.'

766960.M41 / Red Wing. Pythos blockade, Pandorax System

To Shira's starboard side, the frigate *Feinstein* died in a nimbus of blue flame, warp engines torn asunder by the concentrated fire of a dozen Chaos fighter-interceptors. She dipped her control stick, putting her Kestrel into a vertical descent to avoid the attentions of an enemy pilot who had latched onto her tail before pulling up sharply and delivering her pursuer directly into Hyke's crosshairs. The corrupted craft imploded silently as his nose-mounted lascannon shattered the cockpit canopy, allowing the immeasurable pressure of deep space to finish the job.

'What do you reckon, we share that kill?' Shira voxed, moving into formation alongside the wing commander's craft. 'I did all the hard work, you only had to shoot straight.'

'I think I get that one to myself just for saving your skinny ass,' Hyke replied, his voice warping over the comms channel. The Imperial fighter craft's auspexes were being occluded and whatever foul sorcery the enemy was employing was affecting the vox-units too.

The Chaos counter-attack had not been a surprise – visual contact had already been made with the larger vessels before the auspex problems became apparent – but the speed of their assault had caught the Imperial ships on the hop and several were lost before any form of defence could be mounted. The enemy flagship had burst from the Adamantium Fields at full speed, ramming the *Equaliser* and *Sword of Honour*, two Cobra-class destroyers packed in close formation, before either could take evasive manoeuvres. Already the gravitic pull of the asteroid belt was tugging at their drifting shells, claiming them as the latest occupants of the ships' graveyard.

Even Red Wing, seemingly impervious to death during the prior engagements with the Chaos fleet, were two Kestrels down, Goyez and Makita both succumbing to defence turret fire as they sought to assault an iconoclast destroyer.

'Red Wing. Form up on me,' buzzed Hyke across the general vox channel. 'We're going to target that idolator engaging the *Arbitrator*.'

Against a backdrop of stars, the two ships were literally blowing chunks out of each other as their shields failed. It was impossible to miss at such close range. Vast gouges in the hulls of both craft bled atmosphere and crew into the cold blackness and though both were far from inoperable, if they maintained their barrages, destruction was mutually assured.

'Quofe, Vandire, Forczek, Skelmer, Tetsudo, Mkana. Fly cover. Hagen, you're going to target the warp engines with me. Think you can take on something that big?' Under the heat of combat, there were no witty comebacks to the wing commander's unintended innuendo, only distorted confirmations.

'Just keep their interceptors off my back and try to stay out of my line of fire,' Shira replied as the rest of Red Wing fell in line alongside her and Hyke.

Afterburners glowing the brightest orange, the eight Kestrels banked and adjusted formation into a blunt-headed 'V' shape before powering towards the duelling behemoths. A swarm of enemy fighters broke off from their personal dog-fights and strafing runs to target the more obvious threat.

Skelmer was the first to peel off, rapidly cutting his after-burners and allowing the two lead enemy craft to overshoot him, placing themselves directly in front of his deadly weap-ons array. Unlike the Thunderbolt used by planet-based naval wings, the Kestrel forwent autocannons and instead carried extra powercells for the two nose-mounted lascannons. It was one of those lascannons that destroyed the first Chaos flyer, a hellstrike missile the second. Both burned briefly before their onboard oxygen supplies, like the craft themselves, were utterly consumed by the flames.

Another of the Chaos interceptors fell in behind Mkana, but a quick burst from Quofe's lascannon sheared away one of its wings, making it spin away madly before Forczek finished it off with a concentrated pulse from her own nose-mounted weapon.

Vandire and Tetsudo did not fare so well. Isolating one of the enemy fighters, they poured fire at it but to no avail, the swifter craft always ahead of their guns. So intent were they on claiming the kill, neither of them saw the other Chaos pilot coming at them from below. A wave of solid shot broke across the hull of Tetsudo's Kestrel, breaking it into three and spilling its already dead occupant from the cockpit. Van-dire avoided the worst of the autocannon shells but as he banked to avoid absorbing yet more fire, he impacted with the wrecked fore-section of Tetsudo's Kestrel. Embedding in the port-side engine, Vandire lost control and, as he spun recklessly end over end, consciousness. Red Wing watched on helplessly as his bird smashed against the shields of a Chaos destroyer, a brief ripple of energy the only marker of his passing.

'Hagen. Commence your attack run. I have your wing,' said Hyke, his voice adrift in a sea of static. The enemy destroyer loomed large through Shira's canopy. 'The rest of you keep those fighters busy.'

The response from Red Wing was instantaneous. Forczek put one of her hellstrikes straight down the fleshy exhaust port of the craft that had killed Tetsudo while Skelmer did the same to the enemy pilot his two dead comrades had been pursuing in the first place. More of the Chaos fighters converged on their position, but Hyke and Shira were clear of the dogfighting now and heading straight for their objective.

'I'm out of missiles,' Hyke voxed. 'Better make yours count.'

'I bet you have a rack full. You just don't want the embarrassment of missing such a large target,' she voxed back.

'And if you can't hit it, I'm sure the crew of the *Arbitrator* will be embarrassed for you.'

Hyke's words were sobering. Too often the fighter pilots of the fleet sought only personal glory, the pursuit of new kill markings for their hulls their primary driver. It was easy to forget that their real job was to make sure the bigger vessels remained protected.

'When have you ever known me to miss?' Shira said, twisting her control stick and lining her Kestrel up with the port-side of the Chaos destroyer, ready to commence her attack run.

'There's always a first time for everything,' Hyke replied, mimicking Shira's manoeuvre and drawing alongside her, mere metres between the tips of their wings.

Defence turrets opened up all along the length of the hull, but the enemy gunners were chasing ghosts. At near top speed, the two Kestrels evaded the barrage of fire, Hyke shooting his lascannon on full-auto, destroying many of the bizarrely deformed anti-aircraft batteries before they could open up. Alongside him, Shira primed her last two hellstrikes and attempted to get a visual on the hull breach that had exposed the destroyer's warp engines. It didn't take her long, the tell-tale blue glow of the pulsating drives lighting her way like a flare. Pulling up to achieve a better firing angle, Shira eased her pace slightly to give herself longer over the target. Alongside the breach, two turrets rotated towards her Kestrel, both lascannon barrels trained straight upon her. Hyke quickly took care of them.

'You're all clear,' he said, giving Shira the thumbs up from his cockpit as he banked away from the hull of the destroyer.

Narrowing her eyes, Shira flicked the safety cover away from the firing stud and squeezed down with her thumb. Beneath her wing, a missile detached itself, racing straight and true towards the tear in the ship's hull. She pulled her Kestrel up and away sharply, looking back over her shoulder to follow the hellstrike's path. Overshooting the rent by a few agonising metres, it detonated harmlessly near an inactive defence turret, a shallow black crater the only lasting damage.

'Why did you have to go and jinx me?' Shira spat down the vox.

'You'll get it next time,' Hyke encouraged. 'Red Wing. Regroup and prepare to commence second attack run.' Beneath them, the anti-aircraft batteries renewed their barrage.

'No time for that. We can only avoid those turrets for so long and there are more enemy craft inbound.' Another full squadron of Chaos fighters were converging on their position. 'I'm going back in right now.'

'Don't be stupid, Hagen. The turn alone will–'

Shira cut the vox-feed, disinterested in Hyke's admonishment. Knowing what was to come next, she pulled the rebreather away from her face and double-checked that her flight harness was secure. She pulled back on the control stick, putting the Kestrel into a sharp swooping vertical turn. Massive G-forces planted her back into her seat as far as she could go without being pushed through the back of it as she fought to remain conscious. Reaching the apex of the climb, her fighter flipped over and the urge to vomit she'd been suppressing messily overwhelmed her. Now on a collision course with the Chaos destroyer, she forced her eyes to remain open, the gravitic energies she was being subjected to deforming her features and painfully stretching her skin and muscles. With an effort akin to pushing her thumb through a block of lead, she tore the tendons in her hand as the firing stud depressed.

Not needing to see the evidence of the missile striking its target, she jerked the control stick violently towards her, sharply pulling upwards before she followed the hellstrike into the body of the ship. Behind her, a noiseless explosion detonated as the missile tore into the unprotected warp engine ripping it asunder. A bow wave of energy chased her, buffeting her Kestrel and emptying the contents of her stomach again.

Unaware of its own death, the Chaos vessel continued to fire even as thick cracks tore it open and unnatural blue warp energy engulfed it. Sensing an opportunity to inveigle their way into the materium, thousands of daemonic hands and tendrils thrust forth from the gap sliced through reality, clawing at the rapidly disintegrating ship, attempting to gain a hold in the corporeal realm.

Accompanied by the anguished screams of the Neverborn, the warp rift closed as quickly as it came into being, taking the wreck of the destroyer with it.

Groggily, Shira wiped the puke from around her mouth with the sleeve of her flight suit and switched her vox back on.

'...king idiot. You could have died pulling a stunt like that. If you weren't already on a charge once we get back to the *Revenge*, I'd throw you in the brig myself.' Hyke's reprimand seemed incongruous against the backdrop of whoops and hollers from the other four members of Red Wing sharing the same vox channel.

'Hey, Shira. You should put in for a transfer to the *Arbitrator* once you're out of the stockade,' Quofe laughed. 'You'll never have to pay for another drink again as long as you–' His booming voice cut out replaced by static followed by the hiss of three more vox-units suddenly going dead.

Blinking and shaking her head to overcome the adverse effects of her risky loop-the-loop, Shira turned to face the last location of her four fellow flyers. Four explosions briefly bloomed and died, the edges of a dark, jagged shape picked out in the intense orange light.

'No... They're not supposed to be real,' Hyke, who had a better view of the Kestrels' destruction, muttered. 'They're just the ramblings of space jockeys and asteroid miners, the fevered dreams of those who've spent too long in the void. They're not real. They're not real. They're not–'

'What? What aren't supposed to be real?' Shira asked. When she saw what was headed directly for them, she got her answer.

Like a mythical dragon of old, the beast glided through space as if it were riding on warm currents of air, snorting destructive bursts of balefire as it went. A metallic beaked head snaked out from a slender, serpentine body made from the same unholy alloy and its daemonic eyes darted this way and that, seeking out its next prey. Four wicked rending talons protruded from its underside and the inherent wrongness of the thing was completed by the three pairs of wings that were swept forward in antithesis of everything Shira knew about the principles of flight and aerodynamics.

'Heldrake,' Hyke barely managed to utter. 'It's a Heldrake.'

* * *

766960.M41 / Merciless Death, Adamantium Fields, Pandorax System

'LORD IRONGRASP. WE'VE lost the *Perfidious Virtue*,' said one of the hooded bridge crew, flickering psycholithic markers slowly moving in the air in front of him. '*Mutilator, Incarnadine Thirst* and *Blighted Sky* are all reporting catastrophic damage.'

In contrast to the bridge of the *Revenge*, the command centre of the *Merciless Death* had a dark calmness to it, crew and servitors going about their appointed tasks with an almost laconic detachment from the battle raging around them in space. From his command pulpit, Malgar Irongrasp orchestrated the Chaos counter-attack as if by rote, over a thousand years of experience fighting for and against the forces of the Imperium ingraining within him certain automatic responses.

'Have them overload their warp engines and ram larger vessels. Let not their deaths be in vain,' he ordered as if he were sending the ships for a refit rather than to their certain doom. At this stage of the battle, the loss of four destroyers and raiders was a better casualty rate than he had anticipated, twice that number of Imperial Navy vessels having been lost to his guns along with scores of fighters and interceptors. The battle was currently going his way but the two capital ships remained skulking at the back of the Imperial battlefleet, ready to rearm the still numerous wings of attack craft and tip the balance back in their favour.

'Blackheart wishes to address you, lord,' said another hooded figure through a grilled half-face mask. The contempt for the pretender Chaos lord exhibited by both Abaddon and Irongrasp was mirrored by even the lowliest vox-operators of the Black Legion fleet.

'Transfer him to my private channel,' Malgar said. The vox-bead in his ear crackled as the communication from Blackheart's fleet was patched through.

'Impressive, Irongrasp,' Huron said, but only Malgar could hear it. 'I had expected your gambit to have been more costly, but to take down eight of the enemy vessels with the loss of just one of your own? Even I would have been proud of such a feat.'

On the psycholithic display towards the fore of the bridge, three more small icons blinked out swiftly, followed by three larger ones of a different colour.

'Ah, it seems I spoke too soon,' said Huron, obviously witnessing the same thing on his own sensors. 'Still, at least that's three fewer ships that my fleet have to worry about.'

Malgar was unsure whether Blackheart meant the Imperial vessels or the three he had just sacrificed.

'Is your ship in position, Blackheart?' Malgar asked, brushing aside the Red Corsair's attempt to goad him.

'Of course,' he replied, feigning indignation. 'It has been since before you sprung your little trap.'

'Then why don't you stop trying to antagonise me and deliver your surprise to the enemy admiral,' Malgar said, cutting the link.

766960.M41 / The Bridge. Revenge, Pythos blockade, Pandorax System

THROUGH THE OCCULUS, Kranswar witnessed the trio of explosions, each blue halo of rapidly dissipating warp energy signalling the demise of one of his ships.

'We've just lost the *Inviolate*, *Banshee* and *Light of Faith*,' confirmed a helmsman, removing three ship markers from a parchment starchart spread out in front of him.

With these new losses, Kranswar's fleet was down to almost a third of the number of ships he'd had under him when they struck out for Pandorax. The losses of Imperial Guard war machines and personnel were not insubstantial either, and the Lord Admiral was beginning to wonder whether, if they did break through to Pythos, they would have enough manpower to liberate the world. If he and every crewmember on board his ships had to pick up a lasrifle and take the fight down to the planet, he would give the order in an instant if that's what it would take.

'Admiral Blaise wishes to speak with you, Lord Admiral,' called out the vox officer, the single cup of the headset still pressed to his ear.

'Put it over the speakers, Uldar,' Kranswar said, rising from the command throne. The fury in Blaise's voice when it boomed over the vox caused him to sit back down again.

'What in the Emperor's name are you playing at, Kranswar?' the thickly accented voice rang out. Even in the midst of battle, it was delivered with such venom that every man and woman on the bridge of the *Revenge* froze. 'It's a massacre out there. Swallow your pride, you stubborn bastard. Recall the fleet while you still have a fleet to recall.'

All eyes were on the Lord Admiral. He stared off into the distance, out through the occulus. Another explosion ripped noiselessly through the dark. The helmsman removed another piece from the starchart.

'You sent your ships into battle with talk of history ringing in the fleet's ears,' Blaise continued. 'If you don't get those ships back here now and regroup, how do you think history will remember you?' The vox-feed cut out abruptly. Whether by accident or design, nobody on board the *Revenge* could tell.

'He's right,' Kranswar said quietly. The entire bridge crew were still fixated on him, the next words from his mouth were potentially the most important he would ever speak. 'Recall the fleet.'

The glacier of inactivity melted and the volume on the bridge rose as new orders were relayed to the few surviving ships of Battlefleet Demeter. Calculus logi and real space navigators plotted escape vectors for the larger vessels, while the flight decks were told to prepare for returning assault craft. Gunnery stations were put on alert to deal with any of the Chaos ships that had the temerity to follow them back to Gaea.

Kranswar sunk back onto his throne, deflated but not defeated.

'For what it's worth, sir,' said Lieutenant Faisal handing him a sheaf of casualty reports, 'I think you're doing the right thing.'

The Lord Admiral smiled weakly. 'Sometimes, even the right decisions can be made too late,' he said grimly.

'Lord Admiral. We're picking up a new contact. Another ship has just translated in-system and is heading towards our position at speed. It's broadcasting an Imperium identification code, outdated but confirmed,' an ensign said from over near the auspex array. Several of the bridge officers moved to join him.

Kranswar's heart leapt. Reinforcements. Perhaps the day could yet be won. His newfound optimism did not last long.

'It's the *Might of Huron*, sir,' the ensign said dejectedly.

To a man, every member of Battlefleet Demeter knew of

the *Might of Huron* and the reputation of its piratical captain, Huron Blackheart. Many of the worlds under its protection had suffered at the hands of the Red Corsairs and scores of its ships had been lost to the renegade Chapter. Most had been destroyed outright, but those unfortunate enough to be captured were pressed into service under new, traitorous colours. Twice before the *Revenge* had engaged Huron Blackheart's flagship and twice before they'd fought each other to a stalemate. On both occasions, the Imperial vessel had needed to undergo months of repairs before it was starworthy again.

The mere mention of his old adversary seemed to breathe new life into Kranswar, his hunger for battle returning at the sound of Huron Blackheart's name. 'Where is it? I don't have visual confirmation.' Through the occulus, all he could see were the ships of his fleet performing painfully slow turning manoeuvres, harried the entire way by lances of weapons fire.

'It's approaching us from the rear,' replied the ensign. 'Transferring pict feed now.' A previously dark bank of screens strobed into life and a grainy sepia-toned image gradually resolved itself, turning to colour as valves and transistors worked themselves up to operational temperature. The prow of a Slaughter-class cruiser grew ever larger on the monitors, haloed by a rough circle of textured grey.

'What is that?' asked Faisal, furrowing his brow in confusion.

'It looks like it's towing something,' offered another lieutenant.

As the huddle of bridge crew looked on, the image changed and the rapidly moving spacecraft dropped suddenly out of the picture, leaving only the strange spheroid to crowd the visual field. Realisation washed over the crew of the *Revenge* like a tsunami. Mouths hung open in horror and awe at what was about to happen.

His spirit utterly broken, Kranswar dropped to his knees before the image unfolding in front of him. 'Sweet Emperor on the Throne of Terra,' he wept. 'It's an asteroid. The lunatic is going to ram us with an asteroid.'

CHAPTER EIGHT

766960.M41 / Revenge, Pythos blockade, Pandorax System

FROM THE INSTANT the weaponised asteroid crashed into the aft of the *Revenge*, reality became something very different for those on board.

On the crew levels, the handful of personnel fortunate enough to be granted rest during battle footing were flung rudely from their cots, bones shattering and skulls splitting. Those who died from the impact were the fortunate ones, the survivors suffering a drawn-out and lingering death at the tendrils of warp apparitions that bled through the hull of the ship and devoured their souls.

In one of the many galleys on board, a cook who had taken the Emperor's coin to serve on board the *Revenge* by way of escaping justice for the string of murders he had committed on his home world, found himself reshaped and repurposed as a tool of Chaos. Flensed and torn apart by paring knives and cleavers, his muscle and bone were restitched by foul magicks, his skinless body compelled to hunt the corridors of the ship, claiming new victims with the blades he now found in place of fingers.

In the officers' chapel, not a hundred metres from the bridge, a young preacher hung herself with her own robes, unable to cope with the voices of the two children she had not carried to term whispering to her from beyond. Upon finding her body, a fellow ecclesiarch defiled the limp corpse with his own hands, carving blasphemous sigils upon her flesh with his fingernails before ripping out his own eyes and slicing his jugular.

Imperial Guard regiments billeted in the cargo holds like cattle were slaughtered by lesser daemons who materialised in their midst, hundreds of men dead before a weapon was raised in retaliation. Larger, more hideous, entities stalked the lower decks, by now a morass of body parts and otherworldly substances oozing from the very fabric of the ship. In those sections of the ship gouged open by the asteroid, confused accounts of Traitor Astartes boarding parties were exchanged over vox-channels but none were confirmed, communications abruptly ceasing after the initial reports.

The only place where the malign influence of the Arch-enemy was yet to instil itself on board the *Revenge* was the bridge, but from the anarchic scenes taking place there, it was difficult to tell.

Helmsmen and officers alike ran from console to console, checking the distorted returns from auspexes and sensor arrays, while vox-operators tried in vain to make contact with other sections of the ship. Calculus logi spat endless reams of parchment from their portable cogitators, the tacky black ink denoting only nonsense in confused strings of random symbols.

Through the hubbub, Kranswar made out snatches of conversation, all of it insane.

'...turned on each other. Less than twenty of them survived and most of those are...'

'...grew teeth and began chewing away at the bulkhead...'

'...Corsairs boarding parties have breached *Stalwart*. *Might of Huron* moving to...'

'...off his own arm and beat himself to death with it...'

'...says they're in the air filtration pipes. Pink things with...'

Lieutenant Faisal shook Kranswar by the shoulder to get his attention. Ordinarily, that sort of behaviour would have been met with a rebuke, time in the brig and a possible demotion. Right now, none of that seemed to matter.

'Sir, we've lost the lower twenty-seven decks.' The young officer's voice was hoarse. A slick of sweat coated his face and darkened the fabric of his tunic below the armpits.

The Lord Admiral was momentarily confused. The entire ship was going to hell in a tramp freighter and he was being bothered with this?

'Well, have the naval militia or one of the Imperial Guard regiments go and retake them,' he bellowed in irritation.

'No, sir. You misunderstand me,' Faisal replied, confident rather than confrontational. 'We've *literally* lost the lower twenty-seven decks. They're... they're just not there any more.'

Kranswar had no time to process the information, as one of the vox-operators called out to him.

'Lord Admiral. One of the Guard regiments has made contact. Their commander says he wants to speak to you.'

He bounded over from the throne dais and snatched the headset from the woman, speaking into it before he had even put it on properly.

'This is Kranswar. Go ahead.'

'Dashed good fortune you not letting us off the ship,' said the most overtly aristocratic voice the Lord Admiral had ever heard. 'To be absolutely frank, I did consider coming up there and throttling you myself when you refused my request but good job you did, old bean, otherwise you'd be up shit creek without a paddle right about now.'

It was the Vostroyan brigadier. Kranswar involuntarily let out a nervous laugh, partly out of the ridiculousness of the man's turn of phrase, partly out of relief that there were still other survivors on board.

'Good to hear your voice, brigadier. I was beginning to think we were on our own up here,' Kranswar said.

'You almost are, I'm afraid. Bad scene down here, old chap. The Cadians tore each other apart at the first sign of trouble, and the Godesian and Asamantrite regiments are floating past the portholes at the moment, poor bastards.' The brigadier's tone was one of genuine sadness. 'Just us Vostroyans left to mount the counter-attack. Provided you'll let us deploy on board your ship, of course, admiral.'

'Permission granted,' Kranswar said without giving it any thought. 'But I'm not sure how long you'll last out of your tanks.'

It was the brigadier's turn to laugh now, hearty and with more than a hint of relish. 'That's what I'm asking your permission for, old boy. I want to roll my armour out and take the fight right to whatever it is that's tearing your ship apart.'

Kranswar took it in his stride. On a day when an asteroid had been smashed into the back of the *Revenge*, the denizens of the warp had decided to make his lower decks their temporary home and Traitor Legionaries were possibly on their way to take control of his bridge, a titled and overbearing Vostroyan brigadier asking to fight a tank battle on the decks of an Imperial Navy battleship sounded like the sanest idea anybody had ever had in the history of the Imperium.

'Permission granted,' Kranswar said, again without giving it any thought.

766960.M41 / Red Wing. Pythos blockade, Pandorax System

JINKING TO AVOID the razor-sharp tip of the Heldrake's wing, Shira let rip with two pulses from her lascannon. At point-blank range it was impossible to miss the creature, but its thick metal hide merely repelled her shots as if they were pellets from a child's catapult. In her wake, Hyke attempted the same but met with the same results.

'The armour's too thick. It'll take hellstrikes to even scratch it,' Shira voxed in frustration.

'Let's get the fleet back to Gaea first, then we'll rearm and come back for this thing. Until then, keep it occupied and away from the big ships but do not attempt to engage it,' Hyke broadcast over the general channel.

Though only two of Red Wing remained, pilots from other Kestrel wings belonging to the *Revenge* were still operational, along with scattered remnants of the Fury squadrons launched from the *Stalwart*. Believing himself to be the highest ranking pilot still flying, Hyke had assumed leadership of the screening mission to cover the fleet's retreat. Imperial losses had been heavy but the casualties inflicted on the Chaos interceptors were just as brutal and the Navy flyers maintained a numerical advantage over the enemy. There were close to two hundred Kestrels and Furies still involved in the battle by Shira's estimation, but communication between them was almost non-existent thanks to incompatible vox-units and the sorcerous interference.

Oblivious to Hyke's order, a brave, or possibly foolish, Fury crew ran the gauntlet of Chaos interceptors to get in close to the Heldrake. Bigger but carrying the same weapons fit as the single-man Kestrel, the Fury opened up with its wing-mounted lascannons, its complement of missiles already spent earlier in the battle. The rapid fusillade met with predictable results and as the craft spun away to regroup with the rest of the Imperial fighters, the Heldrake thrust out its neck with preternatural quickness, grasping the Fury's tail section between its gargantuan jaws. Exhaling derisorily, it washed the stricken fighter in a stream of baleflame before relinquishing its grip and allowing the blackened shell to drift forever lifeless among the stars.

Emboldened by the presence of the daemonic flyer, the Chaos pilots renewed their assault on the fleeing frigates, destroyers and cruisers. Bereft of missiles, they too were reduced to las and solid shot weapons, seeking to exploit ruptures in the shells of vessels whose shields had failed. Pursued all the way by three Kestrels from Yellow Wing, the double axe-head shape of a Hell Talon got in close to the *Scion of Ultima*, a Sword-class frigate with almost two millennia of service, and set off a ripple of explosions along its quarterdeck, a well-placed shot taking out a tertiary generator used for powering the ship's lighting systems. Larger holes opened up in the hull and, though the culprit was quickly punished by the guns of Yellow Wing, yet more Chaos fighters swarmed the stricken frigate. At the rear of their formation, the Heldrake swerved among them, seeking to reach the head of the pack and claim the kill as its own. Just as it got within range to issue forth its daemonic flame, a dark shape jetted past, missing it by barely a metre and spoiling its aim. Leaving the *Scion of Ultima* to the predation of the Hell Talons, the Heldrake struck out to chase its new target.

'You stay with the fleet,' Shira voxed to Hyke, gunning her Kestrel's engines for all they were worth. 'I'll draw that thing off.'

'Be careful, Shira,' Hyke voxed back, his voice faint. 'There's a round of drinks with your name on it as soon as you're out of the brig.'

'Careful?' she said, dipping the nose of her Kestrel to narrowly avoid an intense burst from the Heldrake's baleflamer.

The temperature in the cockpit rose suddenly and patches of her flight suit ignited, forcing Shira to operate the control stick with one hand while she used the other to pat out the flames. She heaved as the smell of her scorched flesh mingled with the stench of drying vomit.

'I'm always careful,' Shira concluded, not entirely believing her own words.

766960.M41 / Revenge, Pythos blockade, Pandorax System

'THEY'RE DEAD, SIR,' the vox-operator reported solemnly. 'All of them dead.'

The already melancholy atmosphere on the bridge became even more sombre as the fate of the Vostroyan armoured brigade became clear. The initial euphoria at a meaningful fightback had soon given way to anguish as the screams of dying gunners and drivers rang out over the intra-ship vox-network, and all-out despair had taken hold once contact had been lost entirely. Determined to ascertain whether the Imperial Guardsmen had fallen or whether the lack of communication was more Archenemy foul play, Kranswar had deployed a squad of ship militia to get eyes-on confirmation.

'The passageways are littered with wrecks. Tanks torn open by duh... daemons.' Barely into his twenties, the comms man struggled to get the words out. 'Bodies dragged out and – oh, Throne – smeared all over the...' The sentence unfinished, he closed his eyes and issued a plaintive wail.

Since they had last slept, the crew of the *Revenge* had endured more than most citizens of the Imperium, even those pressed into military service, suffered in an entire lifetime. They had met those challenges head-on and despite showing the basic human emotions that come to the fore under periods of extreme duress, they had tempered it with stoicism and grit, never allowing hope to elude them.

Now, even that was gone.

Staring at the faces of his crew, many tear-streaked and sullen, he realised that they were looking to him to give them leadership, to show them light in this time of darkness. Despite leading them to their inevitable deaths, they were offering him a chance at redemption. Clearing his throat, he seized the opportunity.

'The enemy has taken almost everything from us. Comrades, friends, lovers. All now lie dead at their hands. Beyond our hull, the wrecks of almost three-quarters of Battlefleet Demeter are destined to drift eternally, escorted in their silent repose by the ruined frames of Kestrels and Furies, their pilots having laid down their lives so that others had a better chance to survive. Beneath our very feet, dark agents are abroad, slaying with impunity those few brave souls who have found it deep within them to resist, however futile that resistance may be.

'Though the blood of those who served the Imperium so valiantly still drips from the blades and teeth of the servants of the Ruinous Powers, an equal portion of that blood is on my hands too. It was my mistakes that led us to this point, my errors of judgement that have put us in a position where, short of a miracle, victory is now impossible. That miracle will not be coming, for I have not earned it and for that, and for all my errors, I truly apologise.'

With nothing else left to cling to, every soul on the bridge hung on his every word.

'The Emperor will judge me in the next life, of that I am certain, and he will find me wanting, but in this life I have one more action to perform. When I have finished speaking to you, I am going to draw my pistol, leave the bridge and fight my way down to the engine room where I will overload the sub-warp drives and tear the *Revenge* apart. Any crewman wishing to join me is welcome to do so, and given the gravity of our situation, it is perfectly understandable if you would rather spend your final moments in silent prayer or speeding up your journey to the next world.'

Kranswar raised his voice, building the speech to a crescendo.

'They may have taken our lives, robbed us of our sanity and savaged our pride, but by the Emperor, they will not have our ship!'

Kranswar unclasped the holster at his hip, drawing the archaic six-shot stubber by its ornate ivory handle. He opened the cylinder to check that each chamber was loaded with a round and spun it back into position. When he looked back up, he found that he was standing shoulder to shoulder with the entire bridge crew. Even the emotional vox-operator had found the courage to participate in this final, desperate act of defiance and he stood alongside Lieutenant Faisal with a laspistol in his hand.

Kranswar stifled a quiver of his lower lip. In spite of everything, in spite of all the death and horror he had brought upon them, they were still prepared to follow him.

'Come on then!' he cried out, turning to open the ornate wooden doors. 'If they want this ship, they're going to have to pay for it in blood!'

766960.M41 / Red Six. Pythos blockade, Pandorax System

DESPITE THE CAMARADERIE of the pilots' mess and the close bonds that existed between the men and women of each Naval wing – intensified by the fact that they constantly relied upon each other in matters of life or death – the lot of a Kestrel pilot was a lonely one. Forced to spend hours, sometimes days, alone in the cockpit with only your own dark thoughts for company, it took a certain kind of individual to cope with the pressures, both mental and physical.

As Shira Hagen wrestled with the control stick of her fighter, battling to prevent it from entering a terminal spin, she had never felt so lonely nor had her thoughts ever been darker. Far beyond the range of her vox, she had not had contact with anybody else for over an hour, and other than the occasional brief bloom of fire from the direction of Gaea, the only evidence that she wasn't out there alone was the daemonic war engine currently pursuing her in a high stakes game of cat and mouse. Every time the blackness of space lit up, she hoped it was one of the Chaos vessels being scattered to the heavens, but the law of averages dictated that at least a few of them had been Imperial ships. The fact that she didn't put much stock in laws or rules was of little solace.

Coming out of the spin before it could take hold, Shira dipped her wing and banked, tempting the Heldrake with her undercarriage. The creature opened its jaws in anticipation of finally claiming the kill but as its baleflamer spewed molten death, she decelerated rapidly causing the Heldrake to overshoot her. Much to her surprise, she found the beast was directly in her crosshairs.

The Imperial Navy Academy teaches a pilot many things. The unintentional overtaking manoeuvre that Shira had just performed being one of them, how to escape a terminal spin another, the maximum relative speed at which you can come in for a landing onto a moving carrier yet another. But there were many skills and nuggets of information useful to a pilot that the Academy did not pass on: techniques and technical data that even the adepts of the Machine-God, who tend to and preserve the holy flying machines when they are not performing sorties or missions, did not know about. Secret knowledge that could only be acquired by learning them for yourself at the stick of a fighter or by trading with others of the pilot fraternity or sorority. How to reconfigure an ejector seat so that it doesn't kill you the first time it was activated was one such piece of wisdom. So too was the real maximum speed at which you can land a fighter onto a moving carrier while preserving your own life, though not necessarily the integrity of the craft that delivered you there.

Right now, the one piece of forbidden flying lore that was jumping into Shira's mind, bartered from a ten-year veteran with almost a hundred confirmed xenos kills to his name, was how to reroute energy from the Kestrel's power plant to the lascannons. Unlike the Thunderbolt on which it was based, the spacefaring variant eschewed a combustion engine, replacing it with power cells that gave it a far greater range than a fuel-based drive ever could. Although it ran on an isolated circuit to prevent non-essential systems from unnecessarily draining it, those who had forbidden gen on the inner workings of the Kestrel's electrics could channel the power into the nosecannons and cause an effect not unlike fitting a standard Imperial Guard lasrifle with a hotshot power pack. It would drain the fighter's power plant massively but, as Shira's self-appointed mission was to keep the Heldrake away from the fleet, returning to the *Revenge* – if there was a *Revenge* to return to – was hardly a consideration.

Pulling a thick grey wire from its port by her knee, Shira inserted the plug into the neighbouring socket and depressed both firing studs. Bright to the point of retina-searing, twin lances of super-heated energy leapt the gap between Kestrel and Heldrake, impacting against the largest of the three wings along its right-hand side. It stopped dead, forcing Shira to pull up sharply to prevent a collision, and emitted a silent wail. As she looked back over her shoulder, Shira saw the ragged gash she had torn in its wing. Eyes burning brighter than the flame from its mouth, the Heldrake fixed Shira's craft with a murderous glare before renewing its hunt.

Good. She had made it angry.

Game on.

766960.M41 / Revenge, Pythos blockade, Pandorax System

THE IRON TANG of fresh blood filled Kranswar's nostrils, the pained cries of the dying his ears. Struggling to maintain his footing on the metal floor of the corridor slick with vitae, he raised his stubber and directed a shot at the lone Traitor Legionary barring their passage, its gold-trimmed black armour glistening as much as the wet floor. The bullet flew true and straight, striking the Space Marine in the visor over his left eye and shattering it, breaking the spell that had held Kranswar's impromptu militia under its sway.

The journey into the bowels of the ship had been lethal and fraught. Only a handful of the men and women who had followed him off the bridge had made it this far but their numbers had swelled as ratings, stragglers from Imperial Guard regiments and members of the criminal underclass that always took root on a ship the size of the *Revenge*, rallied around the Lord Admiral. Not including the scores of cultists they had exchanged fire and traded blows with, or the half-real horrors that come at them gibbering and slashing, this was the fourth Traitor Legionary they had encountered, and on each occasion the reaction had been the same.

Awe. Pure, unadulterated awe.

Bred millennia ago to serve the Emperor on His mission to reunite the scattered pockets of humanity spread out across the universe, fully half of the Space Marine Legions had turned upon Him, instead swearing fealty to the Master of Mankind's favoured son, Horus Lupercal. Freed from the restraints of servitude to humanity, their methods of fighting grew ever more brutal and the new gods they venerated revealed to them ever more effective methods of killing and subjugation. Horus's rebellion was ultimately defeated but many of his followers survived, fleeing into the warp from where they could wage a long war, chipping away at the Imperium's defences until one day their blasphemous banners would fly over the great palace on Terra. The traitor blocking the corridor wore the colours of the Black Legion, Horus's old brethren, now renamed and re-liveried under the command of his most trusted lieutenant, Abaddon the Despoiler.

Had this Traitor Marine once stood alongside Horus? Had he waged war upon noble Terra, doing battle with beings of legend like Sanguinius, Lorgar and the mighty Russ? Had he been a blight on the Imperium for nigh on ten thousand years, Kranswar wondered? It mattered not. If the three hundred men under the Lord Admiral's command had their way, the black armoured figure's remaining lifespan could be measured in seconds, not millennia.

The report of the stubber echoing along the corridor, the rag-tag band of the *Revenge*'s crew surged forwards, swallowing Kranswar up in the throng. The Space Marine raised his bolter with alarming swiftness, and cut down the first few ranks in a shower of blood and limbs, but the mob carried on charging. Weapon still firing, a wall of bodies collided with the Black Legionnaire, sheer weight of numbers pushing him to the ground. Like a pack of feral dogs they leapt upon him, battering him with anything they had been able to press into service as a maul or shooting him at point-blank range with laspistols and autopistols. A flight officer, his face a scarred jigsaw of lacerations, drove the point of a crowbar through the smashed eye lens, driving it down hard into the traitor's skull and spraying his filthy uniform in a shower of red.

Another Black Legionnaire rounded the corner at the end of the corridor, opening up with a bolter. Some of the charging crowd paused, transfixed by the dark killer before them, but momentum drove those behind them on. The Traitor Marine's rate of fire could not match the rate of attrition, and he too was toppled, drowning under a sea of humanity. Losing grip of his gun, he swung wildly with armoured fists and forearms, each swipe claiming three or four lives, until, battered and bleeding, two surviving Cadians found an opening in the pile of bodies crushing the Space Marine and discharged their lasrifles into him.

Bodies choked the hallway in front of him and as Kranswar climbed over the hill of corpses accompanied by the two Cadians, the lacerated flight officer and a handful of other survivors, the vox-bead in his ear crackled with reports from other ships in the fleet. Sensing its imminent demise, the Chaos fleet had swarmed the *Revenge* and were targeting it with all weapons batteries. The *Stalwart* could not come to her aid as she was currently engaged with the *Might of Huron*, and the rest of the battlefleet were still too far off to lend their strength, since Kranswar had waited too long to recall them from their futile assault. He grinned humourlessly. When he had set out to overload the *Revenge*'s engines, it was purely to prevent it from falling into the enemy's clutches. Now, with so many Chaos vessels in such close proximity, perhaps his ship's final act would be to live up to her name.

Turning the corner from where the second Traitor Astartes had emerged, the doors to the engine room loomed large at the end of the new corridor, glowing pale red in the reflection of the emergency lighting. Setting off at a sprint, he hadn't made it halfway down when a roar of exertion sounded from behind him. Looking back over his shoulder, the mound of dead crew collapsed as the black armoured figure burst out from beneath the array of limbs and torsos, blood leaking from cracks in his helmet and armour. The two Cadians reacted quickest but were no match for the Space Marine's augmented reflexes, bolt pistol in his hand, and both their heads exploded in a shower of crimson mist before their lasrifles were raised.

Panicked shots whizzed past the Black Legionnaire as the last few survivors fought desperately to fell the brute but none of their shots found their target, unlike the traitor who brought down four of the resisting crew with only three rounds. Suppressing the desire to draw his own weapon and turn and face the Space Marine, Kranswar continued his run. If he could get to the engine room and shut the doors behind him, even the post-human strength of the Traitor Astartes would not be able to tear them open. With just metres to go, he stretched out his hand ready to strike the control lever that would cause the twin doors to swing open and admit him to the sanctuary within, but, heralded by the boom of bolt pistol discharge, the bottom half of his right leg disappeared from beneath him and he sprawled to the floor.

Lifting his broken face from the cold metal, Kranswar crawled forwards, each stretch of his arms taking him closer to his goal. Different noises echoed down the corridor, the sound of a magazine being ejected and striking the ground, followed by the clatter of a new one being driven home. He reached out one final time and, making contact with the door, lifted himself up. The lever was mere inches from his grasp when the bolt pistol rang out again, the round striking him a glancing blow at the base of his spine and dropping him to the floor, paralysed.

Preceded by the clang of metal on metal, the Traitor Marine stalked slowly towards the Lord Admiral's prone body. As the vast shadow fell upon him, the vox-bead in Kranswar's ear came alive with excited chatter, a myriad of voices clashing with each other over the airwaves. Closing his eyes, Kranswar concentrated, trying to cut through the background noise and zone in on one strong signal. When he heard the voice of the *Stalwart*'s chief vox-officer and what she was saying, he wished the traitor's second shot had finished him off.

'Multiple contacts reported. New vessels attempting warp translation in our midst. At least a dozen and none transmitting identification codes,' she practically wept, all hope having long since fled.

766960.M41 / Remnants of Revenge and Stalwart fighter wings. Pythos blockade, Pandorax System

DEATH WAS NEVER an easy thing to witness. Be it the violent fiery death of an enemy pilot, the gradual demise of a fellow flyer exposed to radiation or blight, or the peaceful passing of a loved one in their sleep, the snuffing out of a life always left a mark on the soul of any who observed it. Strapped into the seat of his Kestrel, weapons systems spent and power indicator insistently flashing at him to warn him that his engine power was almost exhausted, Barabas Hyke reluctantly prepared to watch the death of the *Revenge*.

Like savannah predators circling a wounded herd animal, the Chaos frigates and destroyers lined up for their share of the *Revenge*'s carcass. Amazingly, tranches of the Emperor-class battleship's shields still held, and though every shot that struck an unprotected section caused massive structural and collateral damage, the majestic vessel clung to life defiantly returning fire from its few remaining defence turrets and torpedo tubes. Despite being wounded, the *Revenge* could still bite back.

Hyke and the few Imperial fighter pilots who had made it back with the bulk of the fleet cruised listlessly on the periphery of the battle. Like their enemy counterparts, the Navy fighters' guns were dry and their missile racks empty, but whereas the Chaos craft had returned to their hangar bays content that their part in the battle was over, the Imperium flyers did not have that luxury. Hyke had ordered the Kestrels to attempt to land on the *Revenge* in the desperate hope that they could rearm and repower, but had to rapidly abandon that plan when it transpired both the primary and secondary launch tubes had mutated into vast maws, tongues languidly flicking into the void and swallowing any craft foolish enough to get too close. All that remained now was for their engines to fail, at which point they would drift on the celestial current until dehydration claimed them.

Of course, before that happened, Hyke was going to order all wings to target one of the larger Chaos vessels and attempt to ram it. If they could make it past the anti-fighter defences, then maybe, just maybe, they could exploit a gap in its shields and slam into the hull. Even then, the chances of destroying the ship would be slim, but at least they'd take some of the enemy with them and their deaths would have counted for something.

'Wing commander? Are you picking up anything odd on your auspex?' A voice cut across the vox. It was Allonsy from Blue Wing.

'I've been picking up nothing but weird since this whole shooting match started,' Hyke replied. 'What's different now?'

'I'm getting ghost returns. Ten... twelve at least. Just blinking in and out.' Allonsy said.

'I'm seeing them too,' said another voice. More confirmations followed.

Hyke, who hadn't so much as glanced at his auspex for hours, such was the effectiveness of the enemy's jamming, peered down at it. Not believing what he was seeing, he used the sleeve of his flight suit to rub the screen. When that didn't alter the reading, he finally believed what his eyes were telling him.

'Throne alive!' he broadcast over the general channel. 'They're going to translate right on top of us. Get out of here now!'

'They must be addled to exit the warp this close to a planetary body,' Allonsy added, his engine ports glowing bright orange as they spooled up.

The expansion of humanity among the stars had only been made possible with the discovery of warp travel, the means by which great distances that would normally take many years, perhaps lifetimes, to traverse could be crossed in a matter of weeks or months. It was an inexact science at best, an uneasy marriage of technology and sorcery that was as likely to leave travellers stranded in the immaterium or deliver them to their destination before they had even set off, as it was to get them to the right place at the right time. Because of its unpredictable and hazardous nature, many safeguards were put in place to reduce the risk of warp travel, chief among them never translating inside a system where the potential existed to emerge too close to a planet and be sucked into its gravity well. Whoever had ordered this warp jump was either very desperate or dangerously foolish. Potentially both.

Oily black ripples coalesced in the fabric of space, denoting the points of egress from the warp, a shimmering wrongness that was painful to look upon. Like the cosmos giving birth to vast metal children, ships tore through the gashes in reality, ten green-hulled leviathans materialising in the heart of the Pandorax System, followed in quick order by a sleek, silver cruiser.

Unable to move out of the way quickly enough, Kestrels and Furies impacted against void shields, disintegrating the instant they made contact with the unimaginable energies. Allonsy, who had been running ahead of the main pack of fighters, avoided the initial collisions but, reeled in by a faster moving capital ship, his Kestrel smashed against the prow shields and was wiped out in a tiny explosion that barely registered among the firmament.

The considerably more experienced, or perhaps luckier, Hyke performed a textbook evasive manoeuvre, banking sharply and rising to make use of a clear space at the centre of the newly arrived fleet. Neither experience nor luck could save him from what happened next.

Another, larger return pulsed on his auspex, almost filling the screen. Turbulence engulfed his Kestrel and the area around him undulated sickeningly. Giving the engines every last drop of power left in the cells, he pulled forward hard on the throttle, almost tearing the lever from its housing. The ghost image on his auspex stabilised and he looked over his shoulder in time to see a massive asteroid coalescing into realspace.

The vibration of protesting engines jarring his body as he coaxed them to perform far in excess of their capabilities, Hyke very nearly outran the magnetic pull of the new arrival but, just as he reached the terminator of the thing's gravity well, his engines sputtered and died, no energy left in the power plant to drive them.

As the gargantuan rock sucked him in, crackling shields waiting to consume both man and starfighter, the last thing Barabas Hyke ever saw was a flotilla of torpedoes racing past him, the same green as the ten capital ships and sporting winged sword insignia on their hulls.

766960.M41 / Revenge, Pythos blockade, Pandorax System

HIS FACE A ruined mess, Kranswar regarded the Black Legionnaire with his one remaining eye as another blow rained down on him. His skull audibly cracked this time though his ability to feel pain had thankfully already deserted him. The Traitor Marine kept the human pinned to the engine room door with one gauntlet while he wound back his other, balled into a fist, preparing to strike a killing blow.

Two things happened then, neither of which made any sense to Kranswar in his current state.

Over the vox, a woman started laughing. Not the hysterical, maniacal cackle of one taken leave of their senses but the genuine, happy laughter of somebody experiencing delight. This was soon joined by other voices adding to the chorus, some cheering, others crying but all out of euphoria rather than fear or sadness. At the same time, a bright light bloomed out of nothingness in the corridor behind the Black Legionnaire forcing Kranswar to close his eye. He did not open it again.

'We're saved!' laughed the chief vox-officer of the *Stalwart*. 'They've come to rescue us all.'

Kranswar couldn't hear her, just as he couldn't witness Supreme Grand Master Kaldor Draigo materialise behind the Traitor Marine and strike down his assailant, taking its black armoured head clean off with a single sword swipe. Neither could he know that all over his ship, squads of Grey Knights were teleporting aboard and commencing the operation to cleanse it of the forces of Chaos. On board the asteroid that had been used to ram the *Revenge*, the entire Dark Angels Chapter had already deployed under the command of Lord Azrael to undo the dark magicks invoked to summon and sustain the aberrations of the warp.

He was not aware of any of this because Lord Admiral Orson Kranswar, captain of the *Revenge* and commander of Battlefleet Demeter, was already dead.

CHAPTER NINE

IN SPITE OF the aches in his bones and muscles, and fatigue from the long hours of maintaining his incantation, Cholgar intoned the words with the same vigour he had the first time he uttered them. Thick black blood streamed from his nostrils and hoarfrost coated the hair on his bare arms, chest and face, but not his head which was entirely smooth save for the two nubs of horns at the point where temple became forehead.

Cholgar was the first of his line to be picked out by the gods to receive the blessing of mutation. His father, his father's father, and every male in his family stretching as far back as anybody could remember, had served the Davinicus Lycae but none had ever advanced beyond the grade of footsoldier, their destiny to end their days by an Imperial Guardsman's bayonet or Space Marine bolt shell. Since birth, Cholgar had been marked for greatness, schooled in the ways of sorcery even before he could talk. Nearly two decades on from the day when the tribal elders took him from the crib, he was finally fulfilling his destiny. His sorcery, combined with that of the hundred or so other cultists filling the hollowed-out chamber within the commandeered asteroid, was creating the right conditions for daemons to dwell within the material realm and assail the Imperial vessel.

The man beside him fell, dark blood trickling from every orifice, steam rising from his corpse as it cooled at an unnatural rate. The air around the dead man thickened and churned, and with a tear that sounded like raw meat being pulled from bone, a hole in reality opened through which stepped one of the Neverborn. An ugly hunched thing, it peered around furtively with bulbous green-grey orbs, before taking possession of the frozen cadaver. Running a fat tongue over the broken remains of crag-like teeth, it stepped back through the portal which crackled closed at its passing. That same fate awaited Cholgar, as it did all of the warlock cabal, though each would gladly embrace it when it came. There was no greater glory for a servant of the Davinicus Lycae than to die knowing their sacrifice allowed beings far more worthy than themselves to walk the materium.

Another cultist took the place of the fallen sorcerer and Cholgar felt a pang of jealousy. The newcomer was no match for him physically – he was shorter and weighed at least ten kilos less than Cholgar – but was the bearer of not two, but three vestigial horns, each longer than his own. Such obvious endorsement from the gods no doubt meant he had the pick of mates in the accommodation cells.

Pushing aside his envy, Cholgar returned his focus to the task in hand. His momentary lapse in concentration had caused him to slip out of harmony with the rest of the cabal, drawing the attention of the overseers who kept a stern eye on proceedings. He had just got his chanting back in time when something else distracted him.

The rime of hoarfrost melted, coating his toned body in a wet sheen and the hairs on his arm pricked up. A new smell rose up, overpowering the scent of blood and sweat emanating from the other cultists, the warm cloying of burning ozone stinging his nostrils.

At the very instant Cholgar figured out what was happening, the laws of physics he had been fighting so hard to rewrite punished him to their full extent.

Materialising several metres above the floor of the asteroid chamber, Brother Balthasar of the Deathwing braced himself for impact. He hit the ground with a moist thud and glanced down to find the remains of something that must have once been vaguely human beneath his feet. Alongside him, a scrawny mutated freak, a concertina of rings around its elongated neck and a trio of horns poking out from a pale, mottled scalp, stared at him wide-eyed. A single burst from Balthasar's storm bolter separated the cultist's torso from the rest of his body.

Around the chamber, similar scenes were being repeated. Scores of Terminator-armour clad Dark Angels blinked into existence over the heads of their targets; those not crushed under the impact of tonnes of ceramite and wargear were cut down by storm bolter, mace or flail. The noise of so many weapons being discharged in the artificial cavern was cacophonous and a rune blinked on Balthasar's visor display to warn him that his armour's noise filters were reaching the limits of their usefulness. It came as no surprise.

A single squad of Deathwing could cleanse an entire space hulk; two could prosecute a small war unaided; five squads – fully half of the Chapter's First Company – would be sufficient to conquer a planet.

Today, for the first time in living memory, the entire Deathwing deployed on the same field of battle at the same time.

The battle, if it could truly be called that, was over in the space of seconds, but that too came as no surprise to Balthasar. Human wreckage lay at the feet of a hundred Dark Angels, the only evidence that any of them had seen combat the crimson smears sullying otherwise pristine tactical dreadnought suits. One cabal of enemy sorcerers lay dead, but many more awaited extermination deeper within the asteroid.

'Onward,' ordered Gabriel, Grand Master of the Deathwing. The sound of boarding torpedoes slamming into the asteroid echoed along the tunnels and punctuated his words. Soon, the rest of the Dark Angels Chapter would deploy alongside their elite brethren. Gabriel raised his Heavenfall Blade, the black sword in stark contrast to his ancient suit of bone-white Terminator plate. 'Show them no mercy!'

766960.M41 / Revenge, Pythos blockade, Pandorax System

WHERE THE DEATHWING had not encountered any serious resistance on board the repurposed asteroid, Supreme Grand Master Kaldor Draigo and the Brotherhood of Grey Knights under his command had found the exact opposite on board the *Revenge*.

Warp rifts had opened throughout the ship and, maintained for hours by forbidden magicks, the *Revenge* was rife with foes drawn forth from the other side of reality. Entire decks now resembled hellish landscapes in mimicry of those worlds deep within the Eye of Terror. Metal transmuted to flesh, machinery shaped into organics, the laws of nature abolished and replaced by the raw stuff of Chaos. It was impossible to move more than a few metres without having to avoid a corpse, hideously broken, primal fear etched on every face.

A daemon skittered rapidly along the ceiling of the corridor towards Draigo, but with a single word he held it there in place, the squad of Paladins advancing behind him eviscerating the thing with sharp bursts from their storm bolters.

More daemons converged on their position, some loping on spindly, misshapen limbs, others blinking into existence among the ranks of the Space Marines. Regardless of how they got there, their fate was the same. Blades flashed, returning them to whence they came in a shower of gore and a chorus of hellish screams. Words of banishment, harshly spoken, took care of the rest, sucked back through the rents in time and space that had birthed them in reality.

Coming to a fork in the ship's corridors, Draigo ordered the Paladins to take the left branch while he veered to the right, deeper into the belly of the ship.

Draigo would not normally lead a Brotherhood into battle himself, but the death of Grand Master Hasimir and the urgency of the situation on Pythos had left him with no alternative but to assume command of the Fifth. With the rest of his Chapter scattered around the Imperium in response to a myriad of daemonic threats, the Supreme Grand Master had not been able to wait for reinforcements from among his own forces, instead opting to enact an old oath sworn to the Grey Knights by the Dark Angels.

Azrael had initially refused to honour the pact, considering it to be tantamount to blackmail. His mind was soon changed when Draigo revealed an interesting nugget of information gleaned from interrogating a Traitor Astartes prisoner and the leader of the Dark Angels committed his entire Chapter to the Pandorax campaign, operational superiority the Grey

Knight's sole concession in exchange for cooperation. Though they were nominally allies, the relationship between the two Chapters had always been fractious, never spilling over into confrontation but coming near on more than one occasion. Being forced to operate so closely together would put that to the test once again, more so in light of the circumstances of their alliance.

Already Azrael had begun the politicking. Daemon hunting being their speciality, the Grey Knights were the logical choice to cleanse the nest of daemons the ship had become but, with only a single Brotherhood to face an entire daemon army, they would ultimately need reinforcing. The Dark Angels would make short work of the warlocks and cultists on board the asteroid before coming to fight alongside their psychic brethren, their superior numbers turning the tide of battle and winning the day. Who the glory covered was of no concern to Draigo. Liberating Pythos and resealing the Damnation Cache was all that mattered. Azrael could score all the points he liked against the Grey Knights as long as the mission was a success.

A noise from further along the corridor gave Draigo pause. The flickering red emergency lights sporadically illuminated a human-shaped figure, curled in the foetal position and weeping uncontrollably. The ball unfurled at the sound of Draigo's thudding footfalls. A man, grey-haired and wrinkled, shivered in fear and looked about to scream when his eyes fixated on the purity seals and holy imagery adorning the Grey Knight's armour.

'You... you're not one of them?' the man said, wide-eyed.

Draigo nodded. 'I am a loyal servant of the Golden Throne and I am here to liberate this ship and her crew.'

'Praise the Emperor! We're saved,' the man said, getting uneasily to his feet. Even at full height he barely reached Draigo's chest. 'Thank you, lord. Thank you.'

Draigo nodded again. The old man set off at pace in the direction from which the Grey Knight had come. Draigo was about to continue his advance when a thought occurred to him, a piece of information he was missing that was not of operational import but useful to know nonetheless.

'What is the name of this ship?' he called after the old man.

'The ship?' the old man said, carefully picking his way

through the bodies carpeting the floor. 'It's called the *Revenge*, lord.'

'Of course it is,' Draigo said with a wry smile, heading deeper into enemy territory.

766960.M41 / Asteroid K27356NV213g (Malefus Murex), Pythos blockade, Pandorax System

BALTHASAR'S POWER FIST connected with the Black Legionnaire's head, smashing open the faceplate to reveal the traitor's visage. Ancient features stared back at the Dark Angel, a defiant grin peeling the lips back from bloodied teeth. Another blow from Balthasar's powerfist quickly removed the smile. The body dropped limply to the ground to join those of his treacherous ilk already vanquished by the Deathwing and the elements of Sixth Company who had joined up with them on their warpath through the asteroid.

'Master Tigrane,' said Gabriel. 'The rest of your company have reached the hull breach and are engaged with traitor forces. Take your men and reinforce their position.'

Though the Master of Sixth Company, along with the three squads fighting alongside him, were already aware of their battle-brothers' situation, Gabriel's instruction was not meant as a slight against Tigrane's leadership or tactical acumen. Both Dark Angels exchanged barely perceptible nods.

'Understood, Master Gabriel,' Tigrane replied, signalling for his troops to move out.

As the green armoured figures made their way out of the chamber, another entered, the dark armour he wore and the crozius arcanum he carried marking him out as a Chaplain. A single black pearl hung from his weapon of office.

Almost twenty Black Legionaries lay dead in the central chamber, joined in oblivion by at least ten times that number of cultists and sorcerers. Interrogator Chaplain Seraphicus moved among the corpses, kneeling beside those in black armour and applying a reductor to their throats to remove their gene-seed. Normally the tool of the Apothecary, when the Dark Angels went into battle against any Traitor Astartes, the brothers of the Reclusiam would also carry one on the orders of the High Interrogator. The fickle nature of alliances among the hordes of Chaos meant that any of the Fallen could have thrown in their lot with any of the countless warbands and armies that blighted the Imperium. Removing the gene-seed of any enemy Space Marine and taking it for testing on the Rock was the only way to be certain that another name could not be struck from the Roster of Caliban.

All across the asteroid, similar scenes played out.

Finding themselves isolated from the rest of Fourth Company, Sergeant Arion and Third Squad held out for over an hour against a much larger force of Black Legionaries and their daemonic allies. Without taking a single casualty, they killed over thirty Traitor Astartes and daemons before Master Boaz and a relief force showed up to help close out the battle. Such was the ferocity of the firefight that when High Interrogator Asmodai arrived once Fourth Company had moved on, he discovered new niches and alcoves had been torn into the rock from sustained bolt shell impacts.

Master Belial of Third Company, shoulder to shoulder with Ezekiel and three other brothers of the Librarius, fought off wave after wave of Khorne berserkers. Their rage heightened by the presence of psykers among the enemy, they smashed ineffectively against psi-shields before being cut to ribbons by bolt pistols and chainswords. Even bolstered by daemonic servants of their master, they could not topple the Dark Angels' defences. When Chaplain Boreas came later to extract the gene-seed from the dead, he found it hard to distinguish which body parts belonged to which dismembered corpse, the ferocity of the berserkers' assault countered in equal measure by the ruthlessness of the defenders.

But for all the acts of selflessness and heroism, not a single member of the Fallen would be found among the numbers of the traitors that day.

Finishing his ministrations, Seraphicus carefully placed the metal cylinder containing the looted gene-seed into a pouch hanging from his waist. As he made to leave, no doubt to remove more progenoids from the slain, he nodded to Gabriel in the same manner as Tigrane had done, but brushed the first two fingers of his right hand across his left cheek just below the eye. It seemingly went unnoticed by the other Terminator-armoured figures but Balthasar furrowed his brow. Being a member of the Deathwing made him privy to all manner of Chapter secrets in excess of his non-ascended battle-brothers but he was still on the periphery of the inner circle. Had Seraphicus made some kind of clandestine signal to Gabriel? How much more forbidden knowledge did the Dark Angels have left for him to learn?

Gabriel turned to address the fifty Deathwing checking their gear and cleaning filth from their armour. Azrael had taken the other half of First Company onboard the stricken ship as soon as it had become clear that the battle to capture the asteroid would be swifter than anticipated and now, with the sounds of battle dying away, Gabriel would lead the remainder to join them.

'Our work here is done, brothers. The Archenemy sorcerers lie dead and broken. Their spells are already fading and the horrors they enabled to gain purchase in this realm weaken by the second.' Gabriel's gaze lingered on Balthasar as he spoke. 'Dozens of the vile Black Legion have been vanquished and their foul barbarism will never again strike fear in the hearts of the loyal. New names will be recorded in the Chapter annals this day, brothers, and we praise them all.'

A great cheer rang out from the ivory-suited warriors. The Master of the Deathwing was still looking directly at Balthasar.

'But although our fight here is at an end, our Grey Knight...' Gabriel paused, probing for the right word. The air filled with pre-teleportation buzz. Winds whipped up from nowhere, billowing the robes of dead cultists. '...allies still require our aid to cleanse the Navy vessel of boarders.'

Already fading as he spoke those last few words, Balthasar swore that the company master nodded at him right before he disappeared.

766960.M41 / Revenge, Pythos blockade, Pandorax System

Driving the Titansword through the daemon's midriff, Draigo did not stop until the hilt made rough contact with armoured hide. Corrosive black-green bile spilled from the thing's guts and it let rip with a senses-shattering scream as it was torn back to the warp, leaving behind it an oily cloud of foul-smelling liquid smoke.

In all directions, Grey Knights were engaged with the servants of the Dark Gods, but direction was somehow meaningless on the lower decks of the *Revenge*, neither fully existing in the material realm nor completely claimed by the malign influence of Chaos. A daemonette stalked towards him across the part metal, part flesh deck yet, impossibly, it was suspended from the ceiling, lilaceous tongue wriggling loose from its jaw and tasting the battle on the air. Draigo and the Knight of the Flame fighting at his shoulder swung their blades in unison, reducing the androgynous beast to a rapidly fading heap of body parts. Still more daemons came at them, the warp portal above them, yet at the same time below them, vomiting forth more blasphemous specimens.

Flashes of psychic messages flashed across Draigo's psyche from others of the Brotherhood in battle across the ship. Castellan Crowe and a dozen Terminators were locked down on the *Revenge*'s hangar deck, a Lord of Skulls and a near-endless tide of Khorne berserkers hampering their attempt to get the flight bays operational again and allow the Navy flyers to land. Justicar Amrythe and his strike squad, tracking a Tzeentchian daemon of no small notoriety, were caught in a localised time loop, reaching the end of the corridor they were advancing along only to find themselves back at the start. Despite being fully aware of their situation, there was nothing they could do about it while the daemon who had cast the spell still lingered on this side of the veil.

Gradually, the nature of the messages changed. Where situations had previously seemed desperate, hope now blossomed in the form of green, black and white armoured saviours. Using their mounts and flyers to full effect, forty brothers of the Ravenwing stormed the hangar decks, sweeping away the warriors of the Blood God in a hurricane of bolter fire and routing even the vast daemonic engine they dubbed 'Crushing Death'. Freed from their chronologic trap, Amrythe and his Justicars discovered the physical shell of their daemonic tormentor and though they found evidence of their allies' involvement in its banishment, the chainaxe wounds that criss-crossed its avian form were a mystery.

In the midst of their own melee, Draigo saw and smelled the tell-tale signs of teleportation, and in the blink of an eye twenty ivory-clad Terminators were in amongst the Purifiers and Paladins he had led into the depths of the *Revenge*. Without pausing to get their bearings, they opened up with their storm bolters, shredding daemon flesh and thinning out the maleficent horde.

'I am Grand Master Gabriel of the Deathwing,' said the Dark Angel alongside Draigo, who, up until moments ago, had not been there. Gabriel's sword flashed through the air decapitating a leaping daemonette.

'Well met, Grand Master. I am Supreme Grand Master Draigo of the Grey Knights,' replied Draigo, his blade claiming the head of another daemonette in mimicry of the Dark Angel's action.

'No introductions are necessary, Master Draigo. Lord Azrael has briefed me well.' There was more than a hint of sarcasm in Gabriel's tone.

Another Deathwing Terminator moved within earshot, backhanding a nurgling into pulp while his storm bolter whirred as it automatically reloaded. 'Can their witchminds close the breech or not?' he asked bluntly.

'Balthasar...' Gabriel said, not in chastisement. The other Terminator moved away again, blasting away at the swarm of daemons now that his weapon had a full complement of ammo.

'What Balthasar meant to say was, are you and your battle-brothers capable of shutting the warp portal?' If any slight was meant by his question, his face, shrouded under the hood of his robes, gave nothing away.

'Yes. It's what we've been trying to do for hours. We just need to be close enough to the portal to enact the ritual.'

'Allow us to clear you a path,' Gabriel said, sweeping his sword in a wide arc and cleaving a pair of daemons who had got a little too close to him. 'Deathwing! On me. The Grey Knights need to reach the portal to be able to close it. We will ensure they get there.'

By rote, the nineteen Dark Angels Terminators took up formation around their commander, despatching Chaotic horrors as they moved into position. Without further instruction, as soon as the last Deathwing was in place, they spread out, pushing the daemons back and opening up a protective envelope in their midst.

'Grey Knights! Forward,' Draigo called out, thrusting the *Titansword* aloft. He moved into the gap opened up by the Dark Angels. A dozen more silver armoured figures rallied around the Chapter relic, its blade blackened by daemon gore. Gabriel turned his head slightly to address Draigo.

'Ready?' asked the Dark Angel.

'Ready,' replied the Grey Knight.

As one, a mass of silver and ivory ceramite surged forwards, a blitzkrieg of bolt shells and blades tearing a route through the pressed mob of daemonettes, nurglings and other less identifiable monstrosities. Even corralled by the shield of Deathwing, the Grey Knights were still a potent fighting unit, the heads and deformed bodies of warp fiends exploding in blue flame at a mere thought from the psychically empowered Space Marines. Those few daemons that did break through the wall of Terminators, or leapt over their heads to get at the Grey Knights, soon met their doom on the end of a force sword.

In short order, the phalanx of Deathwing led Draigo and his brothers directly above/beneath the warp rift and the Dark Angels spread out, their escort mission now becoming one of perimeter control. Tirelessly, they held back the daemonic tide, waves of bloated and spindly bodies smashed apart on a shore of Terminator armour. Balthasar swung unstintingly with his power fist, smiting daemons with every blow, their wrecked forms tossed back against more of their kind. Balthasar's squadmate, Barachiel, left gauntlet shattered and torn, two fingers bitten off at the knuckle, blazed away with his heavy flamer. Daemon-hide burned and shrivelled, greasy smoke billowing as they fled blindly back through the horde, igniting others as they went. Gabriel himself, his black Heavenfall blade rising and falling in ichor-streaked arcs, slew with a veteran's poise, every swing or shot rewarding him with another kill.

At the Dark Angels' backs, the Grey Knights were about their appointed task. Working symbols in the air out of conjured psi-flame, Draigo and two of the Purifiers chanted the Litany of Ensealment while the rest of his brothers vanquished those daemons that were still issuing forth from the tear or any that slipped past the attentions of the Deathwing. Finishing the inverted pentagram that signalled the commencement of the second phase of the ritual, Draigo noticed a change in the mood of the baying horde. The nurglings in particular seemed reluctant to get close to the portal, hanging back and letting the daemonettes get eviscerated on the end of Dark Angels weapons but they too became reticent to attack, forcing the

Deathwing to engage them with ranged weapons. The rate of daemons pouring out of the rift slowed to a halt.

Unheralded, a skeletal hand loomed out of the eddies of the warp, bony fingers taking grasp in reality and dragging through the rest of its emaciated body. Five metres tall and entirely devoid of flesh and muscle, a daemon prince of Nurgle strode through into the materium. Wings, their span the equal of the thing's height, unfurled from its back. Glassy orbs in its inhuman skull regarded Space Marine and daemon alike, and its mouth parted in a grin, the stench of aeons' old death emanating from a breathless exhale.

Draigo was the first to speak. 'J'ian-Lo,' he spat.

The daemon prince turned its head to face Draigo, the crack of bone against bone jarring to all who heard it. Its smile widened in recognition.

'Kaldor Draigo. So good to see you again.' J'ian-Lo's voice was like the scraping of a sarcophagus lid being removed. 'Mortarion sends his regards. He did so want to be here to kill you himself but as you made that an impossibility, he allowed me to have the pleasure instead.'

Moving with a speed beyond the ken of even a Space Marine, J'ian-Lo reached out with a gaunt hand and grabbed Draigo by the shoulder. Before anybody could react, both Grey Knight and daemon prince had disappeared.

766960.M41 / Red Six. Adamantium Fields, Pandorax System

DEBRIS CLANKED AGAINST Shira's Kestrel, every tiny impact from planetary and spacecraft debris pocking the hull. She leaned over to peer out of the cockpit. The kill markings she had fought so hard to attain were patchy, many already obliterated by the tiny rocks. Shira cursed. The way things were going she was unlikely to get the chance to repaint them, let alone add to the tally. The large asteroid she was skirting around lit up in the reflected light of balefire, an unnecessary reminder that the Heldrake was still on her tail.

More red lights lit up on her console as she weaved between two more of the enormous rocks before dipping under the wreck of a Navy frigate. Behind her, her pursuer matched the movement of her craft, its wings swinging backwards and forwards in a rowing motion. A chunk of asteroid separated from a larger body, spinning towards the Heldrake. Without deviating from its course, it engulfed the tank-sized splinter in blue flame, utterly vaporising it.

Shira's plan was a simple one. Kranswar's assertion that the fighter-interceptors could cope within the asteroid field had been sound and so she had led the Heldrake into the Adamantium Fields where its greater speed would be negated. It was far more manoeuvrable than the capital ships of the Chaos blockade but the daemon-flyer was bigger and more cumbersome than a Kestrel and, in theory, should not find it easy to navigate through the mass of cosmic flotsam. That theory had been disproven thus far.

Regardless of whether the Heldrake made it through with her, the final stage of Shira's gambit was to land on Pythos. Despite being in the clutches of an enemy occupation force, she would rather take her chances down there than run out of power in the depths of space and be eaten by a metal dragon or suffocate once her oxygen supply was depleted.

Another ruined ship loomed large in front of her, an enemy destroyer broken apart by a ferocious broadsides attack. Its entire starboard flank was open to the void and an explosion, likely caused by the sub-warp engines taking a direct hit, had gouged through the superstructure right through to port. Seeing the gap, Shira dived sharply and entered a barrel roll, corkscrewing through the hole in the destroyer with barely a metre to spare on either side. The Heldrake once again copied the Kestrel's route, tucking its wings in as it glided through the opening but, being larger than Shira's craft, barely made it. Its sharpened wingtips tore through armoured panels in a shower of grotesquely coloured sparks but momentum drove it through and it emerged on the other side still in one piece. Enraged and still hungry for the hunt, it unfurled its wings and resumed the chase. There was now clear distance between it and Shira.

The rate of impacts against her hull slowed, signalling that she was coming to the edge of the asteroid field. Gently banking around an erratically drifting slab of rock, Pythos, for so long obscured to her, was revealed, the blue and green orb hanging benignly against a backdrop of black. Behind her, the Heldrake broke free of the Adamantium Fields, tiny rocks sliding off its hide like a seabird's feathers repelling water.

Shira checked her instruments trying to ascertain the distance left before she would enter Pythos's orbit, but the auspex, like so many of the Kestrel's gauges and sensors, had automatically shut down to preserve power.

Not daring to open the throttle to its full extent but wary that the Heldrake would soon catch up to her if she maintained her cautious asteroid field speed, Shira pointed the Kestrel towards the largest landmass she could see and coaxed a little more pace out of the engines.

The Heldrake, responding to the brightened flare from the Kestrel's rear, followed in her wake at full pace, long strokes of its wings seemingly pulling at the blanket of space and reeling her in. Without instrumentation to rely on, Shira did a quick mental calculation. If she maintained this speed, and provided the daemon engine could not call on its nefarious patrons for an injection of pace, she should just about make it down to the surface before the Heldrake. Just.

On the threshold of the planet's atmosphere, preluded by a flurry of alarms and warning lights, her engines finally ran out of power.

766960.M41 / Merciless Death, Adamantium Fields, Pandorax System

Malgar Irongrasp had fought enough space battles to know when one was lost. Standing before the occulus on the bridge of *Merciless Death* – literally an eye styled after the Eye of Horus – and looking out over the Fourth, and final, Battle of Sunward Gap, he knew that this time he would be on the losing side.

The wreck of the *Might of Huron* listed uneasily, its contents still being sucked out into the void hours after a Dark Angels battle-barge and the regrouped fighters from the *Stalwart* had pounded it into submission. With the Slaughter-class cruiser's demise guaranteed, the Space Marine ship's assault had been relentless ensuring there was not a scrap of the Red Corsairs' vessel left salvageable. His own ships had fared no better.

Heartless Destroyer had attempted to engage the Dark Angels strike cruiser but, under duress from a trio of Hunter-class destroyers, the Grey Knights vessel had ghosted in on her blindside and crippled her. *Steel Anvil*, bearing massive damage suffered before the arrival of the Space Marine vessels, struck the final blow, its nova cannon cracking open the *Heartless Destroyer*'s spine and setting off a series of catastrophic explosions.

It was not the first time Irongrasp had lost a ship-to-ship conflict. Six hundred years ago he had tasted defeat in an engagement around Cadia, ironically, to the very fleet he now led. Bending his knee before the Warmaster in exchange for his life and swearing fealty, his new loyalty was soon rewarded when he slew Abaddon's former admiral and ascended to command of the Black Legion's primary fleet. If he survived this battle, it would be his last in Black Legion colours. Abaddon the Despoiler brooked no failure from those who served him and should Malgar escape with his life, the *Merciless Death* would need to find a new banner to fly under.

The opportunity to swear allegiance to a new master soon presented itself to the former White Consul.

'Lord Irongrasp. The *Deathblade* is hailing us,' a hooded acolyte seated at a vox-array called out. The *Might of Huron* was the only Red Corsairs' vessel to have fallen to Imperium guns and the *Deathblade*, along with its sister ship, *No Redemption*, and the assorted raiders and destroyers Blackheart had brought to the battle, were keeping the Chaos forces in the fight.

'Put them on loudspeaker,' Malgar replied. Through the occulus two more of his ships disappeared within coronas of blinding light.

'So near yet so far, Irongrasp. A victory so nearly complete turned on its head by the fickle whim of fate. Perhaps if Abaddon had favoured one of the Four, one of the Four would have favoured him in return. Delayed the Dark Angels flotilla in the warp a little longer? Translated them further out from the Pandorax System, maybe?' It was Huron's voice. Malgar had initially thought – willed – him dead in the destruction of the *Might of Huron*, but ever the wily operator, he had led his ships from one of the smaller vessels to make himself a lesser target.

'The day is not entirely lost, Lord Blackheart. The *Merciless Death* is still fully operational and the ships in my fleet are not beyond repair. All are now at your disposal.' There was no guile in Malgar's attempt to save his own skin.

Huron laughed. 'But I need you to cover my escape,

Irongrasp. And besides, your ship is no longer warp-capable.'

'I don't understand,' replied Malgar. He soon did.

'*Deathblade* is readying its plasma batteries!' said a diminutive crewman, a bundle of cables snaking from his head and chest into the console before him.

'Divert shields aft,' Malgar ordered. With the Space Marine fleet attacking the *Merciless Death* head-on, all shield power had been directed fore. Chaos vessels to its rear, the back section of the ship was vulnerable.

Malgar's order came too late. As crew and servitors frantically scrambled to reroute their defences, the weapon bays of the Gothic War veteran glowed white hot. Lances of superheated hydrogen speared through the void, melting the unprotected hull of the far larger vessel and rupturing its warp drives. The *Merciless Death* rocked under the detonations of multiple explosions, secondary blasts still ripping through it by the time Huron addressed the ship again.

'See, Irongrasp? I am nothing if not merciful. Your sub-warp engines are still operational and if you're quick, you can outrun the Dark Angels to Pythos. I'm sure the Warmaster will be pleased to see you.'

Malgar was about to recite a curse, taught to him hundreds of years ago by a Thousand Sons sorcerer, but the line to the *Deathblade* went dead before he could get the words out. Behind the *Merciless Death*, the remnants of the Red Corsairs' fleet turned and fled, trying to put enough distance between them and Gaea before slipping into the warp. Malgar briefly considered following them to draw the Space Marine vessels after Blackheart but it would be futile. The Red Corsairs already had a head start and the *Merciless Death* would be presenting its vulnerable rear to the hunting Dark Angels. Instead, he opted to take Huron's advice.

'All vessels. Make for the Adamantium Fields. We're retreating to Pythos,' he voxed to the fleet. If he could salvage some of the Black Legion ships, perhaps it would put Abaddon in a more forgiving mood. If not, at least he would still be alive to barter for his life.

Without question, the bridge crew ran through the drill of turning the huge craft around. Agonisingly slowly, kilometres of captured Imperial vessel swung around in a wide arc, its prow eventually pointing towards Pythos. As the Dark Angels fleet converged on the handful of surviving traitor ships, Malgar ordered full speed ahead, punching towards the sanctuary of the asteroid field.

'Lord Irongrasp. It's the other vessels in the fleet. They're breaking formation,' said a crewman seated before an auspex. His big eyes were completely jet black, giving the impression of his pupils having swallowed both iris and white. Malgar strode from the rail before the occulus, eager to see for himself. At the centre of the auspex sat the rune denoting the *Merciless Death*, its course a straight line headed directly for the Adamantium Fields. Either side of it, multiple smaller icons headed off at diagonals in all directions. At the fringes of the display sat the ominous red markers of enemy vessels.

'Raise the *Helspite*. I want to speak to Shangsiao Zurmgren. Now,' Irongrasp spat.

'They're refusing all hails, lord,' said the vox-operator after several attempts to raise the fleeing heavy cruiser. The *Helspite*'s rune flickered before disappearing from the auspex.

'*Helspite* has just made warp translation,' said the dark-eyed crewman. More icons pulsed and vanished in quick succession until the *Merciless Death* was the only friendly vessel remaining.

'They've abandoned us. The cowards have fled and abandoned us,' Malgar said, bile rising in his throat. With the other ships gone, the already stricken *Merciless Death* had no escort and the Space Marine vessels would be on her in minutes. 'Launch all fighter wings. Suicide protocols. If any of them try to return to this ship before we are within the asteroid field, you have my permission to shoot them down.'

Moments later the auspex lit up with hundreds of tiny dots, racing towards the edge of the screen. In response, hundreds more in hostile colours swarmed in from the edge, the Imperial fleet scrambling its own fighters to counter the threat. Through the occulus, the Adamantium Fields grew ever closer.

Further explosions rocked the Chaos ship as the swifter Space Marine vessels drew within weapons range. Unimpeded by the suicide pilots now engaged by Imperial Navy fighters, they opened up with prow lances, scorching the *Merciless Death*'s flanks with glancing blows. Irongrasp knew they were not warning shots across his bow; the gunnery teams were finding their range and their next volleys would be deadly.

'Hard to port!' Malgar yelled at the steersman. The mutated brute, more beast than man, pulled the ancient wheel hard to the left and the ship followed suit. Bridge crew grasped for anything to steady themselves as the *Merciless Death* lurched sharply. Through the occulus, two bright beams of energy blazed on by, the Dark Angels vessels missing their target thanks to Malgar's quick manoeuvre. 'Hard to port!' he yelled again.

It was a double-bluff and one he'd used to good effect many times before. The pursuing vessels would be expecting a jinking manoeuvre and would place their next shots expecting him to turn back to starboard. By heading further to port, Malgar was not only avoiding their fire but was moving away from them, putting future shots at the limit of their effective range. The ship pitched again, this time sending crewmen sprawling to the deck and another shot streaked by, missing the *Merciless Death* by a comfortable margin. Before it registered that only a single ship had fired, the prow battery of the other loosed a shot that caught the *Merciless Death* square in the top aft section.

Rocking violently, the ship listed hard under the ensuing explosion, threatening to roll completely before the gravitic compensators kicked in at the last moment. His armoured boots maglocked to the deck, Malgar was the last soul who remained on his feet on the bridge. Ignoring the devastation wrought upon the crew and the fires that had broken out he barked more orders.

'Steersman. Hard to–'

Twin impacts cut him off, the bridge going momentarily dark before the emergency systems sputtered to life. Despite the gloomy half-light he could see that most of the bridge crew were dead. The slab-muscled steersman lay motionless over the wheel, his bestial head split open from forehead to temple.

Malgar crushed the carpet of bodies underfoot as he made his way over to the steering controls but, as yet another direct hit was scored upon the *Merciless Death*, even his maglocked boots and Space Marine physique could not prevent him from being knocked forcefully to the floor. Disentangling himself from the jumble of dead crew, he rose to his feet and struggled on across the rumbling deck. Something filled the circle of the occulus that caused him to stop cold in his tracks.

In the final stages of bringing itself to bear on the helpless Chaos ship, the unmistakable prow of a Space Marine strike cruiser loomed large through the huge glass eye. Tiny explosions flared around it where the suicide fighters launched from *Merciless Death* either smashed against the Dark Angels' shields or were shot down by defence batteries. Movement caught Malgar's attention, a massive turret rotating until its linear accelerator was pointing directly at *Merciless Death*'s bridge.

As the bombardment cannon fired, Malgar Irongrasp – formerly Malgar Eringrisp, White Consuls Master of the Fleet – at last gave in to the inevitable.

766960.M41 / Exterior, Revenge, Pythos blockade, Pandorax System

KALDOR DRAIGO BLINKED back into reality, a fleshless hand still gripping him tight.

Instantly, his suit's systems went into overdrive, runes and icons flashing insistently to warn him of massive changes in temperature and pressure. Inbuilt oxygen reserves kicked in with a low hiss and vibrations rattled through his ancient armour as the soles of his feet automatically maglocked to whatever was beneath him. A noiseless explosion bloomed in the distance causing his visors to darken momentarily, sparing his eyes from damage. When they cleared, Draigo realised where he was.

The vast outlines of Imperial vessels swam through the blackness of space, pursuing fleeing Chaos ships and mopping up the last of the enemy's fighters with their turrets. Stars shimmered, their light reflected from the hulls of the spacefaring behemoths and from the Supreme Grand Master's own armour. J'ian-Lo had teleported them both onto the hull of the *Revenge*.

Diago brought the *Titansword* up in a blur of silver. The upstroke caught the arm gripping him at the wrist, almost severing the filthy bones. His captor's grasp relinquished, the Grey Knight reversed his motion and caught the daemon prince's arm again on the downstroke, splinters of radius and ulna floating free in the void. J'ian-Lo's face formed a snaggletoothed snarl, its visage incongruous without the noise of a roar to accompany it. Balling its fist, it swung its undamaged arm at Draigo's head.

Draigo reacted just in time, the huge knuckle making contact with his pauldron rather than his helmet. He spun at the torso, presenting his other shoulder to J'ian-Lo but his maglocked boots prevented him from being knocked back.

Recovering, Draigo used both hands to slash violently upwards with his weapon, trying to splice the massive daemon through the sternum but his blow was countered. In the blink of an eye, J'ian-Lo's ruined arm reshaped and refashioned itself, flattening and reknitting to form a wide, flat blade of bone. The *Titansword* locked against it, both wielders straining to keep the other's weapon in place, but inevitably the daemon prince's greater strength won out. Overriding his armour's maglock, Draigo took two quick steps backwards. J'ian-Lo's bonesword passed harmlessly through the space the Grey Knight had just vacated and embedded itself in the hull of the *Revenge*.

Too far away to capitalise on the daemon prince's momentary predicament, the Supreme Grand Master instead used the opportunity to assess his surroundings and situation. Crenulations ran for kilometres in each direction, the pattern interrupted by weapons cupolas and sensor arrays until it met either the prow of the ship or the protruding bridge section. The only feature close by that broke the straight line of the hull top was a comms tower, its metallic structure thrusting ten metres upwards from the body of the *Revenge*. Had it been freestanding on the surface of a planet, the comms tower would rightly have been called large but here, in comparison to the Imperial Navy ships and celestial bodies, it paled into insignificance. To Kaldor Draigo it was currently the most important thing in the universe and his best chance of ending the battle with J'ian-Lo swiftly and in his favour.

Breaking into a sprint, Draigo turned and headed for the tower, rhythmically engaging and disengaging the maglock in time with his footfalls, lest he drift off into the void. Freeing its blade-arm, J'ian-Lo grinned and beat its wings to set off in pursuit. The grin soon became another snarl as the daemon prince realised that despite all of the gifts lavished upon it by Nurgle, it too was subject to certain natural laws.

Draigo had surmised that J'ian-Lo had teleported him to

the exterior of the ship not only to separate him from his battle-brothers but also to diminish his arsenal. With sound not able to travel in a vacuum, J'ian-Lo's true name would be useless against him, as would any binding or banishing incantations as it was the hearing, not merely the speaking, from which the power sprung. But lack of sound was the sole boon the void afforded the daemon prince, the absence of both atmosphere and gravity making its wings useless and working to the Grey Knight's advantage instead.

J'ian-Lo dipped his head and gave chase on foot. Already a significant gap had opened up between the favoured of Nurgle and its prey, and this lengthened as the skeletal giant struggled to navigate across the *Revenge*'s bumpy surface. Whereas Draigo could lock himself to the hull without breaking stride, J'ian-Lo had to grip the hull in its claw-like feet with every step it took, talons biting deep into metal. By the time Draigo reached the base of the comms tower, there was over twenty metres between him and the daemon prince.

Finding hand-holds with the ease an ogryn finds food, Draigo clambered up the outside of the tower, his boots gripping the metal as he went. Even in a full suit of Terminator armour, he had almost traversed the structure by the time J'ian-Lo had reached the base.

Looking up at the trapped Space Marine, J'ian-Lo shook its head in pity. All Draigo's foolish gambit had done was strand him at the top of the tower leaving him at the mercy – not that it had any – of one of Nurgle's most blessed. Not bothering to clamber up after him, J'ian-Lo started tearing at the comms tower, trying to separate it from the rest of the *Revenge* and send it floating off into space with Draigo still attached to it.

It was only when the shadow cast by the Grey Knight kept getting larger that J'ian-Lo realised that it was the one who had been led into a trap.

The magnets in his soles inexorably attracted to the vast metal hull of the ship beneath him, Draigo dropped, the hilt of the *Titansword* clasped between both gauntleted hands, blade-tip pointed downwards. Too quick for even a daemon prince to react, Draigo's feet made contact with J'ian-Lo's ribcage at the same instant the blade met its throat. Slamming the giant skeleton to the deck, the Grey Knight's blade slipped through the top of the thing's spine, parting its deformed skull from the rest of its frame. It rolled away into a recess between two crenulations.

Lifting himself from the crouched position he'd landed in, Draigo removed himself from the inert frame of the daemon prince and it drifted away from the hull, floating slowly into the depths of eternity. Steadily, the Supreme Grand Master approached J'ian-Lo's severed head, its bulbous eyes flicking in all directions, mouth moving as if in prayer. When Draigo finally came to stand over it, he realised the head was mouthing the word 'please'. Derisorily, the commander of the Grey Knights order flicked the daemon prince's head away with a swift motion of his foot and looked on impassively as the skull followed the rest of the body out into the blackness.

He opened a vox-link to the *Silver Nemesis*. 'Captain Fischer. This is Supreme Grand Master Draigo. Lock onto my position and teleport me back aboard the *Revenge*.'

SECONDS LATER, THE silvered form of their leader rematerialized amongst the cadre of Purifiers and Paladins, but the scene Draigo returned to was very different from the one he had been so rudely dragged away from.

The noise of combat had abated, the *whoosh* of flamers cremating the corporeal remains of daemons being the only weapon discharge. The suppurating portal had been closed and some semblance of normality had been restored to the lower decks. Patches of bulkhead still retained a living, fleshy quality, but at least it was now possible to distinguish between up and down.

A cheer went up from the assembled Grey Knights when they realised that their leader had been returned to them and as news spread around the ship of Draigo's safe return, his vox link filled with exclamations of relief and joy. Even those members of the Deathwing who had witnessed Draigo's abduction sent respectful nods in his direction, which he returned with equal respect. In his absence, more Dark Angels had made their way down to the lower decks, and green and black armoured figures moved among their First Company brethren. Spying a group of three figures deep in conversation in a darkened corner, Draigo removed his helmet and made to join them.

As he got within several metres of the trio, one of them, a hooded, blue armoured figure with an augmetic eye, gave a subtle gesture with his head in Draigo's direction, causing all conversation to cease. The other two Dark Angels, a Terminator-clad Deathwing and a robed figure with two spiked skulls decorating his backpack, turned to regard the newcomer.

'Supreme Grand Master,' said the robed figure, a finely crafted combi-weapon slung casually at his hip. His armour was scratched and dented, and the tell-tale bite of a chainaxe had taken a chunk of his left pauldron. His arm hung limply at his side and dried blood congealed over a thick rent in the armour over his thigh. He looked as if he had already waged a one-man war.

'Supreme Grand Master,' returned Draigo.

'Brother Gabriel you have already met, and this is Brother Ezekiel of the Librarius,' Azrael said motioning with an open palm towards the blue armoured Dark Angel.

'Well met, Brother Ezekiel. Your reputation precedes you,' said Draigo, genuinely.

The Librarian's crude augmetic eye whirred noisily as it focused on the Grey Knight. 'As does yours, Lord Draigo,' Ezekiel replied, his gaze switching briefly to Azrael, the ghost of a smile creeping across his face.

'You look as if you're going to be keeping your artificers and apothecaries busy for some time to come,' Draigo said. 'Unexpected trouble?'

'Trouble is never unexpected, brother, though the source of this strife was an opponent I had believed long dead.'

Draigo considered pressing for more information but knew it would be futile. Even the Dark Angels' secrets held secrets.

'What about you, brother?' Azrael continued. 'You too bear the mark of combat. Gabriel tells me that a daemon prince took a shine to you and wanted to keep you all to itself.'

Draigo glanced at the pauldron that Azrael was puzzling over. He hadn't noticed before now that the blow from J'ian-Lo had dented the ceramite. The perfect impression of a giant fist adorned the plate.

'An opponent I knew to be still alive but had wished long dead,' Draigo said, matching Azrael's reluctance to divulge any more details than were absolutely necessary. 'Still, that foe is now vanquished and the day is won. You and your brothers have the gratitude of the Grey Knights for your... timely intervention.'

'The battle for the Pandorax System may be over but the war for Pythos has yet to begin,' Azrael said, not acknowledging Draigo's thanks. 'I'm sure there will be plenty of opportunities for you and your brothers to honour the obligation you now owe us.' Although the word remained unspoken, Azrael had made it quite clear that he considered the Grey Knights to now be indebted to the Dark Angels.

Not wishing to rise to the bait, Draigo bid the three Dark Angels farewell and went to rejoin his battle-brothers.

766960.M41 / Red Six. Upper Atmosphere, Pythos

TO ANYBODY LEFT alive on the ground on Pythos, it looked like a meteorite breaching the planet's atmosphere. To Shira Hagen, strapped into the cockpit of the lifeless Kestrel, it felt like she was locked in an incinerator. Her flight suit smouldered, several patches already glowing bright orange with the promise of flame, and sweat dripped from her every pore. Her mouth was dry, her head heavy from dehydration and the massive gravitational forces at play on her body. To top it all, the Heldrake had followed her to Pythos and was still tight on her tail, its powerful wings driving it ever closer to the stricken fighter.

Remembering what she learned on the first day of basic training, and added to over the years with knowledge gleaned from mess rooms and below decks bars, Shira fought against the forces pressing her back in her seat to stick an arm out to release the catch keeping the cockpit shut. She swore, and quickly retracted a burned hand, the atmospheric entry had heated the metal of the craft up to unbearable temperatures. Pulling her hand up into the sleeve of her flight suit, she tried again but the superheated metal had fused to the frame of the cockpit and her only reward was her elasticated cuffs igniting. Patting her arm against her thigh to put out the flames she looked around the cockpit for inspiration, anything that could save her from the twin fates facing her: a crash landing which she had no hope of surviving or being engulfed in daemonic flame. Scores of useless dials and instruments looked back at her.

And also the one thing that might give her a slight chance of survival.

Remembering what she learned on the second day of basic training, and had never discussed with anybody since as, as far as she was aware at least, what she was about to attempt had never been tried by anybody ever before, Shira let a flight suit-covered hand drop to the side of her seat. She fumbled around for a moment before finally locating the small plastic knob atop the end of a lever. The plastic felt malleable, its chemical structure debasing under extreme heat, but it was still intact and, more importantly, still connected to the wing flaps.

The Kestrel was a space-capable variant of the Thunderbolt fighter-interceptor and their basic STCs were almost identical, so much so that systems which were redundant for void use were still fitted lest a Mechanicus cult adept upset the machine-spirits. The rudder on the craft's tail was one such unnecessary feature (though, if the power plant were still active, one that Shira would literally kill to be able to use in her current situation) as was the ejector seat with built-in parachute (again, ironically useful in her current situation if she could get the cockpit open). But the one hangover from the design of the Kestrel's parent that was most akin to breasts on a fish, were the hydraulic wing flaps.

The only reason Shira knew about them at all was because an instructor had told her class how to use them in the case of coming in for a 'hot' landing. Under those 'rare circumstances' where an Imperial Navy vessel had to make a quick warp jump, all of its fighter wings would have to scramble back to the ship, quite often making landings at speed: a 'hot' landing. The practice was not without risk, and even the most careful of pilots could find themselves planting their fighter into a bulkhead or another fighter. One way of mitigating this risk, according to the instructor tutoring Shira at least, was to operate the wing flaps once you were back in the atmosphere of the ship's landing bay, the theory being that the added resistance would 'arrest the craft's forward momentum'. Up until now, it had been a half-remembered theory somewhere at the back of Shira's mind, but right now her forward momentum could really use some arresting.

Straining her neck to twist around and look behind her, Shira saw the fearsome visage of the Heldrake no more than a hundred metres behind her and gaining rapidly. Within seconds, she would be in range of the beast's cone of flame and the temperatures she had been experiencing up until now would feel like a particularly inclement day on Fenris.

The next moment, the view from the cockpit turned to whiteout and steam hissed from the Kestrel's hull. She had hit cloud cover.

'Shit,' she croaked, shocked at hearing the sound of her own voice for the first time in hours. 'Closer to the ground than I thought.'

As quickly as they had descended, the clouds parted and Shira's view filled with the emerald and brown of the jungle below rising up to meet her in a deadly embrace. Fighting for all she was worth against G-force, she twisted her veiny neck. The Heldrake had opened its maw, the pre-flame of its balefire evident on its tongue. It was now or never.

Yanking so hard on the lever that her shoulder popped out of its socket, Shira screamed as the flaps lifted, instantly slowing the Kestrel and pushing her further back into her seat. Ribs fractured and her nose started to bleed as even greater forces abused her body. It took every ounce of her being not to black out. Feeling the heat from the Heldrake's breath weapon, she forced her eyes upwards to see the dark, winged shape overshoot her just as it had done out in space. Unlike in space, its scream of frustration was audible and it pulled out of its dive in time to prevent itself from crashing through the canopies of the tall trees below.

There was to be no such escape for Shira.

Closing her eyes as the top leaves and branches loomed large through the smoke-blackened glass of the cockpit, Shira felt the first few impacts against the hull and wings as tree limbs scraped and tore at the body of the Kestrel that had so very nearly got her to the ground in one piece. She screwed her face up, praying to the God-Emperor and anybody else who would listen that the impact would kill her outright.

When the impact came, it was not at all what she had been expecting.

Instead of a thud followed by a tangle of metal and body parts, there was an almighty splash trailed by the sound of steam rising from the Kestrel's hull. Cautiously, still not quite believing that she had survived, Shira slowly opened her eyes. She could not see much through the cracked and blackened plastiglass of the cockpit but she could see, hear and feel water trickling in through the fissures. By some blind piece of luck, or divine intervention, she had managed to bring herself down into an ocean. Or, more accurately, judging by the colour and smell of the fluid filling up the floor of her craft, a swamp.

Shira tried to unclasp her harness but, realising that they too had fused under the heat of entry, pulled out the combat blade from its scabbard at her waist and cut herself free. She vainly fiddled with the now cooled cockpit lock but met with the same result as before. Even jamming her knife into it and using it like a prybar had no effect. Using her one good arm, she pushed against the frame of the cockpit, hoping that she could somehow force it open. Again, her attempt at escape was futile. The water level had risen to cover her legs and she was struck by the realisation that the soothing cool water that was easing the pain of her multiple burns would soon be the same water that would fill her lungs and kill her.

She gave two final bangs against the roof of the cockpit, no more than half-hearted attempts to shove it open before letting her head loll forward and sobbed. It wasn't fair. She had survived the battles in space, outrun and outmanoeuvred a Heldrake and managed to get a powerless fighter-interceptor down to the planet's surface in one piece but in spite of all that, her final moments were going to be spent waiting to drown. Her sobs turned to laughter as she weighed up the cruel irony of it all.

A new noise made her stop crying and laughing altogether. Over the sound of inrushing water, Shira could hear something moving in the water around the Kestrel. Without warning, a gauntleted fist punched through the glass of the cockpit showering her in tiny fragments and causing the water to flood in at a faster rate. The fist gripped the frame and, after a couple of exploratory tugs, ripped the cockpit away from the rest of the Kestrel. Instantly, Shira was engulfed in the brackish black water. Her first instinct was to kick off and swim away but a massive arm wrapped around her waist and pulled her clear before she had a chance. Belatedly, she held her breath and felt herself being pulled up through the swamp until eventually she broke the surface with a choke and a splutter.

She could hear voices now, muggy and indistinct because her ears were full of water, and she was hoisted out of the wetness and onto soft muddy ground. She tried to open her eyes but glaring sunlight forced her to shut them again. She tried again, this time using her hand as a shield. Rendered as silhouettes against the intense light, two figures stood over her. The first was lithe, taut and obviously female despite her short hair. The other was far bigger, massive shoulder guards and the outline of a backpack clearly indicating he was a Space Marine. Shira instinctively reached for the knife at her belt only to discover it wasn't there, discarded in the cockpit of her sunken Kestrel during her rescue.

The smaller of the two figures stepped forward and knelt down in front of her. Without the light of the sun to frame her, Shira could see that the dark-skinned woman was wearing a green vest and camouflage fatigues, the hilt of a small knife poking out of the waistband. When she spoke it was with a quiet authority.

'I am Tzula Digriiz of the Emperor's Most Holy Ordos,' she said matter of factly. 'Your rescuer here is named Epimetheus and, as I'm sure you've already figured, out he's a Space Marine. Very useful to have around, even if he doesn't generally have much to say.'

Epimetheus stepped forward, the green coated silver of his armour now apparent to Shira. She didn't recognise which Chapter he was from.

'And what about you?' Tzula asked. 'I'm guessing from the fact that you crash-landed here in a fighter and are wearing a flight suit that looks like it has seen many, many better days that you're Navy.'

Shira blinked for a moment, her eyes still adjusting to the light and the rest of her to her situation. 'I'm Shira. Shira Hagen. Pilot first class, assigned to the Imperial Navy battleship *Revenge*.' She paused thoughtfully. 'At least I was. I don't even know if the *Revenge* exists any more.'

Tzula offered the prone woman her hand, which was part of a crude augmetic that replaced the real limb all the way up to the elbow. Shira gripped it and used it to aid herself to her feet.

'Well, Shira Hagen,' Tzula said turning to follow Epimetheus who was already heading into the thick jungle. 'Welcome to Pythos.'

PART FOUR

CHAPTER TEN

THE HELLHAMMER SHELL struck the daemon in the thorax,
tearing through flesh like kindling and exploding its bloated
form in a shower of gore. It remained standing for several
moments, unaware that its existence had been ended, before
collapsing in a smoking heap. Others of its kind simply
ignored the dissolving corpse as the army of the Neverborn
advanced upon the cave-mouth entrance to the hold.

'Reload! Reload!' barked Strike from his command chair
in the Hellhammer. Three burly Catachans heeded his command, one operating the mechanism to open the breech,
the other two hefting an enormous shell into position. It
was a process they had repeated more times than they could
remember in the past year.

Forced to flee Olympax, the 183rd had spread to the four corners of Pythos. Those on foot or in the precious few armoured
vehicles they retained dispersing across the main continent
of Pythos Prime; those on board Valkyries and other flyers
making it as far as the outlying continents and islands. Strike,
along with the handful of men crewing his tank, the inquisitor, the Space Marine and the xenos, had made straight for
Khan's Hold – one of the largest holds to remain in Catachan
hands and barracks for almost two hundred of his troops. It

221

had taken them thirty days to navigate the swamps and thick jungles, battling as much against the environment as the numerous predators who saw the super-heavy tank as good sport. Catachan through and through, the skulls of three would-be attackers adorned the hull of the war machine.

When they reached Khan's Hold, all they found was a charnel house.

Mutilated corpses lined the approach to the vast mining complex, some impaled on thick wooden stakes, others merely discarded on the padded-down earth that formed a crude road. Only weeks earlier, Khan's Hold had been defended from Abaddon's assault, the first victory of any note for the Imperial forces, but now its defenders lay dead and defiled, the hold itself no more than a burned-out shell.

Other Catachan forces made contact with Strike and as the Hellhammer wound its way slowly through the mire and trees towards Thermenos Stronghold, a remote but relatively easy to defend mine in the south of Pythos Prime, Strike's tank became as much a mobile command centre as it was a fearsome weapon of war. From all over the planet, small groups of jungle fighters reported in. A dozen taking refuge in High Peak, twelve men and women to defend a population of almost a thousand; three Valkyries finding sanctuary at Mount Blizzard, the second largest stronghold on the planet now under the protection of fifty Catachans with air support capability; thirty soldiers of Devil's Brigade footslogging for a month to reach the trio of delver-strongholds sited at Glazer's Plateau.

But the tank became so much more than that too – it became a rallying point, a symbol of Pythos's defiance. It had even gained a name – *Traitor's Bane* in honour of the tally of Archenemy it had claimed in its breakout from Olympax. As it rolled through the boggy jungle, refugees from sacked delver-strongholds and Catachan stragglers flocked to it, vox-operators broadcasting around the clock in an effort to round up survivors. By the time Strike rolled up the steep approach to Thermenos Stronghold, over two hundred Catachans and armed civilians marched behind him.

Now the war could begin in earnest.

Leading his troops from his remote base, Strike launched a guerrilla campaign against the occupying forces. Small teams of Catachans harried enemy patrols at every turn, striking from deep cover before dissolving back into the jungle, for all intents invisible to the aggressors. Abaddon's force switched tactics in response and sent out larger parties but, with fewer patrols to protect their assets, the Catachan raiders now had other targets to attack. Like phantoms, they operated behind enemy lines, destroying fuel dumps, arms caches and ammunition stocks before anybody knew they were there. There were no great victories, no grandstand moments for history to remember, but these tiny acts of sabotage and resistance were all that was keeping the Catachans in the war, buying time in the vain hope that reinforcements would one day arrive to liberate Pythos.

Despite all these tiny triumphs, this death by a thousand cuts he was slowly eking out on the invaders, three things still hampered Strike in his shadow war.

Whether by mechanical or mystical means, the enemy had been jamming the vox-signals since the dawn of the campaign, and communication over long distances was almost impossible. The Pythosian miners had their own radio communications network but it operated on short range frequencies, which meant that delver-strongholds had to act as relay stations, passing messages forward from station to station until it reached its intended recipient.

It had been almost a year since Brigstone had evacuated the armour and in all that time no Catachan force had had any kind of contact with them. The enemy had not used any of the vehicles against them, intimating that the ships had not been captured, but his non-appearance was suggesting to Strike that the commander and his precious cargo had fallen prey to one of Pythos's great seaborne predators that made the land-based specimens look like dwarfs.

If the lack of armoured reinforcements was thwarting some of Strike's more ambitious plans to strike back at the Chaos forces, the enemy's ability to bolster their ranks almost at will was amplifying it. The assault on Olympax had only been possible as a result of the armies of the warp being unleashed and Strike had no advance intelligence to either mount an effective defence or carry out a planned and organised evacuation. In a hive city the size of Atika resistance cells should still be able to operate to some degree, no matter how large the occupying force. He knew personally of at least six Catachans who had stayed behind to run insurgency operations after the rest of the regiment had abandoned the capital but, like Brigstone, none of them had been heard from in almost a year.

With the number of warp entities burgeoning in the months since they had set up base at Thermenos, Tzula and Epimetheus had decided to head back to Atika, if not to dam the flow then at the very least to get a handle on the situation. The information they could potentially gather was of vital importance to the resistance effort, but the fighting skills of the inquisitor and the Space Marine had been invaluable since the retreat from Olympax. Strike had objected to their leaving, but ultimately, who was he to question the judgement of representatives of both the Holy Ordos and the Adeptus Astartes?

The pair had barely left each other's side since Epimetheus's miraculous appearance out of the depths of the mountain stronghold – an appearance that the taciturn Space Marine and secretive inquisitor had both declined to explain to him. Though it was beyond all reason that any form of amorous bond had developed between them, it seemed that the armoured giant had assumed the mantle of Tzula's protector.

That protection was something that Strike and the small band of fighters defending Thermenos could do with now. Abaddon had turned his attention from the larger holds and hives and was instead attacking any target that presented itself, regardless of strategic or collateral value. It did not matter if it was a bolthole for Catachan resistance or a safe haven for refugees from one of the cities. The Warmaster of Chaos was dismantling Pythos settlement by settlement and it was inevitable that the time would come when he launched an assault on Thermenos. That time was now.

The dull thud of the hellhammer cannon reverberated around the tank's command compartment, the sound dampeners and recoil suppressors fitted by K'Cee keeping the noise down to tolerable levels. The jokaero, who had not accompanied Tzula back to Atika, loped around the cabin, checking instrument banks and adjusting settings and configurations. Despite all of the enhancements the hairy creature had already made, the tank was still very much a work in progress for him.

More of the disease-carrying monstrosities shambled up

the steep approach to the stronghold, seemingly impervious to the las-fire from the assorted Catachans and militia arrayed behind rocks and barricades close to the entrance. In the wake of the daemons, power-armoured figures ascended the slope: Black Legionnaires and unidentified crimson-clad traitors using the horned beasts as a shield of warp-tainted flesh. Sporadic bolter fire forced the human defenders to seek cover, allowing the Chaos vanguard to gain yet more ground.

Ordering his crew to hold until the last possible moment, Strike waited until the front ranks of rotted daemon flesh were within range of all of the Hellhammer's weapons systems before ordering, 'Fire all weapons.'

Flamers and heavy bolters seared and eviscerated the gangly cyclopses, unholy howls heralding them back to whence they came. Lascannons and autocannons targeted the Traitor Astartes, pinning them back and felling several under the withering barrage. Without the enemy's suppressing fire to contend with, the Catachans and delver militia leapt from cover, setting about any foe not killed outright by the Hellhammer's onslaught. In their diminished state, the fallen daemons were still a formidable threat, slashing away with corroded swords that instantly melted the flesh of anything they came into contact with. One particularly pernicious beast slew nine men before succumbing to its numerous wounds.

Observing from the turret hatch, Strike saw the Traitor Astartes on the move again, clambering from rock to rock on the hillface, using them as cover to reach their objective while the humans were occupied with trying to kill enemies that stubbornly refused to die. 'Advance,' he ordered closing the hatch and returning to his command seat. Tamzarian threw the tank into reverse, moving out from behind the rock wall where it had been hull down and sped down the slope towards the oncoming enemy. Catachans and militiamen threw themselves out of the way as the gargantuan tank moved through them, tearing up the ailing daemons beneath wide tracks.

To the crew inside, it felt as if they were barely moving, the only evidence of progress the gentle jarring every time the Hellhammer crushed a foe. K'Cee's modifications to the tank did not simply extend to the armour and weapons. The Phaeton-pattern Adaptable Thermic Combuster which powered the tank had been souped-up and tuned to such a degree that when Tamzarian had opened her up on one of the plains approaching Thermenos, the Hellhammer had reached a speed of one hundred and seventy-six kilometres per hour before experiencing any significant hull rattle.

Coming to a halt still some fifteen metres away from the new frontline, the tank's Demolisher cannon came to life for the first time during the battle, the siege breaking weapon just as efficient at breaking rocks behind which traitors skulked. Chunks of stone, ceramite armour and body parts were thrown into the air as a result of each cacophonous detonation, dust and shrapnel raining down on the slope. Using the command vehicle as cover, the defenders of Thermenos lent their weapons to the effort, keeping the traitors behind cover so that the heavy calibre weapon could despatch them with impunity.

His veteran ears attuned to the sounds of battle, Strike thought he heard a noise in between the cannon fire.

'Cease fire,' he ordered, much to the puzzlement of the gunners. The big guns fell silent, as did the chatter and whine of the secondary weapon systems. There. Faint, indistinct but undeniably the sound of an engine. He slid back the cover of the view slit but the tiny aperture offered no kind of view. Risking enemy fire, he popped the top hatch and stuck his head out far enough that his eyes came above the top of the rim. The las-fire from the Catachans using the tank as mobile cover had not abated and the Traitor Marines were still hemmed in behind the few rocks left for them to shelter behind. The engine noise was louder now. When Strike moved his gaze to the south-west, the source became clear.

Slamming the hatch behind him, Strike dropped back into the command chair. 'Enemy bombers at two o'clock. Three of them plus a fighter escort,' he explained.

The graveness of their predicament escaped no one. Exposed as they were on the side of the hill, the top of their hull presenting as a near-unmissable target, their chances of surviving the next few minutes were almost zero. 'Get me a firing solution. Now.' Strike cursed himself silently. Had this all been a ruse to draw him out? The enemy force did seem too small to capture a delver-stronghold and the Traitor Astartes had appeared very reluctant to commit fully to the assault.

With barely the sound of motors and gear whirring, the turret turned quickly, hellhammer cannon elevating to the correct angle. The lead gunner's targeting array filled with hostile icons and, with K'Cee's aid, he finessed the dials and mechanisms until a single target sat between the crosshairs. 'Target acquired,' he said turning to the colonel.

'Fire when ready,' Strike acknowledged. Without hesitation the gunner depressed the firing stud, the muffled sound of shell discharge resonating within the compartment.

One of the large red icons instantly blinked out on the gunner's array. 'It's a hit, chief. We got it!' the gunner called out enthusiastically. His joy soon waned. 'The formation's breaking up. They've split the bombers.'

Strike's heart sank. If the enemy had stayed in formation they stood a chance of taking out both bombers. Having to readjust the turret and firing angle to a greater degree, they'd be fortunate if they downed even one more. Without waiting for an order, the lead gunner and K'Cee had another large red icon in their sights. This time, Strike didn't say anything, nodding his affirmation instead. The only hope left to them was that the final bomber missed with its payload and they'd get one more shot. That still left the fighter escort and, with the top of the tank exposed as it was, they would be like target practice to any pilot who could shoot remotely straight.

The tank rocked gently under suppressed recoil. 'Another hit, chief,' the gunner said grimly moments later. To the amazement of all those cooped in the Hellhammer's command compartment, he added, 'The other bomber's gone too. And the fighters. Every one of them just disappeared from the targeting screen.'

Not waiting for confirmation from K'Cee that the instruments were functioning correctly, Strike lifted the top hatch to see for himself if the enemy flyers were still in the sky. The chorus of cheers from his troops and the militia told him that they weren't before the string of black smoke clouds and tumbling debris became apparent. New engine noise filled the skies now. Louder, faster craft and, after the formation of five black flyers flew directly overhead and Strike had taken a good look at their markings, friendlier ones too.

As he watched in awe and relief, four of the flyers peeled off, turning around no doubt to strafe the Traitor Astartes still in cover lower down the slope. The final flyer, a miniature cathedral atop its back just behind the cockpit, veered straight upwards before gracefully flipping over in a corkscrew motion and diving towards the side of the hill. The sheltering traitors broke from the protection of the rocks, the steep angle speeding their descent back down the slope and into the suddenly more attractive protection of the jungle. Pulling out of its plummet at the very last moment, the black liveried flyer deposited its payload in amongst the fleeing enemy from a height of barely five metres. The weapon's effect was not what Strike had expected.

Though devastating to those close to the bomb's point of impact, the larger number of traitors at the edges of its radius appeared to freeze, as if time had stopped briefly, locking them in place. Gradually, their progress sped up, but during the glacial seconds before they had returned to normal pace, the four support fighters had turned back around and slain most of them. A handful of Traitor Astartes had survived the intervention from the Catachans' newfound allies and were almost at the treeline where the rocky hill face became undergrowth. Strike was about to order his troops to pursue them when the shade of the jungle was lit up by actinic light, ten figures in ivory Terminator armour materialising in the space between eye blinks. Another eye blink and they had mown down the retreating Chaos Marines with concentrated bursts from their storm bolters.

Fascinated by what had just occurred, it was some time before Strike realised that his vox-operator, Uclaris, was tugging at the leg of his fatigues. The colonel looked down into the darkness of the command compartment, and saw that the sweaty figure of Uclaris was trying to hand him the handset of a portable vox.

'What is it, Uclaris?' Strike asked, his attention still partly on the armoured figures down at the bottom of the slope who now appeared to be examining the corpses of the dead traitors.

'Somebody on the vox, chief. Claims they're a Lord Azrael of the Dark Angels and insists on speaking only to you.'

787960.M41 / Atika Hive, Pythos

GRIGOR MITTEL, THOUGH he no longer remembered that this had ever been his name, carried the ore like he had been ordered to do. The red Pythosian crystal was stained an ever darker shade, his blood trickling over it from wounds sliced into his arms from the rough edges of the unrefined mineral. Just as Grigor could no longer remember his own name, he could no longer feel pain, and his cuts went both unheeded and untreated.

Beside Grigor, others plodded on, identical lumps of rock held out in front of them. None of them spoke; none of them looked in any direction other than straight ahead; none of them interacted with anything other than the precious cargo they had been told to carry from the mines below to the city above. The city. Was this where he had once lived? The surroundings seemed so familiar yet, like his name, it was impossible to recall.

The man in front of him fell, the weight of the ore too great a burden. Grigor stopped before he tripped over the man now lying inert on the floor. Stopping. Starting. Lifting. Those were the few things Grigor remembered how to do.

Noise from further ahead captured his attention like flame does a moth's and he looked to see two armoured figures moving towards the fallen man. The others alongside him looked too and saw the bloated forms lift the man from the ground and throw him to one side. An arm came off in one of the armoured figure's hands and he laughed a horrible, wet laugh as he tossed the limb on top of the body. Grigor did not know that the laugh was horrible as he could no longer feel horror. Grigor could not feel anything at all. Not any more.

A woman who had been performing some menial task at the side of the walkway out of the mine moved in front of Grigor and lifted the chunk of ore dropped there by the fallen man. Her clothes were filthy and her hair was a mess but none of this registered with Grigor. He no longer had any concept of filthy or messy, just like he no longer had any concept of wood, the night sky or the colour yellow. As the woman hefted the rock up to her chest, her eyes briefly met Grigor's and the slightest spark of recognition flared between them. It was over in an instant and the woman turned to face in the same direction as the rest of the indentured work party. At a barked command from one of the armoured figures, Grigor and the others moved off, conveying the ore to the waiting transporters.

As Grigor passed under the archway that signified where the mine terminated and the city began, sudden movement caught his eye from an alcove in the rocky walls above. Like the look he had shared with the woman in front of him, it was over quickly and, lacking the faculties to either react to or inform anybody of what he had witnessed, Grigor continued onward.

FROM A LEDGE set in the bedrock foundations of Atika Hive, Tzula, Epimetheus and Shira looked on as the procession of plague zombies passed beneath them. The Navy pilot wore a sullen look on her face as a result of having just been admonished by her two companions for wanting to leap down from their hiding place and 'beat the crap' out of the two Plague Marines who had so callously treated the corpse of the dead old man.

'When are you going to understand that these people have been dead for a long time?' Tzula hissed once the last of the zombies and their overseers were gone. 'We can't save them, Shira. They're beyond that now.'

They had been lurking in the shadows of Atika Hive for over two weeks, slowly moving through the shell of the city that now resembled something from within the Eye of Terror more than anything that once belonged to the Imperium of Man. When they had set out from Thermenos many months earlier they had not planned on adding to their number, but when Shira's fighter put down in the swamps less than half a kilometre from where they had made camp and Tzula was able to convince Epimetheus to go in after the Kestrel and rescue the pilot, two became three. Brave to the point of stupidity and with an independent streak as wide as a Baneblade, Tzula had taken an immediate liking to the younger woman. She'd already proved her worth on the march to Atika and her aim with a laspistol was as good as any Imperial Guardsman, as scores of cultists would attest if they were still in any condition to do so. Her lack of patience was becoming a bind, however.

Unlike Epimetheus, who was patience personified.

They had arrived at Atika a month earlier, but the Grey Knight insisted on taking his time to scout the city and find the best point of insertion to minimise their risk of detection.

Eventually locating a sewer outlet pipe that ran into the ocean several kilometres east of the hive, they had crawled the entire way into the city through a stagnant stream of filth and waste. When they made it to the end, Epimetheus had insisted that they wait for three days until he had enough information to determine enemy patrol patterns. Finally emerging from the cess pipe, even the rancid corpse reek of the hive city had smelled like the sweetest air Tzula and Shira had ever breathed.

Despite all the time they had spent together in the intervening months, Tzula still knew very little about the ancient Space Marine. Rather than wasting her time by verbalising ten thousand years of Imperial history, Tzula had let Epimetheus probe her mind to gather the information he needed to get up to speed. In return, he had offered nothing. One evening before they had met Shira, Tzula had deployed some of her more subtle Inquisition interrogation techniques, the kind where the person being interrogated does not realise it is happening. Either Epimetheus was wise to what she was doing or he had been conditioned to resist neurolinguistic questioning.

The only response she did get from the Space Marine was when she asked if he had fought during the Horus Heresy, and even that was nothing more than a close of his eyes and a slight nod.

'I know, but I feel so useless hiding out in the shadows like this. Surely there's something we can do?' Shira still wore the same flight suit she had been wearing when she had crash-landed, but with adjustments to the legs and sleeves to make it more comfortable to wear in Pythos's hot climate. Patches of scar tissue puckered over her legs and arms where they were visible beneath the crude cuts of the fabric and her neck looked like that of a much older woman where the healing process had wrinkled the flesh. A belt hung loose at her waist, a holstered laspistol on one hip, her predator-styled helmet on the other.

'We *are* doing something,' the normally silent, normally helmeted Epimetheus intoned in a bass whisper. Though Shira would swear that she and Epimetheus had shared many conversations in the time she had been a member of their little band, these were actually the most words the Grey Knight had ever spoken to her, all previous occasions being Shira talking at the Space Marine rather than with him. Yet more testimony to his patience and her brashness. 'We're going to find out what's going on here and we're going to put an end to it.' There was an intensity to his words but laced with kindness. He could not chastise the woman for wanting to do something to help.

'You think it's more than a mining operation they're running here?'

Ever since they had arrived in Atika it had been gnawing away at Tzula why the invaders had turned to extracting the Pythosian crystal. There were rare examples of forge worlds falling to Chaos and continuing to produce las-weaponry, but most converts brought their own with them when they turned or looted them from the corpses of dead Guardsmen. Her strongest theory was that Strike's resistance was so effective that Abaddon's army was forced to resupply and rearm itself from what resources they could find on the planet they now held. That thought at least helped Tzula sleep, on those rare occasions when she could grab rest so far into enemy territory.

'I *know* it's more than a mining operation they're conducting in Atika. This city was built atop the Damnation Cache. A conduit by which daemons can enter the material realm lies somewhere beneath us.'

Tzula looked at him agog. 'You know the location of the Damnation Cache and only now do you decide to share that information? How long have you known?'

'My memory is eidetic so I have "known" its location ever since I first came out of my sus-an coma.'

'You were in a coma?' said Shira, who up until this point had looked on like a child watching her parents bickering. Both Epimetheus and Tzula turned and gave her looks that implied most convincingly that she would be better off keeping her mouth shut for the next few minutes. 'It's just you never mentioned anything about that to me...' she added, sheepishly.

'So if you've known ever since you woke up, why didn't you let Strike know? He could have mounted an assault.' Tzula fought hard to keep her voice at a level that wouldn't carry.

'As brave and able as the colonel and his regiment are, they don't have the numbers to pose any real threat to Abaddon and his army. Strike's guerrilla campaign is the optimum course of action at this point while we wait for reinforcements. Besides, even if the Catachans could fight their way through to the Cache, how would they close it?'

'How would we?'

Epimetheus pointed to the hilt poking out of Tzula's waistband. She reached down with her artificial hand and brushed her fingers over the hilt. 'The blade...'

'The blade is much more than you know it to be, Tzula Digriiz. I have perused your thoughts and even your considerable knowledge is but a mere fraction of all there is to know of this knife. Its powers and uses are myriad, walking between worlds perhaps its greatest, but its capacity for destruction knows no limits in the right hands.' He paused. 'Or the wrong ones.'

'Corpulax said something similar about the Hellfire Stone. That it was "all things to all men".'

'Had the Plague Marine succeeded in planting the blade into that stone, the peril faced by Pythos would be far greater indeed. Your actions in retrieving the knife may be the only reason that we are able to stand here now speaking like this. The only reason that Strike still lurks in the jungle nibbling away at the enemy's numbers and supply lines.'

Tzula smiled. 'I was just doing my job.'

'As you continue to do now by keeping it out of the hands of the Archenemy.'

'Except we've brought it right to their doorstep.'

'I doubt even Abaddon would think to look for it right under his own nose.'

Tzula gave a whispered snigger. 'You still haven't answered my original question. Why didn't you find out the location of the Damnation Cache sooner?'

A look that Tzula interpreted to be shame blanketed the Space Marine's craggy, ancient face. He pulled the maglocked helm from his hip and clamped it back into place over his head. Although the rest of his armour still bore traces of green where time had embellished it, the headgear had now reverted to its original silver sheen.

'I didn't think anybody would be foolish enough to build a city on top of it,' he said.

'But Strike told you he thought the pack of daemons that captured Olympax originated from here.'

'Like I said,' he said rising from his haunches, 'I didn't think anybody would be foolish enough to put a city right on top of it.' He moved past Shira and onto the ledge that would eventually lead them down to the mine entrance. The pilot sat there with her jaw slack, the information she had taken in too much to process all at once.

'And you,' Tzula said, pointing at Shira playfully with one finger of her augmetic hand. 'Forget everything you just heard,' she added, following Epimetheus down towards the hidden depths of Atika.

788960.M41 / Dark Angels Landing Zone. 1,013 kilometres south of Mount Olympax, Pythos

COLONEL STRIKE STEPPED down the ramp of *Traitor's Bane* to find his route to the waiting Land Raider flanked by twenty green armoured Space Marines spaced at precise intervals. All of them helmeted, they stood stock still as the colonel crossed the distance between his own tank and Lord Azrael's.

It had been three days since the Dark Angels' relief force had landed, and in that time Strike had received reports from strongholds all over Pythos detailing their liberation by Space Marine forces. No corner of the world remained untouched by the Dark Angels presence, and the high count of combat actions they had undertaken since arriving in orbit made Strike think that the entire Chapter had deployed to liberate the planet. Seeing the number of tanks, flyers, heavy weapons and troops that were making planetfall on the southern plains of Pythos Prime only confirmed that.

Overhead, Thunderhawks engaged their retro boosters, slowing their ascent and hovering motionless barely a metre above the savannah, disgorging combat-ready squads of Space Marines before returning to orbit. Some way back from Azrael's Land Raider, two figures with servo-arms protruding from their backs – Techmarines – fussed over a newly landed drop pod. After administering the correct blessings and key code, the massive craft opened like a flower blooming to reveal the Dreadnought within. It stomped forward ponderously and, after a brief inspection from the two Techmarines, strode off to join two others of its kind already freed of their confines.

Sergeants calmly relayed orders to their squads before mounting Rhinos or bikes and heading off in the direction of their next mission flanked by tanks and land speeders. Sub-orbital jetfighters – Nephilim classification if the vox-chatter was accurate – formed contrails high in the clear blue sky, eyes open for signs of enemy movement and ready to strike should a target present itself.

A loud boom sounded from off in the distance and Strike halted sharply, spinning on his heel in time to witness a mushroom cloud pluming upwards from several hundred kilometres away. Orbital bombardments had been a regular occurrence since the Space Marines' arrival, targeting conglomerations of daemons when the orbiting vessels detected them out in the open, but this was the closest Strike had been to one. None of the Dark Angels honour guard paid it any heed, remaining locked at attention and staring dead ahead.

Moments later, a gust of wind blew through the savannah, swaying the tall grass. The breeze felt cool on Strike's arms, drying the near-permanent sheen of sweat there and he suddenly felt self-conscious; he was about to meet the Chapter Master of the Dark Angels, scions of one of the great founding Legions that pre-dated the Horus Heresy, and he was going to do so in torn fatigues and a blood-stained vest.

When he reached the base of the Land Raider's boarding ramp, he was almost pleased to see that Lord Azrael was in a similar state to him, armour split open in places and once fine cloak shredded and stained. He paused on the threshold, waiting for the Dark Angel to finish speaking to another Space Marine. He kept Strike waiting for what seemed to the Catachan like an age, motioning to markers on a hololithic map and gesticulating insistently to the other Space Marine. Eventually, Azrael noticed the colonel waiting patiently at the rear of the tank and broke off his conversation.

'Colonel Strike,' Azrael said, a smile that was more business-like than warm forcing its way onto his lips. 'At last I have the pleasure of meeting the hero of Pythos.' Behind the Catachan, the two squads of Dark Angels broke ranks in perfect choreography and returned to their duties.

'My lord, this really wasn't necessary,' Strike replied.

'Nonsense. If it wasn't for the actions of your men and the leadership you've shown, there wouldn't be a planet left for us to liberate.' It was the other Space Marine who spoke now, and for the first time Strike noticed that he was wearing different armour from Lord Azrael. Not only was it Terminator pattern but it was silver too and covered in strips of parchment and purity seals. It wasn't just the armour that marked him out as different. He radiated something that made Strike feel uneasy, the same feeling he had felt in his brief time around Inquisitor Dinalt's astropath, and later, Epimetheus. Was this a Librarian? Strike had already seen Dark Angels in green, black and white armour; perhaps the fabled Space Marine psykers wore silver to denote their rank and station.

'This is Grand Master Draigo,' said Azrael.

'*Supreme* Grand Master Draigo,' Draigo corrected.

'Of course,' Azrael replied.

Though far from being an expert on Space Marines, Strike was an excellent judge of people. Right now, he could not shake the feeling that not only were Azrael and Draigo not of the same Chapter, but neither could stand to be in the presence of the other. 'Enough of the pleasantries. Lord Draigo and I are about to return to orbit to coordinate the liberation of Pythos and would like you to accompany us to assume command of the Imperial Guard forces that will begin landing in the next few hours.'

'I am flattered, my lords, but I am only a colonel. Surely there are higher ranking officers in the liberation fleet?' Strike said, taken aback at the offer.

'Hundreds of them,' Azrael replied. 'But none of them with the jungle fighting experience or knowledge of the terrain to lead this campaign effectively. Up until now this has been your war, Strike. I see no reason for that to change now.'

Strike considered his response. 'Permission to speak freely, my lords?' he asked, his voice not betraying the nervousness he felt.

'By all means. Frankness is a trait much admired by the Dark Angels,' Azrael said. He regarded the Catachan a little more intently.

'With all respect, my jungle fighting experience and knowledge of the terrain would be put to better use down here,' Strike said. 'If there are others among the regiments in orbit who have led campaigns before, I'd urge you to call upon them to coordinate the Guard effort on Pythos. My place is leading my men from the front.'

Draigo's face darkened, his brow furrowing in the manner of somebody not used to being told no. Azrael by contrast warmed to Strike in that moment.

'Your candour is both noted and appreciated, colonel. My battle-brothers who have already fought alongside your men are full of tales regarding their valour and if half the stories they have told about you are true, I would be pleased to keep you at the spearhead of the resistance effort.'

'Once again you flatter me, lord. I was not without aid though.'

'You mean Inquisitor Dinalt? It was his distress call that called us here. I presume he is dead, otherwise he would have already made contact,' said Draigo.

Strike smiled a little at hearing this. Mack's sacrifice hadn't been in vain after all. 'Yes, my lord,' Strike said, noticing for the first time the stylised 'I' of the Inquisition emblazoned over Draigo's breast. 'One of his apprentices turned out to be a traitor and led him to his death. She's dead too along with most of his cohort. His other apprentice, Tzula, is still alive. At least she was the last time I saw her.'

He neglected to mention that K'Cee still survived. He'd left the simian genius back at Thermenos until he could get a handle on how the Dark Angels would react to a xenos life form, no matter how useful and loyal, operating as part of an Imperial Guard command structure.

'And the Space Marine still lives,' Strike added, almost as an afterthought.

Draigo and Azrael turned to each other and locked gazes.

'A Space Marine? What Space Marine?' Draigo asked switching his attention to Strike.

'He showed up right before we made our escape from Olympax. Took down a daemon single-handed and allowed us to escape. I presumed he had been sent in advance of the full liberation force.'

'We made all haste to Pandorax as soon as we received the distress call. *We* are the advance of the liberation force,' Draigo said.

'This Space Marine?' Azrael asked. 'What colour armour was he wearing?'

Draigo shot his counterpart a suspicious look.

'It was green. Like yours but darker,' Strike said gesturing to the Dark Angel. 'But that was just moss and lichen that had formed upon it with age. Where patches had worn away, it was the same colour as yours.' He pointed now at Draigo. 'It was a similar size and pattern too, but archaic. Looked like the same kind you see in the paintings and frescoes of Imperial cathedrals.'

'Did this Space Marine have a name? Do you know which Chapter he was from?' Azrael's latest questions were not delivered with the same intensity as the first, as if Strike's answer had assuaged him.

'I barely spoke to him, my lord, and his armour bore no heraldry or insignia. In the weeks he travelled with us he spoke almost exclusively to Tzula. Chose to keep himself to himself. I did hear her refer to him as "Epimetheus" on one occasion though.'

Draigo's face wore a look of shock that passed within an instant. Azrael noticed it, Strike did not.

'You have our gratitude, Colonel Strike, both for the information you have imparted and your resistance efforts in the months since Pythos fell. Go now and lead your men into glorious battle,' Draigo said.

It felt to Strike as if he was being ushered away before he could reveal any more about the mystery Space Marine. Not that he had anything else to reveal.

Strike bowed reverently to the two Space Marines, internalising his chastisement at not having done the same when bidden to enter the Land Raider. He was about to leave when he found the courage to speak again. 'My lords, if I might be so bold?'

Both Space Marines looked at him implacably.

'You say there are Imperial Guard regiments awaiting deployment from orbit?' Strike asked.

'That is correct,' Azrael said. 'Three entire regiments survived the void war that allowed us to break through to Pythos and will make planetfall by dusk. A dozen more regiments, mainly Cadian, are due to warp translate in the next day for immediate deployment.'

'Could I request that the newly arrived regiments be kept in orbit for a few days before entering combat?'

'I'll certainly consider it provided you can demonstrate

sound reasoning for such a bizarre request,' Azrael said archly.

'Travel through the warp is draining for a man, even a soldier of the Imperial Guard. They're not whole again for some
time afterwards. It's as if their body has arrived but they're
waiting for their soul to catch up with them.'

Strike's belief stemmed from old Catachan superstition but
other Guard regiments he had encountered over the years
held similar beliefs, and experience had taught him there was
more than a sliver of truth to it. It was bad enough that regiments without death world backgrounds were being thrown
at Pythos and the colonel saw no reason to compound that
misery by sending warp-lagged soldiers into the fray. 'If any
were needed for imminent operations, I will gladly send the
183rd in their place.'

'I have witnessed the same phenomena myself among
humans who have fought alongside me in the past,' Azrael
said. 'Provided your troops will fill in for them, I will acqui-
esce to your request. Now, was there anything else before you
finally take your leave of us?'

'Just one more thing, Lord Azrael. Could you have the fleet
scan the Pythosian oceans?'

'Once again, I'm sure you have a good reason for asking
such a thing but could you please enlighten me why?'

Strike turned away briefly and ran the edge of his hand
against his sweat-slicked forehead. He looked back at the
Supreme Grand Master of the Dark Angels before speaking
again. 'Because a year ago I sent an entire mechanised brigade
to sea and I haven't heard from them since.'

CHAPTER ELEVEN

801960.M41 / The Underhive. Atika, Pythos

SHIRA STOOD UP in the miners' hut and clasped the fingers of both hands together, raising them towards the ceiling in a full body-length stretch. After weeks of crawling around on her belly and traversing tunnels at a stoop, the discovery of the workers' refuge had been a welcome one and even Tzula seemed to appreciate the respite from sneaking around and clinging to the shadows. The dry ration packs they'd taken with them from Thermenos had run out weeks ago and the food they had obtained in the city above was almost at an end. As well as a concealed shelter, the hut had provided canned provisions and wafers of processed grain that had not yet become too mouldy to consume.

Dropping her arms to her sides and twisting several times at the hip, Shira accepted the remnants of a can of unspecified – and unidentifiable – fruit from Tzula. She sat down next to Epimetheus who was standing at the metal structure's single window, a position he had barely moved from since they entered the hut more than two days ago. It was pitch black both inside and out, no natural light filtered so far down into the tunnels beneath the hive and the miners' discarded lantern was left unlit to prevent it drawing the attention of any passing patrols. Shira assumed that his enhanced Space

Marine vision would enable him to see what he was looking for, whatever that was.

'What are you looking for?' she vocalised after spending some time staring at the same point Epimetheus was fixated on but seeing only darkness. Although hidden and muffled by the corrugated metal walls, she was careful to keep her voice as low as possible.

'Patrols,' Epimetheus said not averting his stare. 'In approximately two minutes' time, two guards will walk along the tunnel that runs alongside the hut. They will be in visual contact for less than thirty seconds but it will be nearly an hour before they pass this way again. Once they have passed and there is clear distance between us, we shall emerge and move further down the tunnel to another hiding place I found yesterday.'

Twice Epimetheus had left the hut, both times shortly after Plague Marines had passed by on patrol and on each occasion he had been gone barely any time at all.

'You think this tunnel leads down to the Cache?' Tzula asked, sipping from the last dregs of water in her canteen. This too she offered to Shira when she had finished. The pilot refused, instead slurping the juice from the bottom of the can of fruit.

'No cultists have come along here since we began our descent and the patrols are more frequent than along any of the other tunnels we tried. Plague zombies are led down here but we haven't seen any of them come back up, not even transporting ore,' said the Grey Knight.

'But the cache is a repository of daemons and thankfully we haven't seen any of those. It could be something else down there? Something else they're trying to protect?' countered Tzula.

'If it is, we'll find out what it is and find a way to destroy it if needs be.'

Though stealth had been their watchword since descending into Atika's mine levels, Epimetheus had begun to communicate more with the two women. Only a week ago he wouldn't have shared that they were moving on to their next hiding place until the very last moment and neither would he discuss what he was thinking. He would simply lead and expect Tzula and Shira to blindly follow, in the dark both literally and figuratively. They all knew the risk they were taking just by being here, even Shira who had asked, and been told, about the knife while Epimetheus was away on one of his scouting missions. If they were discovered by a patrol, simply killing them wouldn't be enough. As soon as their disappearance was noticed, the tunnels would flood with Traitor Astartes and the blade would soon be forfeit. The slow, patient approach was the right way to proceed and Shira had learned to accept this, although she still found it difficult.

Epimetheus held up a gauntleted hand to silence his two companions. Tzula froze, the lid of her canteen only half screwed back on. Shira gently pulled the fruit can away from her lips and angled her head slightly so that she could see out of the window. Two beams of muggy brown half-light played across the tunnel floor, widening as the bearers of the sources grew closer. Illuminated solely by the backwash from the torches mounted atop their bolters, two Plague Marines clomped past, their ill-fitting power armour causing echoes with every step. Even poorly lit and visible briefly through the window, the sight of their distended bulk repulsed Shira. She had seen many things she wished she could forget since she had taken off from the *Revenge* and every new day brought with it fresh horrors for her to contend with.

As if caught in amber, the three figures in the hut listened as the echoes grew fainter as the patrol moved further away. When all sound had ceased carrying, Epimetheus lowered his hand.

'Now we go,' he said.

THEIR PROGRESS WAS methodical as they passed through the dark.

Weapons drawn, one of them would advance a couple of metres being careful not to trip over any rocks underfoot or unduly disturb the scree before halting and allowing the next in line to move up alongside them, followed by the next. The last to move up would be the first to move on and this pattern was repeated until they reached their destination.

The next bolthole Epimetheus had selected for them was only fifty metres from the miners' hut, but at this rate of movement they would barely make it before the patrol doubled back on itself and came this way again. Better to get there slowly rather than give their presence away.

Shira shivered involuntarily. The modifications she had made to her flight suit had been necessary in the jungle, tolerable in the hive city but, deep below ground level, she regretted the moment she had gone at it with Tzula's combat knife. At least the cold was keeping her alert. Or so she thought.

Creeping up on the spot where Epimetheus and Tzula already were, she continued forward several paces, eyes down so that her dark-adjusted vision could pick out any obstacles. Planting her front foot down, the toe cap of her boot became visible to her. Too late she realised that she had stepped into a beam of light. Snapping her head upwards she was dazzled by the light from a torch, the glare so intense that she could not make out who, or what, was carrying it. She would have bet a month's booze rations it was a Traitor Marine.

+Stay perfectly still and whatever you do, do not discharge your weapon.+ Epimetheus's voice invading her head caused Shira to stifle a gasp, instead coming out as a tiny squeak. +Control your breathing and even if he looks directly at you, do not move, do not turn away.+

Shira did not know what was frightening her the most: the no doubt heavily armed enemy moving towards her or Epimetheus speaking directly into her mind. The wielder of the light and the corrupted boltgun it was attached to revealed itself as another Plague Marine, the beam stabbing like a spear through the darkness and pinning Shira in place. As he moved closer, Shira had to fight for mastery of her gag reflex as the smell emanating from the follower of the Plague God became so thick on the air she could taste it. Flies buzzed around him like a pestilent cloud and as he drew alongside, oblivious to her presence, several of them landed on Shira and crawled over her flesh. The Plague Marine moved past her and Shira prepared herself for the inevitable shoot-out when he spotted her two companions higher up the tunnel.

+Stay still. Don't move until I say you can.+

Shira had no idea how long she stood immobile in that passage. The clank of armour soon diminished in the distance but it was unbearable minutes before Epimetheus spoke to her again. This time he used his voice.

'All clear.'

Shira gave a long exhale, partly out of relief and partly out of holding her breath for so long. She turned to her companions who were cautiously picking their way over to her, dark shapes camouflaged against the gloom. Epimetheus lifted a hand up in front of him and Shira could see that it was shining with the faintest blue glow, delineating his features.

'Thank you,' she whispered. There was cold steam rising from the Space Marine's chiselled cheeks and dark fluid trickled from one of his nostrils. 'You have a–' Shira said.

Epimetheus swept his hand up to his top lip, catching the drop of blood before it could hit the ground. 'Thank you, Shira,' he said before continuing down the tunnel and waiting for her and Tzula to follow him.

808960.M41 / The Underhive. Atika, Pythos

TZULA LOST ALL track of time during the days they spent below ground. Up in the hive it had been possible to distinguish between night and day cycles, sunlight bleeding in through cracks in the structure where it had been damaged during the initial assault. Now she couldn't tell whether it was morning or night, afternoon or evening. She couldn't even work out the date.

Food and water had been easier to find up there too. Abandoned hab blocks and communal eating areas had offered up supplies, most of it still edible, and Tzula and Shira had been able to refill their packs several times over. Water, while not in abundance in the deserted hive, was still available unlike down in the mines where they had to rely on coming across seams that had worked their way down from the surface. It didn't inspire confidence in her that the water passed through ground that was no longer free of the taint of Chaos, but the alternative to drinking it was to die of dehydration. Each time she woke, she would find herself irrationally checking her arms and legs for scales and from time to time would run her fingers across her scalp checking for horns and protrusions before she realised she was doing it.

Fortunately for her and Shira, Epimetheus had no such base needs, other than a drink of water that by her, possibly flawed, estimation he took every four days or so. He was a Space Marine who, if he was to be believed (and Tzula had no reason not to believe him), had spent ten millennia standing sentinel over the final seal of a gateway into the warp. The thought of that made her astonished that he actually needed air to breathe, let alone an infrequent drink of water.

'Something's happening down there,' the Grey Knight said. They were beyond the mines now and into a new section of tunnels that plague zombie slaves still worked on with crude tools, illuminated by the flickering light of braziers and fire-baskets. High above the cavern floor, at the lip of a tunnel system that corkscrewed hundreds of metres down into the bedrock, the three of them could hear the echo of a thousand and more pickaxes tapping away, widening the tunnel that was already large enough to move a small Titan through. The slaves worked unstintingly. Tzula had been up there for hours and in that time not a single one had missed a stroke, carving out rock at a pace to rival industrial-scale mining drills.

She noticed the activity that Epimetheus had referred to. A small band of figures had entered from a side chamber and were awaiting a squad of Plague Marines approaching from the opposite direction, a struggling human prisoner shackled between them. A horde of plague zombies staggered behind them, many gripping pickaxes and other tools – fresh slaves to bolster the mining effort. A grim smile cracked Tzula's features when she realised who was at the head of the first group.

'Corpulax,' she whispered venomously.

Shira gave Tzula a quizzical look.

'He murdered my master and a very good friend,' she said. 'One of his agents was responsible for this too.' She held up her replacement arm.

Shira nodded her understanding. 'What are they doing?' she asked.

The cries of the struggling prisoner grew louder, increasing to a volume that battled with the reverberation of tools around the vast underground cave. He pulled at his restraints but his protestations were ineffective. Pulled to the ground by his captors, his ruined face left a bloody smear across the rock floor as he was dragged the final distance to be brought before Corpulax. The smaller, robed individuals flanking him formed a circle around the prone, wailing man and struck up a chant. The sound was distant and faint but Shira clamped her hands over her ears to block out the blasphemous words. Bile rose in Tzula's gorge but she did not turn away, despite knowing what was about to happen.

The incantation ceased and, with a tear of parting flesh and snapping bone, the captive unfurled and unfolded, reshaped like organic putty until he took on a new form. Shira turned her head away, looking towards Tzula with an uncomfortable look on her face.

'What are they doing to him?' Shira asked, swallowing dryly.

'Communion,' Epimetheus said. 'It's how the followers of the Plague God communicate over great distances. They create a flesh golem of who they want to speak to and converse with them directly without the need for an astropath or sorcerer to act as a medium.'

'Who is Corpulax speaking to? Abaddon?' asked Tzula.

'I don't know. Certainly Traitor Astartes of some ilk judging by the shape of the golem, but they are speaking too quietly for even my enhanced hearing to pick out their words above the noise of the tools.'

'Can't you use your psychic abilities to listen in?' Shira suggested.

'It's not that simple. Those are sorcerers down there. Not powerful enough to register my presence but likely more than able to sense me if I start tapping into the warp.'

'We have no way of hearing what they're saying?' Tzula asked.

'Short of going down there and standing right next to them? No.'

Tzula was caught off-guard by Epimetheus's response. It was the first time she had heard him exhibit sarcasm and she didn't need his ability to read minds to know that he was frustrated. 'So we just have to sit here and watch? Spend Emperor knows how many more weeks, lurking in the shadows,' she said with equal irritation.

Epimetheus rounded on her, his previously infinite amount of patience finally having found their limit but aborted his retort. He stared over Tzula's shoulder.

'Where did Shira go?'

SHIRA CROUCHED AT the mouth of the side-tunnel waiting for the procession of plague zombies heading down the tunnel to pass her by. Once the back markers were in line with her, she popped up out of the darkened nook and took her place among their ranks, mimicking their vacant look and shambling gait. Her ragged outfit was covered in dried vomit, filth and burn marks, she hadn't bathed in well over a month and her breath stank like promethium from where ketosis had set in from burning her own body fat for energy. She fitted right in.

Forcing her way to the centre of the mass of slaves, she snatched a pickaxe out of the hands of one of the zombies. He stopped briefly, those behind him having to change course like a rock splitting a stream. He looked down blankly at his hands, then at his fellow thralls passing him by before continuing on as if nothing had happened.

When they got close enough to the mine face, the mass broke apart, heading for gaps in the throng already at work. Shira attached herself to a group making for an unworked section barely a few metres from Corpulax and the flesh golem. She hoped it would be close enough to hear over the din of excavation.

She was almost in position when one of the sorcerers, a scrawny thing with filed teeth and mottled, almost-orange skin, turned and looked her dead in the eye.

'SHE'S GOING TO give us away,' Epimetheus whispered. He and Tzula had looked on, powerless to stop the hot-headed pilot, as she had pilfered the axe and blended in with the press of bodies. For a while it had looked like her gamble was going to pay off but now one of Corpulax's spellweavers had taken a very unhealthy interest in her. 'I'm going to have to ware her.'

She had never experienced it herself but Tzula knew of the process. It was a form of possession practised by the most powerful psykers whereby a vessel, usually willing, would play host to their psyche for a period of time. The psyker would have complete control over the vessel's body and would be able to see, hear and feel everything he or she could. It was not a safe process. Tzula had heard tales of those being worn never being able to regain their own consciousness leading to madness and even death. Those who survived the process unscathed were still altered, as if they were no longer a whole person.

'But if you use your gifts, *you'll* give us away,' Tzula said.

'And if I don't, that sorcerer is going to realise Shira isn't what she seems. Those plague zombies are under the sway of another's will. Their souls have been discarded, hollowed out so that their actions can be dictated by a higher power. If I ware her, her signature in the warp won't register as her own and there's a chance that sorcerer will assume she's part of the horde. There's no guarantee it will work but if I do nothing, she'll be dead or captured within seconds. Us not long after.'

Tzula felt the temperature drop beside her, Epimetheus's breath condensing as he prepared to hijack Shira's body.

TO HER CREDIT, Shira did not panic as those yellowed eyes bored into her. The sorcerer sniffed like a feral predator catching the scent of blood on the wind but did not break from his chanting, now a low murmur. The others of his ilk seemed oblivious to their comrade's concerns, eyes fixed on the transmogrified flesh whose form they were striving to maintain.

Shira could never remember what happened next, a six-minute gap in her life that eluded recall for the rest of her life. She was always aware of the presence of that absence but like all holes, it was impossible to grasp.

As all control of herself was stolen from her, the last memory she formed before waking up back on the overlook, Tzula mopping her brow with the hem of a filthy vest, was of Epimetheus speaking softly into her mind.

+This will all be over soon.+

THE DAVINICUS LYCAE cultist standing to his left was starting to distract Corpulax. Although he was maintaining the chant needed to keep the doppelganger in the form of Huron Blackheart, the sorcerer had turned away to stare at the plague zombie miners. One in particular was the focus of his attention and Corpulax was about to pause the communion to deal with him when the errant cultist returned his focus back to his appointed task, the sceptical aspect to his expression melting away.

'The Warmaster trusts me, Plague Lord. Why is it that you do not share his faith?' Huron said through lips that were not his own.

Corpulax emitted a moist chuckle. 'The only faith I have is in Great Nurgleth, not in a pirate who switches his loyalty based on which direction the most favourable wind is blowing.'

'Right now, my loyalty lies with Abaddon. I have already proven my worth to him in this campaign and continue to do so.'

'Ah, yes. Of course. The cabal you have hidden among the Imperial fleet, sustaining the conditions for our daemonic allies to move freely on the surface of Pythos. Tell me, Blackheart, how did you manage to pull that off right under the enemy's nose?'

'Like you said, Plague Lord, I am a pirate. Capturing ships is a speciality of mine and a supply vessel is hardly going to arouse suspicions as long as it keeps supplying the fleet and the Imperial Guard regiments.'

'That many psykers on board is bound to draw attention. The entire Dark Angels Librarius is here on Pythos and a Grey Knights strike cruiser lingers in orbit.'

'Abaddon has called upon the services of my cabal because he knows of its power. More than keeping conditions ripe for the Neverborn they are masking their own presence, nestling the ship in a fold in the warp. The Imperial fleet is so large that nobody will notice it missing as long as the flow of rations is maintained.'

Reluctantly, Corpulax showed how impressed he was.

'All I require now is the taint you promised to deliver,' Huron continued. 'I have holds full of food that awaits poisoning.'

'The first batch is almost complete and will be with you in weeks. Production has been quicker than anticipated and I've already switched some of the slaves over to the mining effort.'

'The Emerald Cave is still not open?'

'You keep your end of the bargain, Blackheart, and by the time the fleet is wiped out the Cave will be open and its prisoner freed.'

'For your sake I hope that is true, Plague Lord.'

'And for your sake, I hope Lord Abaddon grants you a swift death when he realises it is his mantle you covet.'

The simulacrum sneered. 'All things in time, Plague Lord. All things in time.'

The chanting of the cultists wound down, causing the flesh golem to fall apart, splashing to the floor of the cavern in a wet, bloody mess. The Plague Marines who had escorted the prisoner to Corpulax headed back in the direction from which they came, leaving a trio behind to keep watch on the plague zombie slaves. The Plague Lord, flanked by the robed cultists, returned to the side chamber, lingering on the threshold as the sorcerers walked past him. When the last one reached the doorway, the ochre-skinned cultist who had almost undone Shira, Corpulax placed his skeletal hand on the man's shoulder, turning him to dust which fell slowly to the floor of the subterranean cavern.

JUST AS EPIMETHEUS had seen and heard everything Shira had, so too had Tzula. The inquisitor already knew that the Space Marine possessed a prodigious amount of psychic talent, but being able to simultaneously ware somebody and establish a telepathic link with a second person placed him right at the top end of the spectrum. And although she would rather have not heard most of what she had, she could not help but feel uplifted.

Dark Angels. Grey Knights. Here on Pythos. Part of what she felt was naked relief that a liberation army had arrived, but the other part was that Liall's sacrifice hadn't been for nothing. She had seen so many good people die futile deaths in her service to the Golden Throne, lives violently snuffed out without achieving any of their potential or leaving a lasting mark. Liall's victory may have been small, pyrrhic and unsung, but if it led to the reconquest of the planet and the knife being kept out of the Archenemy's clutches, ultimately it would have been worth it.

None of that would matter if they couldn't get Shira out of there.

The three Plague Marines prowled the periphery of the enthralled workforce, bloated fingers poised over the triggers of their corrupted bolters. Unstintingly, the plague zombies chipped away at the rockface, pickaxes rising and falling in a tireless rhythm, never venturing away from the small area in which they operated. The only slaves who did move were those who cleared the rubble away, piling it high off to the sides so that it didn't hinder the miners. And that gave Tzula an idea.

+Be ready to move her,+ she sent over the still active telepathic link to Epimetheus. She picked up a fist-sized stone and held it up for the Grey Knight to see it. Still holding his attention on waring Shira, he nodded his understanding which made Tzula wonder whether he had figured out what her plan was from her gesture or if he had read her thoughts. She reeled her arm back, took aim, and launched the rock silently over the heads of the guards and indentured workers.

In her formative years, as well as the beast riding skills she had developed as a result of her privileged upbringing, Tzula had excelled at most forms of sport and athletic endeavour. Gymnastics had been her forte, making her initial career choice much easier along with making her popular with the opposite sex. Almost as good as her suppleness and flexibility was her ability to throw a ball accurately and powerfully, and before she had taken her first steps along the criminal path, she had rejected several offers to play competitive sport professionally. Opportunities to practise this particular skill set had been few and far between during her time in Dinalt's employ, but thankfully for Shira, the muscle-memory was not easily forgotten.

Catching a high pile of rubble just below its summit, the hurled missile dislodged several larger rocks setting them rolling down the incline, unsettling others as they went. More followed them down until, with a low rumble, the entire pile collapsed burying a group of unaware, unfeeling slaves beneath an avalanche of rock. None of the other plague zombies reacted, continuing about their business as they would for all eternity if their bodies didn't give out first.

Tzula knew that the Plague Marines would not be distracted for long, but that did not matter. By the time they had dug the pickaxes out from underneath the mess of debris and corpses and redistributed them to empty-handed zombies, Shira was already back in the safety of the side-tunnel and making her way back to her two waiting companions.

820960.M41 / The Deathglades. Thirteen kilometres south of Atika, Pythos

EPIMETHEUS HAD PROMISED Tzula answers once they had escaped from the hive city and now, as he stood guard on their camp perimeter while Shira roasted the carcass of an animal they had captured before night fell, she was determined to get them.

Their flight from Atika had been as stealthy as their insertion, right up until the final few hours. Wanting to sow discontent among the enemy ranks, the three of them had silently murdered a string of cultists, clumsily hiding the bodies in the hope that they would be found once they were clear of the city. With evidence of intruders within the walls of Atika, fewer personnel would be spared for jungle patrols, making their getaway from the capital and return to Imperial lines easier.

The intelligence they had gathered changed everything and needed to be reported to Strike and the newly arrived Space Marines. Rather than hiding in the shadows deep in the bowels of the city, the information they held needed to be shared and acted upon. Strike still believed that the population of Atika was safe in the caverns, but the reality was that all of them were dead, reanimated to serve new dark masters. The site of the Damnation Cache was in those same tunnels but the three of them had not been able to get close to it. Was that to do with the excavation work? The planet was infested with daemons so they must have been getting out from under the city somehow. Huron Blackheart had a coven of sorcerers in orbit making sure that the daemons could exist in the material realm once they were free of the Cache and, most pressing of all, had set a plan in motion to poison the food supply for the entire human element of the liberation force.

'So, what did Corpulax mean when he talked about freeing the prisoner in the Emerald Cave? Was that somebody you put there, back then?' Tzula had so many questions but this seemed as good a place for her to start as any. The Grey Knight turned to face her, unstartled yet she had made no sound in her approach.

He was about to speak, no doubt to fob her off with a cryptic half-answer or point-blank refusal, but when he caught sight of the stern look she was giving him in the wan light of Shira's small fire, he motioned for her to sit down. She planted herself on top of a fallen log and Epimetheus crouched down in front of her, bolt pistol in hand ready for the slightest sign of danger.

'You have knowledge of the Grey Knights and have fought alongside them in the past. That much I have gleaned from your memories.' His use of the word 'them' rather than 'us' struck Tzula as odd, but that was only the latest question she could add to a very long list. 'The current incarnation of my Chapter is the militant arm of a branch of the Inquisition known as the Ordo Malleus, a specialist organisation of daemon hunters fiercely loyal to the Throne and humanity.'

Tzula nodded her affirmation.

'Ten thousand years ago, things were different. Your Inquisition was a fledgling operation, mistrusted even by those who sanctioned it and yet to splinter into its disparate factions. Barely a hundred men and women wore its mark and barely half that again were aware of its existence. One of its primary functions at the time was to root out those sympathisers to Horus who still sat at the heart of Terra and were inveigled in the rebuilding of the shattered Imperium. To find, prosecute and execute all those who would jeopardise its future and seek to plunge it back into anarchy.

'But these hidden remnants of Horus's betrayal of the Emperor paled next to the visible ones. Across the galaxy, forces still loyal to the arch-traitor continued to fight the war he had declared, razing planets and claiming dominion over vast tranches of human worlds. The forbidden knowledge shown to Horus that had been the catalyst for his fall from grace bore other more sinister fruit, and dwellers from the other side were now abroad in the material realm. Though many believed the word to be childish and loaded with superstition, they came to be called daemons. Whatever name given to them, their threat to existence itself was all too apparent. At points all across the galaxy, the materium had been worn thin and the veil between realities torn open. The Eye of Terror blinked open, casting its malign gaze on the destruction so freshly wrought and worlds after worlds became conduits for the unreal to enter the real.'

'Like Pythos?' Tzula ventured.

'Like Pythos,' Epimetheus confirmed. 'The loyal Legions were diminished, their fighting strength a paltry fraction of its pinnacle and their primarchs dead or at each other's throats in the power vacuum that followed the Emperor's internment in the Golden Throne. While the Emperor had foreseen the myriad dangers humanity faced and created the Legions in his own image to combat them, even He could not have anticipated the monstrous forces now unleashed upon the Imperium. While the Legions had been bred to fight wars on the material realm, this new foe could battle on the immaterial front too, rendering Space Marines little more effective than the common soldier when it came to psychic war.

'Many of the Legions had once welcomed psykers into their ranks but an edict barring his sons from utilising the potential of their warp-gifted troops had been passed in the years before Horus's betrayal and endorsed by the Emperor himself. Denied the one weapon that could reasonably have altered the course of the opening stages of the civil war, in time the primarchs came to see its true power and the loyal Legions gladly welcomed Librarians among their number once again. But one man had always known the capability of that weapon and had foreseen a time when humanity would need to fight the powers of the warp with powers born of the warp.

'The Regent of Terra, a man who had served at the right hand of the Emperor for as long as anybody could remember, had been gathering to him men and women with particular talents since the end of the Great Crusade. At first working for him in an informal, secretive and ad hoc capacity, with the enemy at the gates of the Imperial Palace he shared his vision with the Emperor and brought before him twelve beings of unswerving virtue who he had recruited on his master's behalf. Four of those would become the founders of your Inquisition but the other eight, all Space Marines of differing Legions and unparalleled psykers in their own right, would become the eight founding members of the Grey Knights – the first Grand Masters of the Chapter.'

Tzula was rapt. She knew snippets of this from conversations with Lord Dinalt, but to hear it from somebody who had been alive so close to the events, possibly even lived through them, was a singular privilege.

'For years, the Regent had occluded the moon of Titan from the eyes of both friend and foe, covertly building a fortress-monastery and equipping it with forbidden technologies and secret training facilities to prepare the new Chapter in its role defending the Imperium from daemonic incursion. In addition to the eight, thousands of others had been taken to the hidden satellite to serve as ancillaries, serfs and the recruits that would form the original Brotherhoods. The Regent's final gift to the Chapter that would be his most enduring legacy was the gift of time. Using his own considerable psychic talents he removed Titan from time as well as space, granting us long years in which to prepare for the longer war that would await us upon our return.

'When we did finally take our place back in the Imperium, less than a decade had passed in real time, but for the warriors of Titan many centuries had elapsed. Men who were young during the twilight days of the war against Horus were now older than the oldest surviving veterans of the fragmenting Legions. Those eight who had previously worn armour of a different colour had accrued more years than even the most ancient and venerable of Dreadnoughts.'

He paused now, as if what he had just uttered had led him to a new realisation.

'The galaxy was still in turmoil. Primarchs bickered over how best to prevent a rebellion on the scale of Horus's from ever happening again, while the defeated traitors preyed upon worlds still loyal to the Golden Throne, as did newly emboldened xenos races. But against this backdrop, the malign influence of the warp had not dwindled – if anything, it had intensified – and the Grey Knights threw themselves straight into the fray. The rips in reality were still shedding horrors, cults had sprung up in every segmentum hoping to gain their patron's favour by summoning forth the Neverborn, and there were still worlds where doorways remained open into the warp.'

'Like Pythos.'

'Like Pythos,' Epimetheus said matching Tzula's tone. 'It was one of the first missions the Grey Knights ever undertook. Three entire Brotherhoods and a quarter of a million Imperial Army soldiers set out to close the Damnation Cache, a warp rift that had been opened during the early days of the war against Horus. It had supplied the traitor forces with allies throughout the campaign, and with turncoat Legions fleeing towards the Eye of Terror the daemons now turned their attention to the worlds surrounding Pythos, seeking to claim them as their own and establish their own debased realm on the material plane. Four entire systems had already succumbed when we got here, and it took years to fight our way across them and finally reach Pythos, harried every step of the way by a daemonic army that would have rivalled the Ultramarines at their peak for sheer numbers. By the time

we made planetfall, our own ranks had already been deci-
mated and the Imperial Army regiments accompanying us
were down to less than half strength.

'The war to close the Cache was long and bloody. For every
daemon we despatched, another would step from beyond to
take its place while our numbers continued to decline. Faced
with certain defeat that would eventually condemn an entire
subsector to unholy servitude, Supreme Grand Master Janus
took the only course of action left open to him. Ordering all
surviving Grey Knights and Imperial Army soldiers to launch
a diversionary assault, the Supreme Grand Master led a small
group of Grey Knights through the maze of tunnels that led
to the Cache, fighting their way through wave upon wave of
daemons before finally incanting the ritual of binding and
sealing the rift shut. Every daemon the Cache had spewed
forth was recalled in that instant, drawn inexorably back no
matter how far they had ventured from Pythos. And that
should have been the end of it.'

'The prisoner in the Emerald Cave?' Tzula said.

'The entities from the Cache were not the only ones present
on this world. Drawn by the promise of a daemonic paradise,
others of their kind had sought Pythos out. Many of them
were of the lower orders, barely cogent things that served as
foot soldiers for those who were especially blessed by their
patrons, but one in particular was more formidable than
any of the others. A greater daemon who served the Plague
God, he tore through us with abandon and still we died even
though the Cache had been closed. The thing was nameless
to us so we did not have the power to banish him, but our
combined psychic might was enough to bind him and seal
him in one of the vast chambers. A chamber where instead of
red Pythosian crystal, green gems studded the walls.

'Of the three hundred Grey Knights who had set out from
Titan to cleanse Pythos, barely twenty of us survived. The
Imperial Army regiments fared worse, wiped out to a man
during the final battle to subdue the Great Unclean One. With
no athame to keep it permanently closed, it was decided to
hide seven seals around the planet, each one different and
only able to be undone in a specific order. Over the final seal
a guard was to be placed, a volunteer from among the surviving Grey Knights.'

Epimetheus's story tailed off but Tzula had already filled in the blanks. Except one.

'What's an athame?' she asked.

Epimetheus chuckled, only the second sign of emotion Tzula had seen him exhibit. 'Such power in your grasp and you don't even know its name. *That* is an athame.' He pointed at the blade tucked into her waistband.

'And this is what we're going to use to close the Damnation Cache?'

'No. It's what *you* are going to use to close the Damnation Cache.'

'I don't understand,' Tzula said.

'There is a ship full of sorcerers hidden up there enabling whatever crawls from the Cache to maintain its presence on this side of the veil. To compound matters, there are rations on board that ship destined for Imperial forces that will be poisoned by the time they reach them. I am going to go there and destroy it. You are going to return to Strike and inform him that the population of Atika is dead and the city can be bombarded from orbit.'

'We can get a message to Strike some other way. I'm coming with you.'

'That message is too vital not to be delivered in person. If we chance a vox-message or courier we risk it being intercepted and losing the element of surprise. I can't trust getting a message to him telepathically as there are so many enemy psykers on this planet one of them may intercept it merely by being in proximity.' He looked away from her. 'Besides, there's a strong possibility this is a one-way mission.'

'Don't be ridiculous. Why does it have to be a suicide mission?'

'Because I have to ensure all of those sorcerers are dead and the only way to guarantee that is to destroy the ship.'

'But you don't have to be on it,' Tzula urged.

'I have to be certain.'

'Well, it's a good job you've got no way of getting up there, isn't it?' Tzula scoffed.

'He has a pilot. All he needs now is a ship,' said Shira from out of a mouth half-full of roasted animal. Tzula hadn't heard her approaching.

'How long have you been there? What did you hear?' Tzula snapped.

'Emperor. Titan. Daemons. Emeralds,' Shira was trying to speak and swallow simultaneously. 'He's right though. From the sound of things that ship does need destroying before the big daemon pit thing can be closed,' she finished, gulping down a barely chewed hunk of meat.

Tzula got up and turned her back on Shira and the Space Marine, heading back towards the fire, arms folded.

'And hey, if I go with him you can be sure he's coming back,' Shira added.

Tzula stopped and turned back to the pilot, face split in a wide grin. Shira's cockiness was becoming infectious.

'Well, in that case,' Tzula said. 'I suppose I'd better tell you where you can find a shuttle.'

822960.M41 / The Deathglades. Forty-four kilometres south of Atika, Pythos

THE THREE OF them stood at the crossroads of the jungle trail, an awkward farewell about to take place.

They had travelled together for the past two days, their route shared, but now it was time to go their separate ways; Epimetheus and Shira towards Olympax and the shuttle hidden in the jungle near there; Tzula towards Thermenos and the last known location of Strike and the bulk of the Catachan force. It was dry season on Pythos, a period that lasted no more than a few weeks but allowed the jungle floor to dry out and prevent swamps from turning into lakes and landmasses becoming one with the oceans. The track beneath their feet was scorched and cracked, the cessation of rainfall accompanied by an increase in temperature and a welcome drop in humidity.

Many days' travel still lay ahead of them and the two women had divided the little remaining food and water between them. Tzula had insisted that Shira take more as it would be difficult to hunt and forage around Olympax if it was still held by daemons. The pilot reluctantly agreed but insisted that Tzula take all of the remaining power packs for the laspistols because Epimetheus would no longer be around to protect the inquisitor.

Tzula was the first to break the prolonged silence that hung between them.

'You're absolutely sure about this? It's not too late to change your mind and come with me. Let the Dark Angels or your brother Grey Knights deal with that rogue supply ship instead.' It was half-hearted at best. She knew Epimetheus was following the best course of action and that any delay would put the liberation of Pythos at risk.

'I am certain, Tzula Digriiz.' His verbosity of two nights before had been an aberration and he had barely spoken to either of his companions on their trek through the jungle.

'Try to get him there in one piece.' This she aimed at Shira. The pilot nodded and stepped forward, looking for a moment as if she was going to throw her arms around Tzula and hug her. At the last moment she remembered that Tzula was an inquisitor and bailed out of the attempted embrace. She thrust out her hand instead, clumsily gripping the other woman's augmetic and shaking it weakly.

'You take care of yourself,' Shira said, still holding onto Tzula's metal hand. While circumstance had thrown them together and Shira had nearly got her killed, captured or worse several times over, Tzula had built up a rapport with the woman and would miss her company. If Shira could fly as well as she could talk, Tzula had no doubt that she would get Epimetheus on board that ship.

'I put the shuttle down a couple of kilometres east of Olympax. It's camouflaged with leaves and branches and I activated the cloak. That should have been enough to stop it from being seen by anybody passing that way, but if you're actively looking for it, it shouldn't be too difficult to find.' Shira finally let go of her hand. 'Epimetheus has the access and override codes.'

'How come he gets the codes and I don't?' Shira asked.

'Because they're both thirty digit alphanumeric strings. I can give them to you if you like?'

'No. That's fine,' Shira said. She moved back alongside the towering Space Marine and picked up her pack from the trail. Slinging it casually over one shoulder, she set off along the branch of the path that led towards Olympax. 'See you soon,' she called back to Tzula.

'The Emperor protects,' Tzula replied.

'It has been a pleasure to fight alongside you, Tzula,' Epimetheus said, making the sign of the aquila with his hands across his breastplate. 'The Emperor protects.'

Tzula reflected his gesture. 'The Emperor protects,' she said. Epimetheus turned and, with only a few of his giant strides, caught up to Shira.

Tzula hefted her pack and prepared to follow her own path when she called after the Space Marine. For all his openness two nights before, there was still one question that remained unanswered. 'Epimetheus?'

He stopped and looked back down the trail.

'Why have you been so reluctant to see your Grey Knights brothers again?'

Epimetheus grinned. 'What makes you so certain it is my brothers in the Grey Knights I have no desire to see again?' he said before catching up to Shira.

As the murk of the jungle swallowed him up, Tzula knew it would be the last time she ever saw him.

CHAPTER TWELVE

825960.M41 / Imperial Forward Command. Thermenos Stronghold, Pythos

'WHEN ARE YOU going to realise your tactics aren't working?'

Kaldor Draigo slid the data-slate across the unfurled map spread over the table. It came to rest next to the icons of three delver-strongholds, red 'X's scored through them to denote their destruction. Azrael picked the tablet up to see the previous day's casualty figures scrolling across it in flickering green type.

'Eight hundred lost at Bakira, over three hundred unaccounted for at Awgreave and both holds lost. Abaddon is hitting us where we are weakest and continues to exact a heavy toll. Your rapid reaction approach isn't working. We need to go on the offensive. We need to take Atika,' Draigo said, banging his meaty fist against the thick metal table.

The assembled Imperial Guard commanders looked uneasy at this display of dissent, despite having witnessed it almost every day since the Pythos campaign had begun. For months Draigo had been petitioning for an orbital bombardment of the planetary capital, and for months Azrael had ignored him. Early in the fighting it had become obvious to the Grey Knight that the source of the daemonic forces lay beneath Atika and his preferred strategy was to cut off the enemy's supply of combatants at source. The Dark Angel disagreed.

263

Atika had been home to the largest concentration of people on the planet and Strike's forethought to send them to shelter in the cave system had likely saved them all. Draigo countered that nothing had been heard from the hive since the day it fell but Azrael argued that until they had conclusive proof to the contrary, they were to assume the inhabitants of Atika were still alive. It was as if Azrael was making a very public show of preserving human life in front of the commanders of the liberation force.

The irony was not lost on Draigo. He knew how ruthless the Supreme Grand Master of the Dark Angels could be to protect his Chapter's precious secrets, how many human lives he would shed to preserve its privacy. Draigo could make informed guesses as to the nature of those secrets, but it was his knowledge of the methods the Dark Angels employed to keep them that had ultimately ensured they honoured the ancient pact struck with the Grey Knights.

'Abaddon is the one prosecuting this campaign, and like myself he is leading it from the front,' Azrael retorted. The battle-damaged state of his armour bore testimony to the amount of action he had seen. 'Rapid reaction achieves two goals. It protects the lives of Imperial Guard troops and it will lead us to Abaddon. If we remove the head of the enemy, the body will soon die.'

'And in the meantime the Damnation Cache keeps building him an army of daemons while we keep chasing our tails,' the Grey Knight scoffed.

As was usual at these strategy discussions, the Imperial Guard representatives were simply bystanders, an uneasy audience to the constant clashes between the two Space Marine commanders. Only one among them had the testicular fortitude to stand up to the Supreme Grand Masters, let alone speak at these meetings.

'What were the enemy casualty figures for yesterday?' Colonel Strike asked. Though he had refused the position of overall Imperial Guard Commander of the Pythos Reconquest Force, both Azrael and Draigo had insisted that he form part of the forward command structure on the ground. A Cadian colonel by the name of Kardine sat up in the fleet controlling troop deployments, supply lines and rotations, but for all intents and purposes Strike was in charge of Imperial Guard combat operations on Pythos, albeit in deference to the two Chapter Masters.

Azrael looked at the slate once again. 'Twenty-two Traitor Legion fatalities. Half that number again in confirmed daemon kills. At least a thousand cultists slain.'

'We're not making a dent in their numbers. If we keep throwing men at defending the mines like this, we won't be able to hold out much longer. Fighting a war of attrition will only lead to defeat.' The other Imperial Guardsmen seated around the table fidgeted and looked at each other nervously. There was no love lost between Strike and his peers. Since the reconquest force had arrived on Pythos, the Catachans had suffered casualty rates way below those of the other regiments, the enemy avoiding those holds defended by the death worlders. Strike had also refused to rotate his men out and give them downtime back in the fleet, choosing instead to keep them on the frontlines, something the 183rd had accepted without dissent.

'And what would your suggested course of action be, colonel?' asked Azrael without malice. The Supreme Grand Master of the Dark Angels was the arch-pragmatist and, if he could be shown a better way to fight this war, that is how he would fight it. Of all those around the table, Strike would be the most likely to find the key that would unlock the war, Draigo excepted. Though Azrael had an intense personal dislike for his Grey Knights counterpart, his pragmatism did at least allow him to recognise that, in matters of warfare at least, he was his equal.

'The Space Marine and inquisitor have failed to report in,' Strike said. Draigo and Azrael both bristled at the mention of Epimetheus. 'We have to assume that they, like the population of Atika, are dead. I agree with Lord Draigo. An orbital bombardment of the hive followed by a ground assault is the only way we can win this war.'

Whether Azrael would have ever heeded the colonel's advice would remain another secret of a man who had come to embody the word. A blue armoured Dark Angel strode into the command room, slipping back his hood as he did so to reveal a freshly shorn pate. He was young, no more than thirty certainly, and his intense green eyes seemed to stray off into the distance as if he was looking for something beyond his vision.

'Codicier Turmiel. You bring news?' Azrael asked.

The Librarian nodded respectfully to his Supreme Grand Master before doing the same towards Draigo. The Grey Knight returned the gesture. 'I do, Lord Azrael. We have received a request for reinforcements from Master Gabriel at Mount Dhume. The hold there has been attacked by a small force of Black Legion. They have been under fire for many hours already.'

'Gabriel has thirty Deathwing with him as well as several thousand Imperial Guard. Why is he requesting reinforcements? Has the jungle heat sapped him of his courage?' Azrael replied.

'No, Lord Azrael,' Turmiel cast his gaze around the assembled Imperial Guard commanders. Strike felt as if the Librarian was staring straight through him, as if he wasn't there. 'He has visual confirmation that Abaddon himself is leading the assault.'

826960.M41 / The Deathglades. Sixty-three kilometres south-west of Atika, Pythos

THEY BROKE CAMP as the first rays of dawn filtered through the canopies high above. Tzula put out the dying embers of a camp fire before sweeping the ashes away with her feet, not wishing to leave any sign of their passing for enemy patrols. Within minutes of waking, they were back on the jungle trail again, following the path to Thermenos that had been revealed by the receding swamp waters.

Her new travelling companions were understandably grim faced, being the last four survivors of the Catachan platoon stationed at Mortenshold, a small delver-stronghold on the eastern edge of the Olympax range. Despite its proximity to Atika, Mortenshold had avoided the attention of the Chaos forces until three nights ago when a Black Legion raiding party, backed up by gibbering warp-bred monstrosities, struck under cover of darkness, killing almost fifty Imperial Guardsmen and the squad of Dark Angels posted with them. Tzula had witnessed the assault from where she had slept that night. At first she had thought it to be an unseasonal storm, mistaking the distant pop of grenade and missile detonation for thunder, but the sporadic flashes of light from high up in the mountains could not be confused with lightning.

She had considered deviating from her route to check for survivors but she knew it would be futile. Experience told her that if the hold was in enemy hands there would be nobody friendly left in there alive. Besides, without Epimetheus around, she was less inclined to do anything that would risk the athame falling into the clutches of the enemy.

As it transpired, the survivors of Mortenshold had found her, rather than the other way around. Late on the evening following the far-off lights on the mountain, just as she was looking to make camp for the night, Tzula was surprised by a knife at her throat and a well-toned forearm at the back of her neck. Fortunately for her, the four Catachans had been stalking her for the best part of an hour without her being aware, during which time the sergeant among them, Magrik, had recognised Tzula from the battle for Atika docks. Rather than being cautious, sneaking up behind her and putting an unsheathed fang to her throat was Magrik's way of saying hello.

None of the banter Tzula would usually associate with a group of Catachans was evident among this bunch, and they tromped through the undergrowth without ever sharing a quip or joke. Their combat readiness was undiminished however, lasrifles raised to just above waist height ready to be aimed at the slightest sign of movement. Enemy units were the greatest danger they now faced in the jungles of Pythos, but although much of the native fauna had been hunted for sport by daemons, many hungry predators still lurked within the bush.

The pink rays of sunrise were giving way to the yellow lances of early morning when Magrik signalled for them to get into cover. The other three Catachans – Trondar, Santarini and the veteran Gdolni – made for the far side of the trail and dissolved into the green. Tzula and Magrik sought refuge behind the thick trunk of an ancient redwood. The sergeant cocked her head, positioning her ear to capture any sound carrying on the almost imperceptible breeze. Picking up on something, she turned to Tzula and motioned in the direction she thought it was coming from.

Had Magrik been a man, she would have been described as grizzled, sharp lines cut deep into a face sculpted by battle. Being a woman, the more patronising way she would undoubtedly be described would be she had 'had a hard life'. Magrik was a Catachan. She hadn't lived a hard life, she had lived life hard.

Tzula turned her ear towards the light wind. Almost immediately, she heard the sound of engines. Lots of engines.

Magrik dropped to her haunches, placing her palm on the ground. Whatever she felt vibrating through the jungle floor did not impress her. Rising to her feet, she unclipped a pair of grenades from the bandolier slung diagonally across her torso and passed one to Tzula.

'War engines. Plenty of them,' she said in that hushed but at the same time loud tone all Catachans seemed to adopt when combat was imminent. 'Don't throw it at the hull because it'll bounce off. Roll it under the chassis. The armour is usually weaker underneath.'

Abaddon's capacity to deploy war machines had been remarkable since the earliest days of the invasion and was the primary reason the Catachans had chosen to fight the war in the delver-strongholds which were inaccessible to the daemon engines and other tracked monstrosities. With so many now deployed on the planet, Abaddon must have established a forge on Pythos for their creation.

Across the wide track, the other Catachans followed Magrik's lead, priming grenades and awaiting their targets. If their attack went true to form, the Catachans would have melted back into the jungle before the front ranks of vehicles were destroyed, barring passage to those behind until the wrecks were moved clear. It may not stop the column's advance but it would certainly slow it down.

The bass rumble grew louder and the vibrations that Magrik had felt with the palm of her hand, Tzula could now feel jarring up through her legs. Magrik looked concerned.

'More of them than I thought,' the Catachan sergeant lamented, picking another grenade from the bandolier. She couldn't say anything else as the growl of engines became a fully fledged roar, stifling the possibility of any other noise. 'A hell of a lot more than I thought,' Tzula saw Magrik mouth.

Sooner than any of them expected, the barrel of something massive poked its way over the brow of a ridge, collapsing trees as it went.

Magrik's cry of 'Now!' lost beneath the din, Tzula stepped out from cover ready to destroy whatever the fearsome gun was attached to.

826960.M41 / Delver-stronghold 2761/b.
Mount Dhume, Pythos

THE THUNDERHAWK SWUNG wide around the mountain peak, banking right as it did so and granting Azrael his first view of the battle raging below. Thick black smoke drifted across the shallow incline that led up to the entrance of the mine, billowing from the wrecks of two Rhinos, spiked, corrupted imitations of the Dark Angels' own troop carriers. Black armoured corpses dotted the slope along with countless more Imperial Guard. Much to Azrael's consternation, several in the ivory of the Deathwing also lay among them. Bursts of muzzle-flare highlighted the positions of the traitors advancing towards the hold, their shots returned by a wall of fire from the cave's mouth and from behind cover along the approach.

Alongside him in the cockpit, standing behind the two pilots, Kaldor Draigo witnessed the same scene. The Dark Angels' response had been the very definition of rapid, calling in all available forces from the holds close to Thermenos and being in the air within three hours of receiving the call from Gabriel. Though the entire Chapter was not deploying as it had done to liberate the *Revenge*, over half their number were now in the air above Mount Dhume preparing to defend the hold and kill Abaddon the Despoiler, a blight on the Imperium since the time of the Emperor. At their flanks flew hundreds of Valkyries, their troop holds crammed with Imperial Guardsmen ready to lend their guns to the effort. High above them all, guardian angels in the truest sense of the word, a score of Dark Talons flew escort.

To Draigo's chagrin, his Brotherhood of Grey Knights, seldom used thus far in the Pythos campaign, would not be taking part in the battle.

Ignoring the Grey Knight Supreme Grand Master's request to be allowed time to get his battle-brothers planetside, Azrael had insisted that speed was of the essence, that Abaddon could not be allowed to slip through their grasp. Draigo was convinced that it was only because he was present when the message was relayed to Azrael that the Dark Angel had deigned to allow him to take part in this mission. Had the report come in while he was with the fleet he would have been none the wiser, another secret Azrael would have kept to himself.

'I still think this is reckless, Azrael,' Draigo snarled. 'You're committing too large a force. What if this is a feint and it enables Abaddon to launch assaults on those holds you've left undefended? Take a look down there. Does that look like an army strong enough to capture a hold from thirty Terminators and a few battalions of Imperial Guard? Or does it look more like an army just strong enough to hold out until reinforcements can arrive to bolster the defenders?'

'That works in our favour. If he elects to spread his forces so thinly, there is little chance of his forces being strengthened before our battle is through. Even if we do lose a few holds, it will be a small price to pay for the elimination of Abaddon.'

Azrael pointed to a large plateau behind the Black Legion lines. 'Put us down over there,' he instructed the pilot.

'If it even is Abaddon leading this assault,' Draigo retorted.

'If the Grand Master of my First Company says that Abaddon is here then he is here,' Azrael snapped, as if it was his own reliability that the Grey Knight were casting doubt upon.

'Then the real question we have to ask ourselves,' Draigo said, making ready his wargear so that he could enter the fray the moment the Thunderhawk doors opened, 'is *why* is he here?'

RISING FROM COVER, Balthasar's storm bolter erupted in a hail of shells, scattering the Black Legionnaires converging on his position. Beside him, five Mordians, their once pristine blue uniforms coated in the dust of the distant world on which they had been sent to fight and the blood of their comrades, rose up from behind the upturned mining cart and opened up with their lasrifles. One of the traitors went down under Balthasar's fire and was finished off by the Guardsmen peppering their fallen enemy with concentrated bursts.

Another of the Traitor Marines, a brute almost the same size in his ancient power armour as Balthasar was in his Terminator suit, tore open two of the Mordians with a pair of shots from his bolter. Convulsing and almost split in half, both men were dead before they hit the ground. Balthasar recognised this one. It was the same warrior who had slain Brother Jephael earlier in the day, mercilessly gunning him down as he rushed to the aid of a stricken Deathwing.

Balthasar grinned. Like all of his order, he strove for vengeance above all else, a vengeance that had grown ever darker as he had advanced through the Dark Angels' ranks. Already he had been made privy to the most guarded secret of his Chapter, that during the galactic civil war of ten millennia ago, over half of what was then the Dark Angels Legion threw in their lot with the Ruinous Powers, shunning both Emperor and primarch. In the few years since he had ascended to the Deathwing, he had already taken part in several hunts for these erstwhile battle-brothers, the Fallen as they are known amongst the Chapter's inner circle, and more than once had returned to the Rock as part of one of their guard details. The Dark Angels were patient hunters, playing the long game of centuries to capture their prey, but sometimes the universe had a way of offering up the chance for instant vengeance. The enemy facing him was not one of the Fallen but Jephael would soon be avenged.

On the periphery of his vision, one of the other Black Legionnaires took aim at Balthasar with his bolter, but the Deathwing raised his storm bolter and obliterated the traitor's faceplate before he could return fire. Drawing his power sword, Balthasar ignited the blade and swung at Jephael's killer, ruining his bolter with the downstroke and gouging a furrow in his breastplate with the return. Bereft of his gun, the Traitor Marine drew the chainblade hung at his thigh and revved it into life, preparing to duel with the Dark Angel.

Seeing what was happening, and eager to grant Balthasar some measure of rectitude for their brother's death, other Deathwings stepped from cover and engaged the now regrouping Black Legionnaires, inspiring more of the heads-down Mordians to abandon their cover and do likewise. Shoulder to shoulder, Gabriel and Barachiel drove back an embryonic counter-assault, shredding three of the dark-armoured traitors with a concerted volley.

Balthasar's sword was a blur of blue energy, sweeping through the air with a crackle of energy. At the last moment, the Black Legionnaire raised his own blade, countering the blow in a shower of chainblade teeth. The two warriors pushed against each other, both weapons protesting at the strain being placed upon them. Though wearing only the ancient armour that may have once been painted in the colours of the Luna Wolves, then the Sons of Horus, the traitor's strength matched that of Balthasar, augmented as it was by a suit of tactical dreadnought armour. Servos and muscles straining, the Deathwing allowed himself to be driven back, overbalancing the Chaos Marine slightly. Dragging his power sword away from the squealing chainsword, Balthasar drew back the energy-tinged blade and swept with it once again. Momentum his temporary master, the traitor stepped forwards into the blow but, in defiance of his bulk, spun away from the Dark Angel's blade. The tip of Balthasar's weapon caught the Black Legionnaire around the waist, gouging a deep furrow in his armour from which spilled crimson that stained the jet of the ceramite.

The traitor did not bellow in rage like a lackey of the Blood God, nor did he revel in his own pain like a follower of the Prince of Pleasure, instead bringing his weapon back to the guard position and awaiting the next riposte like the consummate warrior he evidently was. A moment later, *was* became the operative word.

The ground in front of the Traitor Marine threw up dust where the rock had been turned to powder, tiny explosions impacting every two metres or so racing towards him. The heavy bolter shells reached the Black Legionnaire and, instead of dust, a cloud of blood and viscera filled the air, a dozen rounds disintegrating him in the space of seconds. His body fell forwards, helmeted head crashing down in front of Balthasar's feet and the Deathwing drove his power sword down into the traitor's skull, being careful to avoid damaging the gene-seed in the throat.

Tugging his blade from the corpse, Balthasar turned to find the source of the Black Legionnaire's demise and found the sky full of Dark Angels and Imperial Navy flyers breaking over the cover of the mountains. At their head was *Roar of Vengeance*, most ancient of all the Dark Angels Thunderhawks and, when he deployed with the Chapter, personal transport of Supreme Grand Master Azrael. As it got closer, Balthasar saw that the barrels of the nose-mounted heavy bolters were still smoking and he raised his blade in salute and gratitude. Being denied his victory in personal combat was not an issue, Jephael's slayer had been vanquished and vengeance belonged to the Dark Angels. As *Roar of Vengeance* swept low, Azrael returned the salute from the cockpit.

Sheathing his sword, Balthasar sprinted down the slope, storm bolter blazing, to help secure the landing zone.

826960.M41 / Inquisition Shuttle Virtuous. Imperial Fleet, Pandorax System

'I STILL DON'T see anything,' Shira said, leaning forward in the pilot's seat to peer out through the cockpit window. All around her, lights flashed and dials spun on consoles and instrument arrays, the purpose or function of which she had little idea. The shuttle that Tzula had left in the jungle was a very different craft from a Kestrel and though the principles of flying it were the same, she was sure there were systems that would aid their journey that she was in complete ignorance of. She had managed to get the cloaking system working at least and, as they glided between the monolithic chips of the Pythos Reconquest Fleet, they did so unseen.

'It's not what you can see,' Epimetheus said, standing over the co-pilot's seat that was far too tiny to accommodate him. 'It's what you can't.'

Shira turned to look at the Space Marine. 'That's not very helpful, you know?' she said.

'Here. Look again,' he said.

Shira turned back, feeling a tingling sensation around her eyes as she did so. Although he had only used his powers on Shira on a couple of occasions, she found it disconcerting that he never asked or gave warning that he was about to do so. The 'possession' he carried out a couple of days ago was particularly invasive and Shira had not fully recovered from its effects, a weird feeling she could neither pinpoint nor shake.

'I'm sorry but this *is* necessary,' Epimetheus said, if not reading her thoughts then certainly sensing her discomfort. 'Can you see it now?'

A purple haze forming on the periphery of her vision, Shira squinted and, as if looking down a tunnel, the vague impression of… something resolved itself.

'I think so,' she said. 'It's like somebody has torn off a strip

of space and has put it in the wrong place, like it's not supposed to be there.'

Epimetheus smiled. 'Precisely. Now, can you take us in
closer?'

Up close, the outline of the *Lamentation* – the call sign the
ship was broadcasting – certainly resembled that of a Nep-
tune-class supply frigate, but one that had been covered in a
blanket made from the void. The dips and grooves of the vessel's hull could be made out along with the bumps and rises
of sensor arrays and comms equipment; it wasn't so much
that the ship was invisible, it was more like space had been
wrapped around it.

'There should be a landing bay towards the rear of the ship.
Bring the shuttle down on top of the hull and I'll insert from
the outside,' Epimetheus said causing Shira to frown. 'Too
risky to attempt a landing on board. If they don't have the bay
guarded, the arrival sensors will trigger on board the bridge
and tip them off.'

Satisfied with the Space Marine's reasoning, she slowed
the shuttle's velocity trying to find a clear patch of hull to
set down upon. Seeing a spot at the very rear of the ship that
appeared smoother than the rest, she went to engage the
landing gear. Out of habit, she reached down underneath
the console to find the release lever but, realising she wasn't
at the controls of a Kestrel, sat back up again and studied the
myriad controls blinking at her.

'Is there a problem?' Epimetheus said after Shira had guided
the shuttle over the rear of the *Lamentation* and turned one
hundred and eighty degrees to fly back along the hull.

'No. No problem here,' she said dismissively, eyes flitting this
way and that, scanning the unfamiliar icons and runes of the
shuttle for any control that might operate the landing gear.

'If you're looking for the landing gear,' Epimetheus said,
leaning forwards over the co-pilot's chair and stretching out
an arm, 'it's this one here.' He stabbed one of the flashing
buttons with a huge finger. The suppressed whirr of three
magnetised feet emerging from the bottom of the shuttle
followed.

'That's the one I was going to press,' Shira said not very
convincingly.

'Of course you were,' Epimetheus replied, smiling. He unlocked his helmet from his thigh and put it over his head, sealing it in place with a hiss of pressure. 'As soon as I'm clear, head back to Pythos and find Tzula and Strike. If this goes to plan, they should be gearing up to assault Atika by the time you find them.'

'But–' Shira said.

'No "buts", Shira. That's an order.'

Leaving no room for protest, Epimetheus stepped through into the shuttle's rear chamber and made ready to disembark.

826960.M41 / Delver-stronghold 2761/b.
Mount Dhume, Pythos

THE HELLHAMMER CANNON erupted into a riot of noise and explosive fury before the Valkyries carrying it had even begun their landing.

In the command compartment Strike directed the crew in the reloading and firing, not aiming for specific targets but instead laying down a carpet of suppressing fire to cover the approach of the combined Catachan and Dark Angels forces. Still several metres above the landing, the four Valkyries that had transported it from Thermenos released the thick metal chains suspending *Traitor's Bane* between them and the tank dropped, cracking open the rocky terrain beneath. Thanks to the impact suppression system that K'Cee had overhauled, to the occupants of the tank it felt as though they had landed on sand. The jokaero thrust out his lower jaw and nodded his head in satisfaction as the tank sped towards the enemy position the instant it was on the ground, all weapons blazing.

A Rhino flipped violently into the air, its flaming husk crashing back down on the two Black Legionnaires who had been using it as cover. The barrel of the Hellhammer's main gun spun to target a second Rhino causing the half dozen traitors behind it to beat a hasty retreat. Two never made it from the armoured personnel carrier's shadow, cut down by bolter fire from a squad of Dark Angels deploying on jump packs from a rapidly moving Thunderhawk. The handful who avoided their comrades' fate were driven onto the plasma cannon of *Corvex*, superheated hydrogen burning through armour and roasting the flesh and organs of those beneath. The Master of the Ravenwing gracefully turned his jetbike through one hundred and eighty degrees, skimming back over the smouldering Traitor Marines to finish off any survivors.

Heartened by the arrival of reinforcements, the Mordian soldiers taking cover at the entrance of the mine charged down the approach, trapping the Chaos forces between a wave of green on one side, a tide of blue on the other. In amongst the Mordians, Gabriel and the Deathwing roused the Imperial Guardsmen, their white armour sticking out like surf at the head of a tidal wave.

The Black Legion caught between them didn't stand a chance.

From a view slit in *Traitor's Bane*, Strike watched as the approach to the mine head became a cauldron of las and bolter fire. With no way out, the few remaining Black Legionnaires attempted a desperate rearguard, fighting back to back, mowing down Guardsmen by the score. But to no avail.

Azrael and Draigo at their head, power-armoured figures pushed through the throng of humans, some shoved bodily out of the way by Dark Angels eager to claim their kills. From the rear, the Deathwing converged, penning in the last few Black Legionnaires.

There were no offers of clemency from either side, no appeals for weapons to be laid down or terms of surrender proposed. Nobody begged for their life to be spared and not a single one of them stopped fighting until the breath had fled from their lungs and their hearts had stopped beating. Less than three minutes after *Roar of Vengeance* had crested the peak of Mount Dhume, the Black Legion had been defeated.

It had been a rout. If Azrael had only brought a third of the force with him – a quarter even – it would still have been a resounding victory, but the Supreme Grand Master of the Dark Angels did not look pleased. Standing over the corpses of the slain Black Legionnaires a heated exchange was taking place between Azrael, Draigo and Gabriel. Enemy bodies were kicked over onto their backs and helmets cracked open with sword tips, revealing their faces for identification. Not supplying the result that Azrael had been looking for, he went face-to-face with Gabriel, simmering resentment threatening to boil over into violence. Gabriel stood his ground. Moments later, Azrael broke off from the confrontation and raised his head skywards.

'Abaddon! Show yourself. Come and face me on the field of battle instead of cowering behind rocks like the craven traitor you are,' Azrael bellowed. He spun around slowly, looking at the surrounding peaks and outcrops for signs of movement. All about him, human and Space Marine eyes did the same.

The echo from the Dark Angel's words had almost faded to nothing when the silhouette of a huge figure, right arm terminating in a crackling power claw, appeared on a promontory high above the battlefield. He raised his other arm, sword in hand, but it was not in salute. It was in threat. Abaddon brought the blade down in a chopping motion.

Inside *Traitor's Bane*, the hairs on the back of Strike's arms rose and the tang of scorched ozone carried on the air.

826960.M41 / Lamentation. Imperial Fleet, Pandorax System

As HE HAD surmised, Epimetheus's insertion onto the supply vessel had been without incident. The landing bay was empty, save for a few Chaos fighter-interceptors that could be used to eliminate any Imperial craft that took too much of an interest in the *Lamentation* or, more likely, for escape if Corpulax and Huron Blackheart's scheme went awry. No guards had been posted and there was very little sign of recent activity.

Deeper into the ship, things had taken on a very different complexion. Corpses of the crew had been left to rot where they had been butchered, many with wounds to the back of the head and torso where they had been shot from behind. Just as Epimetheus was boarding via stealth, it appeared the raiders who had taken this vessel had done so too. Where wounds from attacks from the rear weren't apparent, throats had been slit to prevent the victim from crying out for help.

But it was the dead who were the lucky ones.

As in Atika plague zombies lurched along the corridors, but instead of rock and ore, they carried vials and containers, food and poison with which to taint the fleet's provisions. Unlike Atika, their overseers wore crimson armour, the red crudely painted over whatever colour their armour originally was.

Red Corsairs. Rather than have Tzula explain who Huron Blackheart was, Epimetheus had been able to extract the information directly from her mind but what he had found there appalled him. Bad enough that Horus had turned half of the Emperor's Legions ten thousand years ago but for it to still happen today, often willingly, was difficult to comprehend. Were the false promises of the Dark Powers still that attractive after all that history had taught? No matter. Vengeance ran in Epimetheus's blood and soon, when the ship was destroyed, vengeance would be his, regardless of the cost.

Epimetheus was forced to keep to the shadows and seek cover in cabins and crew dormitories to avoid detection. Though his desire to throttle these turncoats was immense, the last thing he wanted to do was tip the pirates off about his presence on board and his progress towards his goal was both slow and measured.

His psychic gifts had revealed two locations on the ship where sorcerous activity was at its most intense. The first was amidships while the other was several decks lower down, but both burned like beacon fires in the warp. According to a parchment schematic of the ship he had discovered in one of the officers' cabins, the first was on the route he needed to take to reach the second so that was where he was headed.

The closer he got, the more the ship began to alter. At first, it was simply a rime of hoarfrost dappling the metal of the bulkhead, but this gradually gave way to the metal itself taking on a new aspect and bizarre fronds descending from the ceiling like polyps. The plague zombies and their overseers became less frequent, as if this part of the ship had been shunned due to the changes wrought upon it and their mystical nature.

The psychic resonance grew stronger and Epimetheus drew his bolt pistol, safe in the knowledge that if he were to use it, nobody other than those on the receiving end of the contents of its magazine would be able to hear it. His back to an ice-sheened wall, he sidled along it, approaching an open hatchway from which he could hear voices. In such close proximity of others gifted by othersight, he had to strain to keep his presence in the warp occluded. Reaching the threshold, he risked a surreptitious glance into the room beyond.

Four Chaos sorcerers stood facing each other in a circle at the centre of the chamber. The walls and floor were even more misshapen than the approaching corridors, and leering daemonic faces filled every surface, observing the scene dispassionately with unblinking, lidless eyes.

All the sorcerers carried staves, as different from each other as their bearers. The one with his back to Epimetheus wore armour of iridescent purple, trimmed with silver and black hair that tumbled over ornate pauldrons. His staff was made of the darkest wood, almost black in colour, and it was inset along its length with human-sized eyes, each blinking out of time with the others.

Next to him was an emaciated figure, his unadorned, unpainted power armour too large for his diminished frame. His face was wrinkled like the bark of a dead tree and his completely bloodshot eyes and the clumps of wispy hair that dotted his scalp lent him the aspect of one who had paid a high price for his dalliances with the warp. The staff in his hand, as simple as his armour yet greyed and carbonised by fire, served to reinforce this.

Opposite him was a sorcerer who was obviously a follower of the Plague God. Though still recognisable as power armour, the plates no longer resembled ceramite and were instead coated in a scabrous material criss-crossed in a network of translucent veins through which flowed pus and other noxious fluids. His face appeared to be was painted white, but just beneath the surface capillaries and burst blood vessels gave it a pale violet hue, the same colour as his staff which looked like a length of solidified intestine.

The final sorcerer stood a head taller than the others, and in him Epimetheus recognised something. Under different circumstances, ones where the Imperium had not been torn asunder by civil strife in millennia past, the Grey Knight might have called him a kindred spirit, another who could recall times past as if it was only yesterday. The traitor's armour was the exact twin of Epimetheus's own set of Cataphractii but, whereas the Grey Knight's suit was silver tarnished by a few remaining patches of green, the sorcerer's was blue and gold. Even hooded and in unfamiliar livery, Epimetheus could still recognise his features as being that of a Prosperan, one of the Thousand Sons sorcerer elite.

Epimetheus was preparing to burst into the chamber and kill all four of them before they could react when the son of Magnus tapped his ornate staff twice on the floor and uttered a single word in a language Epimetheus didn't understand.

When he swung around the corner, bolt pistol raised, all he found was the after image of teleportation and the whiff of seared ozone.

826960.M41 / Delver-stronghold 2761/b. Mount Dhume, Pythos

A THOUSAND GUNS were raised and aimed at the same target. Exposed on the outcrop of rock, the Chaos Warmaster, no matter how formidable his reputation, no matter how high his cunning, had no escape.

Escape was not his intention.

In a crackle of warp-spawned lightning, four figures appeared alongside Abaddon. In the same instant that Azrael gave the order to open fire, one of the newcomers, a shrivelled thing in unmarked power armour, erected a protective kine dome, the parabola of blue energy nullifying las-fire and deflecting solid rounds. Almost a hundred Imperial Guardsmen and Space Marines alike had fallen under the reflected barrage before Azrael directed them to cease firing.

Beneath the dome, the three other armoured figures raised staves in the air and commenced a noiseless chant. A violent wind blew through the mountain approach, kicking up dust powerful enough to tear skin and strip paint from ceramite. Overhead, roiling clouds appeared in the previously clear sky, a purple and grey mass moving as if time had been sped up.

Strike had watched all this unfold from the command compartment of *Traitor's Bane* with a mixture of fear and wonder. He did not need to be warptouched to know that the four newcomers to the battlefield were sorcerers, just as he didn't need the tactical acumen of a Space Marine Chapter Master to know that Draigo was right. They had been lured into a trap.

'Strike,' Azrael's voice blared from the vox.

'Yes, lord?' Strike replied, dropping back into his command chair.

'Target the outcrop. If we can't breach the kine shield then, by the Lion, we can damn well bring him down by other means.' The venom in the Dark Angel's voice was palpable.

'Acknowledged, lord,' Strike said. He turned to his tank crew. 'You heard Lord Azrael. Bring the demolisher cannon to bear and aim for the base of the ridge.'

K'Cee bounded down from where he was sitting and went

to join the demolisher gunner at the front of the compartment. Between them they had the firing solution in seconds and, accompanied by the grind of servos, swung the mighty gun around.

'Fire when ready,' Strike called over to them, not waiting for the weapon to be aimed before giving the order. The demolisher cannon fixed into position with a satisfied clank but the next sound Strike heard wasn't the thud of the weapon firing that he had expected. From somewhere above came a noise like cartilage tearing.

'What the-' Strike's question was drowned beneath the boom of the siege cannon discharging. He scrambled back up the turret ladder to inspect the aftermath of the shot only to find, to his confusion and dismay, that the crag was still intact and the five Chaos Marines along with it. What was more bewildering was that he hadn't heard the detonation of the demolisher shell. He popped the hatch and stuck his head out of the tank.

A sea of humanity, most of it wearing Mordian blue, flowed past the Hellhammer, running in abject terror towards the landing zone. Bolters opened up from the Dark Angels positions and were soon joined by the chatter of heavier weapons. An immense shadow passed over the tank and Strike looked skyward to discover the target of the Space Marines' fire and the source of the Mordians' fear.

Vast wings beating with a sound like thunder, a Skulltaker – or Bloodthirster as Draigo had corrected him on more than one occasion – hovered over the battlefield, demolisher shell in one hand from where he had obviously plucked it out of the air. Half the size again of the one that appeared near Olympax, it snarled in rage before throwing the ordnance down among the fleeing Guardsmen. The ensuing explosion rocked *Traitor's Bane* and showered it with debris, both organic and inorganic, forcing Strike to take cover under the turret hatch. He was about to call down to the gunners to target the daemon with the main gun when more of the tearing noises emanated from the sky. In between clouds the colour of bruises, incisions in reality opened, the stuff of the warp bleeding through into realspace.

It started raining daemons.

CHAPTER THIRTEEN

THE LAST OF the cultists died as easily as the previous eight, the force halberd severing her thread to life as easily as it parted her head from her shoulders.

Already the thick warpfrost was receding from the mess hall they had turned into an improvised ceremonial chamber, and the buzzing Epimetheus felt in his skull when in close proximity to other psykers abated. These nine had been powerful in matters of the warp, of that there was no doubt, but both physically and mentally they had been no match for the Grey Knight. With their demise, the daemons using the Damnation Cache as a conduit into the material realm would struggle to gain a toehold in reality. Now they would have to expend more of their energies merely existing, making them weaker to physical assault. If Tzula had been able to reach the commanders of the Reconquest Force, they now had a fighting chance of taking Atika and resealing the Cache.

With a burst of blue flame from his gauntleted hand, Epimetheus set the corpses alight, taking his leave of the chamber which was already filling with the stink of burning flesh. The cultists had died too swiftly to raise any alarm so he still had stealth in his armoury and reaching the *Lamentation*'s engines was going to be a lot easier without Red Corsairs guard details stalking him.

Following the source of the constant hum and vibration that reverberated through the ship, Epimetheus slunk through the dark places, avoiding the plague zombies carrying their cargo back and forth, as oblivious to his presence as they were to everything else. The only time he had had to employ violence was when he finally reached the doors to the enginarium and found a guard posted there, the crimson paint doing a poor job of disguising his former allegiance to the Imperial Fists. The Grey Knight called upon his telekinetic abilities to move the corpse of a crewmember slain when the ship was taken. It slammed into the bulkhead with a resounding thud loud enough to be heard over the engines and, while the Red Corsair's back was turned investigating the noise, Epimetheus moved up behind him and opened his throat with a swift motion of his combat blade. He lingered over the corpse a moment, appalled that a Space Marine descended from a Legion who had given so much to stifle treachery could have turned traitor himself, before burning through the lock mechanism with warpfire and pushing open the doors to the enginarium.

The *Lamentation* was a small ship compared to others of the fleet, but the engine needed to power it through the void took up fully a third of its bulk, and the Space Marine felt dwarfed as he stood before the immense throbbing structure. The heat it threw off would have killed an unaugmented human not wearing protective clothing and Epimetheus pulled the helmet from his hip and clamped it in place to prevent his flesh from burning. A bank of instruments sat off to one side, lights and dials gently flashing and spinning to denote the ship was at rest, and Epimetheus strode over to study them. The sheer number of indicators and controls was baffling and it took him several minutes to deduce what did what. Eventually, settling on a T-bar lever that even he would need both hands to operate, he took a deep breath and pushed it all the way upwards.

Epimetheus hadn't been sure what to expect. The very concept of overloading a spaceship engine suggested to him that it would go nova very quickly, melting down almost instantaneously and obliterating the vessel and all on board. Instead, the thrum of the engine rose in pitch and several of the dials crept to the right, moving from sections marked in green through a spectrum that terminated in red.

Epimetheus had been moulded in the image of his primarch, remoulded in the image of the Emperor upon his ascension to the Grey Knights and blessed with enormous psychic talent. When he had set out on this mission he had assumed it to be one-way and was willing to sacrifice his all to ensure its success. If he did not have to needlessly lay down his life then he wasn't going to do so. He checked the dials again to see how fast they were moving and calculated that he had just over thirty minutes to get back to the landing bay and commandeer one of the ships there to try and make it back to Pythos. Hopefully, with all of the confusion a ship blowing up in their midst was going to cause, the fleet would be too busy to notice a tiny fighter sporting the colours of the Red Corsairs speeding towards Pythos. He gripped the lever again and pushed it further upwards, wrenching it from its housing before tossing it away. By the time anybody else realised that the engine was going to blow, they wouldn't be able to do anything about it.

He turned to leave but discovered that he was no longer alone in the enginarium. Clad in red and black armour haloed by a spiked golden arch sat atop his backpack, stood a figure he only recognised from Tzula's memory: Huron Blackheart.

In one hand he held a massive power axe, already activated and bristling with energy, while his other was covered by a taloned power fist, similarly ready for battle. At his feet, a strange creature loitered, its maw a mess of misshapen teeth, its leathery pale orange hide mottled with brown pustules. He could see both of them with his eyes but neither registered as presences in the warp, which had allowed the Tyrant of Badab to get the drop on him.

'So,' Huron said, raising his axe and charging the Grey Knight, 'who do we have here?'

826960.M41 / Delver-stronghold 2761/b. Mount Dhume, Pythos

THE SCREAMS OF dying men drowned out the wails of the horrors birthing into reality. The daemons were indiscriminate, caring not who they slaughtered and Mordian and Catachan died alongside Dark Angels, no pecking order being applied to the killing. Some turned upon each other, the lure of fresh souls not great enough to outweigh settling old scores or challenging those more favoured by their patrons.

Winged fiends flew overhead, engaging the Dark Talons that still flew air cover, macabre dogfights sporadically breaking out and filling the sky with bursts of explosions and low hanging vapour trails. Thunderhawks struggled to get airborne, their hulls caked with bloated and clawed horrors. Dark Angels armed with flamers bathed them in fire but they too soon found themselves buried under a morass of the Neverborn, stripping away armour and tearing at the flesh beneath. Those Imperial Guardsmen not run mad by the sight of things that should not be walking among them, fought in vain, their lasrifles no match for iron-tough hide. Some had made it back to the shelter of the mine but they were merely delaying the inevitable. As soon as the daemons had massacred those who had stood and fought, their turn to die would come.

Their differences set aside for the sake of battle, Azrael and Draigo fought shoulder to shoulder, the *Titansword* and the *Sword of Secrets* rising and falling in concert, despatching daemons back to whence they came. The Supreme Grand Masters' armour was streaked with gore, and a heap of rapidly dissolving corpses lay in a ring around them.

It served as no warning to others of their kind as still the Neverborn drove at the two Space Marines, looking for one or the other to falter and grant them an opening.

Behind them, *Traitor's Bane* traversed the slope slowly, the mobile fortress shredding and broiling daemons with its weapons and crushing them beneath its treads, but those it killed were a mere drop in the ocean compared to the numbers still spewing forth from the portals. Realising its threat, a pack of lithe daemons targeted the Hellhammer, their vaguely feminine forms scrabbling over the hull with claws and blades in place of hands.

'They're right on top of us!' Tamzarian called out.

'We need to burn them off,' Strike answered. 'Can we turn the flamers on ourself?'

'Negative, chief,' one of the gunners replied. 'They don't have the firing arc.'

K'Cee, who had been fiddling with a bundle of cables behind one of the auspexes, loped over to Strike's command chair and pointed at one of the buttons he had added to the armrest. Many of the modifications the jokaero had made to the tank were purely cosmetic – a flange here, some filigree there – and the number of extra buttons K'Cee had added purely for the sake of symmetry or aesthetics had become the bane of Tamzarian's life. This one, however, appeared to do something and he was most insistent that the colonel press it. Which he did.

The hull of the Hellhammer lit up as millions of volts of electricity passed through it, frying the boarders and turning their white skin and violet hair the darkest black. Their remains tumbled from the hull, breaking like charcoal on the hard ground.

Enraged, the Bloodthirster turned its attention to Strike's command vehicle, swatting other winged daemons out of the way like flies as it tore towards the Hellhammer.

'Target it with the demolisher and hellhammer but stagger the shots by a split second,' Strike ordered, peering out through the view slit. Two shots followed soon after, their report blending into one due to their proximity.

Without pause, the Bloodthirster caught the first shell in its powerful grasp, its fingers leaving an impression on the tough metal casing but, distracted, it was too slow to react to the second which caught it square in one of its meaty flanks. Time seemed to freeze for a moment, and all on the battlefield stared enraptured as the massive daemon tumbled out of the sky. It twisted mid-fall and landed crouched on its feet, the force of impact breaking open the ground beneath it and felt as far away as Atika and Thermenos. It rose from its haunches and raised its head to the clouds before emitting a deep bellow of rage and pain. It looked back towards the Hellhammer and charged.

Lesser daemons struggled to get out of the way, and those unfortunate enough to be caught in the Bloodthirster's path were either trampled underfoot or picked up and slung bodily at the tank. Achieving a pace that nothing of its size and bulk should reasonably reach, it launched itself into the air, axe raised above its head ready to smash it through the body of *Traitor's Bane*.

* * *

826960.M41 / Lamentation. Imperial Fleet, Pandorax System

'NOT VERY TALKATIVE, are we?' Huron Blackheart commented, sweeping his power axe through the space Epimetheus had just vacated.

The Grey Knight countered with a riposte from his halberd, the buzz of energy becoming a crackle as the two power fields met. He said nothing.

'Come now. At least tell me which Chapter sired you so I can have your corpse shipped back to them.' Huron pulled his axe away and swung again but his blow was again blocked by Epimetheus's weapon. 'Or wear your hide as a banner the next time I face them in battle.'

Epimetheus went on the attack this time, a flurry of strikes aimed at Huron's body but each one met by the head or haft of the traitor's axe. Whatever had blinded him to Blackheart's presence was inhibiting him from using his psychic abilities, and the Grey Knight was now reliant on only his skill with a physical weapon to see him through this battle. The creature that had been at Huron's heel was perched on a railing designed to prevent crewmen from falling into the vast chasm surrounding the engine and was looking on disinterestedly. Epimetheus couldn't pinpoint it, but he was certain the wretched thing was blanking out his powers.

'I do not recognise your colour scheme and you bear no markings on your armour. Are you a renegade like me?' Huron said, switching tack and attempting an uppercut with his power fist, which Epimetheus knocked away with the haft of his halberd. 'Because I can always make use of somebody like you, particularly in light of your gifts.'

Epimetheus broke his silence. 'I'd rather die here on this ship than throw in my lot with you.' He gripped the halberd in both hands and was using it two-handed like a staff, blocking Huron's blows with the base and attacking with the head. He struck a glancing blow to the traitor's thigh, cracking the ceramite, but Blackheart immediately retaliated with an attack of his own that struck Epimetheus on the pauldron, taking off the surface layer of verdigris and moss that still coated it.

'Interesting,' the former Astral Claw said. 'Are you an Iron Hand? No, still too much flesh to you, not enough augmetics. A Silver Skull? Perhaps not. You didn't spend months consulting the innards of dead animals before deciding whether to fight me.'

Epimetheus said nothing and let his weapon do the talking instead. Three blows aimed for the head, all parried by Blackheart's axe.

'Or are you a Grey Knight? The Hamadrya here tells me that your psychic abilities are off the scale. Nothing it can't keep in check, naturally, but impressive nonetheless.' Blackheart aimed a blow at Epimetheus's midriff. The Grey Knight stepped back allowing the power fist to pass through thin air and lunged with his halberd, narrowly missing the traitor's head.

'Yes, I think that's it. You are a Knight of Titan. A daemon hunter. Be sure to give my regards to Mordrak the next time you see him. I hear he holds quite the torch for me.' Blackheart took a step back from Epimetheus, giving himself more room to swing his axe which met with the adamantium haft of the Grey Knight's weapon.

'What I don't understand is the armour. A suit like that is a Chapter relic and should be worn by a Chapter Master. You are certainly not Kaldor Draigo so why do you wear the suit? What marks you out as being so special?' His axe head clipped Epimetheus's pauldron again. 'But that's not a relic to you, is it? You've always worn it. I can smell the millennia on you, Grey Knight. That same stink of the ages that emanates from Abaddon and his ilk.'

Epimetheus's blows came harder now, his choler up. Had Blackheart really figured all of this out from the state and pattern of his armour or had his familiar read him? If it was powerful enough to suppress his psychic powers, then it was likely able to brush the surface of his mind without him knowing. The Grey Knight was relentless, forcing Huron onto the back foot. The Red Corsair's swipes were purely defensive now, driven back by Epimetheus's onslaught.

'I've hit a nerve haven't I, Grey Knight? Not only are you ancient, but you were one of the first to wear the silver of the Grey Knights. More than that you were one of the–'

Overreaching slightly to block a thrust of the halberd, Epimetheus took full advantage and struck Blackheart on the back of the bicep forcing him to drop his axe. Swinging the pole arm back around low, he smashed the haft against the back of

Huron's calf, dropping the traitor to the floor. In an instant, Epimetheus was over him, halberd tip poised to carve open the Red Corsair's throat.

Blackheart laughed. 'As much as I've enjoyed our very one-sided conversation, it really is time for me to leave. If you hurry, you might be able to make it back to the hangar and steal that ship you were planning to escape on.' He started to dematerialise. 'Until next time, Da–'

Epimetheus slammed the halberd down but it connected only with bulkhead, Huron Blackheart having already escaped. He flicked the weapon up and around towards the rail but the Red Corsair's familiar had gone too. Warning sirens wailed and emergency lighting kicked in pitching the enginarium into a red gloom. He checked the dials on the instrument array and saw that they had all crept up into the orange zone. His duel with Blackheart had wasted valuable time but there was still a chance he could escape the *Lamentation*.

Locking his halberd to his back, Epimetheus sprinted from the enginarium.

826960.M41 / Delver-stronghold 2761/b.
Mount Dhume, Pythos

TAMZARIAN THREW THE tank into reverse, desperate to avoid the mighty axe head bearing down on them, but *Traitor's Bane* had barely moved before the Bloodthirster's weapon hit. The clang of metal on metal reverberated around the command compartment but the hull held out, a long dent in the thick armour – much to K'Cee's chagrin – the only damage.

Without waiting for orders, the gunners let loose with all weapons, peppering the daemon's hide with bolter and las-fire and igniting small fires across its wings and torso with the flamers, but this only enraged it further.

The loaders slammed another hellhammer round into the main cannon but just as it was about to be fired, Strike called out, 'Hold your fire!'

The crew all looked at him dumbfounded.

'We know we can take hits from that thing's axe. How do you think we'd do against one of our own shells?' A murmur of agreement and understanding rippled around the compartment. It did not last long. 'Tamzarian. Full ahead. We're going to ram it.'

'But, chief–' the driver said.

'It's not open to debate, trooper. Open that throttle and put us into that Skulltaker. The rest of you, keep those sponson guns firing.'

Slamming the gear lever out of reverse, Tamzarian pushed forward on the throttle, propelling the tank forwards in a burst of acceleration. Smaller daemons caught under the treads but did nothing to impede the Hellhammer's movement as it sped inexorably towards the Bloodthirster. The daemon did not attempt to get out of the way, did not beat its enormous wings and take to the air but stood its ground. As *Traitor's Bane* crashed into it, the thing was actually smiling.

The sound of impact was too great for K'Cee's noise dampeners to compensate for and as the tank ground onwards with the daemon pinned to the front of its hull, the echo still rang out, painful to all those crewing the Hellhammer. The Bloodthirster raised its axe once again, gripping the side of the tank with its free hand, and brought it down upon the turret, shearing off the searchlight mounted there and leaving a gouge in the armour the twin of its earlier blow.

Before it had a chance to bring it down again, Strike smashed his fist into the button on the armrest of his chair lighting up the outside of *Traitor's Bane* in a nimbus of electrical energy. The Bloodthirster cried out, its body convulsing and shuddering under the massive voltage passing through it. Its skin blistered and smouldered and the hair on its head and face ignited, smoke pouring over the still moving tank.

Without warning, the electrical field cut out.

Strike mashed the button repeatedly but to no avail. The system was as dead as they soon would be. K'Cee tore a cover away from beneath one of the control consoles and slid underneath it on his back, pulling at cables and wires in an attempt to get it working again.

'Slam on,' Strike ordered. 'Dead halt, now!'

Not questioning the colonel, Tamzarian yanked back hard on the brake lever, instantly bringing the tank to a stop from a speed in excess of a hundred kilometres per hour. Thanks to the jokaero's ministrations, none of the occupants of *Traitor's Bane* felt any of the ill effects of such a rapid deceleration. The same could not be said of the Bloodthirster.

It launched from the body of the Hellhammer, velocity

driving it through the air for over fifty metres before it hit the ground and skidded the same distance again, bowling over its smaller daemonic cousins on its way. For several moments, it lay there unmoving, smoke still rising from its form. Just when Strike thought it was vanquished, it stirred, dragging itself to its feet and thrusting its fearsome axe towards the heavens. Bellowing a war cry, it dipped its head and charged, the ground beneath it cracking open with every stride.

'Full ahead. Ram it again,' Strike said calmly.

In time with the sponson weapons opening up, Tamzarian milked the power plant for all it was worth, launching like a rocket towards the daemon. An unstoppable force on its way to meet an immovable object. Its rage focused on the tank speeding towards it, the Bloodthirster shrugged off the bolter and las-shots impacting against it and built up a head of speed. Mere metres from collision, it threw itself into the air. Axe held aloft in both hands, it drove the warpforged blade down, this time splitting the top layer of armour across the front of the hull. Standing astride the turret, the claws of its feet dug deep into the metal to prevent it from being bucked off as it rained blows down upon the Hellhammer.

'Any time now would be good, K'Cee,' Strike said. The jokaero slid out from under the console and gave a frustrated shrug before burying himself in wires and circuitry again.

ACROSS THE BATTLEFIELD, the Imperial infantry and Space Marines were faring little better than the stricken super-heavy tank. The ruined corpses of Mordians and Catachans carpeted the approach to the delver-stronghold, the smaller winged daemons having taken to snatching Guardsmen up before dropping them from a great height onto their comrades below. Those few able to mount any kind of defence found themselves woefully underarmed, lasrifles virtually ineffective against their daemonic foes.

Gabriel and the Deathwing had regrouped in the face of the surprise attack, and though they had been fighting to protect stronghold 2761/b for far longer than their brethren, their defence was as spirited as when it first began. Corralled in a circle, their storm bolters glowed red from overuse, forcing them to alternate between ranged and close combat weapons. Several of their number lay dead, their ancient suits of

Terminator armour split open by claw and fang, and those who fought on all laboured under grievous wounds.

Above them, the Dark Talons struggled to provide effective air support, harried constantly by the winged daemons still spilling forth from the portals. The handful who had attempted strafing runs soon found themselves the target of daemons on the ground and plumes of thick black smoke billowed upwards from numerous crash sites. The only effective aerial response the Dark Angels had been able to mount was Sammael's jetbike and the destructive power of his underslung plasma cannon, but he now found himself having to cope with the attentions of two bloated monstrosities clinging to the body of the *Corvex*.

Azrael and Draigo had distinguished themselves, as would be expected of Space Marines of their position and status, but even they were hard pressed to fend off such a sustained assault. The Grey Knight bled from a head wound, his Larraman's Organ struggling to seal the deep gouge yet still he fought on, the gore-streaked blade of the *Titansword* keeping the ravening horde at bay. Azrael's cloak was nothing but rags and his armour was pierced across his thigh. The right greave was missing altogether, stripped away by daemonic claws, and congealed blood coated his forearm. Like his counterpart, he continued to slay the Neverborn with abandon but the weight of numbers was threatening to consume both Supreme Grand Masters.

THE BLOODTHIRSTER HAMMERED on the hull of *Traitor's Bane*, the rhythmic beating of the axe splitting armour and destroying weapons. Inside, the crew awaited the inevitable while Tamzarian swung the steering controls sharply left and right to throw the unwanted rider from its back. Another heavy blow struck the turret, the rending of the armour as loud as the creature's incessant grunts and cries of fury, quickly followed by another, this time cracking all the way through and sending daylight leaking into the darkened confines.

'Drop the rear hatch, Tamzarian,' Strike called. 'We're going to have to bail out.'

Above him, more light bled in, the Bloodthirster tearing back the torn plates to create an opening big enough for him to get at the nuisance tank's occupants. Fully aware of the futility of the act, Strike drew his laspistol and aimed it at the daemon who was peering down through the aperture. The Bloodthirster snorted derisorily and reached down, unbothered by the pinpricks of las-fire aimed at its head and face. Suddenly, as if scooped away by some invisible force, the daemon was gone, replaced by the report of artillery fire. Lots of artillery fire.

Being careful not to slice himself open on the sharp edges of torn armour plating, Strike lifted himself up and looked out from the ruined turret.

Colonel Strike was not a man given over to open displays of emotion – a lifetime in the 183rd and growing up with nine elder brothers for company saw to that – but what he was greeted by as he emerged from *Traitor's Bane* almost made him weep.

Tanks.

Hundreds upon hundreds of tanks.

826960.M41 / Lamentation. Imperial Fleet, Pandorax System

ALL NOTIONS OF stealth abandoned on his hurried journey back through the supply ship, Epimetheus put two rounds from his bolt pistol through the head of the Red Corsair barring his way.

The plague zombies he had been escorting continued on in ignorance that their overseer had been killed and Epimetheus barged his way through them, causing more than one to spill the container it was carrying, contaminated dry ration packs tumbling to the deck. Unsure of what to do, the mindless slaves looked around aimlessly until they too took bolt rounds to the head, another of Huron's traitors emerging from a corridor and opening fire in the direction of the fleeing Grey Knight. Without breaking stride, Epimetheus turned his torso and fired from the hip, a single shot striking his would-be killer in the throat and felling him. The alarms grew more insistent and a female voice speaking High Gothic intoned a continuous warning, urging anybody left on board to abandon ship.

Rounding the next corner, Epimetheus almost ran into two more Red Corsairs attempting to do exactly that. The first he took down with his bolt pistol, the second with his mind, stabbing out through the immaterium with a psi-lance and lobotomising the Traitor Marine. He hurdled the quivering figure and raced towards the hangar bay. Shoulder barging the doors open, he was instantly assailed by the smell of smoke and the crackle of fire.

The fighter-interceptors that had been berthed here upon his arrival were ablaze, each one at an advanced stage of consumption by the inferno and certainly in no fit state to fly. Around them lay the corpses of cultists who had likely fled here to use the craft to flee the ailing *Lamentation*, skulls ruined by what appeared to be las-fire. At the far end of the landing bay, sitting atop the sleek roof of the shuttle that had delivered Epimetheus here, was the source of this carnage.

'I thought you'd need a ride back,' Shira said cheerfully, sliding down from the top of the shuttle onto the already open boarding ramp.

'And I thought I told you to get out of here,' Epimetheus retorted, his anger barely tempered by relief.

'I never was very good at following orders,' Shira countered, disappearing into the shuttle.

Shaking his head, Epimetheus followed her up the ramp.

A MINUTE LATER, the Inquisition shuttle burst clear of the *Lamentation* and back out among the fleet. The general vox-channels were abuzz with talk of the supply ship that had seemingly appeared from nowhere in their midst not long earlier, and Shira put out a general call informing the Imperial vessels to avoid it along with a précis of the reason why. Hurriedly, admirals and captains ordered their ships away from the doomed craft.

The two closest frigates had just finished their evasive manoeuvres when the *Lamentation*'s sub-warp engines finally reached critical point and the hijacked ship exploded with the brightness of a small sun. Chunks of debris scattered in all directions, many burning up against the shields of the fleet, accompanied by a cosmic shockwave that buffeted the smaller vessels like a storm surge tossing driftwood.

Shira fought with the controls of the shuttle, turbulence threatening to force it into a terminal spin but, with help from the Ordos-funded automated systems, she retained control and kept the craft level until the swell abated. Once she was certain that the threat had passed, she switched most of the systems over to auto and turned to Epimetheus who was stood at the rear of the cockpit, his armoured form too bulky for any of the seats.

'I was listening in on the vox-traffic while I was waiting for you. That Catachan colonel you and Tzula talked about has set up a base at one of the strongholds south-east of Atika. The Dark Angels are operating out of there too. Three Navy fighter wings are among the reconquest force and I'm sure they'd be better off with somebody of my obvious skills flying with them.' She looked at Epimetheus hopefully. 'What do you say? Should I make for there?'

The Grey Knight removed his helmet and looked back at her, staring her dead in the eyes. 'And it has nothing to do with the Heldrake that's been reported attacking patrols and strongholds across the southern peninsula of Pythos Prime? The one with the ragged wing?'

Revenge. That was exactly the reason why Shira wanted to make for the Imperial base and get back into combat. But she had only found out that 'Ragwing', as the vox-operators were calling it, was terrorising Pythos from a broadcast she had picked up less than an hour ago.

'You know, it's so creepy when you do that,' she said, crossing her arms over her chest and gripping her shoulders. 'So? Shall I land us there?'

The Space Marine looked thoughtful for a moment, weighing up the options. 'Put us down in the far north of the continent. There are strongholds there that could use our aid.'

This was something else he had got from reading Shira and the vox-chatter she had absorbed. The Dark Angels were concentrating their forces in the south leaving Imperial Guard regiments to garrison the more remote strongholds.

Sighing, she turned back to the controls and adjusted their course.

826960.M41 / Delver-stronghold 2761/b. Mount Dhume, Pythos

STRIKE CLAMBERED FROM the back of the Hellhammer, following his crew out of the stricken vehicle. K'Cee shambled alongside him, blinking in the daylight after spending so long in the darkened confines of *Traitor's Bane*.

The rumble of tanks was overwhelming, not only the noise but the nauseating bass rumble that heralded their coming. Scores of vehicles were rolling into the landing zone with many more behind them in an armoured column stretching back as far as Strike could see. Baneblades, Shadowswords, Leman Russ, Hellhounds, Vanquishers, Executioners; tanks of almost every pattern currently in service with the Imperial Guard. Most sported the camo green livery of the 183rd, but in amongst their number were grey and plain green hulled tanks – Vostroyan and Cadian judging by their markings.

Daemons fell by the dozen to their cannons, returned to the warp in a crescendo of explosive fury. Some of the smaller ones panicked and turned to flee, running into a wall of fire from the Dark Angels and emboldened Guardsmen advancing down the slope. The greater daemons held no such terror of the Imperial armour and sought to engage them, clawing and rending with daemonic appendages.

A grotesque horned thing, its four arms ending in crab-like claws and vicious spikes, tore at a Hellhound ripping open the crew compartment and slicing at the Cadians inside. The gunner, paralysed with fear, maintained his grip on the trigger of the flamethrower bathing the blessed of the Pleasure God in ignited promethium. The daemon revelled in the pain, moaning in ecstasy as its flesh sizzled and cracked, but its rapture was short-lived. The flames from the engulfed Keeper of Secrets caught the tanks supplying the flamethrower, exploding them in a powerful burst that evaporated the greater daemon and other lesser ones that were caught in the blast radius.

The Bloodthirster that had crippled *Traitor's Bane* was in a bad shape, its left arm and wing shorn away entirely by the tank shell that had flung it from the hull of the Hellhammer. Recovering its axe, it roared in the direction of a Catachan Baneblade, knocking Guardsmen, Space Marines and daemons to the ground with its force. It charged, but got no more than a few metres before more shells struck it, taking its other arm and a good chunk of its torso. It slumped to its knees, bellowing in defiance as more ordnance eviscerated it. Howling its rage to the last, two of the Deathwing moved in and finished the beast off with their blades.

'Find somewhere to hide,' Strike yelled to the jokaero over

the sound of tank fire. K'Cee was a genius with weapons and machines, but combat was not his forte and Strike still wasn't certain how the Dark Angels would react to a xenos in their midst. Picking up discarded lasrifles as he went, K'Cee loped over to a large rock and took up position behind it.

Retrieving a heavy flamer from beneath the body of a dead Mordian, Strike burned a path through the battlefield, fighting his way to the two Chapter Masters still battling alongside one another. The way they fought was like warfare made art, each stroke of their swords measured and precise, painting the ground around them in ichor and gore.

'It seems you've found your tanks, colonel,' Azrael said, ramming the tip of the *Sword of Secrets* into a daemon's gullet. 'Or rather your tanks found you.'

'These aren't just mine,' Strike replied, frying a pink multi-limbed monstrosity with a quick burst of flame. 'Half the armour on Pythos must be rolling in here.'

The advancing column showed no sign of ending. The landing zone was already filling up and the approach to stronghold 2761/b was lined with tanks driving the daemons caught before them onto the guns of the waiting Dark Angels, Mordians and Catachans. Above them, another rent opened in the sky, spewing forth more of the Neverborn.

'Our reinforcements are finite, but I fear the enemy's are not,' Draigo said. A diseased, taloned hand reached for Azrael's face, but the Grey Knight separated it from its owner's arm before it could do any damage. The next swing of his blade opened the daemon's guts, maggots spilling to the ground in a sickening shower. 'If we cannot get those portals closed, all this will come to naught.'

High above the battle, the four sorcerers continued to weave their debased magicks under the watchful eye of Abaddon. If the recent turn of events had given him cause for concern, he wasn't showing it.

'Leave it to me,' Strike said, breaking off from the two Space Marines and clearing a route with a wide sweep of his flamer. Giving short bursts of his weapon to keep the horde at bay, he crossed the hundred metres or so between him and the Baneblade that had accounted for the Bloodthirster, using the tanks advancing on the delver-stronghold as cover. Other Imperial Guardsmen had the same idea and, behind each one, he found Catachans pleased to see that their leader was not only alive but in the thick of the action.

Reaching the slow moving Baneblade, he clambered up the skirt, his feet finding purchase on the huge rivets holding it in place, and crawled over to the turret. Heaving himself up to the hatch, he banged on it with the butt of his flamer. Almost instantly, the hatch popped open and a familiar face greeted him along with the business end of a laspistol.

'Good to see you, Brigstone,' Strike said dryly. 'I was beginning to think you were going to sit out this entire war.'

'Sorry about that, chief,' Brigstone replied, helping the colonel down into the tank. 'We couldn't get the damn voxes to work. I think we're being jammed or something. Been sat twiddling our thumbs on an island in the middle of the ocean for months.'

'What made you come back now?' asked Strike. The interior of the Baneblade was almost identical to that of *Traitor's Bane*, minus K'Cee's enhancements.

'We saw drop pods coming down on Pythos Prime and figured it for a liberation force or more enemy troops. Either way, with dry season starting it meant we could get the tanks through the jungle. Hooked up with a couple of mechanised brigades we ran into on the way down. Said something big was going down at Mount Dhume and they were headed here to help out.'

'Well, you took your time about it.' Strike's tone relaxed.

'Would have been here sooner, chief, but we ran into a bunch of heroes up the road. Thought we were enemy war machines and decided to ambush us. Fortunately, they only took out a few track links but it cost us a good few hours getting them repaired.'

'How many times do I have to apologise for that, commander?' said a woman from out of the darkened rear of the command compartment. She stepped forward and Strike saw that it was Tzula. Filthy and sporting a few more scars than the last time he had seen her but most definitely the junior interrogator. 'Hello, colonel. Still managing to find trouble, I see.'

'Likewise,' Strike said with a grin. 'Are you alone?' he added, his face becoming grim.

Tzula's features hardened. 'Huron Blackheart infiltrated a

supply ship in the Imperial fleet and was planning to contaminate our supply line. He had a coven of sorcerers on board masking its presence and maintaining the conditions on Pythos for the daemons to exist in realspace. I'd guess from the rate they're dying out there that Epimetheus's mission to destroy it was a success.'

'Did he…?' Strike asked.

There was a long pause before Tzula answered. 'I don't know. He certainly thought it was a one-way mission.'

Strike nodded solemnly. 'Well, if he did sacrifice himself, let's make it count for something.' He turned to the commander. 'Brigstone, I have a new target for your guns.'

FROM HIS VANTAGE point high up on the mountain approach, Abaddon looked on as his army of daemons was taken apart.

For kilometres in every direction, corporeal metal and daemon flesh clashed, artillery and armour pitched against tooth and claw. It was a sight he had beheld a thousand times before on a thousand battlefields across thousands of years, but very rarely had he presided over a defeat. The battle was still underway and the price exacted from the lackeys of the False Emperor was high, but millennia of experience cried out to him that the day was lost.

Beside him the sorcerer willing the kine shield into being faltered, the huge exertion too much for a body already wracked by the ravages of the warp. Unnatural smoke poured from the gaps in his ill-fitting armour and issued forth from his mouth, nose and tear ducts. Convulsing maniacally, the moisture in his body fled, his skin cracking and wrinkling like time speeded up. The warp barrier he had erected flickered and died, and his desiccated husk tumbled from the outcrop and turned to dust as it hit the hard ground below.

The other sorcerers looked at each other uneasily but continued with their ritual, not wishing to anger the Warmaster to whom their master had been eager to loan their services.

From the heart of the melee, Abaddon saw the turret of a tank traverse, the super-heavy taking aim in his direction. The commander of the Black Legion took this as his cue to leave, pulling a teleportation activator from a pouch at his waist and slipping his thumb over the trigger stud. This battle was indeed forfeit, and likely it would turn the course of the war for Pythos, leading to the ultimate defeat for the forces of Chaos.

It mattered not to Abaddon. To him the war was merely a distraction that would lead him to a far greater prize.

As the shell ejected from the end of the Baneblade's barrel in a burst of muzzle flare, he stabbed his armoured thumb down on the activator. By the time the round hit, killing the trio of sorcerers and turning the promontory into a shower of debris, Abaddon the Despoiler was already gone.

THE BATTLE FOR Stronghold 2761/b would last another thirty-nine hours. Azrael and Draigo fought it to the very last second.

Starved of fresh daemons to bolster their forces, those stranded on the material side of the veil became desperate and attempted to break through the rolling blockade of armour moving towards them. Wave after wave of the Neverborn fell to the Imperial guns but their kindred clambered over the corpses of the fallen, tearing and rending at the wall of steel. Free of the monsters clinging to their hulls, the Thunder-hawks and Valkyries took to the air, picking off the daemons from above. The vital role they played in the battle saved many a tank crew, but the losses of Imperial armour were so immense that, a decade later, when an Adeptus Mechanicus team arrived to salvage the wrecks, casualties were measured in tonnage rather than numbers.

The enemy's forces and spirits broken, the battle devolved into smaller conflicts. A pack of Tzeentchian lesser daemons broke through to the minehead and massacred the Mordians taking cover there. Balthasar and two of his Deathwing brethren led a combined force of Catachans and Mordians into the depths of the stronghold. By first light the next morning, not a single daemon still persisted in the darkness.

With air superiority re-established, Sammael hunted down any daemon foolhardy enough to venture off the ground. The deadly plasma cannon fitted to the undercarriage of *Corvex* was fired so often that it overheated and melted down within hours, necessitating a refit from the Dark Angels Techmarines once the jetbike was back on board the Rock. It would be six days before the weapon had cooled sufficiently to be worked upon.

Bereft of his mobile command centre, Strike, along with

Tzula and Magrick's adhoc squad, scoured the battlefield, targeting those daemons too nimble for the guns of the tanks. A new honour was added to the 183rd's banner in the days following the battle commemorating their bravery and sacrifice. The colonel's pride was only dented by the loss of Magrick who survived the Battle of Stronghold 2761/b but died of horrific injuries she suffered taking down a daemonette single-handed. Her fang would be ever present at Strike's hip until the war for Pythos was over.

The two Supreme Grand Masters never drifted more than a few metres apart, matching each other kill for kill. Ideologically poles apart, in the simple matter of slaying the foes of the Imperium, they were entirely attuned. The Imperial Guardsmen who were privileged enough to witness them fight that day would carry with them stories from war zone to war zone of the two killing machines who fought for nigh on a day and a half without pause, putting paid to creatures from beyond nightmare without fear nor mercy.

The last daemon to fall to their blades was an enormous bloated thing, its putrid form generating a miasma of stench and filth that clogged the filters of Space Marine power armour and stripped flesh from bone. With the Imperial Guard ineffective against such a foe, the entirety of the remaining Dark Angels and Draigo engaged the thing for hours, constantly hampered by the smaller daemons and plague golems that separated from the main bulk of the Great Unclean One. Its eventual demise came when a trio of Nephilim jetfighters unleashed their full complement of blacksword missiles, felling the titanic daemon. The two Chapter Masters struck simultaneously, the Grey Knight piercing its chest, the Dark Angel driving the *Sword of Secrets* through its skull. Leaping clear of the flailing horror, it played out its death throes as it melted into a bubbling pool of bubonic sludge, permanently staining the slopes of Mount Dhume.

With all foes vanquished, the Space Marines marched from the field of battle, the veneration and praise of their Imperial Guard allies sounding out across the Pythosian night.

'YOUR STUBBORNNESS ALMOST cost us this war. It is high time you saw reason and ordered an assault on Atika,' Draigo said, his voice loud enough to be heard by the Deathwing sitting on board *Roar of Vengeance* waiting for it to take off.

Any common ground the two Supreme Grand Masters had found, any bond they had formed, had been left on the battlefield. Alongside him at the foot of the Thunderhawk's boarding ramp, Azrael bristled.

'Next time we'll be ready for that tactic if Abaddon employs it again. It's high time the Grey Knights saw action on Pythos instead of kicking their heels up in the fleet.' That was the closest to an admission that the Dark Angel was wrong Draigo would get, even if Azrael had twisted it to cast the Grey Knights in a poor light.

'And next time he'll strike at a more remote stronghold inaccessible to the Imperial Guard tanks and negate that advantage. We have to stop being reactive and take the battle to Abaddon, starting with Atika.'

'I brought my Chapter here in response to your call for aid to save the population of Pythos, not condemn it. While there's still a chance that the citizens of Atika still live, I shall not risk a direct assault.'

'That's not an issue, my lord,' said a voice unfamiliar to the Dark Angel. Strike and a dark-skinned woman dressed in Catachan fatigues, vest and bandana approached the idling Thunderhawk. 'The entire population of Atika is dead. Or as good as,' Tzula finished.

'It is good to see you again, Junior Interrogator Digriiz. I had feared you dead,' Draigo said. 'My condolences on the loss of your master. He was a fine man and a great servant of the Golden Throne.'

'Thank you, Lord Draigo. It is my wish to honour his memory by completing his mission here and destroying the Damnation Cache,' Tzula said, bowing slightly.

'And you have the... weapon, I trust?' Draigo said.

Azrael cast a sideways look at the Grey Knight but was not drawn to enquire further.

'I have, Lord Draigo,' Tzula said, tucking her hand into the waistband of her fatigues and surreptitiously pointing to the hilt of the athame with her thumb.

'This reunion is all very touching but if the girl has intelligence regarding the state of Atika then I wish to hear it,' Azrael snapped.

'As you wish, my lord,' Tzula said, bowing to the Dark

Angel before explaining what she had discovered in Atika. She spared none of the detail regarding the population's fate, the plot to contaminate the Imperial rations and the coven hidden among the fleet. When it came to Epimetheus, she said as little as possible.

When she had finished, Azrael simply regarded her with a penetrating stare. 'And this mysterious Space Marine? This Epimetheus. Where is he now?'

Tzula was about to say that she believed him to have perished in the operation to destroy the hijacked supply ship when Draigo intervened. 'That's hardly the issue here, Azrael. The souls of Atika are lost. Even worse, they have been ensorcelled and enslaved to help the Archenemy's cause. There is nothing to hold us back. We *must* attack.'

Azrael looked to Strike who nodded his agreement with the Grey Knight's assessment. The commander of the Dark Angels turned and stamped off up the ramp. When he reached the threshold of the troop compartment, he halted and spun on his heel.

'Very well, but we do this on my terms and at a time of my choosing. Have your Brotherhood be ready for the assault on the capital as soon as I issue the command. You and your men too, colonel,' he said before the ramp retracted and the hatch slammed shut behind him.

As *Roar of Vengeance* sped its way skywards back towards the Rock awaiting it in orbit, Draigo and Strike were already issuing the orders that would ensure Atika burned.

INTERLUDE

826960.M41 / No Redemption. Geo-stationary orbit around Kylix, Pandorax System

HURON BLACKHEART MATERIALISED in the middle of the *No Redemption*'s bridge, a rush of displaced air and crackle of warp energies presaging his arrival. The Hamadrya slunk between his legs, its eyes glowing in the darkened confines of the Murder-class cruiser's command deck. Several of the Red Corsairs present acknowledged Huron's arrival but continued about their business without ceremony.

A figure in battle-damaged Terminator armour, patches of black and yellow still evident beneath the red betraying his former allegiance to the Scythes of the Emperor, approached him. 'Shall we prepare the fleet to make for Pythos, Lord Blackheart?'

'Not yet, Remulus, though the way the war for the planet is turning, we will be needed there before long.' The Hamadrya melted into the darkness as Huron strode forward, casually tossing his axe to the deck. From the shadows twisted, mutated things emerged squabbling over which one of them would transport the precious thing to their master's arming chamber. 'I need to speak with Abaddon immediately.'

'As you wish,' Remulus said signalling to a human member of the crew to carry out their master's bidding.

Blackheart addressed some of the other renegade Space

Marines, former Astral Claws and his most trusted lieutenants, but trust was a commodity rarely traded among their number. He briefly appraised them of the fate of the *Lamentation* and issued orders for the next phase of the Red Corsairs involvement in the Pythos campaign while they brought him up to speed with the intelligence they had been receiving from the death world. After several minutes, Remulus interrupted them.

'We've been able to reach the Warmaster, Lord Blackheart.'

Huron dismissed his captains and followed the Terminator over to a flickering hololith, a diminutive facsimile of Abaddon being broadcast from the surface of Pythos.

'If you've only contacted me to gloat about the failure of the ambush at the mine, I shall wipe you and your renegades from the face of the galaxy with such totality that even the footnotes of history books will neglect to remember you, usurper.' The threat in Abaddon's voice was backed by a confidence that left none who heard his words in any doubt of their veracity.

'Far from it, Abaddon. Considering that you have no interest whatsoever in holding the planet, the...' Huron paused, knowing that if he selected his next few words incorrectly he would likely be dooming the Red Corsairs to a blood feud with the Black Legion that they were not yet in a position to contest. '...limited success of your operation has probably extended the war on Pythos, giving you longer to find that what you seek. Or is *who* you seek more accurate, Warmaster?'

Abaddon smirked, a grin that had condemned a thousand worlds crossing his lips. 'And what would you know of it, pirate?'

'More than you think. I've found what you're looking for and left him undamaged for you.' It was Blackheart's turn to grin now. 'Better yet, I know how you can capture him.'

The hololith flickered, the image of Abaddon briefly cutting in and out. When it resolved again, the Warmaster's body language had relaxed, his tone conciliatory.

'Tell me more, Blackheart.'

PART FIVE

CHAPTER
FOURTEEN

085961.M41 / Atika Hive, Pythos

GRIGOR MITTEL SET down the lump of ore he had carried up from the bowels of Atika and turned to repeat the journey. He did not know, nor care, how many times he had done this before, nor did he have any concept of how long he had been doing it for. Under the possession of the plague zombie virus, he merely existed, held somewhere between life and death to carry out the whim of others.

His body had deteriorated during his long months of servitude, but he had not noticed. Fingers were missing on both hands, the skin on his chest had worn through to bone and the flesh of his cheek was torn, a ragged hole through which his yellowed teeth poked. His clothes, like those of the others who laboured under the curse, were threadbare and frayed, leaving him almost naked, but Grigor did not feel the cold deep down in the mine tunnels. He could no longer feel anything at all.

Something brushed past his arm causing him to stop. He looked to his side to see a woman, though Grigor could no longer distinguish gender just as he had no gauge of age or race, shamble past him. He looked at her, for a fleeting moment experiencing a rush of recognition. She too stopped, turning to meet Grigor's gaze. Their eyes locked, dead stares regarding each other vacantly until, barely perceptibly, the corner of her mouth turned upwards a fraction. It was a smile, but Grigor could no longer recognise it as such.

The moment was cruelly ended by the lash of the overseer's whip, gouging flesh from Grigor's back and snaking out to rip the woman's hand from the end of her arm. Grigor started to move again, not out of fear or pain but from some base imperative that told him the whip meant move. He stepped over the woman's severed hand, looking down as he did so to see a slim band of metal wrapped around one of the fingers.

Grigor no longer knew that the ring signified the union between two lovers, and he no longer knew that it was he who was wed to the woman, or that her name was Katalina. He could not remember that they had met three years ago when she had joined his mining team along with a new influx of settlers from Gaea. He could not remember that the governor himself had presided over their union or that it had taken place on the Feast of the Emperor's Ascension, revellers greeting them in the streets of the hive city and wishing them well for the future. He could not remember that in the weeks before Pythos fell they were talking of starting a family and of moving to Gaea where they would work on Katalina's family farm to raise enough money to build a home of their own.

He could not remember any of this because Abaddon's invasion had robbed him of everything he held dear, just as it had robbed an entire world of its liberty and its population of their humanity.

He heard another noise now, louder than the whip, and stopped. Everybody stopped. If he still had the faculty for description, he might have described the sound as a high-pitched whine but he did not so to Grigor it was only noise. He looked to the woman, some strange urge compelling him to do so, and she looked back. The noise became something different and he took his eyes off the woman not knowing it would be the last time he would ever see her.

When he looked up, the sky was on fire.

* * *

FROM ORBIT, THE missiles rained down upon the capital of Pythos. The hive city that had stood for over five thousand years was reduced to rubble and ash in a matter of minutes. In the wake of Atika's destruction, the fleet turned its attention to the surrounding swampland and jungle, burning away the forestation and evaporating the wetlands, leaving behind a glassaic plain that tanks could use to reach the ruins of the city now that the rains had come again.

Azrael had been true to his word about assaulting the city, but stuck just as rigidly to his assertion that it would be on his terms. Despite repeated petitions from Draigo, the Supreme Grand Master of the Dark Angels had continued to stall, prosecuting operations against enemy supply lines and concentrations of war machines before committing to the attack on Atika.

Strike was torn. Draigo's aggressive stance had a lot of merit and it would have potentially neutered the flow of daemons from the Damnation Cache a lot sooner, but Azrael's approach had virtually eliminated the threat of allies coming to the aid of the invaders now trapped in the tunnels beneath the rubble. It had also allowed fresh Imperial Guard regiments to make their way to the Pandorax System, along with elements of Legio Crucius who had deigned to send a complement of Warhound Titans to aid in the reconquest of Pythos. On a purely selfish note, Strike had been glad of the extra time to prepare for the battle as it had given K'Cee time to work on *Traitor's Bane* and get the mobile fortress operational again.

Steam still rising from the incinerated ground, the Hell-hammer rolled along at the head of an armoured column the likes of which had been very rarely assembled since the days of the Horus Heresy. An entire Cadian armoured division, supported by two mobile artillery divisions followed behind the remaining Catachan tanks, along with a similar sized detachment of Vostroyan tanks. Interspersed among the countless Leman Russ variants were the pride of any armoured regiment, the super-heavy tanks. Many sported the colours of the Cadians, Catachans and Vostroyans but by far the bulk of them were in the livery of the First Palladius armoured company, nicknamed 'The Thunderers' on account of their exclusive deployment of Baneblades, Doomhammers and other gargantuan armoured vehicles. The only things larger on the battlefield were the Warhounds striding along at their flanks.

In the skies over the tanks and walkers, high above the low-lying fog from the cooking off of the swamps, flew close to a thousand Valkyries ready to deliver infantry directly to the frontline. At a higher altitude soared the Thunderbolts and Lightnings of the Imperial Navy wings alongside the Dark Talons and Nephilims of the Dark Angels. Their brothers waited out in space ready to drop from the skies when the time was right but the Chapter's entire complement of fighter-interceptors and bombers deployed in support of the Imperial Guard.

From the command seat of *Traitor's Bane*, Strike listened in on the vox-traffic passing between the regiments, formations being coordinated and reports coming in from forward scouts. With visibility so poor, they were reliant on instruments and the eyes in the sky for navigation, but occasionally agitated messages were exchanged between crews who had inadvertently collided with one another. They were lucky they could communicate at all. Another benefit to Azrael's delay had been the recapture of Hollowfal and an end to the enemy jamming Imperial signals.

An insistent beeping sounded from the vox denoting a priority one incoming transmission. Strike killed all other communications and switched channels.

'Are your tanks in position, colonel?' came Azrael's voice, crackling over the ancient vox-unit.

Strike looked to one of the auspex operators who gave him the thumbs up.

'Yes, Lord Azrael. We'll be able to begin bombardment as soon as you are on the ground.'

'Very well. Commencing deployment now.'

The Battle for Atika had finally begun.

BALTHASAR SWUNG HIS blade, paring open the belly of the daemon leaping at him. The thing crashed to the ground with a wail, fading from reality before it had a chance to bleed out. He slashed again, taking the heads from a pair of pale svelte things with malformed claws in place of hands. They too disappeared, leaving no trace of a corpse behind.

'Save some for the rest of us, brother,' said Gabriel, fighting at Balthasar's shoulder. The company master of the Death-wing blazed away with his storm bolter, allowing the younger Dark Angel to pick off any Neverborn that got too close to them.

'Why don't you tell that to them? There'll be no glory left for anybody else at the rate they're eliminating these things.' Dragging his blade through the torso of a minor plague daemon, he finished the motion by directing his sword tip to a group fighting several hundred metres away.

Resplendent in their pristine silver Terminator armour, a squad of Grey Knights Paladins put the enemy to rout with their witchflame. Balls of white-hot fire launched from their fists, like heavy flamers given human form, but the devastation wrought by their psychic assault was far in excess of any mere weapon. Those caught by the full blast of the attack were incinerated instantly, ghoulish white outlines of their forms forever etched upon the ground. Even those on the edge of the blast area died quickly, the smallest flame soon spreading and engulfing the larger daemons arrayed against the Imperial forces.

'If only we'd had a few of those at 2761/b then perhaps our losses would not have been so great,' Gabriel said, taking aim at a daemon before blowing it apart with two well-placed shots.

'That sounds like sedition to me, master. Questioning the tactics of the Supreme Grand Master,' Balthasar teased. While their structure followed the Codex Astartes almost to the letter – ten companies, First Company granted Terminator armour, Tenth Company being the Scouts – the Dark Angels operated unlike any other Space Marine Chapter. Their First Company – the Deathwing – went to war exclusively in their Terminator armour and it was always painted bone white in contrast to the green and black armour of their brethren in the other nine companies. They were also privy to the Chapter's darkest secrets and, among others of the Deathwing at least, were able to share their thoughts on all matters openly.

'Lord Azrael and I have already had a full and frank debate about the merits of his tactics that day, Balthasar. Each battle, be it a victory, loss or grinding stalemate, teaches us all something, even the Supreme Grand Master. The day we stop learning is the day the Apothecaries apply the reductor to our corpses.'

Gabriel ceased firing, waiting for his weapon to reload. One of the pink, horned abominations saw an opportunity and leapt at the Dark Angel from his blindside. Gabriel brought his weapon up in a vicious arc, snapping the thing's neck with a sickening crack. 'Besides, I think you're jealous.' His weapon barked to life.

'Jealous? In what way?' Balthasar asked.

'I've seen the way you revel in the kill, the controlled fury with which you strike down our foes. You live for battle, Balthasar, and constantly seek better ways to wage war. Your body is already a finely-tuned killing machine, but you know how much more you could achieve if your mind was as potent a weapon too.'

Balthasar said nothing, instead bringing his own storm bolter to bear and ploughing through a throng of daemons, chopping away with the sword in his other hand leaving Gabriel wondering whether he had hit a nerve.

IN THE TROOP hold of the Stormraven, Tzula watched the pict feed of the battle taking place on the ground below.

Hundreds of thousands of Imperial Guard marched across the Plain of Glass – as many of the regiments had named it – towards the ring of steel formed by the Imperial armour. With the tank bombardment as cover, they would soon move up to relieve the Dark Angels and Grey Knights forces already engaged with the daemonic horde, allowing the Space Marines to breach the tunnels beneath Atika and take the war underground. The entirety of the Dark Angels Tenth Company had infiltrated the tunnels over a week ago and, accompanied by Castellan Crowe of the Grey Knights and a squad of Purifiers, had sealed off all routes from the Atikan underhive to the surface bar one. The largest tunnel had been left open to allow the Titans and tanks access to the subterranean battlefield, the big guns needed to handle whatever horrors the enemy kept lurking in the deeps.

Thoughts of the underhive led Tzula to wondering about Epimetheus and Shira, and what fate had befallen them. The Grey Knight never had any intention of joining up with the main reconquest force for reasons Tzula believed she had figured out, but Shira's failure to reappear was a puzzle to her. The Heldrake she was seemingly obsessed with had been spotted all over Pythos, and the junior interrogator thought the pilot would have jumped at the chance to get in the cockpit of a Navy flyer and renew the duel. She had a suspicion they had not been idle. Uncorroborated reports had been coming into Imperial Command for months of a mysterious silver ghost coming to the aid of besieged strongholds, appearing as if from nowhere – or, as one report dismissed on account of the eyewitness's lack of sobriety put it, 'out of an invisible spaceship' – at the eleventh hour and helping to fight off the attackers.

'To arms, brothers,' said Draigo, taking his eyes from the same pict screen Tzula had been watching and locking his helmet in place. The other five Grey Knights seated in the troop compartment did likewise. Tzula fastened the last two clasps on her new bodyglove and checked over her plasma pistol, augmetic arm whirring gently as she did so.

'Lord Azrael has kept you in orbit and out of the battle thus far for fear you would shame his Dark Angels.' Draigo stood up. The other Grey Knights did likewise. The timbre of the Stormraven's engines altered as it commenced its vertical descent. Still several metres from the ground, the rear hatch descended and Draigo moved to the rear of the hold. 'Let us now make his fear manifest,' he said, leaping from the back of the hovering troop carrier.

The five other silver-clad Terminators followed him down, each one slamming onto the superheated ground below, shattering it like porcelain. Tzula was the last one out of the Stormraven, waiting for it to get closer to the ground before leaping out and landing in a forward roll, pistol raised. She instantly squeezed off a shot, making ruin of a crimson doglike creature waiting to pounce upon her. Gunfire from behind her cut down the rest of its pack and she turned to see Imperial Guardsmen charging through the gaps in the tank formation. She was unable to suppress a smile when she saw it was the Catachans at the head of the charge, their jungle-green attire taking on an orange hue in the light of airbursts and cannon flare from the artillery.

In a manoeuvre that looked like it had been choreographed, the Dark Angels and Grey Knights disengaged from their daemonic foes and pushed on towards the only remaining entrance to Atika while their human allies vacated the gap they had left. The ring of steel broke apart, scores of Leman Russes moving in to supply armoured support to the Guardsmen while the super-heavies rolled in after the Space Marines, mowing down any foe too slow to get out of their way. The artillery continued to shell the area leading to the underhive, clearing the path of daemons for the Space Marines to pass unhindered. Missile batteries launched volley after volley at the airborne horrors, any they missed being picked off by circling Valkyries and Thunderhawks.

Behind Imperial lines, more shuttles and troop landers deposited Guardsmen onto Pythos before speeding back up to the fleet to repeat the process. Where Catachans, Cadians and Vostroyans already engaged the forces of Abaddon, troops from Krieg and yet more Cadians swelled their ranks. For the first time since the war for Pythos began, the forces of the Imperium outnumbered those of Chaos.

It would not last long.

Struggling to keep up with the massive strides being taken by Draigo and his brothers, Tzula had to break into a sprint, swinging her pistol from side to side, jetting plasma at anything unnatural that stepped within range. The Space Marine vanguard had already reached the vast opening that led down to the mines beneath the former hive city and were engaged in fierce combat with the entities still emerging from the depths. Azrael was at the head of the Dark Angels and quickly renewed his battle bond with his Grey Knights opposite number, the two Supreme Grand Masters picking up from where they had left off at 2761/b and throwing themselves into the fray with ruthless abandon.

The surge of daemons from below was relentless, and though the combined Chapters butchered many, it was not without cost. A Knight of the Flame found himself cut off from the rest of his squad, surrounded by bloodthirsty canids not unlike those Tzula had already encountered. His psychic abilities having no effect on the Khornate hounds, both his flesh and soul were devoured within their fangs before his brothers struck the beasts down in their vengeance.

Nearby, a Dark Angels sergeant in the black of the Ravenwing succumbed to the rampage of a daemonic chariot, its hideous rider chanting from a blasphemous tome atop a spiked disc drawn along by a pair of noisome serpents on a wave of warpflame. Trying to outrun the infernal vehicle on his bike, the chariot drew alongside, slamming into the Dark Angel and bucking him from the saddle. Before he had a chance to react and lift himself from the ground, the two screaming horrors bathed him in flame, turning him to nothing more than a pile of ash in an instant. Too fast for the Ravenwing, his murderer could not outrun the tank shell that blew it to pieces while the Space Marine's corpse was still afire.

New combatants started to flood the battlefield from the tunnel mouth, a trickle that quickly became a surge. Moving slowly, their collective consciousness under the sway of a higher power, plague zombies joined the throng of daemons, the undead soon outnumbering the living. Whereas the thralls Tzula had encountered many months earlier in Atika had been benign, these possessed a malevolent aspect, clawing and biting at anybody who got in their way. Individually, it was a simple matter to avoid them, but packed together tightly in packs it was almost impossible to escape their clutches. Thousands of Guardsmen fell to the horde only to be reborn immediately as mindless soldiers intent on killing their former comrades. Grey Knights and Dark Angels too went down under the weight of numbers, armour torn away to allow the plague zombies access to the flesh beneath. Mercifully, the genetic enhancements that protected Space Marines from disease in life continued to function in death, preventing their corpses from reanimating and turning on their brothers.

The tanks turned their guns on the largest concentrations of undead, a ceaseless fusillade ripping open the walking cadavers and tearing up craters into which the mindless slaves fell, clambering over each other in their attempts to scale the sheer walls. Those not killed, who lost limbs or other body parts from the blast, simply carried onwards, crawling in some cases where legs had been blown off. The only ones that stayed down were those who had suffered cranial injuries or lost their head altogether.

In the space of a few minutes, hundreds of thousands of plague zombies spilled out of Atika, the flow showing no signs of abating. In among them, larger figures emerged, firing upon the loyal Space Marines from behind a wall of the undead. Seemingly unnoticed in the melee, the Plague Marines killed almost at will, the little return fire they did receive soaked up by their shields of rotting flesh. But Tzula noticed them, just like she noticed the taller shape at the rear of the horde, giving out orders and guiding his slave army.

Casually shooting the head from a plague zombie, Tzula set off in the direction of her new target, muttering a single word under her breath.

'Corpulax.'

085961.M41 / Piraeus Stronghold. 4,218 kilometres north-east of Atika, Pythos

SHIRA SQUEEZED OFF her final shot, the laspistol power pack dying along with the cultist she had aimed for. His body slumped to the ground alongside the seven others she had picked off from her vantage point on a ledge several metres above the tunnel. She ejected the spent cell and slammed another one home before dropping to the ground in search of new targets.

Further down the mineshaft, Epimetheus finished his duel with the final Black Legionnaire, his force halberd bifurcating the Traitor Marine with a wail of sparking energy and the wrench of tearing bone. The two halves of the ruined body had not ceased twitching by the time Shira caught up to the Grey Knight.

'Is that the last of them?' Shira asked, swinging a boot at part of the corpse and kicking it derisorily.

Epimetheus knelt down and rifled through the pouches and containers strapped around the dead Traitor Marine's waist. He pulled out a couple of grenades and a handful of bolt shells, adding them to his own kit. 'That's the last of anyone. I'm not detecting any signs of life, no presences registering in the warp.'

Confirmation, not that either of them needed it, came when they entered the next cavern and found the hold's defenders dead at the mine face, a desperate last stand that had come to nothing. The bodies of hundreds of Cadian Whiteshields, boy soldiers pressed into the service of the Emperor, lay intermingled with those of the miners, few of them any older than the Imperial Guardsmen they had died alongside. They had given a good account of themselves – the lifeless forms of scores of dead cultists attested to that – but their defence had been doomed to failure because of the presence of Traitor Astartes among the aggressors.

It was an all too familiar sight to Shira and the Grey Knight. For months they had been operating across the north of Pythos's main continent, responding to distress calls from Imperial Guard and militia units coming under attack from enemy raiding parties. Rather than concentrate his forces on one coordinated offensive against a single delver-stronghold, Abaddon had instead opted to launch smaller assaults against clusters of mines, synchronised so that the Imperial forces garrisoned there could not come to each other's aid. The strategy had been ruthlessly effective. For every stronghold Epimetheus and Shira made it to in time to aid its defence, two more would be lost. With the battle to retake Atika underway, there would be no reinforcements to bolster the Imperial Guard, and despite the Warmaster teetering on the verge of defeat in the war for Pythos, he could still strike with impunity in the north.

Grimly, Shira and Epimetheus set about piling up the bodies ready for burning.

'So what are you going to do when all this is over?'

Shira's question caught the Grey Knight off-guard. Her chatter was ordinarily banal, often centred around asking him if he had met specific figures from the age of the Horus Heresy, or about Space Marine bodily functions or lack thereof.

'I mean, when the war is over,' she added, hacking her way through the thick undergrowth as they made their way back to the shuttle.

'If all that you and Tzula have told me is true, the war is never over. The Imperium of Man is in a constant state of conflict. There will always be battles to fight,' Epimetheus answered, hoping that would be the end of it.

'That's not really an answer,' she smirked. 'Do you plan on rejoining your Chapter or are we going to keep our double act together? The Silver Ghost and his daring sidekick, flying around the galaxy coming to the aid of those who need it most.'

Epimetheus reached out in front of them, grasping a low-hanging bough that was barring their way and tore it from the trunk of the mighty redwood as if it were nothing more than a twig. 'It is no longer my Chapter. In some regards very little has changed, but the Imperium has moved on in the last ten thousand years. I am a man out of time, a throwback. I probably have more in common with Abaddon than I do the modern Space Marine.' He stared off into the distance, almost wistful. 'When the enemy is driven from the face of Pythos and the Damnation Cache has been resealed, I plan to leave here and make my way into the Maelstrom. I shall take the fight to the enemy and do what I was bred to do.'

'I knew you'd keep our little team-up going,' Shira said, coming to the shuttle they had left cloaked beneath a gargantuan tree, its trunk as wide as the flyer was long.

Epimetheus punched in a string of numbers onto a barely visible external keypad. The camouflage faded away to reveal the sleek black hull of the craft, its side hatch slowly dropping to the ground to form a boarding ramp. Shira made to climb up it but Epimetheus halted her. 'It is something I must do alone. The Maelstrom is a deadly place littered with daemon worlds that make Pythos look like a pleasure planet. Without the correct psychic wards in place, its denizens would tear your soul apart as easily as cast eyes upon you. A simple laspistol would be no defence there.'

Shira looked as if she had just taken a punch to the gut. Though he could read minds, reading people had never been one of Epimetheus's strengths. In the months he had spent around the pilot, he had learned one way of dealing with her, however.

'But you are a very good shot with it,' he said. 'Almost as good as you are a pilot.'

'Yeah? Well, you're a lousy liar,' Shira sniggered climbing up the boarding ramp. 'And besides, don't think you'll be rid of me anytime soon. There's still plenty of war left on Pythos.'

Her point was punctuated by the crackle of the vox.

'This is Lieutenant Korbienev of the Cadian 99th. Murranz Hold is under attack. I repeat Murranz Hold is–' The panicked voice drowned in a sea of static.

'See?' Shira said, strapping herself into the pilot's seat.

Five minutes later, the Silver Ghost was airborne, racing south to do what he was bred to do.

* * *

085961.M41 / Atika Hive, Pythos

TZULA WAS NOT the only one to notice Corpulax's presence on the battlefield.

Carving through the plague zombie horde, one of the Deathwing had also spotted the Plague Lord and was making his way to engage him. In their ivory Terminator armour, the Dark Angels First Company all looked alike, except for those few who forewent helmets. Tzula had been trained by some of the finest analytical and observational minds at the Ordo Malleus's disposal and, being more than a casual observer, had noted the positioning of the three purity seals running along his left greave on the sole occasion she had met this particular Dark Angel. His name was Balthasar. Not that it mattered. She would reach Corpulax first and avenge Dinalt's death.

Coming up on the traitor's blindside, she took aim with the plasma pistol and pulled the trigger while still several metres away. Instead of taking his head off as she'd intended, her shot struck two of the ever-shifting mass of thralls who got in the way.

Corpulax turned to find the source of the attack. When his eyes found Tzula amongst the press of undead flesh, he gave a sickly, wet grin.

'I had a feeling we would meet again, you and I,' he said through a throat full of mucus. 'You took what is rightfully mine and I demand to have it back.'

Instinctively, Tzula looked down at the knife tucked into her belt.

'Have you really been so foolish to keep it on you? Delivered it right into my grasp?' With a gesture Corpulax parted the plague zombies standing between them, giving him a clear view of the junior interrogator. 'Yes you have, and saved me the trouble of torturing you for its location. Bring it here, girl, and your death will be swift. Make me fight for it and you'll beg me to kill you a thousand times over before I allow you to die.'

'It'll be sticking between your ribs before that day ever comes. This is for my master.' Tzula fired again, but Corpulax countered with another gesture, moving the plague zombies back into her line of sight. Broiled necrotic flesh and limbs tumbled to the ground.

'How very touching. You seek to avenge Dinalt's death. You've been spending too much time around these Dark Angels. Vengeance blinds them too.' The Plague Lord's bolter barked to life, forcing Tzula to dive and roll. His gun tracked her movements, the shots felling thralls but leaving the figure in the black bodyglove unscathed. Coming out of her roll, Tzula swung the pistol around but her shot only despatched more of the mindless slaves.

'And what do you know of the Dark Angels, traitor?' Balthasar's shadow fell across Tzula and she threw herself to one side as he opened up with his storm bolter. The shield of walking corpses continued to do their job, gobbets of shredded dead flesh all that hit Corpulax.

'This one's not too bright, is he? Or maybe his lust for vengeance has literally blinded him.' Corpulax opened up a channel through the plague zombies to allow Balthasar a good look at him. The Deathwing hesitated for a fraction of a second, his rate of fire faltering as he saw the Plague Lord clearly for the first time. 'That's right, we were once brothers, you and I. You could almost say we were Legion, couldn't you?'

Balthasar's fire intensified, but his shots were wayward. It looked to Tzula as if the Deathwing was enraged, fighting angry.

'Don't worry. Your dirty little secrets are safe with me.' Corpulax waved his skeletal hand again, this time making a claw as he did so. Every plague zombie in a fifty-metre radius broke off from swarming Imperial Guardsmen or clogging up tank treads and converged on the Dark Angel and junior interrogator. 'But you'll soon be taking yours to the grave, "brother"'.

Balthasar drew his power sword and swung it in a wide arc. Heedless to the danger, the mindless thralls walked onto his blade while others of their kind were shredded by his storm bolter. Tzula drew her combat knife and stabbed away at the cloying mass one-handed, her plasma pistol glowing and dangerously close to overheating in the other. Arms, legs and heads parted company with their owners in a storm of carnage, yet the throng did not abate.

The corpulent black armoured figure moved among his servants, a pathway opening before him then closing just as quickly in his wake. The bolter hung at his side, the mind-controlled crowd his weapon of choice now. As he drew closer to the beleaguered pair, he raised his fleshless hand.

'His hand! Don't let it touch you,' Tzula yelled, straining her vocal cords to be heard over the incessant din of battle.

In a blur of steel and energy, Balthasar brought his power sword upwards, tearing through any plague zombie unfortunate enough to be in its way before making contact with Corpulax's wrist. The Plague Lord threw his head to the sky and let out a howl, its moist bass momentarily drowning out the sound of artillery fire and daemonic chatter. Balthasar's sword died in his hand, the energy field sputtering and dissipating. Even devoid of power, the blade's sharp edges were lethal, carving up undead as the Dark Angel tried to press home his advantage and plough through the tightly packed bodies to reach Corpulax.

Although his hand had been severed, the Plague Marine retained control of the horde, rotting forms moving into position behind him to cover his escape. Balthasar fought relentlessly to reach the traitor, smashing thralls out of the way with his fists and the pommel of his sword but it was all in vain. For every metre of ground he won, Corpulax drew ever closer to the safety of Atika.

The vox-bead in Tzula's ear awoke. It was Azrael's voice. 'All forces pull back. There are too many of them. We're going to blast them from orbit.'

Still slashing and firing, she started to retreat but halted when she realised that Balthasar was still heading in the opposite direction. 'You heard Lord Azrael. We're retreating so the horde can be bombed from space. You have to move. Now.'

The Dark Angel stopped, nonchalantly swinging an elbow and taking the heads from a pair of zombies who had ventured too close to him. Away in the distance, the red and white Chapter symbol of the Consecrators stark against the black of his relic armour, Corpulax was swallowed up by the darkness of Atika.

'Balthasar,' Tzula urged. Tanks reversed past her at speed, clearing the way for the Space Marines and Guardsmen following behind.

Sheathing his sword, Balthasar turned and ran after the junior interrogator, the deep blue of the twilight sky already streaked by white contrails heralding the death to come.

CHAPTER FIFTEEN

152961.M41 / The Underhive. Atika, Pythos

CORPULAX EMPTIED THE magazine of his bolter into the prone form of the Dark Angels Scout, the shredded body convulsing under every impact. Blood gushed from suppurating wounds, coating the green armour in a layer of crimson and pooling around the twitching Space Marine. Reports of yet more bolters sounded from further along the tunnel, the Scout's squadmates having been cornered by the cadre of Plague Marines accompanying Corpulax and meeting the same fate.

The Plague Lord revelled in the kills, not so much in the act itself but in what they represented. For months the Scouts had been operating ahead of the main contingent of Dark Angels and Grey Knights, locating and destroying ammo dumps, guiding forces to sacrifice sites and reconnoitring plague zombie activity. Seemingly able to become one with the darkness, the Dark Angels Tenth Company struck with impunity, often gone before the Chaos forces had realised they had ever been there, and with a trail of corpses to mark their leaving. These kills were merely five weighed against the hundreds inflicted upon his forces, but it was five fewer pairs of eyes to gather intelligence for the enemy. Five fewer warm bodies that could uncover the location of the Emerald Cave, especially as it was so close to being opened.

The clank of armour heralded the return of the Plague Marines, their bloated shapes resolving out of the gloom, all reloading their bolters. Corpulax made to do the same, reaching down with his free hand to take a clip from his belt only to remember that he no longer had a free hand. All these weeks later it still felt as if it was there. The Deathwing's power sword had cauterised the wound, denying Corpulax the pleasure of having the stump fester as a constant reminder of its loss. Gripping his bolter under his armpit, he used his other hand to retrieve fresh ammo and slide it home before wielding the weapon once again. A sudden noise from the darkness soon had him raising it again.

Oblivious to the gun aimed at her head, the Davinicus Lycae leader was almost forehead to barrel with it when Corpulax spoke. 'You shouldn't go sneaking around in the dark like that, Dormenendra, I could have blown your head off.' This was a stretch of the truth. Corpulax's enhanced vision had identified the cultist leader while she was still many metres away, even in the pitch blackness.

'I beg your forgiveness, Plague Lord. I did not mean to startle you.' The woman's deferential tone drew wet chuckles from the Plague Marines. More followed when she fell to both knees before Corpulax.

'As flattering as it is, I gather you didn't come all the way down here just to prostrate yourself before me. Have you news?' For a cult that had persisted in one form or another since the time of the Horus Heresy, the Davinicus Lycae got through figureheads at a prodigious rate. Dormenendra was the latest cultist to have ascended to the head of the cult, those who had assumed the mantle since Morphidae having either fallen to the predations of the planet, the enemy or ambitious pretenders from within their own ranks. Corpulax had a grudging respect for the woman as, in her case, she had assumed the role by means of the latter.

Dormenendra raised her horned head to look upon the Plague Lord before lifting herself to her feet. Despite the elongated growths from her temples, she barely came up to Corpulax's chest.

'I do, my lord,' she said. 'The Emerald Cave has been breached.'

* * *

IN HIS CENTURIES of existence, Corpulax had seen many things in service to both his masters. As a loyal Space Marine fighting in the name of the Emperor he had witnessed the Exterminatus of worlds, the destruction of xenos races and entire cultures brought to their knees. In his second life, reborn as a scion of the Plague God, he had travelled deep within the Eye of Terror to seek audience with daemons, inflicted pain beyond the ken of man and presided over butchery on an epic scale.

What he saw before him in the Emerald Cave made all that came before it pale as if to nothing.

Colossal in the truest sense of the word, the Prisoner from the Emerald Cave virtually filled its confines. The top of its head – or what passed for a head – almost scraped the top of the cavern, and its corpulent bulk spilled nearly to each wall. Its mottled blubber bubbled and pulsed, a sheen of stagnant moisture, like toxic sweat, reflecting the green light of the glowing gems embedded in the walls. Smaller versions of itself detached from its hide, bursting free from pustules in a shower of stinking fluid. Some were immediately subsumed back into the whole, while others squabbled and fought, trying to catch the attention and favour of their progenitor. Others became food, the host growing fat tentacles and scooping them up, dropping them into maws it could form at will.

Awed at this sight that no mortal – no post-mortal – had witnessed for almost ten millennia, Corpulax fell to his knees as Dormenendra had done before him not an hour earlier. Even fully armoured and with his enhanced physique, augmented greatly by his patron's gifts, Corpulax looked like an ant before a demigod. Curious, two of the recently detached spawn slid down their creator's flesh to take a closer look at the supplicatory figure at his feet, probing and prodding Corpulax with foetid appendages. Where the bickering of its children had failed to gain notice, this pair of errant progeny succeeded and the immense daemon sprouted a plethora of eyes where its bulk met the floor of its prison, intrigued by the minuscule worshipper.

Corpulax raised his head slightly to be greeted by the wall of eyes. 'Oh, Great One,' he said ignoring the attentions of the two smaller daemons. 'I am here to free you from this prison where you have dwelt ere long so that you may go once more into the galaxy and subject it to your grand design.'

The eyes blinked but registered neither comprehension nor confusion. Corpulax wasn't even sure how a being such as this communicated. Verbally? Psychically?

He would soon have an answer.

Sprouting a pair of tentacles, the Greater Daemon grabbed the two things harassing the Plague Marine and swallowed them back into its body, their distended forms becoming one with the host again. From the same spot his tormentors had disappeared into, a mouth formed, a fat tongue sitting between two rows of rotten, sharpened teeth. The maw inhaled, drawing in the musty air of the cavern and held it in for a while before blowing it back out again in a green-brown miasma. The cloud enveloped Corpulax, one of the many toxins in the heady cocktail instantly paralysing him, rooting him to the spot where he knelt.

Manifold diseases, viruses and infections coursed through him, mingling freely with those he already played host to, mutating and evolving, giving birth to new forms of sickness never before imagined, let alone unleashed. In the hours before he regained full control of his body, these contagions would ravage him and speak of the great plan that the Prisoner from the Emerald Cave had for the galaxy, septic harbingers of the time of malady that awaited humanity.

Taking brief control of his beleaguered immune system, Corpulax fought against his rebelling body for just long enough to force a smile to his lips.

HIGH ABOVE, UNSEEN by eyes either post-human or daemonic, a shape only a few shades darker than the emerald of the cavern walls peeled itself from the mouth of the tunnel it had used to spy upon proceedings. Turning around in the narrow confines, Scout Sergeant Namaan began the long crawl back to inform Lord Azrael of what he had witnessed.

153961.M41 / Jala Hold. Two hundred and eighty-seven kilometres north-east of Atika, Pythos

THOUGH HIS OCCULOBE had already enabled Epimetheus to see the damage caused to Jala Hold from over twenty kilometres away, he had still insisted that Shira put the shuttle down so he could inspect it close up.

Thick black smoke swirled around him as he ascended the slope towards the mine entrance, inky fronds dancing around his now almost entirely silver armour as the backwash from the shuttle's engines blew across the rocky approach. Fat flames licked from the cave mouth, the entire underground complex completely engulfed, but of the arsonists there was no sign. Even in his armoured state, the heat was too much for the ancient Grey Knight, and he stood his ground thirty paces away from the blaze, the orange light making his Terminator suit appear bronze as he turned about to survey the devastation. Despite his vision being obscured by the dark plume, he still spotted what he was looking for.

To his left, a blackened figure lay face down on the ground, a pistol clutched in one hand. At first, Epimetheus took the dark hue to be cindered flesh but as he got closer and saw that the Cadian's uniform had not been claimed by the fire, he realised it was only soot coating the corpse. Kneeling down, he rolled the dead Imperial Guard officer over. Unspoilt by the smoke, the front of the man's tunic was torn in five places, dried blood surrounding each deep gash that had been cut all the way through to bone. Four of them ran parallel but the fifth, not as deep as the others, was offset, running across the Cadian's flank where the others had ripped at his torso.

In ancient times, superstitious cultures believed that those who had died a violent death retained an image of their killer upon their retina, a victim's indictment of their killer from beyond the threshold of life. In the tens of thousands of years that had elapsed since then, that belief had been disproven but it did not mean that the dead man could not tell any tales. Like all superstitions, it had a grain of truth to it and while the eyes of the recently deceased could not offer up the identity of the Imperial Guardsman's murderer, his mind could. Closing his eyes to aid concentration, Epimetheus reached out to read the corpse's mind.

He knew the answer before the image flashed into his mind. It was the same image he had seen from nearly fifty dead men at over a dozen burned-out holds in the past week.

Abaddon.

The Warmaster's actions had ceased making sense. From the vox-traffic he and Shira had been monitoring, the enemy were effectively fighting a last stand yet Abaddon had neither rushed to their aid nor fled the planet, instead choosing to carry out pointless raids on isolated delver-strongholds that no longer held any strategic value. It seemed to be only one group carrying out these attacks, always one step ahead of Epimetheus and always gone from the scene by the time he and Shira arrived, heading to the next massacre. It was impossible to predict the exact location of these attacks, but it was always in the same general direction.

It was almost as if he was being left a trail to follow. A trail that was heading southwards, ever closer to Atika. The Grey Knight was reluctant to engage with the main Imperial Reconquest Force but if Abaddon was planning to reinforce his beleaguered forces beneath the planetary capital, Epimetheus would be left with little option.

Lifting the body up, Epimetheus took a few steps forward and hurled it unceremoniously into the flames, the inferno hungrily consuming it in an instant. By the time he had made it back to the shuttle, even the bone had turned to ash, such was the intensity of the fire fuelled by mining machinery and promethium stores.

'No survivors?' Shira asked from the controls. She had asked that question a lot recently and had received the same answer.

Epimetheus said nothing, instead simply shaking his head as he seated himself at the rear of the crew compartment, contemplating the Warmaster's plan as Shira sent the shuttle skywards.

153961.M41 / The Underhive. Atika, Pythos

THE BLADE SLID under Balthasar's flesh, peeling the skin away from the muscle beneath. Pain suppressors flooded his system along with coagulants and clotting agents as the knife burrowed deeper, probing through the meat of the Dark Angel's forearm. Finding its target, the wielder twisted the scalpel, loosening the foreign object from where it was embedded between the fibres before stabbing it with the tip of the surgical instrument. Careful not to cause any more damage than he had done on the way in, Apothecary Rephial slowly withdrew the sliver of blight grenade shrapnel, the shard festering and hissing as it made contact with the stale air of the subterranean cavern. He placed it alongside dozens more onto a metal tray beside the slab of stone he was using as a makeshift operating table.

'That's the last of it,' the Apothecary said. His skin was dark orange, weathered and lined, a remnant of his early years on a desert world before his recruitment into the Dark Angels, and his Gothic was heavily accented. The planet had supplied many neophyte Space Marines down the years – Balthasar had served in the same squad as two of them during his time in Fifth Company – and though it had a reputation for breeding doughty fighters, Rephial was the first to join the ranks of the Apothecarion. 'Try not to stand in front of any grenades for a while, alright?'

Balthasar grimaced, partly out of pain, partly out of the Apothecary's attempt at a joke. A Space Marine's lot was a grim one, of constant warfare and eternal strife. Brothers they had served alongside for several lifetimes of an ordinary human could be wiped out in the blink of an eye, and death's shadow was permanently upon them. It was an existence bereft of levity and any attempt at humour was awkward and forced.

'It was Master Gabriel who stepped in front of this particular grenade, not I,' Balthasar said, sitting upright and examining the lattice of cuts across his arms. He patted his face experimentally, not wishing to reopen the lacerations on his cheeks. 'How is he?'

'Ask him yourself. He is out of his sus-an coma and Brother Raguel has almost concluded his ministrations.' The Apothecary gestured to another ad hoc surgical station on the opposite side of the dimly lit chamber.

Nodding his thanks to Rephial, Balthasar slid from the stone table while the Apothecary moved on to treat more of the wounded Dark Angels strewn about his own field hospital. Already close to thirty Space Marines sat or lay on the raised tablets or rough floor and word had come through that more were on their way.

The months since the initial assault had been a bloody grind, the labyrinth of tunnels beneath the former hive city a deathtrap of blind corners, dead ends and cave-ins. Marauding packs of daemons prowled the benighted depths and Traitor Astartes and cultists lay in wait, ready to spring ambushes or collapse tunnels on top of the Imperial attackers. Almost an entire company of Dark Angels had been lost since the underground war commenced, many still entombed beneath rubble. Azrael had redeployed elements of Tenth Company to operate in a purely search and rescue capacity, locating survivors and pulling them from under the rocks.

The Grey Knights had fared little better, the daemonic host reserving especial hatred for the psychic Knights. In any joint operations between the two Chapters, it was always the silver armoured Space Marines who bore the worst of the casualties rather than those clad in green, white or black. Draigo's Brotherhood was still a viable and potent force but was now down to three-quarters of its initial strength.

It was the soldiery of the Imperial Guard who had fared worst, however. The lack of any natural light this far beneath the surface of Pythos made it almost impossible for the unaugmented humans to fight unless it was alongside armour equipped with searchlights or other forms of illumination. Many of the tank brigades were out of action waiting for the necessary parts to arrive in-system to allow them to be upgraded for underground combat, but some mechanised units were already able to operate in the wider tunnels with impunity. Curiously, the entire armoured complement of the Catachan 183rd had been in the thick of the action right from the start, light arrays based around the abundant crystal found beneath Pythos fitted to all of their vehicles within days of the first shots being fired.

But the war below ground needed to be fought regardless of the conditions and so hundreds of thousands of human soldiers were ordered into the tunnels to bolster the Dark Angels and Grey Knights forces. Many of them would never see daylight again, rent apart by claws of daemons or feasted upon by an army of the undead intent on defending the Damnation Cache and the Emerald Cavern. A high proportion of those who did feel the rays of Pythos's sun on their skin again did so only briefly before being shuttled off back to the fleet where they died lingering deaths on board medical frigates.

The Imperial Guardsmen who had been fighting alongside Balthasar and Gabriel belonged in the former category. Following up on reports from Dark Angels Scouts, the two Deathwing had accompanied a unit of Cadians through a maze of tunnels leading to a sacrificial chamber where Plague Marines and cultists had been seen escorting prisoners. The intelligence regarding the use of the cavern had been accurate but when they arrived, there was no sign of any Traitor Astartes, only a coven of warptouched enacting some form of grotesque ritual.

Their slaughter was straightforward, economical use of the two Terminators' storm bolters turning the stagnant air crimson, but, in a final act of defiance, one of the sorcerers detonated a blight grenade before he perished. Spotting the danger before anybody else, Gabriel put his body between the blast and the unarmoured Guardsmen, bearing the full brunt of the toxic explosion. Despite all of his Emperor-gifted boons, all of his augmentation and conditioning, the Master of the Deathwing was still too slow. The bizarre shrunken head fragmented sending shrapnel flying inexorably towards weak human flesh, killing a few of the Cadians outright but condemning the rest to a slow, agonising death. Still able to walk, Balthasar had dragged the comatose form of his company master back through almost twenty kilometres of tunnels before sending help for the stricken Guardsmen.

'It would seem you saved my life again, Brother Balthasar,' Gabriel said as he noticed the younger Space Marine approach. Raguel was pulling shards of grenade from the Master of the Deathwing's chest. His scalpel bore deep into the flesh but the veteran did not flinch. 'You are making quite a habit of that.'

'It was you who shielded me from the blast, master. If not for that, Rephial might have had to use his reductor rather than his scalpel on me.'

Gabriel smiled despite Raguel's hand being sunk to the knuckles in his pectoral, probing around for an errant sliver of blight grenade. 'Let's call it honours even.'

Balthasar returned the grin.

'The Cadians. Did they…?' Gabriel asked.

'Most of them survived, though all were wounded.' Balthasar didn't need to add that they had likely all died in transit back to the fleet, the merest sliver of shrapnel being enough to seal their fate.

Gabriel sighed. 'A pity. Sadder still that we did not find any of the Plague Marines the Scouts reported.'

The muscles in Balthasar's cheeks tightened and he broke eye contact with his company master. Raguel at last found the piece of grenade he had been seeking and removed it, adding it to a pile of similar fragments.

'All done here,' Raguel said. His pale skin was in stark contrast to that of his counterpart, his alabaster complexion lending him an aspect not dissimilar to that of a Space Marine of the Raven Guard. 'I'm going to request that you be kept away from the frontline for two days to allow your body to recover. I've spent the past seventeen hours taking almost an entire grenade out of you, and those wounds will need time to mesh.'

'And I shall politely request that Lord Azrael decline your request. You have my gratitude for your care and attention, Brother Raguel, but I must now ask that you leave Brother Balthasar and I to our discussion.' There was no malice to his tone, but he fixed the Apothecary with a hard stare.

Raguel nodded his confirmation and took his leave. It was obvious that the company master wished to talk business. Deathwing business.

'Care to tell me what troubles you, brother?' Gabriel said, lifting himself to a sitting position.

'What makes you think something is troubling me?' Balthasar retorted, a little too quickly.

'You have been in a constant state of pensiveness ever since we came below ground. Distracted. You should have been as quick to react as I to that grenade, but instead you hesitated.' Gabriel paused. 'You act as if you're carrying a burden. A secret perhaps?'

The tell registered on Balthasar's face immediately. 'I had wished to speak to a Chaplain about it but the campaign has not let up for an instant these past few months. The brief time I have spent in the company of our brothers from the Reclusiam has been battling at their side.'

'I am no Chaplain, brother, but I am a capable listener if you wish to unburden yourself upon me. You know that you may speak freely.' Gabriel's body language relaxed.

Balthasar took a breath. He was a relative newcomer to the ranks of the Deathwing and had only navigated the first few curves of the Dark Angels' inner circle. There were secrets he knew that would rock the Imperium to its core should they come out, but at the same time he had scarcely plumbed the depths of his Chapter's mysteries.

'It was just prior to the second orbital bombardment, when the Plain of Glass clogged with the half-dead. In among the carnage and confusion I saw someone, a black armoured Traitor Astartes who now swears fealty to the Plague God. The inquisitor, she spotted him too and we both engaged him in combat. I severed his arm but he was able to escape before the bombs dropped.'

'You know the protocol for dealing with the Fallen,' Gabriel hissed. 'This should have been reported straight away.'

Balthasar lowered his voice. 'It was not one of the Fallen. Well, not exactly.'

'What do you mean "not exactly"? He was either one of our erstwhile brothers or he wasn't.'

'He was not a Dark Angel who had turned traitor, but he bore the markings of another of the Unforgiven. I saw them as clear I can see you now. The inquisitor confirmed it too when I spoke to her after, but she was unaware of his lineage or affiliation to us. The traitor was responsible for the murder of her former master and she desires vengeance.'

Gabriel's eye were locked on Balthasar. 'Which Chapter?'

'The Consecrators.' There was an uneasy pause. 'I know the protocols for the location, capture and interrogation of the Fallen, but I do not know the procedure when the traitor comes from within our own ranks. What should I do, Master Gabriel?'

'You?' Gabriel said after some thought. '*You* do nothing.'

'But his betrayal is an indelible mark upon our honour. It cannot go unpunished.'

'And it won't. There are protocols in place for this eventuality, but your level of ascension is not yet sufficient for you to be privy to them.'

'But I was the one who discovered him. Surely that–'

'That counts for nothing. The matter will be dealt with,' Gabriel interrupted.

Balthasar was about to protest further when Apothecary Raguel approached them again.

'My apologies, Master Gabriel. Brother Balthasar. We've received word from Lord Azrael that the enemy have breached the Emerald Cave. He's ordered every battle-ready Dark Angel to rally there.' He looked the company master up and down. 'I suppose I'd be wasting my breath asking you to sit this one out?'

Gabriel snorted. 'We shall not speak of this again, Brother Balthasar,' he said, leaping down from the stone table. 'Serf! Bring me my armour.'

THE STENCH INSIDE *Traitor's Bane* was as potent as any of the gas-based weapons the forces of the Archenemy had thus far deployed in the underground war. Tzula had taken to wearing her bandana as a facemask to block it out.

Months of fighting without respite had taken their toll, and the crew of the Hellhammer were filthy and dishevelled. With all water strictly rationed for drinking, none of them had showered in weeks and the reek of sweat freely mingled with the odour of burnt oil and engine fumes. Even if there had been a break in the combat sufficient enough to open some of the hatches and air the tank out, it would have done no good. The still, dank air of the subterranean tunnels would do nothing to displace the smell.

There were small mercies. Imperial tanks – even super-heavy ones – did not come fitted with internal latrines, so certain bodily functions occurred outside of their confines, but that was not without its dangers. Tamzarian and three other crew members had been eviscerated by a lurking lesser daemon the previous week when they'd left the protection of *Traitor's Bane* to answer the call of nature.

Though the smell was constant and oppressive, Tzula knew that ultimately it was not going to kill her... unlike the pack of daemons that had just detached themselves from the darkness and were clambering over the tank's hull.

The tapping of claws on metal echoed around the crew compartment, audible above the chug of the power plant and the grinding of the tracks. K'Cee had done an almost impossible job in getting the Hellhammer operational again, but the jokaero's hard work was in danger of being undone, something he emoted frantically from the driver's seat he now occupied.

'*Tindalos*, this is *Traitor's Bane*,' Strike voxed. The colonel, replete with the thick beard he had sported throughout the jungle campaign, remained calm. 'Get these things off us.'

'Affirmative, chief,' came the response through the compartment speakers.

From behind the Hellhammer a smaller tank broke

formation, overtaking several others in the armoured column to draw alongside the command vehicle. Turning its turret to face *Traitor's Bane*, the Hellhound let loose with its inferno cannon, dousing the super-heavy in flame. While its thick armour plating could withstand the intense heat, the flesh of its unwanted passengers could not and the host of daemons expired in a cloud of fire and chorus of otherworldly screams.

It was a tactic Strike and the other tank commanders had been using to great success since the underground war had begun, albeit one discovered by accident when a Hellhound got a little too close to both a fire daemon and a boarded Baneblade.

'Good work, *Tindalos*,' Strike enthused through the vox. 'Maintain position along the flanks of the column. You too, *Fuego Diablo*, *Fire of Sanctity* and *Hell's Fury*. We're getting close to the cave now and I don't want you stuck in traffic if we encounter any more of those things.'

Three more Hellhounds separated from the line of tanks running two and three abreast through the tunnels of Atika.

This far down, the passages and caverns were enormous, generations of excavation having bored them large enough for heavy mining vehicles – and by default, tanks and Warhound Titans – to operate unimpeded. Scouts, both human and Space Marine, had reported that there were much smaller tunnels driving deeper towards the planet's core and yet richer mineral deposits. These branches pre-dated the Imperial miners' tunnels by many millennia and were so narrow and low they suggested they were dug by a diminutive race, long since disappeared from the face – and depths – of Pythos, perhaps even the Imperium.

Tzula shifted position within the compartment, keeping her arms out alongside her lest the rocking motion of the tank take her feet from beneath her. K'Cee had improved the handling and suspension to such a degree that *Traitor's Bane* could move at speeds close to two hundred kilometres per hour without the occupants being aware they were moving. Despite their urgency to reach the Emerald Cave, K'Cee had to limit his speed to much lower than that to allow the other tanks to keep up, much to the jokaero's chagrin.

'This is it, isn't it?' Tzula said, gripping tightly to the back of the command chair. She had to raise her voice to be heard over the rumble of engines and hard ground passing rapidly beneath them.

'Feels that way,' the colonel agreed. 'One way or another, this is the final battle for Atika, for the whole of Pythos. For good or for ill, Lord Azrael is committing all of the Imperial forces to this assault, and if what we heard in the briefing is true, that still might not be enough.'

Once the location of the Emerald Cave and the nature of its occupant had been revealed to the Grand Master of the Dark Angels, he had not hesitated in gathering all forces fighting the underground war, along with many of those tasked with protecting the lone entrance to the underhive, to rally on the threshold ready for an assault on the abomination and its spawn. Even when information reached Lord Azrael during the briefing that the location of the Damnation Cache had also been determined, he did not deviate from his course of action. To the surprise of all the human commanders present, Lord Draigo had been vehement in his support of the Dark Angel's strategy. The denizens of the Cache had been contained to the planet, and the fleet in orbit could blast the planet to smithereens should that situation somehow change. If the Prisoner from the Emerald Cave were allowed his freedom, even Exterminatus would not guarantee its destruction.

Close to a thousand Space Marines, a quarter of a million Imperial Guard and tens of thousands of tonnes of armoured vehicles might not be enough either, but to the two Space Marines leading the Pythos campaign it represented their best chance of victory.

'Regardless of the outcome, colonel, it's been a pleasure to fight alongside you. You have the gratitude of the Ordo.' Tzula held out her unaugmented arm to perform the traditional Catachan salute.

Strike smiled, locking hands and forearm with the woman. 'Likewise. And the Ordo has my gratitude also.'

'Oh,' said Tzula, taken aback. 'Why is that?'

'Because if you hadn't shown up here like you did, I wouldn't have thought a damn thing was wrong. When Abaddon arrived he would have taken the planet in minutes. And your boy, the astropath, he's the reason reinforcements ever got here. If not for him, Emperor knows how many worlds would have fallen to the onslaught of daemons.'

Tzula returned his smile and broke off the salute. She was glad that somebody else had recognised how vital Liall's sacrifice had been. She was about to honour the valour of his men when a screech from K'Cee interrupted them. The jokaero was slowing the Hellhammer down and gesticulating in front of him. Strike clambered up to the turret and peered through a viewslit.

'We're here,' he said.

THROUGHOUT THE BLOODY history of the Imperium of Man, countless battles have been fought: first for the cause of expansion, then to counter betrayal and lastly for the sake of survival. Trillions of souls on all sides of these battles have perished, and the fields upon which their lives were laid down are as varied as the armies themselves. Death worlds. Craftworlds. Tomb worlds. Ice worlds. Desert worlds. Water worlds. Worlds ravaged by the inexorable hunger of the tyranids. Worlds warped by the malign power of daemons and their consorts. On board satellites, orbital stations and spaceships. Even in the void itself. But in all that time there was one battlefield that the Imperium had found itself waging war over less frequently than most.

During the time of the Great Crusade, and Horus's betrayal that followed, some of the largest and longest underground campaigns found their way into Imperium annals. In the deepest recesses of the Rock, the Dark Angels themselves retained scripture to the war fought in the mines below a planet called Sarosh, where the agents of the warp made themselves known before their true nature was yet fully comprehended. At Calth, the Ultramarines played out a decade-long war of attrition with the Word Bearers Legion after the once verdant planet's surface was rendered an irradiated wasteland by traitor bombs and missiles. The ensuing guerrilla campaign neutered both armies for the remainder of the Horus Heresy and whittled down the strength of both Legions to a mere fraction of their previous strength.

In more recent times, the Space Wolves had fought alongside the Inquisition across a system called the Hollow Worlds, a string of planets each interlaced by underground tunnel networks, while the Blood Angels, Exorcists, Raven Guard and Doom Eagles had all experienced subterranean conflict under the auspices of their current Chapter Masters.

Never, in all that time, had a single underground battle been fought on the scale of the one about to be contested beneath the surface of Pythos.

The entire strength of the Dark Angels Chapter, close to nine hundred Space Marines along with the various bikes, speeders and personnel carriers that had survived the war above, stood alongside eighty of their Grey Knights cousins. Behind them came the massed ranks of the Imperial Guard, the few thousand surviving Catachans at the head of a far larger force of Cadians, Mordians, Vostroyans as well as other less distinguished regiments and Pythosian miners who had taken up arms in defence of their home world. Intermingled with the infantry were the tanks and artillery, mobile fortresses and mobile missile platforms ready to rain death down upon the daemonic host that awaited them.

The stale air above them was displaced by the engines of more than a hundred hovering Valkyries providing welcome relief from the stifling heat for the assembled human troops. Getting them this deep into the mines had been a logistical challenge but, with the caverns now the sizes of small nations, they could fly unfettered to provide much needed air support. Watching over all of this like dark sentinels were the Warhound Titans of Legio Crucius, stationary as they awaited the address of Supreme Grand Master Azrael but ready to explode into destructive life at a mere thought from their noble princeps.

From the promontory where his command Land Raider was berthed, Azrael too looked out over the vast army at his command, all of them waiting to hear his words, to be sent into battle with the inspiration of one of the Emperor's finest ringing in their ears. Although his vantage granted a view over the top of everyone and everything in the cavern – save the flyers and the Titans – he clambered atop the hull of the Land Raider to provide a focal point for the assembled masses and opened up his vox-link.

'Loyal servants of the Emperor, today we commence the final battle for Pythos, the last drive to liberate this world from the yoke of daemonic intrusion and banish the aggressors from this planet.' He did not look upon the Dark Angels as he spoke, nor the Grey Knights. They needed no words of encouragement or comfort to face the horrors ahead. These words were for the human soldiers, those men expected to display the same courage as the Space Marines but without the physical and mental attributes to prevent fear from taking hold of them in the crucible of battle. As far as his enhanced eyes could see, the Guardsmen stood rapt on his every word, the external speakers of the hulking Legio war machines rebroadcasting his speech on their external speakers.

'Some of you have fought this war for longer than others and have done so with a valour that has become the envy of your peers.' He looked to the remnants of the 183rd. 'By rights your war should be over already, and if not for your jungle fighting prowess it would have been long ago, but the Emperor must call upon you again. Will you answer that call, men of Catachan? Will you raise arms once more in the Emperor's name and vanquish his foes in the name of the Golden Throne?'

The cheer in the affirmative that followed belied the depleted strength of the death world regiment, each man and woman raising their voice to fill the void of fallen comrades.

Azrael turned his focus to the militia. 'Others have a greater stake in the coming battle than simply eradicating the warpspawn, for some of you call this world home and seek vengeance for its occupation. Let me tell you, men of Pythos, vengeance is the purest of all reasons to wage war and where your lack of fighting experience may fail you, let your desire for retribution spur you on.'

The bedraggled miners, some of them armed only with makeshift hand weapons rather than guns, chanted the name of their planet and the Emperor. A few even called out the Lord of the Dark Angels' name.

'A great many of you have experienced first-hand what the population of Pythos has had to endure for nigh on these past two years.' Azrael's gaze fell upon the Cadians and Mordians. 'You know what it is like for the boot of the enemy to tread roughshod over the soil of your home world, to have your Emperor-given liberty torn cruelly from your grasp. Remember this as you fight. Carry that knowledge in your hearts as you drive these invaders from this world, lest next time it be your own that falls to them.'

There were more cheers. More exaltations of the God-Emperor's name.

At last he regarded his own troops. 'But know that you do not go to face this enemy alone. The Sons of the Lion will be among you and know that we will not falter, we will not break. When your courage deserts you, look to us to lead the way forward and just as we will not fail you, the same is expected in return.'

As one, nine hundred Space Marines gave voice to their primarch's honorific.

Azrael's eyes found the silver-clad figures in the throng. 'Though many of you thought them nothing more than a myth, an order long passed into history or mere children's tales, the Grey Knights fight alongside us all this day and their zeal and proficiency is very real, let me assure you of that.' Draigo looked up from where he had solemnly been staring dead ahead and shared a nod with his Dark Angels counterpart. 'Their psychic ability will shield you from witchery, and their blades and halberds will strike straight and true for the heart of the enemy.'

Cries of 'For the Emperor' and 'Titan' followed in his wake.

'And let us not forget the great Warhounds of Legio Crucius who have so graciously lent us their might. For millennia these noble war engines, these god machines, have routed the foes of the Imperium and struck terror in the hearts of all those that would oppose them. Truly are we blessed that they take the field with us this day to defend our lives and inspire us all.'

War horns sounded in chorus, their atonal dirge forming the accompaniment for the cheers and chants emanating from below them. They were still blaring as Azrael concluded his speech.

'Let us go now to battle. Let us go now to vengeance. Let us go now to the liberation of Pythos and let us go now to victory!'

Leaping down from the hull, he boarded the Land Raider, the driver heading for the cavern exit while the rear hatch was still swinging shut. Behind the Supreme Grand Master of the Dark Angels, over a quarter of a million men followed into the daemon-infested hell that awaited them.

CHAPTER SIXTEEN

157961.M41 / The Emerald Cave. Atika, Pythos

THE CADUCADES BATTALION of the Fourth Cadian Regiment had a fearsome reputation for warfare, justified time and time again by their valorous actions in the name of the Emperor. As with all Cadian soldiery, they were taken before puberty and forced to survive on the deadly island chain from which they took their name, but unlike their rank and file counterparts, the men and women of Caducades Battalion didn't just survive against the wild landscape and horrors that dwelled there.

They thrived.

Eking out a wild existence well into their teenage years, eventually the call would come to rejoin the fold and take their place in the elite of the Fourth Cadian. Many answered that call and joined five hundred similar souls in the charcoal grey and tan camouflage pattern only their battalion were allowed to don by order of the Lord Castellan himself. Those who refused to take up the uniform were allowed to remain on the islands, yet another threat for potential Imperial Guardsmen to negotiate.

The roll of honour for the Caducades Battalion could put that of entire Cadian regiments to shame. Their banner sported the iconography of no fewer than three Space Marine

Chapters who had granted that honour after fighting along-side them, and the symbols of Battlefleet Cadia and Legio Astorum sat proudly among them. Before Pandorax, they had fought a brutal two year-long campaign to liberate a string of moons to the galactic east of their home world and, after their arrival on Pythos, were the sole non-Catachan force to suffer no casualties as a result of the lethal plant and wildlife, their formative years having left them in good stead for death world combat.

At the Battle for the Emerald Cave they lasted less than a minute.

The mouth of the cave, and the tunnel leading to it, was more than wide and high enough to grant egress to war machines and flyers, but its girth was finite, allowing only one Warhound or two Valkyries safely through at a time. The infantry of the Imperial Guard could comfortably march through fifty abreast, but with two hundred and fifty thousand souls, along with artillery and armour rolling in support, to get into position the going had been slow. Almost four days into the battle, a fifth of the Imperial forces were still to deploy into the chamber.

The Dark Angels and Grey Knights had been at the van of the assault, ploughing through the ranks of minor daemons at the fore of the enemy and establishing a beachhead from where their human allies could launch their own attacks. Impatient at the delay in getting into the fight, the Caducades Battalion had pushed their way to the front of the Cadian Fourth's number in an effort to be the first of their regiment to reach the staging zone, their ingrained savagery coming to the fore as they clubbed aside their fellows with the butts of their rifles. It was this impatience that would be their undoing.

Screaming battle cries and profanities, the thousand-strong force swept through into the Emerald Cave, lasrifles and autorifles raised to bring death to the enemies they had waited so long to smite. In spite of all Azrael's fine words at the dawn of the battle and the horrors they had witnessed merely by dint of being citizens of Cadia, the first thing they did upon entering the chamber was freeze in terror.

Where the army of the Imperium numbered a quarter of a million, the daemonic horde easily matched it. Bloated things the size of Space Marines shambled awkwardly across the cave, batting aside Guardsmen with pendulous, distended arms and raking at tank armour with broken claws, pestilence dripping from their tips. In among them skittered smaller horrors, emaciated husks with exposed ribs and patchy flesh, mouths stuffed full of multiple sets of crooked, rotten teeth. Their diminutive stature made them no less deadly, however, and their fearsome maws bit through both flesh and steel with ease. Plague Marines too fought among the enemy host, their positions easy to spot by the masses of plague zombies they used as rotting meat shields, firing unimpeded from behind their undead protective walls. It was over all of this that the true source of the Caducades Battalion's fear presided.

Immense in its stature, the Prisoner from the Emerald Cave dwarfed all before it, including the black and white liveried Warhounds of Legio Crucius that were vainly unloading their guns at it. Its hide constantly shifting beneath the miasma of disease and filth that oozed from every pore, the daemon altered its form to respond to any threat ranged against it. A Valkyrie hovered in front of the thing's chest – at least where its chest would have been had it allowed itself form – and prepped its missile batteries to let loose a salvo at one of the beast's many spontaneously generated eyes. Aware of the craft's intent, the area around the organ stretched and transformed becoming a grotesque approximation of an arm that lunged and grabbed the stationary flyer, gripping it so tightly that escape was no longer within its capabilities. With a crunch of metal, the Prisoner from the Emerald Cave wound in the appendage, swallowing the stricken Imperial flyer in a maw that an instant earlier had been the eye they were targeting.

Whether by accident or design, it was the monster's next act that would ensure the Caducades Battalion would never get to add to their roll of honour. The patch of blubber beneath the pseudo-mouth undulated and heaved violently, the roiling folds of fat swelling the pseudo-lips as if they were trying to contain what was within. With a guttural roar, the maw expelled its contents in a torrent of jet black vomit.

The warpbred physiology of the blessed of Nurgle had taken the remnants of the Valkyrie – its mechanical components, its hull, its fuel, the organic matter of the human crew – and transformed it into something new, something horrific, something deadly. The shower of hot, dark filth cascaded across the Emerald Cave, over the heads of battling Guardsmen and daemons and engulfed the troops of the Cadian 4th's elite battalion along with anybody else unlucky enough to be standing in proximity. The viscous bile clung to them like tar, eating away at the charcoal and tan they so proudly bore and the weak flesh and organs beneath, the battle cries and expletives of moments before giving way to the wails of the dying.

Their banner with its now meaningless honours was the last trace of the Caducades Battalion to disappear, consumed by the corrosive mass of the men and women who had once fought so bravely beneath it.

'GET THOSE LEMAN Russ over here and clear the staging area,' Grand Master Gabriel called out. 'You there. Have your men fill the breech. Don't let the enemy retake the beachhead or we'll never get the rest of our forces through.'

The Mordian major being addressed by the Deathwing stood rooted to the spot, the shock of seeing half his men turned to mush in the same attack that wiped out the Caducades Battalion still sinking in. The trio of Leman Russ showed no such hesitation, firing their engines and rolling towards the sticky remains of the Guardsmen the daemon had wiped out. Their dozer blades already pitted from the four previous occasions they had been called upon to carry out this grisly task. The three tanks pushed the bubbling goo to one side ready for the Mordians to step in and hold the line.

'Did your ears melt in the attack, major, or are you intentionally disobeying an order from the Grand Master of the Deathwing?'

Despite four days of constant fighting there was no harshness to Balthasar's tone. It wasn't needed. The sight of the ivory-clad Terminator looming over him was enough to scare the Mordian back into lucidity, and within moments blue uniforms filled the void left by grey and brown.

Their reaction came just in time. Sensing an opportunity to stem the flow of Imperial Guard, a phalanx of plague-riddled beasts charged the staging area, tearing and hurling any defenders that got in their way. Balthasar, Gabriel and the rest of the Deathwing squad assigned to secure the cave entrance were the first to react, storm bolters blazing in a withering hail of fire. The front ranks succumbed to the onslaught, but their kindred behind them simply bounded over the bodies and drove onwards. The Leman Russes joined the attack, their turrets having finally rotated into firing position and the drumming of their guns sounded out a tattoo, throwing up daemonic limbs and entrails with every beat. Emboldened, the Mordians and elements of the Cadian 4th who were flooding into the Emerald Cave opened up with their guns, picking out any of the fiends fortunate enough to avoid the guns of the Dark Angels and the tanks.

Gabriel stood firm, his storm bolter taking down enemies at range, his humming power sword carving through any that ventured into its deadly arc. His armour, already in a poor state of repair before the battle as a result of the grenade explosion, was battered and cracked. The once-pristine ivory was streaked with the red of blood, black of fire and green and brown of daemonic filth, and the vambrace of his sword arm was missing entirely, the exposed skin a mess of scars and welts where ichor from his victims had gushed down the hilt of his blade. Balthasar noticed that the Crux Terminatus the Grand Master bore on his left pauldron was cracked and hoped that it was not a poor augur of events to come. But that wasn't all he noticed.

'Master Gabriel!' Balthasar called out, seeing the dark shadow moving through the press of daemons on the older Space Marine's blindside. Scattering the weaker of its kind and panicked Guardsman alike, the hulking daemon pounded over the rocky ground at speed, building to a head before launching its bulk into the air directly at the Master of the Deathwing. At the last moment, Gabriel took two quick steps backwards, the space where the daemon had expected to connect with the Deathwing now occupied by the glowing blue metal of a power sword. The ultra-sharp blade caught the monster square in the gut, momentum passing him through the blade as opposed to vice versa. Without altering the angle of his gun, Gabriel continued to fire as the bisected parts of the daemon passed through its arc, gobbets of rancid matter gouging from its flesh with the impact of every bolt shell. The two separated halves of the beast hit the floor with a wet thud, the unnatural liquids no longer contained within its form leaving a blood-like smear in its wake. They had not yet come to a stop when Brother Barachiel stepped up with his heavy flamer and doused the remains in cleansing fire.

'I think that most definitely squares us now,' Gabriel voxed over a closed channel to Balthasar.

The other Deathwing did not have time to formulate a response. Through the channel created by the forerunner, more of the gargantuan daemons surged forwards, each closer in size to a Dreadnought than the Terminators they bore down on. Storm bolters were mag-locked to armour as power swords and maces were drawn to be wielded two-handed against the rotting hulks.

The first crashed into the Imperial line, Balthasar and Gabriel simultaneously swiping low with their blades and taking the legs from beneath it. It lurched to the ground with a thud to be instantly set upon by Cadians and Mordians who shot it at close range with their rifles or ripped it open with bayonets.

Not all of the defenders were as successful. Further along the line, Brother Casatiel, a veteran Deathwing Knight of more than two centuries' service, found himself isolated by two of the monstrosities. Valiantly swinging his Mace of Absolution, the robed Terminator stove in the skull of one of them, felling it like so much dead timber, but the other slapped aside the weapon as Casatiel attempted to connect with the backswing. Its other massive arm drove over its head in a windmill motion and smashed against the Dark Angel's head, knocking it back to an unnatural angle with the sickening crunch. The veteran was dead before the daemon's other arm swung back and punched him forcefully from his feet.

Witnessing the demise of the Space Marine, the Catachan crews of the Leman Russ – now abandoned, as deadly to ally as enemy at such close quarters – fearlessly rushed his killer, their dulled blades tip down in their fists. A dozen figures in jungle camouflage assaulted the towering beast as if it were a wall to be scaled like their first day in basic training. Using their knives to gain purchase, they clambered over it, spilling its brackish vitae with every motion of their blades. By the time they had brought it to its knees and Barachiel had bathed it in flame to finish it off, fully half of their number lay dead or dying.

Casualties were heavy but the line held and the staging area remained clear. Brother Golathiel, a Deathwing Knight so large in stature that the Apothecaries speculated he might be a genetic throwback to the days of the Great Crusade, rallied the Mordians at the brunt of the fighting, going so far as to assume direct command when their major fell to one of the massive beasts. Bereft of his mace, the enormous Space Marine took one of the daemons down barehanded, pummelling it to a pulp under a rain of mighty blows, while the Mordians saw off another through the combined efforts of a hundred men, some of whom survived the encounter.

Dardariel and Mendrion butchered another two between them. Squadmates since their days in Tenth Company, the innate understanding they shared made them a formidable force on the battlefield, so much so that it had not escaped the eye of Master Ezekiel or the brothers of the Reclusiam who had ascended them to the Deathwing as soon as openings became available.

Narcariel. Thaddiel. Paderion. Yimguel. All of the Deathwing handpicked by Gabriel to defend the staging area covered themselves in glory, just as they covered themselves in the rank filth of the enemy. Ten of the brutes fell to the Space Marines and their human allies, putting the smaller daemons to rout, but this was merely a skirmish, one of thousands that formed the Battle for the Emerald Cave, and that was not yet won. For every daemon slain at the hands of the reconquest force, the thing that should not be at the heart of the chamber spawned two more in its place.

Balthasar was mopping up stragglers alongside Barachiel when the vox in his helmet crackled to life with the voice of Supreme Grand Master Azrael.

'Deathwing. To me,' he said. His tone was as inspiring as it had been when he had given his speech before the start of the battle. 'This ends now.'

THE HEAT INSIDE *Traitor's Bane* was so oppressive that Tzula regretted ever requisitioning a new bodyglove and pined instead for the Catachan fatigues and vest she had worn before the reconquest force arrived.

With so many daemons packed so tightly into the Emerald Cave, Strike had assigned a Hellhound to protect each of the super-heavies from boarders. *Tindalos* ran alongside the Hell-hammer, bathing its hull with fire every few minutes to burn away the conglomeration of fiends climbing over its armour, allowing *Traitor's Bane* to concentrate on mowing down the enemy beneath its tracks and obliterating them with its fearsome arsenal.

So far the tactic had worked for Strike, but some of the other tanks under his command had not fared so well. Four Stormswords were lost on the first day of the battle through friendly fire incidents, stray shots from the larger tank taking out their escorts' promethium reserves, allowing the daemons unhindered progress through their thick hulls, and the same number of Baneblades – including Brigstone's – had suffered similar fates since.

Fortunately for the affable tank commander, *Traitor's Bane* had been operating nearby when his own vehicle's end came and he now sat at the controls of his commanding officer's tank, manipulating the ancient controls as easily as if he had been fused with the machine like a Titan princeps. At Brigstone's feet, K'Cee slept with his head on a pile of scrunched-up tunics, the three days he had spent at the controls having taken thier physical toll on the xenos. Nearby, other crewmen rested now that the operators of the destroyed Baneblade had relieved them. Neither the sound of the jokae-ro's snoring nor the battle raging outside barred them from the welcome embrace of slumber.

Strike, his thick beard drenched with sweat, peered out through the slit in the turret.

'Are we winning?' Tzula asked from her position at one of the sponson guns. She had felt much like a spare part for most of the action and had been happy to relieve a gunner when the opportunity arose.

'Winning. Losing. Drawing. It depends where you look and how you look at it.' The colonel sounded uncharacteristically philosophical, which Tzula put down to exhaustion. Even the great Colonel 'Death' Strike needed rest once in a while and when the rest of the crew awoke, she was going to pull rank and place Brigstone in temporary charge of *Traitor's Bane* while Strike got some well-earned sleep. Well, she would try at least.

'We're keeping the foot soldiers contained but that big

bastard keeps spawning reinforcements as fast as we kill them,' he continued. 'Unless we take it down, we're only delaying the inevitable.'

'The Grey Knights will deal with it,' she replied, squeezing the firing controls and wiping out a pack of daemons with the lascannon. 'They did it before, thousands of years ago. I have every faith they can do it again.'

'The Grey Knights can't get close enough to it. If you think we're having a hard time with these monsters, they have it ten times worse. The things are singling them out. Targeting them. They know the threat they pose to their master and are dealing with it.'

Tzula looked out through her own viewslit and made out the silvered forms of a squad of Purifiers, harried by four times their number of daemons, some winged and striking at them from the air. Tzula readjusted her aim and took one of the winged horrors down, followed by another, then another. She couldn't risk targeting the daemons on the ground in case she hit the Grey Knights, but at least she had helped make the odds a little fairer.

'So what do you suggest we do?' she asked. Both Azrael and Draigo would be prepared to hear Strike out if he had an alternative plan and Tzula would lend her Inquisitorial authority if it was required to help change minds.

Strike jumped down from the turret. 'What if we had a weapon that could kill it? What if we'd had that weapon all along?'

Tzula stopped firing and turned to face him. 'You mean the athame? The knife?'

'Why not? If what you've told me about it is accurate, then it's more than powerful enough to cope with that thing. Tear a portal and send it through.'

'But it could end up anywhere. We might end up trading one war zone for another. Or worse.'

'Then stab the bastard with it.'

'If the Grey Knights can't get anywhere near it, what makes you think we can?'

Strike never got to answer.

'Chief. The vox-light's flashing. Somebody's trying to raise us,' Brigstone said, keeping both hands on the controls but motioning at a console with his head.

Strike turned away from Tzula and lifted the handset. '*Traitor's Bane*. Go ahead.'

'Colonel Strike,' Lord Azrael said over the weak, crackling link. 'I have need of you. We're going after the daemon.'

157961.M41 / The Mouth of the Underhive. Atika, Pythos

LIEUTENANT RANN OBERWALD sipped from his mug of recaff as he stood listening to the rain pounding against the tarp over his head. Pythos's dry season had given way to monsoon season with a vengeance, and even after weeks of constant downpour the sky still had plenty left in reserve.

As part of the Eighth Cadian Recon Regiment, Oberwald had served on three different worlds now – including his own – but he had never experienced rain like this. It didn't fall as drops but instead in sheets, walls of water cascading from above. It was warm too and despite breaking the oppressive Pythosian humidity, it did nothing to diminish the heat. The one upside to the inclement weather that the lieutenant had found was that men who had spent months fighting on the planet without bathing could now shower at will, much to the relief of all.

Alongside him, two other officers drank from identical Munitorum issue tin cups speculating about the battle taking place many kilometres beneath their feet. All Imperial Guard forces on the planet and in orbit had been called upon for the assault on the Emerald Cave, but Colonel Strike had the prudence to leave a sizable force topside. With only one way in or out of the underhive, the Catachan hadn't wanted to risk reinforcements sweeping down to surprise them from the rear or, just as deadly, collapsing the tunnel entrance.

The two Cadian recon regiments deployed to Pythos were both the most lightly armed and armoured troops on the planet, and while that had been a boon during the jungle campaign, they were not well suited for the close confines fighting of the underground portion of the war. Lots had been drawn to determine whether it would be the Eighth or Third recon regiment that would defend the mouth of the underhive, with the loser scattering their forces to outlying delver-strongholds to allow Guardsmen better suited to up close subterranean fighting to join the assault. Oberwald was glad it had been the Eighth that had prevailed. Though most of the enemy forces were engaged down below, contact had been lost with many of the surrounding mines and the garbled snatches of vox-traffic the Eighth had been able to pick up gave the impression that the Third had literally and figuratively drawn the short straw.

Oberwald was about to join in the conversation when a new sound became evident in amongst the drumming and splashing of the fat raindrops. Through the falling torrent, he could make out pinpricks of light in the distance. He reached back into the Salamander Scout vehicle to which the make-shift rain shelter was attached and retrieved his magnoculars, setting them to his eyes and adjusting the magnification.

Tanks. No, not tanks, Oberwald realised as the image sharpened, armoured personnel carriers but not like the Chimera variant he rode into battle. These were Space Marine pattern vehicles – Rhinos and Land Raiders. This confused him briefly. The Dark Angels and Grey Knights were fighting in the underhive, so who did these belong to?

He sharpened the magnification and got his answer.

Dropping the magnoculars which smashed on impact with the rocky ground, Oberwald ran out through the rain, skidding and falling in his desperation to reach a vox-operator and issue a warning before it was too late.

157961.M41 / Vortras Hold. Twenty-nine kilometres north of Atika, Pythos

SHIRA BROUGHT THE shuttle around in an arc maintaining the holding pattern she was flying in an effort to find a landing zone. Vortras Hold was perched at the peak of a high mountain, all of its approaches sheer boulder-strewn slopes that made it impossible for any land vehicle to traverse or flyer to put down. Ideally, she would have landed the craft directly in the cave mouth that formed the mine entrance but, like so many others she had seen recently, it was billowing thick black smoke from fires lit in its depths. Considering how difficult it was to get to Vortras Hold, especially in light of the torrential downpour, somebody had gone to a lot of effort to destroy it.

'There's nowhere to put down,' Shira said, taking her hands from the controls for a moment to shrug her shoulders. 'I could try to land lower down the slopes and let you climb up but we both know you won't find any survivors. The auspex isn't returning any signs of life and if this was the work of the Black Legion, they hardly have a reputation for leaving anybody alive.'

Epimetheus considered this briefly. 'One more pass but lower this time. The smoke is so thick that it may have obscured a landing site. Use the engines to disperse it.'

Shira shrugged again and prepared to do as he asked. A burst of static from the vox followed by a distorted, frantic voice halted her.

'This is Lieutenant Oberwald of the Eighth Cadian Recon to all Imperial forces. The entrance to the underhive is under attack. I repeat, the entrance to the underhive is under attack. Black Legion.' A pause, the hiss of interference. 'Oh, sweet Emperor no! He is with them. Abaddon is here. Send help, Throne damn you. We're being massac–' There was a drawn-out scream followed by the hollow fizz of a dead channel.

Shira turned to Epimetheus. She knew how reluctant the Grey Knight was to link up with the Space Marine forces on Pythos, yet here was a distress call that would lead them to the same battlefront.

Epimetheus did not hesitate. 'Go,' he said.

Shira broke the holding pattern and pointed the shuttle south, speeding Epimetheus to a meeting that he had hoped to avoid.

157961.M41 / The Emerald Cave. Atika, Pythos

THE PLAN, THOUGH it involved the movement and participation of tens of thousands of troops not to mention Titans, tanks and flyers, was a deceptively simple one and, in principle, Draigo agreed with it.

With the Grey Knights unable to get close enough to the gargantuan daemon to banish it, Azrael had decided to use that to their advantage. Instead of leading the assault on the beast, Draigo and his men would provide a diversion, drawing the bulk of the daemon forces away while Azrael and the Deathwing vanquished the Prisoner from the Emerald Cave. It would also require the Titans and tanks to distract the beast, and the combined forces of the Imperial Guard to keep the smaller daemons at bay while the Dark Angels got close enough.

'And what makes you think *you* can slay this daemon, Azrael?' Draigo said when the Supreme Grand Master of the Dark Angels had finished outlining his plan. 'It would take the Emperor himself to best it in personal combat.'

'Then if that's what it takes,' he said drawing the *Sword of Secrets* from his hip and pointing the diamond-sharp tip at Gabriel's shoulder. 'My apologies, brother. I do this out of necessity and mean you no disrespect.' He stabbed into the Master of the Deathwing's already cracked Crux Terminatus and broke it open, catching the tiny sliver of bright metal that fell from it. He took a bolt round from a pouch at his waist and raised it to his lips. For a moment it looked to those around him as if he was kissing the shell, but when he lowered it they could see that his acidic saliva had melted away some of the casing. Taking the fragment of shimmering metal from his other hand, he pushed it onto the shell with his thumb, fusing the two together.

'Brother Gabriel's armour is the most ancient of all the Deathwing's suits, forged upon the anvils of the Rock in the days when the Emperor was already interred upon his throne, but the Legions had not yet been divided. From Terra came a gift to all those Legions who had remained loyal in the face of Horus's perfidy, a section of the Emperor's own armour so that it may be incorporated into the newly forged Terminator suits of his true sons. The Dark Angels took delivery of the Emperor's right gauntlet, and over the coming decades over a thousand suits of armour were fashioned incorporating metal from his battle plate in the pauldrons. Many of those suits were gifted to our noble successors when Lords Dorn and Guilliman broke the Space Marines down into smaller Chapters, and though most have been lost down the millennia, some of our brothers still go to battle in armour bearing those original Crux Terminatus.'

Draigo did not think it would be appropriate to point out to his Dark Angels counterpart that *all* Grey Knight Cruxes held a shard of the One True Armour. Nor did he think the time right to challenge Azrael's use of the word 'brother' rather than 'cousin' when referring to the Dark Angels successors.

Azrael held the shell between his thumb and forefinger and held it up. 'This shell is bound with a portion of the gauntlet that struck down Horus. Just as it laid low the arch-traitor so too will it eradicate this putrid scion of the Plague God.'

Awe and reverence passed across the faces of the crowd listening to Azrael's briefing. The remaining Deathwing – now numbering barely seventy – were all in attendance along with eight Dark Angels company masters, Dashiel of the Ninth having succumbed to grievous wounds earlier in the battle. Draigo, Strike and Tzula rounded out the impromptu war council.

'Even if you could get close enough, how do you plan to fire that shell inside it? That thing can absorb tank shells in its flesh and spit them back out,' Draigo challenged.

Azrael redrew his sword, its blade as dark as midnight. 'The Heavenfall Blades can part stone as if it were wood. Daemon hide will be no match for it.' Flanking the Supreme Grand Master, Gabriel and the eight green armoured company masters placed their hands on the pommels of their own swords.

Draigo failed to look impressed. 'Stone is one thing, daemon flesh is another entirely. The beast is clad in the stuff of the warp. Those swords will be no better than an Apothecary's needle against it.'

'And what would you suggest, Grey Knight?' Azrael said rounding on Draigo. 'Trapping it down here again so that somebody else can deal with the problem in ten thousand years' time?'

Draigo bit back a retort. Beside him Tzula was giving him a sideways look. He opened a psychic link with her.

+What is it, junior interrogator?+ he sent.

+The athame. If it can part reality surely it can carve through daemon flesh?+ she replied.

+The knife is attuned to the warp so in theory, yes it could do that.+

+Then we have to use it.+

+You would reveal it to the Dark Angels?+

+What choice do we have?+

Draigo paused, mulling things over. +Be wary. A man like Azrael could put an artefact like that to many uses.+ He broke off the link. Tzula gave him a solemn nod, her face a mask of confidence.

'Lord Azrael. I believe I may have a weapon that may be of use,' Tzula said, deftly sliding the athame from where it was tucked into her belt.

The Lord of the Dark Angels looked at her impassively. 'Is this some sort of jest? If a Heavenfall Blade is incapable of doing the job, what use is that primitive tool?'

'Please, Lord Azrael. Hear me out.'

Tzula explained to the Dark Angels how she and Dinalt had studied the weapon, sought it out and obtained it from the clutches of the upstart tau in the name of the Imperium. She told them of its purpose and how the enemy had sought it out when she brought it to Pythos, slaying her master and other loyal servants of the Ordos in their desire to obtain it for their own dark purposes. Through it all she was very careful to keep any mention of Epimetheus out of her tale, certain she had fathomed the root of his reticence to join up with the Space Marine contingent of the reconquest force.

When she had finished, Azrael eyed her intently. 'And you chose to keep this a secret from us?'

'Oh please, Azrael,' Draigo interjected. 'If I didn't think my ribcage was already fractured, I'd laugh. Don't you dare to presume to lecture anybody on guarding secrets.'

'I am an inquisitor of the Ordo Malleus, Lord Azrael. Secrets are my stock in trade as much as they are yours,' Tzula said.

'Is there anything else regarding this campaign that you have been keeping from us, junior interrogator?' Azrael replied. It was obvious to Draigo that the Dark Angel was trying to pry information from her about the elusive Grey Knight. Tzula was too canny to fall for this.

'Other than the xenos life form I brought here with me that is currently driving Colonel Strike's tank? No, I think I've told you everything.'

Strike shot her a nervous glance.

'Please don't mock me, girl. My patience is already worn parchment thin.' He placed the shell back in its pouch and held out his hand. 'Now, give me the knife.'

Draigo stepped forward, forming a barrier between the Dark Angel and Tzula. 'The knife stays with Junior Interrogator Digriiz. Both of us will be accompanying you on the mission.'

The company masters' hands reached once again for the hilts of their swords. Azrael held up his palm to stop them. 'As you wish, Lord Draigo, but please, try not to get in our way.'

He dismissed the assembly, Tzula and Strike returning

to *Traitor's Bane* which had formed part of the ring of steel surrounding the war council, the Dark Angels back to the frontlines. As Azrael was about to join them, Draigo, who had hung back, addressed him.

'A moment of your time, Lord Azrael.' It was not a request. The Dark Angel approached him, coming to a halt just within what the Grey Knight would term his personal space.

'Make this quick, Grey Knight. I have a daemon to slay.'

'I feel it only fair that I deliver you a warning.'

'A warning,' Azrael said, a full smile cracking his stern features. 'What could you possibly want to warn me about?'

'The knife,' Draigo said, inching forward so that he was practically nose-to-nose with the Dark Angel. 'I know of its value and now so do you. As a loyal servant of the Golden Throne, I know you will do all within your power to ensure that it is still in the junior interrogator's grasp at the end of the battle and that no harm has come to her.'

'That sounds more like an appeal than a warning.' The Dark Angel was so close that Draigo could smell the tang of corroded metal still evident on his breath.

'I'm getting to that part. If the blade goes missing, or the girl dies, I shall bypass Titan on my way back from here and head straight to Terra where I shall demand, and be granted, audience with the High Lords.'

'I sincerely doubt that the High Lords of Terra would concern themselves over the misplacement of some museum piece,' Azrael scoffed.

'Perhaps not,' Draigo replied, his pauldron brushing against the Dark Angel's as he barged his way past him. 'But I'm certain they'd like to know what you have locked in those dungeons beneath the Rock.'

As he strode away, he didn't need to call upon his psychic abilities to know exactly what Azrael was thinking.

CHAPTER
SEVENTEEN

157961.M41 / The Emerald Cave. Atika, Pythos

THE SOUND OF mighty warhorns echoing through the Emerald Cave signalled the start of the final phase of the battle.

Behind the bass fanfare marched the six Warhound Titans in the black and white of Legio Crucius, spreading out across the enormous cavern to attack the beast at its heart from multiple angles. Even stacked one on top of another, the towering war engines would not have reached the gem-encrusted ceiling, and the air above them was thick with Valkyries flying patrols to prevent winged daemons getting too close to the ancient Titans.

Beneath their feet, the super-heavy tanks of the Imperial Guard rumbled into position flanked by a complement of Hellhounds and Demolishers to ensure that their larger cousins did not get overrun. Foot soldiers maintained tight formations marshalled by the green armoured giants of the Dark Angels, picking off targets of opportunity as curiosity got the better of some of the lesser daemons and they ventured too far from their own lines.

Their armour almost the same colour as the Dark Angels

under the reflected light of the emeralds, the Grey Knights took up their own position apart from the main bulk of the Imperial Army. Already packs of the Neverborn were prowling towards them, hackles up in response to the presence of the psychic daemon hunters.

At their head marched Azrael, accompanied by an honour guard of his Chapter Masters and First Company, blades already drawn to face the inevitable onslaught. In among them, two other figures walked, one clad in the silver Terminator plate of the Grey Knights, the other a dark-skinned human woman, dwarfed by the armoured figures around her.

The warhorns ceased and, as one, the Imperial guns opened fire.

THE OPENING BARRAGE was immense. Large calibre weapons sought out the Prisoner from the Emerald Cave, those shells not subsumed into its body knocking away huge gobbets of flesh that turned into daemons before they hit the ground. Mouths formed spontaneously over its hide, some swallowing inbound artillery before spitting it back in the direction it had come from, others forming macabre grins to emote the thing's enjoyment of the punishment being meted out upon it.

In response, those daemons already within the chamber charged the Imperial lines, many of them singling out the Grey Knights, their presence in the warp a shining beacon to those from the other side of reality. From behind the silver armoured figures, tanks rolled, Leman Russ and their myriad variants assigned to augment the psychic Space Marines presenting such a tempting target to the daemonic horde. Their main guns blasted huge gaps in the ranks of the Neverborn, and those that survived the bombardment ended up crushed beneath tracks or impaled on the spikes of dozer blades. A few made it through the wall of steel only to run into a wall of psychic energy erected by the combined minds of Grey Knights squads. Fewer still made it past the warp barrier, those that did find their brief existence in the materium ended by the blade of a force sword or halberd.

Tens of thousands of Imperial Guard surged forward to meet the army of lesser daemons head-on, their numbers swelled by the monstrosities raining down from above as the big guns continued to pound away at their master. The men and women of Catachan, Cadia, Krieg, Mordian and many other worlds besides turned their fear into anger, filling the air with the sound of las-fire and the stench of scorched daemon flesh.

From the flanks of the battle, Corpulax looked on with increasing concern. The lesser daemons meant nothing to him, and as long as the Prisoner from the Emerald Cave could keep supplying an endless stream of them, the Imperial Guard would succumb in the end. The Grey Knights had been neutered, so small a force struggling to contend with the increased attention from the Neverborn and was not able to mount any form of attack on the blessed of Nurgle. Even the Titans and the tanks presented no more than an inconvenience to it and would run out of ammunition eventually, making them easy prey.

But there was one element of the enemy they faced that was starting to pose a real threat. Singular in their purpose, the ivory figures of the Deathwing cut a swathe through the sea of daemons, intent on reaching the Prisoner from the Emerald Cave. Corpulax doubted that even warriors as formidable as the Dark Angels' elite could do the daemon any true harm, but he could not take the risk. He had fought so hard to do his patron's bidding in freeing it and had been promised so much in return. Nothing would deny him his just reward, and if it meant that he had to despatch these Dark Angels personally because the Prisoner's minions were unable to, so be it.

Ordering his cadre of Plague Marines to follow him, Corpulax waded into the battle.

157961.M41 / Approaching the Mouth of the Underhive. Atika, Pythos

UNLIKE VORTRAS HOLD, the approach to Atika presented numerous clear landing spots, the previously steep and foreboding terrain now vitrified by the orbital assault. Through the torrential rain streaming over the shuttle's front viewport, Shira could pick out immobile dark shapes on the ground, some of them glowing with the red-orange of a recently extinguished blaze. Sheet lightning panned across the sky, illuminating the scene below and Shira briefly saw that the shapes were in fact the burned-out shells of tanks or personnel carriers. Scores and scores of them.

'Put us down near the cave mouth,' Epimetheus ordered.

Shira banked the craft right and was preparing to deploy the landing gear when the console in front of her lit up with flashing lights. An alarm wailed insistently.

'What's wrong?' Epimetheus asked, his level tones in stark contrast to the panic Shira felt rising within her.

'There's something coming up behind us,' she said checking an auspex. 'Something quick.'

'Missile?'

'I don't think so. A shuttle like this should have automatic countermeasures.' She checked the auspex again. 'Besides, this is too big to be a missile.'

'Can you outrun it?'

'Judging by the speed it's gaining on us, no.' Shira tugged back on the steering controls. 'But I can outmanoeuvre it.' The shuttle veered steeply upwards and Shira frantically strapped herself in with one hand while using the other to loop the craft over in a wide arc. Epimetheus didn't move, the boots of his armour maglocked to the floor of the crew compartment.

Pulling out of the flip, Shira levelled the controls, positioning the shuttle above and behind the craft that had been stalking them. The pursuer was now the pursued. The next flash of lightning revealed the exact nature of what they were chasing.

Irregular gold lattice lay atop a serpentine body of dark metal, a head like that of a dragon at one end, a short tail at the other. Beneath its snaking torso sat two sets of wicked claws, tipped with talons the size of a normal human. From its flanks, three pairs of reversed wings protruded, pulling back in rhythm and propelling it through the air like an oared boat through water. One of those wings – the foremost on the beast's right – had an ugly hole torn through it, a wound Shira herself had caused.

'Ragwing,' she mouthed under her breath.

As if responding to the pilot's sobriquet for it, the Heldrake curved its prehensile body and tucked in one set of wings, gliding back around itself with much greater finesse than Shira had managed with her stunt. Facing the onrushing shuttle, it opened its jaws, the early promise of balefire lapping at its metal jaws. It exhaled before Shira had time to react, the narrow jet of flame heading straight for the Inquisition craft.

More alarms sounded in the crew compartment as the warp-born fire licked over the hull, but Shira entered a steep dive before it could entirely engulf the craft, zipping under the Heldrake. Steam rose from the exterior as the monsoon extinguished the small fires that had attempted to take hold. Her manoeuvre had spared them catastrophic damage but it had placed the daemon engine behind them again.

'I'm going to pass back around again, low to the ground,' Shira called back to the Grey Knight. 'You're going to have to bail out when I'm near to the entrance.'

'But what about Ragwing? This thing is barely armed and we can't compete with it for speed,' Epimetheus said.

Shira grinned at his use of the name she had given the beast. Perhaps he had been listening all those times she had regaled him with the tale of how she outran and outwitted it. 'I survived against this thing the last time I went up against it; this time I mean to bring it down. Unless your psychic gifts extend to sprouting wings, you're no use to me up here.'

Epimetheus nodded. 'You don't have to go in too low,' he said, clamping his helmet in place. 'I may not know how to fly, but I do know how to land.'

'Oh, that's priceless,' Shira laughed, pulling the controls from side to side erratically, weaving the craft in an irregular pattern. 'Our touching farewell and you finally develop a sense of humour.' She stabbed at the control for the rear hatch. Warm air and rain blew into the crew compartment seconds later.

'Good luck,' she called over her shoulder. The Grey Knight stood framing the open hatchway, his hands gripping the frame. A burst of blue balefire silhouetted him against the darkening evening sky. In a blink he was gone.

Shira hit the door control again and the hatch retracted. Pulling back on the controls, she made for the open skies and away from Atika. As she ploughed the shuttle through the thick grey cloud cover, a familiar voice invaded her mind for one last time.

+Good luck, Shira.+

EPIMETHEUS TUCKED HIS arms and legs in as the ground quickly came up to meet him. It had been ten thousand years since he had free-fallen from a moving craft – in the days before he had sworn his new oaths and his gene-seed swapped out for that containing the Emperor's own biological material – but the memory of it came easily to him.

His shoulder hit first, shattering the glassaic ground under the force of impact and opening a wide crater. Momentum carrying him on, he rolled, limbs still tight to his body to prevent them snapping or snagging until finally coming to rest some twenty-five metres from where he had made landfall. He lifted himself quickly to his feet, drawing his scavenged bolter in the same movement and tracked it around in a full circle, alert for any signs of Abaddon and his Black Legionnaires. Satisfied that there were none, he made his way to the tunnel mouth, weapon still raised and using the steaming wrecks of vehicles as cover.

Eviscerated corpses lay strewn haphazardly across the smooth floor and draped over burned-out frames of Chimera and Leman Russ variants. True to what he had seen of the Black Legion's handiwork in the preceding weeks, this was a total massacre, though on a vastly greater scale to any of the lightly garrisoned delver-strongholds. Through the lashing rain, as far as even augmented eyes could see, an entire regiment lay butchered, the downpour washing their blood into narrow gullies that bisected the battlefield like veins. *Almost* an entire regiment.

Noise and movement in the distance drew Epimetheus's attention and he raised his bolter to his shoulder, looking out over the wide body and barrel to find its source. Proceeding cautiously, he stepped over the dead as he followed the sound. As he got closer two voices became apparent, one weak and little more than a hoarse whisper, the other deep, resonant and distorted by static.

'Please…' the quiet voice said. 'Ab… Abaddon is in the… underhive. Kill… killed us all. You have… have to stop him…'

'What are his numbers?' came the vox-distorted response.

'They hit… us so quickly. Hard… hard to tell.' The man's voice was laboured. Breathing, let alone speaking, was a supreme effort for him. 'Doz… dozens? Hundreds…?'

The second voice was lower this time, as if the speaker had turned away to address somebody else. The noise in the background sounded like a mighty battle was raging. 'Don't be a fool, Azrael. If the Black Legion are sweeping in behind us, we have to meet their assault.'

Epimetheus could make out another voice replying but his enhanced hearing couldn't discern the exact words.

'Well, you and your Dark Angels can die and your damned secrets with you,' the voice at the end of the vox-link raged. 'I am withdrawing my Grey Knights to meet the threat.'

Epimetheus was now close enough to see the owner of the first voice. A human lay slumped against the side of a semi-intact scout vehicle, a vox-receiver held limply to his mouth. His tunic was soaked, not only with rainwater but with blood too, the white chevrons denoting his rank of lieutenant stained red. The lower half of his body was missing from the waist down and his face was as pale as the moon rising overhead. He noticed Epimetheus approaching and grew more animated, thick black liquid spilling from his mouth as he spoke.

'No... no. Sweet Emperor, please... have mercy,' the man spluttered. As Epimetheus drew nearer, his tone changed to one of serenity. 'You... you aren't Black Legion. You're one of... of them. You're a... a Grey Knight.' His eyes grew wide and in that instant he finally gave in to his wounds, one last long exhale presaging his journey into oblivion. The vox, which had remained open, sprang rudely to life.

'Who is that? Why have you fled the battle? This is Supreme Grand Master Draigo. Answer me, Emperor damn you!' the other voice boomed. After a pause filled by the static addled noise of combat, it added, more calmly, 'Lord Epimetheus?'

Epimetheus crouched down, closing the dead man's eyes with one hand and picking up the vox-receiver with the other. He lingered for a moment.

'Lord Epimetheus? Is that you?' Draigo said again.

Epimetheus raised the handset, tiny in his huge hands, but let it drop again. Getting to his feet he opened a mind link with the Chapter Master of the Grey Knights.

+Well met, Master Draigo,+ he sent. +From what Tzula tells me, the Brotherhoods have a worthy commander.+

+By the Throne!+ Draigo's mind voice was full of reverence. +It *is* you, returned to us after all these years.+

+I am returned to no one. It was my sworn oath to remain here in slumber watching over the seals. Those seals are now broken and, though I am released of my oath, I am still duty bound to ensure that this world does not fall to Chaos and become a haven for the Neverborn.+

+But you are one of the–+

+Who I am and what I was is of no relevance. All that matters now is closing the Damnation Cache and dealing with what was released from the Emerald Cave.+

+You have done both of those things before, but you choose not to aid us in our hour of need?+ Draigo's reverence started to secede to frustration. +Why do you abandon us?+

+I have not abandoned you. I came here to deal with Abaddon and his Black Legion dogs who are snapping at your heels. You already have the means to vanquish the daemon and close the Cache.+

+The athame.+

+And Tzula. She does not know it, but I have implanted within her the knowledge she needs to use the knife to seal the portal. She will not be able to recall what she has done once she has committed the act, but the information will bury itself in her psyche should it be needed again.+

+And the daemon?+

+Azrael's plan is sound. You only have to get close enough to the daemon to carry it out.+

+How could you know of the Dark Angel's plan? It was never discussed by vox so you could not have intercepted it.+

A pause followed by realisation.

+The scriptures are true.+ The awe returned to Draigo's mind voice. +Your psychic power levels are prodigious.+

+I have been privy to Azrael's thoughts ever since he arrived on Pythos.+

+Hence your reluctance to reveal your presence to him.+

+What would you know of that?+ Epimetheus countered.

+Not nearly enough. But if you wish to share what you have found in the recesses of his mind…+

Some vestige of Epimetheus's former loyalties rose to the fore. +All men have secrets and Azrael is entitled to his. Just like I know about your future, Kaldor Draigo, and choose to keep that knowledge from you.+

+My future?+ Draigo sent. +What happens to me in the future?+

+You will find out soon enough as you will be the one to live it.+ Epimetheus replied. +We waste time with this discussion. I will go and hold Abaddon off. You use the time I buy you to banish the daemon and reseal the Cache. Farewell, Kaldor Draigo.+

Abruptly, Epimetheus cut the mind link. Hoisting his bolter in both hands, the ancient Grey Knight set off through the rain in pursuit of Abaddon.

157961.M41 / The Emerald Cave. Atika, Pythos

BLOOD CASCADED FROM Draigo's nose, the strain of maintaining a psychic sanctuary around himself and Tzula whilst simultaneously battling off a cohort of daemons and engaging in communion was exacting its toll.

In his shadow, the junior interrogator fired away relentlessly with her plasma pistol, each clean headshot accounting for another of the Neverborn. Her bodyglove was torn open across her stomach and thighs and she bled from gashes to her arms and chest. The athame remained safely tucked into her belt.

'You looked distracted for a moment there,' Tzula said, drawing in closer to the Grey Knight to make herself heard. 'Having second thoughts about withdrawing to face Abaddon?'

The *Titansword* flashed through the air, bifurcating a daemon that had strayed within the shield generated by his mind. 'No need. A friend of yours is taking care of that.'

Even in the midst of battle she spared a grin.

Draigo swung his blade again, taking an enemy down on both the front and backstroke. It was like stamping his feet to clear water from a lake; no matter how many he killed, more would flood in to take their place. 'This is getting us nowhere. With me.'

Pushing the boundary of his sanctuary further out, he wielded the *Titansword* one-handed, raising the storm bolter mounted on his other arm and blasted a path through the daemons through to where Azrael was fighting nearby. Gibbering fiends tried to move in to plug the void but fell under the concentrated fire of the Grey Knight and the inquisitor, those not eliminated by plasma blast or bolt shell impaled on the end of his sword or smashed out of the way by storm shield.

'What changed your mind, Grand Master?' Azrael scoffed as Draigo took up position alongside him. As they had done several times already during the Pandorax campaign, the *Sword of Secrets* and the *Titansword* rose and fell in union, slick with the gore of daemons. At his other shoulder, Gabriel fought with an identical vigour and relish.

The Grey Knight ignored him. 'We're bogged down here. For every metre we take, they push us back two.'

'If we could get the teleporters to work this far underground this would have been over long ago. What do you suggest, Draigo?' Azrael sounded as if he was genuinely open to ideas.

'On the *Revenge*. Your Deathwing formed a cordon around my Grey Knights to get them to the warp rifts on the lower decks. There are more daemons here but you have more Terminators too.'

The Supreme Grand Master of the Dark Angels thought about this for a moment but no more. 'Gabriel. Form two circles. You have command of the outer, I the inner.'

'As you wish, Lord Azrael,' Gabriel said. At his signal, close to seventy Terminators formed two concentric rings. The bulk took up position in the outer, a smaller number including Draigo, Tzula, Azrael and the company masters, in the inner. It was a formation the Dark Angels had utilised in combat for millennia and it was the work of mere seconds before they were all in position, the gap between the two armoured rings cleared of daemons.

At another signal from Gabriel, the outer circle started to move, not only forwards but in a spinning motion too. The inner circle moved in time with them, guns aimed high to deal with any winged daemons or those scrambling over others to bypass the wall of Terminators. Warp lightning leapt from Draigo's fingertips, turning any daemon it came into contact with to ash. The Deathwing alongside him muttered a curse under his breath and the Grey Knight realised that it was Balthasar, the one he had encountered on board the *Revenge* when he first met Gabriel. The Terminator was helmeted, but Draigo recognised him by the wave of repulsion and unease he emanated.

Their progress through the horde was slow but at least it was progress, each metre hard earned and paid for in the hellish blood of the Neverborn. Barely any ivory remained visible of the armour of the Deathwing, each one of them coated from head to foot in unnaturally coloured gore. Even the silver of Draigo's own Terminator suit was dulled by the foul, stinking liquid.

The Titans and tanks continued to pound away, the colossal daemon seemingly oblivious and impervious to their weapons. Fledgling horrors oozed from his body like sweat, a continual slick that provided fresh fodder for the Imperial guns or new reapers for their souls depending on where they were drawn forth from the immaterium.

As quickly as the Imperial forces had gained the upper hand, the battle turned against them.

Whether it was a reluctance to take any further part in the conflict on the part of its machine spirit, the incorrect prayers incanted over it or simple malfunction, the plasma blaster of one of the Warhound Titans ceased firing. Detecting an opportunity, the daemon sprouted a clump of fat tentacles which it thrust towards the ailing Titan. The war machine brought its other arm to bear but only managed to rattle off a handful of shots before the vulcan mega-bolter seized, the *clack clack* of a jammed shell issuing forth in place of the roar of full automatic fire. The probing limbs clasped hold of the Warhound, wrapping around it massive arms to stop them from being used as cudgels, acrid steam rising from where corrosive slime met the ancient metal of its body. Servos and motors screeched in protest as the princeps fought to prevent his charge from being dragged into the beast and subsumed into the daemonic mass.

The fleshy tentacles stretched as the Titan struggled to move backwards until, just as it seemed it was breaking free, the tendrils suddenly withdrew. Momentum did the rest.

Packed tightly into the confines of the Emerald Cave, neither daemon nor Imperial Guardsman could move quickly enough to avoid the felled Warhound. Like one of the mighty redwoods from the jungle above, it crashed backwards obliterating anything unfortunate enough to be caught underneath it. A Baneblade and its Hellhound escort were crushed under the Titan's massive head, the ensuing explosion wiping out everything in a five hundred metre radius and setting light to the prone god machine.

Unfazed by the loss of such a mighty ally, Draigo and the Dark Angels fought on relentlessly but the nature of their enemy changed. Instead of the lesser daemons and spawn of the Prisoner, plague zombies swarmed the twin rings of ceramite, sheer weight of numbers impeding their progress. The Terminator directly in front of Draigo went down, a hole punched clean through his helmet, blood fountaining from the exit wound. His brother alongside him took a round to the shoulder, spinning him backwards but not causing enough damage to remove him from the fight. Draigo followed the report of the bolters back to their source.

'Plague Marines!' he called, spotting the misshapen armoured forms lurking in amongst their undead minions. Almost taking his warning to be an order, the Deathwing shifted their formation, those among their number armed with close combat weapons and storm shields forming a tighter outer ring to fend off the zombies, the rest firing over their brothers' shoulders at the Traitor Marines.

All forward movement ceased as yet more plague zombies hemmed in the Space Marines, tearing away armour to expose the weaker flesh beneath. Anything became a weapon as Draigo and the Dark Angels swung out elbows and knees, rotted limbs and organs popping with each blow.

The Dark Angel who had taken the shot to the shoulder shuddered as two more rounds found their mark, the first squarely into his chest, the other blasting out the lower half of his torso. Instantly, the plague zombie horde was upon him, dragging him to the ground and revealing his killer.

A rusted, serrated blade in one remaining hand, the Plague Marine strode boldly forward, fixated on Tzula, who had remained by Draigo's side. The junior interrogator let off two quick shots of her plasma pistol which her target evaded with an ease belying his bloated form.

'Corpulax,' she stated plainly to Draigo. The muzzle of her pistol was glowing from overuse and her Catachan blade flashed in her other hand, stabbing viciously at anything that came within arm's reach.

Ignoring the Grey Knight, the Plague Lord carved through the ranks of his own thralls to get at Tzula. Draigo swung the *Titansword* but it snagged against the throng, plague zombies packed in so tight that the dead remained on their feet to serve as further impediment to the Space Marines. Just as Corpulax was about to lunge for the junior interrogator, warp lightning shot forth from Draigo's free hand, knocking the Traitor Marine backwards.

'It would seem there's always a knight around to save you, Tzula,' Corpulax said, disentangling himself from the undead mass. 'And this one wears shining armour,' he added, looking Draigo up and down.

The Grey Knight let rip with another salvo of crackling blue energy from his fingertips, but Corpulax merely waved his hand to dissipate it.

'My god favours me, Grey Knight. You won't find me as easy to kill as these daemons or my thralls,' Corpulax sneered, the knife in his hand lengthening and broadening organically under the malign influence of the warp until it was a match for Draigo's own blade.

Raising his sword high, the Plague Lord charged the Supreme Grand Master of the Grey Knights, a benediction to his foul master rasping wetly from his dead lips.

'RIGHT TURN, K'CEE,' Strike called from the command seat.

The jokaero swung the controls and the tank veered off in the direction of the oncoming daemons the colonel had espied through the viewslit. A slight vibration resonated through the tank as the majority of them were crushed beneath the tracks, the combined efforts of the sponson-mounted flamers and *Tindalos*'s main gun accounting for those not flattened.

Traitor's Bane's main turret swung around, the hellhammer cannon firing back in the direction from which the tank had come, annihilating a pursuing pack of plague-touched Neverborn. The demolisher cannon did likewise to a second wave of horrors approaching from the front while heavy bolters and flamers continued to despatch anything getting too close.

With almost two full crews on board, *Traitor's Bane* was operating at peak efficiency, its guns only falling silent when all of its immediate targets had been killed. Leaving K'Cee to drive once again, Brigstone had formed part of the loading team for the Hellhammer's primary weapon system, and as soon as one empty casing had been cleared from the breech, he was there straight away with a fresh shell.

To Strike, it was just like old times. Brigstone had been a loader on the first ever tank he had commanded, a Leman Russ Eradicator named *Longfang*, and the man's indefatigability had seen them through many deadly battles. The enemy back then had been orks, rather than the vile servants of the Plague God, and at that moment Strike would have given anything – even his cherished Catachan fang – to have been back on any of those worlds fighting under open skies instead of trapped deep underground in a ready-made tomb.

'We're almost out of shells,' Brigstone called out to Strike, slotting a massive hellhammer round home with the aid of another Catachan before slamming shut the breech. Crates were stacked precariously around him but only two bore unopened seals.

'Concentrate fire from the demolisher,' Strike called back. The secondary gun was a far more common armament on Imperial tanks than the hellhammer cannon and over the course of the Battle for the Emerald Cave, Strike and his crew had been able to salvage a reasonable number of demolisher shells. 'That should see us through the next few hours.'

Moments later, the ordnance situation became the least of their worries.

A nearby detonation rocked *Traitor's Bane* with such violence that Brigstone, the other loaders and anybody else not seated slammed to the hard metal floor. Pulling back the slider of a viewslit, Strike witnessed the tail end of the explosion that had engulfed *Tindalos*, a plume of orange flame rising high from its blazing hull. Whether the lightly armoured prome-thium tank had taken a direct hit, a backdraught had fed flame back along the inferno cannon or daemons had some-how boarded it and detonated it from within was impossible to fathom and irrelevant. *Tindalos* was now a flaming wreck and *Traitor's Bane* had lost its close support.

Like ocean-bound predators smelling blood in the water, shoals of the Neverborn started to circle the stricken tanks. The heavy flamers, heavy bolters and lascannons swung about to meet the new threat, any daemon caught within their arc of fire either eviscerated or evaporated, but there were too many for even *Traitor's Bane*'s formidable weaponry to cope with. The ominous scraping of claws over armour echoed through the crew compartment and clawed footfalls tapped out like an agonised metronome counting down the time until the beasts would be within.

Strike mashed his fist onto the control that electrified the hull but nothing happened. K'Cee shrieked and gesticulated from the driver's seat, and though Strike couldn't understand exactly what the jokaero was trying to communicate, he got the gist: it no longer worked.

The xenos's protestations took on a more urgent tone as the sound of tearing metal issued from the rear of tank, shortly followed by the grind of the Hellhammer coming abruptly to a halt. Despite the language barrier, it was perfectly clear to Strike what K'Cee was now trying to tell him: the daemons had taken out the engine.

Launching out of his seat, K'Cee tore away one of the panels below a control console and slid underneath it. He re-emerged moments later and gestured to Brigstone with all four elongated fingers of one hand in the universal gesture for 'pass me a wrench'. Brigstone tossed the tool to the jokaero and took K'Cee's place in the driver's seat, vainly applying pressure to pedals and controls to coax some power out of the dormant war machine.

All the while, the sound of daemonic clawing and rending grew in intensity.

157961.M41 / Thirty kilometres north of Atika, Pythos

DESPITE LACKING THE manoeuvrability of a Kestrel, under Shira's control the Inquisition shuttle was doing things she swore it was never designed for.

Hugging the canopies of the tall trees, she waited for a break in the blur of green rushing beneath her and dropped beneath the cover. She weaved the craft through the thick trunks, sometimes banking the craft onto its side to slip through the tighter gaps.

The jungle behind her lit up in a riot of blue flame, the chasing Heldrake's impatience at finding an opening of its own forcing it to burn a point of egress. The shuttle's auspex flashed repeatedly, alerting Shira that her pursuer was now within fifty metres of her and gaining. It opened its jaws, the promise of yet more balefire flickering across its maw, and sent a funnel of intense heat in the direction of the shuttle. At the last moment, the broad leaves above her gave way to clear skies and she burst out of the jungle, now ablaze with daemonic fire, and back out into the rain.

Behind her, the Heldrake wailed in frustration, its vast form erupting from the flame and steam, doggedly sticking to her tail.

For a craft designed to carry some of the Imperium's finest and most loyal servants often into hostile environments, whoever had put the shuttle together had incorporated one major flaw – all of the weapons systems pointed forwards. At first glance, the sleek black-hulled craft could be mistaken for a civilian vessel, having no outward signs of offensive capability. On closer inspection it became apparent that the two recesses on the nose were both lascannons and the exhaust ports protruding from either side were flamers designed to protect the shuttle from interference on the ground. But the real *pièce de résistance* was the hellstrike missile concealed alongside the landing gear.

As with most of the craft's systems, Shira had discovered it through trial and error on those missions where Epimetheus had deemed it too dangerous for her to accompany him. Fortunately, the button she had pressed just deployed the missile and neither activated nor launched it. It was a simple process of elimination that had led her to find that particular switch.

She briefly considered turning the shuttle around and ramming the hellstrike straight down Ragwing's throat, but quickly ruled it out. Not only would she be putting herself directly into the path and range of its flame weapon, but if she missed she would have blown her one chance at bringing the Heldrake down.

But that didn't mean she was entirely without hope or options.

Veering off in a north-easterly direction, Shira flew for all she was worth towards the nearest mountain range. With a snort of warpfire, Ragwing followed.

157961.M41 / The Underhive. Atika, Pythos

THE COMBINATION OF total recall and enhanced vision made navigating the benighted tunnels beneath Atika a simple task for Epimetheus. He had already walked this way twice, once ten thousand years ago at the head of a hundred Grey Knights, the second time very recently as part of a much smaller group. If he was not familiar with the route or his eidetic memory had somehow failed him, the advanced light-capturing capabilities of his occulobe were revealing the path to him as if it were merely twilight rather than pitch black.

He came to a halt at a flat section where the shaft widened and knelt down, dipping his fingers in a stream of dark liquid running across the stone floor and sniffing them. Blood. Following the trail back to behind a boulder against one of the walls, he found a Cadian in the same uniform as those dead up above, almost split in two from a wound that ran from groin to throat, ran down by Abaddon and his Black Legionnaires as he tried to raise the alarm. Rising from a crouch, Epimetheus swore to himself that this would be the last servant of the Emperor the Warmaster slew on Pythos.

Reaching his full height, a sudden bout of vertigo afflicted the Grey Knight forcing him to thrust out an arm to steady himself. His head ached in a way that his pain suppressors were unable to deal with and a sickening buzzing and tingling lashed across his temporal lobe. Not since the days before the Emperor came to his home world and he swore his first oaths as a Space Marine had he felt pain of this magnitude and had never expected to feel its like again. He pulled off his helmet in case his ancient Terminator suit was malfunctioning, but the pain and dizziness did not abate. He regulated his breathing but to no avail, the pain intensifying rather than dissipating.

Gas, he thought. Either some build-up of subterranean fumes so toxic it affected even a Space Marine's genhanced physiology or an Archenemy trap.

It was a trap, just not the kind Epimetheus suspected.

Turning to head back to the surface, the Grey Knight had only taken a few steps when a shape detached itself threateningly from the darkness. Instinctively, Epimetheus drew upon his gifts but the well was dry, his link to the warp severed. Without flinching, he raised his bolter and put three rounds through the head of his concealed would-be assassin. Two more figures resolved out of the black, one of whom Epimetheus put down immediately, but the other was able to get off a shot before meeting with the same fate as his comrade. The bolt round struck Epimetheus in the knee, shattering armour and bone, dropping him to a crouch once again. More figures shifted in the gloom but there was another enemy he was fighting against. It felt as if his own powers had turned against him, killing him instead of saving him. The closer the shadows got, the more severe the pain became.

Epimetheus squeezed off two more shots, the heavy thud of power armour against rock signifying both were fatal. He was lining up a third when he was struck on the wrist, the shot not penetrating all the way through his Cataphractii plate but enough to send his bolter skidding away down the tunnel. He tried to rise, desperate to retrieve it, but was assailed by more gunfire, two rounds finding their way through his armour at the chest and shoulder, another to devastating effect on his other knee. His secondary heart kicked in and his system flushed with pain-killing agents, calming his physical wounds but doing nothing to intervene in the war within his mind. His brain felt like it was made of glass, every burst of gunfire shattering it.

His attackers revealed themselves, the black armour and gold livery of their battered armour denoting their allegiance to Abaddon and his Black Legion. Three of them held chains at the end of which were tethered beasts, feral things crawling on all fours. It pained him to do so but Epimetheus forced himself to look upon them. Only then did he realise that they were not animals at all, they were human, or, in the case of one of them, something approaching human.

One was female, completely naked and covered in filth, her hair and nails long and unkempt. Her face could be considered beautiful by human standards but Epimetheus found it difficult to look upon her, her very presence this close to him making him want to completely and utterly destroy her. The other two were both male, in a similar state of undress but whereas one of them had a primitive aspect to his features – as if he was a genetic throwback to an earlier stage of evolution – the other was something different, something not human.

Covered entirely in tough scaled hide, the thing skulked on four simian legs, straining on its leash to reach what it considered to be prey. Its humanoid face showed intelligence and a bulbous tongue ran across twin sets of needle-sharp teeth as if in anticipation of a feast. Its orange, glowing eyes were fixed on Epimetheus, but the Grey Knight could not hold its gaze, convulsions wracking his body the instant he made eye contact.

Blanks.

Though the pinnacle of human power is psychic ability married with the enhanced genetics of a Space Marine, even a being so mighty can be laid low by a blank, an aberration scarcer than a psyker upon the worlds of the Imperium. Able to negate the most potent of mental abilities, the blank – or blacksoul as the Grey Knights referred to them – was uncomfortable for even normal humans to be around, excruciatingly painful for those touched by the warp. At the time of Horus's rebellion, the Emperor maintained an entire cadre of such beings – the Sisters of Silence – but to find more than one in the same planetary sector, let alone the same planet, was unheard of. This was no freak occurrence; somebody had engineered this. Somebody had brought three blanks to Pythos specifically to nullify Epimetheus.

The Black Legionnaires parted and Abaddon stepped out of the darkness.

CHAPTER EIGHTEEN

157961.M41 / The Emerald Cave. Atika, Pythos

STEEL FASHIONED ON the anvils of Titan clashed against the serrated edge of a blade forged deep within the Eye of Terror, the strength of both wielders locking together the two swords that were anathema to each other. Like oppositely charged magnets each weapon fought to repel the other, the air around the duel heavy with electrical charge and the stink of ozone.

The two warriors broke from each other, Draigo swinging the *Titansword* around and clearing the surrounding area of plague zombies, Corpulax summoning yet more of his thralls to him. Nearby, Tzula lashed out with both combat knife and plasma pistol, keeping the horde at bay.

The din of combat had not subsided, but where the air had once been full of the boom of artillery fire and the discharge of heavy ordnance, now the ululating cries of daemons and low moan of the undead drowned it out. Many kilometres away, the Brotherhood of which Draigo had taken temporary command continued to engage the Neverborn, thousands of them converging on the Grey Knights' position. His Space Marines fought with the same freshness and zeal as they had at the dawn of the battle, but the first inklings of concern were seeping into the psychic link the Supreme Grand Master maintained with his troops. Thankfully few Grey Knights had fallen thus far but the Imperial Guard tanks had borne the brunt of the daemons' assault, leaving them virtually bereft of armoured support.

Azrael and his Dark Angels fared little better. Those in the immediate vicinity were now fighting on two fronts – up close and personal with the overwhelming press of plague zombies and at range with the Traitor Marines. Not a single Deathwing or company master remained unscathed and Azrael himself bled from a vicious claw wound to his torso. The squads scattered throughout the Emerald Cave found themselves hunkered down behind the cover of transport vehicles or rock formations, any daemons not able to get close enough to the Grey Knights seeking out the Sons of the Lion instead.

It was in the air where the most success had been made. With fewer of the winged daemons than those confined to the ground, air superiority had been established and Thunderhawks and Valkyries rained down death from above while Sammael pursued and eliminated any of the Neverborn with the temerity to challenge their aerial dominance. It had not come entirely without cost, as the smoking wrecks of more than a dozen Imperial flyers bore testimony to.

The Plague Lord came at Draigo again, but the Grey Knight turned aside the blow with his own blade and drove his elbow into the back of Corpulax's head. The *Titansword* flashed with reflected emerald light as it swept in a blur towards the traitor's head but at the last moment Corpulax threw a plague zombie bodily in the way, which exploded in a shower of blood and innards as Draigo's sword connected with it.

Lifting a gore-drenched arm, the Grey Knight opened up at close range with his storm bolter but with a flick of his hand, Corpulax put a putrid barrier between him and Draigo, another coat of stinking crimson atop silver armour the only outcome. Back and forth it went, Draigo countering every thrust and swipe aimed at him, the Plague Lord sacrificing his thralls to defend the Grey Knight's attacks.

Eventually something had to give.

Unseen among the stack of limbs and severed body parts, a gruesome collage adorning the floor of the Emerald Cave, the upper half of a plague zombie continued its progress towards the Grey Knight. Unnoticed by Draigo, who was too preoccupied by the attentions of Corpulax and his other minions, it dragged itself along on decaying arms leaving bloody smears behind it as it pulled its body closer to its intended victim. Reaching one of Draigo's massive armoured greaves, it raised itself up, biting and clawing at the weak point at the back of the Supreme Grand Master's knee.

Draigo looked down for a split second, drawing his blade backwards and impaling the half-zombie on its tip, but this was the opening Corpulax had been seeking. Spinning his sword so it was point down, he stabbed at Draigo's calf, the serrated edge biting through ceramite and into the huge muscle beneath. Hamstrung, the Grey Knight fell to one knee with a grunt of pain. Corpulax was upon him instantly, sword-tip pressed against Draigo's throat.

'A fine duel, Grey Knight, but there was only ever going to be one victor.' Corpulax applied pressure to the hilt of his weapon, Draigo's armour sizzling under its acidic touch. 'Consider yourself fortunate that I will allow you to live on as one of my thralls.'

A call rang out from where the Dark Angels were engaging the Plague Marines. 'Draigo!' bellowed Azrael, futilely trying to carve his way to his stricken counterpart.

Corpulax's grip on his sword relaxed slightly, grim realisation apparent on his face. 'Draigo? No, this cannot be. The Four have such plans for you, such a role you have yet to play.' He tightened his hold of the blade again. 'No. I shall not be robbed of this. If you truly are part of a greater scheme then why–'

Draigo never got to find out why. With a crackle of energy, a power sword slid through the air taking Corpulax's other hand at the wrist, still gripping the sword as it fell to the ground with a clang. Behind the sword came a mass of stained ivory ceramite, crashing into the Plague Lord and knocking him to the ground. The Deathwing raised his sword for another attack but Corpulax had lost a hand, not his senses, and plague zombies flooded in to fill the space between them. Under cover of his thralls, Corpulax got to his feet and retreated through the ranks of the undead. Accepting Draigo's nod of gratitude, Balthasar set off in pursuit.

Tzula came alongside Draigo again and the Space Marine lifted himself erect, his wound already knitting thanks to his accelerated healing process.

'How bad is it?' the junior interrogator asked, her plasma pistol finally having given out, forcing her to resort to a scavenged bolt pistol for defence.

'The muscle feels like it's almost completely shorn through and the blade was laced with toxins that are inhibiting its repair.' He blazed away with the last few shots from his storm bolter until it returned a hollow *clack* signifying it was empty. 'I can stand but I won't be able to move freely until an Apothecary has taken a look at it.'

Despite Corpulax fleeing, neither the plague zombies nor his Traitor Marine cohort relented in their attack. A Dark Angels company master in tattered robes was hit in the side of the neck; the arterial flow was quickly stemmed but in his weakened state he was dragged down by undead hands, armour torn from him so they could feast on what lay inside it. Their superior armour no advantage, the Deathwing too fell under fire from the Plague Marines. In the space of as many seconds, three died, their breastplates and helmets giving in under a sustained barrage from a heavy bolter. It was only the psychic sanctuary Draigo had put back in place that prevented him and Tzula from sharing their doom.

The shift in tactics had come so close to succeeding but the intervention of the Plague Marines had brought them to the threshold of defeat. Their forces already depleted, Dark Angels were dying in droves and still the Prisoner from the Emerald Cave persisted, his ever burgeoning offspring ploughing their way through the mass of zombies to help strike the final blows.

There was one last option open to Draigo. He would probably die in the process, his soul given up as a banquet for those beyond the threshold, but it was the only chance they had.

Sheathing the *Titansword*, Draigo closed his eyes.

CHINKS OF EMERALD light filtered in through the roof of the Hellhammer, cracks forming in its armoured hull where talons and claws widened the gaps between plates, tearing away the outer layers to reveal the prey within.

K'Cee worked furiously beneath the console, stripping out wires and fibre bundles, reconfiguring them and soldering them back in place with heat from one of the many rings that adorned his long, slender fingers. Strike and the others knew that the jokaero's efforts were in vain; the daemons had crippled the engine and short of stepping outside their rapidly diminishing armoured cocoon and, getting under the hood, *Traitor's Bane* was not going anywhere.

A loud crunching sound was followed up by brighter green light flooding the crew compartment. Strike looked up to see that a hole the size of a man's head had been gouged through the side of the turret, a pustule-riddled arm reaching experimentally inside.

'K'Cee,' Strike said, gripping one of the xenos's furry knees and shaking it to get his attention. K'Cee shot out from the darkened recess, wrench raised threateningly.

'We have to bail out.' Strike pointed to the daemonic limb reaching around blindly above them.

In sheer frustration, the jokaero bashed away at the console with the wrench then paused with a hopeful look on his face that his percussive maintenance had yielded results. When he was certain that even this hadn't coaxed any final vestige of life out of the tank, he flung the tool at the flailing arm, screeching with delight when it struck the wrist with a satisfying crack.

There was another crunch of metal and the red gloom of emergency lighting gave way entirely to the jade from without, but this breach of their confines was the planned opening of the rear hatch rather than the violent attention of the swarming Neverborn. Brigstone tossed Strike a lasrifle and the two Catachan officers, along with K'Cee, followed the rest of the crew out into the cavern.

Seen through the tiny rectangular aperture of a tank viewslit, the Battle for the Emerald Cave had been a gruesome sight to behold. Exposed to the full panorama, the experience was soul-crushing. The screams of the dying were virtually indistinguishable from the howls of their daemonic killers, sounds that would keep the men and women who heard them awake at night for the rest of their lives. Corpses, both human and warpborn, festooned the cavern floor, the stone dyed a deep red from the blood and other matter that had leaked from the lifeless, the grisly by-product of war. Those wounded that lived on cried out for mercy, for their comrades to grant them a swift end and spare them from the virulent horrors eating away at their bodies, the lingering deaths that would wrack them with pain until they breathed their last.

Smoke hung in palls over the battlefield, endless banks of promethium fumes from the burning wrecks of tanks and fly-ers. Strike was glad of it, not only to cover their retreat from *Traitor's Bane*, but for the smell masking the rank odour of the Plague God's servants and the four days' worth of Impe-rial dead.

Weapons fire, sudden and loud, drew the colonel's atten-tion. Through the smoke, muzzle flare from multiple heavy bolters and red beams of lascannon fire emanated from the silhouette of what was unmistakably a Baneblade. The dae-mons closing in on Strike and his crew collapsed under the barrage, the corpses convulsing under sustained fire as the tank's rear hatch dropped to allow the fleeing Catachans on board.

With K'Cee bounding along on all fours several metres back, Strike sprinted towards their saviour, a Mars-pattern super-heavy in the urban camouflage colour scheme of the Tenth Cadian Armoured regiment. He had just placed the first of his standard Imperial Guard issue boots on the metal ramp when a roar from behind him had him spinning, the butt of his lasrifle reflexively coming up to his shoulder.

A horned, one-eyed monstrosity had placed itself between K'Cee and the Baneblade, too close to be targeted by the tank's weapons systems. Strike and the other Catachans opened up with their guns but their shots bounced harmlessly off the thing's thick, rancid hide. It loomed over the xenos and bel-lowed again, its breath so heavy with stench that what came out of its mouth was the same grey-green as its flesh. Raising its crude, heavy blade above its head, it made ready to finish the jokaero.

K'Cee didn't flinch. Extending a single finger, another of his rings was revealed to be a lethal weapon, a vast fountain of flame shooting forth from it, engulfing the daemon. The creature thrashed and flailed as its mottled skin melted under the intense heat, dropping to the ground with a howl in a futile attempt to douse the cleansing fire.

Seemingly oblivious to what he had done, K'Cee contin-ued to lope forwards without any urgency whatsoever. He clambered aboard the waiting Baneblade which moved off at speed before the rear hatch had closed.

While Strike remonstrated vociferously with the Cadian tank commander who believed the hairy orange alien who had just boarded his tank to be an enemy agent, K'Cee stared back at the rapidly disappearing Hellhammer, wiping the dampness away from the fur on his cheeks.

IN THE LONG and storied history of the six hundredth and sixty-sixth Chapter of the Adeptus Astartes, what Draigo was about to do had only been attempted on a handful of occasions, each time at great personal cost to the individual performing it.

During the 33rd millennium, Supreme Grand Master Tethys had performed the feat and spent the next one hundred and twelve days in a coma. Upon awakening, his psychic abilities were so diminished that he had to pass over his mantle as Chapter Master and lived out the rest of his days tending to memorials for the fallen in the Dead Fields.

Two thousand years later, a battle-brother of no small potential by the name of Hiermeno would attempt the same feat. His actions that day saved the lives of more than a billion souls who would otherwise have succumbed to daemonic predation but of the Grey Knight himself no trace was left, warp energy burning him out and consuming him entirely.

Most recently, Brother-Captain Stern had pulled off the same feat on a much smaller scale than Draigo was attempting during the cleansing of a world recently emerged from the Eye of Terror. The captain survived his ordeal and ensured the mission was a success, but he and his Brotherhood spent most of the next year on Titan training new recruits while they recuperated from their psychic exertions.

Reaching out through the mental storm raging around him, Kaldor Draigo spoke directly into the minds of his temporary charges, preparing them for what was to come. The Supreme Grand Master felt his resolve strengthen as each Grey Knight of the Fifth Brotherhood accepted what he was about to do unflinchingly and loaned him a small portion of their psychic might.

His eyes firmly closed, Draigo began to chant. The sanctuary he had been maintaining dropped as he diverted his power elsewhere, and a cadre of opportunistic daemons charged him, scenting an easy target. Tzula blazed away with her bolt pistol, taking the first rank down before the gun returned the sound of metal striking metal, her last clip having run dry. One of the Neverborn leapt towards her, and she held her combat blade locked against her chest in both hands – if this was how her battle was going to end, she was going to take her killer with her – but the daemon was barely off the ground when it was torn to pieces by storm bolter shells. She turned to look upon her saviour, the battered form of Gabriel despatching another trio of daemons before tossing the junior interrogator a fresh bolt pistol that had been maglocked to the shattered thigh of his armour.

With the Grand Master of the Deathwing alongside her, Tzula continued to keep the horde at bay. Draigo's incantation grew in volume and the temperature around him plummeted, blue-white frost forming across his worn Terminator plate. A wind blew up out of nowhere so powerful that it pushed and dragged corpses across the floor of the cave and generated tiny tornadoes that harassed both friend and foe alike. The Grey Knight's body convulsed violently, and azure smoke trickled from the joints and cracks in his armour. He thrust his face skywards, muscles taut with warp energy coursing through them, and cried out the same phrase three times over.

The litany he had chanted was in an archaic language, unfathomable by the layperson and difficult to hear. The final five words that he called out thrice over were in High Gothic and all who heard them knew their meaning.

'Come to me, my brothers!'

With a deafening crack of reality being parted and a blinding flash of intense white light, the seventy remaining Grey Knights of the Fifth Brotherhood appeared at Draigo's side. The displacement of air sent out a shockwave, a wall of concussive force that knocked all in its path to the ground. Daemons and plague zombies fell in droves, as did the Dark Angels. The Grey Knights sprayed the area with gunfire, slaughtering their prone enemies before they could rise.

Castellan Crowe rushed to Draigo's side, the stricken Supreme Grand Master still on his knees, wisps of blue smoke pouring from his mouth and nostrils. Ignoring the aid being offered him, Draigo stared right past the Castellan to where Tzula had come to rest alongside his Dark Angel counterpart.

'The daemon...' Draigo croaked before collapsing back into Crowe's waiting arms.

Reacting quickest, Azrael hauled himself to his feet before lifting Tzula to hers. Their path to the daemon clear, the inquisitor and the Dark Angel set off to finish the Battle for the Emerald Cave.

157961.M41 / Forty-two kilometres north-east of Atika, Pythos

DIVING DOWN INTO the ravine, scorching balefire licked the rear of the shuttle triggering yet more alarms in the crew compartment. The shrill wail quickly subsided as the heavy rain continued to pummel at the ship's hull, stifling any fire before it could take hold.

Jerking at the controls, Shira jinked the craft from side to side and erratically altered her altitude, sometimes coming within metres of the trees whizzing by beneath her, other times faking that she was pulling out of the gulley altogether. The Heldrake was hot on her tail, so close that every issue from its breath weapon scored at least a glancing hit. The only thing preventing the shuttle from becoming a fireball was Shira's skill as a pilot and the torrential downpour. She didn't know how much longer she could rely on either.

The ravine bent sharply to the right and Shira was glad of the curve, her turn presenting the Heldrake with a smaller target. Practically on its side, the shuttle arced widely around the bend, levelling out high above a new valley. As if to let Shira know that it was still close behind her, the Heldrake sent another blast of blue flame in her direction; not as close as its previous attack but enough to raise the temperature within the craft by double digits.

The combination of inclement weather and failing daylight meant Shira had to rely on her instruments to navigate, and as sensors fed their data into the navigational auspex, a pleasing sight resolved itself on a screen in front of her. The chasm she was in narrowed to a bottleneck, just wide enough for a single craft to fly through, before widening back out again. She was still several kilometres away and wouldn't be able to manoeuvre the shuttle while aiming the missile but this was the opening she had been looking for.

Throwing the shuttle around wildly, Shira called upon

every trick in her extensive repertoire to put more distance between her and the faster flying Heldrake. Every extra metre she gained was potentially the difference between life and death, and she fought hard for each one of them. At one point, she flew so close to the trees below that the cover for the landing gear was shorn away and a grating sound echoed around the crew compartment as branches scraped along the undercarriage. Ragwing fared even worse, its claws snagging on canopies in its effort to match Shira's altitude. By the time it had extricated itself from the tops of the trees, Shira was already spinning upwards in a controlled barrel roll.

Coming out of her final flip she checked the auspex again. She had indeed lengthened the gap, but wasn't sure it was enough to keep the Heldrake off her back for long enough to get her shot away. She had done all she could, the rest was up to fate.

Sheet lightning lit up the sky and the outline of the narrow pass loomed large ahead of her. Activating the control to lower the missile into its firing position, she brought the shuttle steady. Under normal circumstances she would have engaged the hunter-killer's guidance system and let that do the hard work for her, but that would tip the Heldrake off about her plan; this had to be done manually at the very last moment to maintain the element of surprise. Her finger hovered over the launch button.

More alarms sounded and the temperature rose sharply, the otherworldly stink of warpfire and scorched paint forcing Shira to suppress a gag. She glanced at the auspex again to see the Heldrake had eaten up the distance she had gained and was now closer than ever. Whether it had been holding something back in reserve or had called upon whichever foul god it worshipped for its acceleration spurt, she would never know. The one thing she was sure of was that another blast like that would certainly finish her off.

Ignoring the now constant wail of klaxons, Shira hung on until the last possible moment before slamming her fist down on the launch control. The missile left its housing with a *whoosh*, but that sound was soon swallowed up by the louder roar of the Heldrake and the crackle of flame engulfing the Inquisition shuttle. Shira pulled back on the controls, hopelessly trying to lift the craft over the shower of rock and scree about to rain down from the mountaintops.

The missile hit home and the twilight sky lit up brighter than a lightning flash, but Shira wasn't paying attention. Her focus was on the two engine status lights that were flashing bright red on the console before her, telling her they were both dead. Debris cascaded down, bouncing off the outside of the powerless shuttle that was heading rapidly for the ground trailing fire in its wake.

THE BOON OF its sudden burst of speed instantly becoming a curse, the Heldrake was flying too fast to avoid the avalanche. Tucking in its vulnerable wings, it darted through the shower of stones and boulders like a rocket, debris bouncing off its form as it cried out in pain, still airborne as it emerged through the other side.

Taking perch atop a nearby summit, the Heldrake looked on as its prey broke through the thick canopies down below before crashing to the ground in a blue streak. From thousands of metres above, the initial fire looked tiny, but moments later the crashed ship erupted in an explosion, a thick column of sapphire flame rising high into the darkening sky.

Satisfied that nothing could have survived the blast, the Heldrake took wing, considerably slower than before thanks to the grave damage inflicted upon it.

157961.M41 / The Emerald Cave. Atika, Pythos

LUNGS BURNING IN her chest, lactic acid flushing through every muscle in her body, Tzula fought against her exertions of the past four days with the same determination she had battled whatever the Archenemy had thrown at her.

Already outpacing her, Azrael ran on ahead, his sword lashing out from side to side, killing any foe with the temerity to try and get up. The Grey Knights and Dark Angels provided the pair of them with covering fire, any Plague Marine or daemon not dealt with by the *Sword of Secrets* ruthlessly mowed down in a hail of bolter fire.

Reacting to the shift in the battle, the bloated horror yielded yet more facsimiles, sliding down its blubber to enter the fray and defend their progenitor. They too found Azrael's blade and Space Marine bolters too much of a match for them.

With just a few metres left to cover, half a dozen of the

things detached themselves from the base of the host, putting themselves directly in Tzula and Azrael's route. The Lord of the Dark Angels didn't miss a beat, sweeping out his sword to take out half of them before bundling into the remainder and slamming them hard to the ground.

'Go! Go!' he called out to Tzula as she sprinted past him.

The distance to the Prisoner from the Emerald Cave eroded to nothing, and Tzula slid the athame out from her belt, gripping its crude hilt tightly. She blinked – just a standard, involuntary bodily response – and in that instant another of the horrific copies formed to bar her path. Fatty tendrils sprouted from its misshapen body, probing their way towards the inquisitor.

Calling upon years of gymnastics training from some of the finest physical tutors at the Ordo Malleus's disposal, Tzula pushed down hard on her back foot, launching herself over the top of the newly formed daemon. Her foot landed on what would have been its head, had the thing obeyed any basic laws of physiology, and sprang off again, stifling a scream as the toxic ooze coating its hide ate through the thick leather of her boots and stung her flesh. Somersaulting, she clasped both hands around the blade, stabbing down hard as she emerged from her flip.

The point of the blade parted daemon hide as easily as paper, a long gouge opening up as Tzula allowed gravity to pull her downwards. Filth spilled from the wound and Tzula vomited violently when she reached the ground as maggots, flies and the gestational larvae of things best left unknown gushed from the slit.

'Azrael!' she yelled, arm around her gut to prevent any more of its contents from being expelled.

From beneath the triumvirate of daemons attempting to subsume the Supreme Grand Master of the Dark Angels a gauntleted hand emerged gripping *Lion's Wrath*, one of the most finely crafted combi-weapons in the Imperium and a veteran of even more battles than its current wielder. His hand steady, Azrael engaged the bolter portion of the weapon and squeezed the firing stud.

When she looked back upon the battle in her later years, Tzula was never certain whether she actually witnessed what she saw next or whether the toxic stench from the daemon had caused her to hallucinate.

Time slowed around her, the bolt shell clearing the end of Azrael's weapon seeming to take an age. Muzzle flare issued forth in its wake more like a serene glow than the violent orange expulsion she was accustomed to seeing and the shell shimmered with that same light as it flew inexorably towards the daemon. The part that always gave her pause, always made her doubt the veracity of her own experience when she would later recount the tale, was in that last instant before the round found its mark it appeared to have wings, altering its course ever so slightly to enter through the rent rather than bounce harmlessly off the daemon's skin.

Her perceptions sped up again, the report of Azrael's weapon still ringing in her ears, and she staggered backwards looking up at the cyclopean daemon.

She had seen Neverborn vanquished before, even prior to her experiences of recent months, and no two ever left the mortal realm in quite the same way. Some exploded in a shower of gore, taking with them as many souls as possible in one final cruel act. Others merely dissipated, their passing leaving no trace of their ever existing save the trail of corpses the Neverborn inevitably leave in their wake. Others still go noisily, cursing their banisher, pleading for clemency or offering undreamt of riches and power in exchange for their continued material existence.

The Prisoner from the Emerald Cave did none of these things.

Deflating like a child's punctured kick-toy, the daemon's flesh sloughed from its frame releasing the detritus Tzula had witnessed when she had opened it up. Billions of maggots oozed across the floor of the cavern and thick black clouds of flies took flight, indistinguishable from the palls of smoke hovering overhead. The embryonic horrors flailed on the hard ground, bereft of the amniotic sustenance of their incubator, quickly dying and becoming fodder for the tide of maggots. Its offspring, those daemons formed from the raw stuff of the host, withered and died in the same way, the toxins that coated them corroding the stone, leaving craters behind as markers of their passing.

Tzula shook her head in an attempt to clear the fug that had gripped her and wiped her stinging eyes. Slightly unsteady on her feet, she made her way over to Azrael who was flicking the corrosive sludge left behind by the dissipated daemons from his greaves and gauntlets.

Tzula was about to laud him for his shot when he spoke first.

'I don't care if it was the heat of battle, junior interrogator,' he snarled, shaking loose a glob of acidic goo from his boot. 'The correct way to address me is *Lord* Azrael.'

Drawing his sword, the Supreme Grand Master of the Dark Angels headed in the direction of the Deathwing who were dealing with the few Plague Marines and zombies that remained.

Shaking her head in disbelief, Tzula tucked the athame back in her belt and followed him.

157961.M41 / The Underhive. Atika, Pythos

THE PAIN IN his head had built to such a level that Epimetheus wanted to grab one of the nearby rocks and break open his own skull to relieve the pressure. The buzzing and throbbing was so intense that he was finding it hard to focus on Abaddon's words.

'So,' the Warmaster said, leaning forwards and gripping the Grey Knight roughly beneath the chin. 'Which one are you?'

Epimetheus said nothing.

'Mute are you? I'd make the most of our conversation if I were you, Epimetheus, because you won't have a tongue for very much longer.' Abaddon moved his hand away from Epimetheus's face and turned away from him. 'I know you aren't my erstwhile brother because I watched him die, nor are you one of the other traitors Malcador recruited so that narrows it down.'

Struggling through the agony, Epimetheus locked Abaddon with a baleful stare.

The Warmaster turned back to meet his gaze. 'Have we met before? Did we once fight alongside each other as brothers, you and I, or was it later, trading shots from opposing battle lines?'

Epimetheus maintained eye contact but remained silent. Abaddon switched his line of questioning again.

'Are you the Ultramarine?' He leaned forwards, inspecting Epimetheus's features. 'No. Too obvious. Besides, you don't have that look about you.'

Abaddon peered deeply into Epimetheus's eyes, as if he was trying to see what lay behind them. He started to laugh, coldly and entirely devoid of mirth.

'Oh, the irony...' He leaned in closer, his nose practically touching the Grey Knight's. 'The brother of ten who became a brother of eight. Azrael and his whelps would tear this planet apart if they knew who you were.'

Epimetheus didn't flinch. He held Abaddon's gaze, unblinking.

The Warmaster backed away. Without taking his eyes off the Grey Knight, he gestured for one of his Black Legionnaires to come forward. A black and gold figure emerged from the dark holding out a portable vox-unit which he passed to Abaddon.

'Huron,' he said, the handset crackling as he activated it. 'Get me off this rock. My mission is complete.'

There was a long crackle of static followed by a tinny voice. 'As you wish, Warmaster. The extraction will commence the instant you are back on the surface.'

Killing the link, Abaddon handed the vox back. Epimetheus's brow furrowed a fraction, almost imperceptible but apparent even in the gloom to one with the enhanced senses of a Space Marine.

'I know what you're thinking, Epimetheus,' Abaddon said. 'The Damnation Cache. The Prisoner in the Emerald Cave. Why am I abandoning this world while there is still a chance that my war could still be won?'

Abaddon crouched down.

'This was never my war, but it was convenient for me to fight it. Corpulax and his lackeys wanted the Emerald Cave opening to set free the daemon within and gain favour with Nurgle. I doubt that without the aid of my Black Legion he will be successful in that venture but, should his god spare him, the Plague Lord and his warband are bound by oath to join me on my next Black Crusade.

'The Davinicus Lycae wanted to reopen the Damnation Cache and get their hands on one of those accursed blades. For millennia, they have been honour bound to the Black Legion and all true sons of Cthonia, and they sought our aid in this matter. While the prospect of an endless army of daemons sallying forth into the Imperium is an appealing one to me, using a campaign on Pythos as a distraction to see whether the whispers in the warp were true was an opportunity too good to pass up.'

Epimetheus finally broke his silence. 'What whispers?'

Abaddon smiled, obviously pleased that the Grey Knight had relinquished his quietude. 'That a psyker of prodigious power dwelt here. Many took that to mean the Prisoner who you trapped here ten thousand years ago, but the Davinicus Lycae held a different theory based upon the snatches of information that left this world after you first came here. They believed that when the Grey Knights sealed shut the Cache and trapped the Prisoner in his tomb they left one of their own behind to watch over this world. The most powerful among their number. One of their founding brothers.'

Epimetheus's eyes narrowed slightly.

'Don't worry, it's not *only* your psychic abilities I'm interested in.' The Warmaster raised a hand to Epimetheus's neck and tapped it with two fingers right where the progenoid sat beneath the flesh. 'It's your genetic legacy I want too.'

The realisation carved through the pain granting Epimetheus a moment of clarity.

The Grey Knight was about to cry out his defiance when Abaddon's fist made contact with Epimetheus's forehead and everything went black.

157961.M41 / Forty-two kilometres north-east of Atika, Pythos

THE RAIN HAD subsided to little more than a drizzle by the time Shira moved out from the crash site.

She had spent her first hour on the ground sheltering at the base of a mighty redwood, partly to be out of the rain, partly to be out of sight of Ragwing who she was convinced would be circling overhead waiting for her to emerge. Confident that she was neither going to get drenched nor be picked off by the enraged Heldrake, she had salvaged what she could from the steaming wreck – which turned out to be very little – and fashioned a basic crutch from twisted metal and fallen branches to allow her to move on the ankle she had broken in the crash. Her ribs throbbed from where the harness had prevented her from dying in the impact and her shoulder was badly bruised from where she had used it to ram open the shuttle door seconds before the craft exploded.

But at least she was alive to take another shot at Ragwing. Provided Tzula didn't kill her first for breaking the shuttle, of course.

Putting all her weight onto her good foot, Shira began the long hobble back towards Atika.

158961.M41 / The Emerald Cave. Atika, Pythos

AZRAEL WAS ENGAGED in deep conversation with Apothecary Rephial as Balthasar approached, prisoner in tow. The two Dark Angels halted their discussion of casualty figures and gene-seed retrieval ratios and drew their weapons as the Terminator drew closer. Gabriel and Interrogator-Chaplain Asmodai did likewise, moving to the Supreme Grand Master's side when the identity of the captive became apparent.

'Apothecary Rephial, Master Zadakiel and Fifth Company have been leading the clean-up operation for the past day and almost all of them are walking wounded. Have Master Belial and Third Company relieve them and see to their wounds,' Azrael said, his subtext plain.

'As you wish, my lord,' Rephial said. His armour was as battered and gore-streaked as any of the other Dark Angels, his ability to kill the equal of his capacity to cure. As he walked past Balthasar, he gave the Deathwing an appreciative nod.

'A prisoner for you, Lord Asmodai,' Balthasar said, tugging on the chains he had used to bind Corpulax and dragging the Traitor Marine unceremoniously to the hard ground. Whereas previously he had only been missing his hands, now both of his arms were gone entirely, the shackles wrapped tightly around his throat. 'I apologise that he is no longer in one piece.'

Asmodai said nothing, the crackle of his crozius arcanum doing his talking for him.

'With your leave, my lords...' Balthasar acknowledged his three superiors before turning on his heel.

'Brother Balthasar, you should witness this,' Azrael said. Balthasar halted and spun to face them again.

'Lord Azrael, he is not ready,' Gabriel protested.

Azrael raised a hand, bare flesh visible where daemonic acid had corroded his gauntlet. 'Perhaps not, Gabriel, but he has earned this.'

The Master of the Deathwing nodded his assent, first to

Azrael then to Balthasar. Corpulax laughed, the look on his face that of an arrogant victor rather than a defeated foe.

'It's always secrets with you, isn't it?' Corpulax sneered. 'Trying to keep a lid on the shame you've borne all these long millennia. Not wanting anybody to know about the Dark Angels treachery, including your own brothers. I was one of you, once, one of "the Unforgiven", putting my life on the line day in and day out in the name of the Lion and the Emperor, and what did I get for it?'

None of the Dark Angels answered, their visages masks of disdain.

'I got treated like a child at the supper table, asked to leave when the grown-ups wanted to speak, just like you did to your Apothecary. For years I put up with it, never questioning, never querying. Carrying out my orders even when it meant abandoning the people we were supposed to be protecting to carry out our own petty agenda or entering into conflict with our own allies. And for what? To protect a few pathetic secrets.'

Corpulax laughed again.

'Do you know what the joke of it is? The punch line to all this? You're only keeping it a secret from yourselves. You don't think the Fallen share their path to enlightenment with those who rally to their banners, with those they bend their knee to? All who dwell within the Eye are privy to your secrets, know of your ancient betrayal and what you do with those former Dark Angels you hunt down and capture.'

Asmodai's crozius blazed angrily.

'We know about your dungeons, and how you make us try to repent, the "techniques" you employ to extract confessions and assuage your bruised pride. I've even spoken to the one you let slip from your grasp, the only prisoner ever to escape from beneath the Rock.'

The Dark Angels looked cagily at one another. The look that passed between Azrael and Asmodai was particularly loaded.

'More secrets? Or has that not happened yet? The way time passes within the Eye that's entirely possible.'

He let out a long, wet chuckle.

'No matter. You can throw me in there, try to break me but it won't work. My new master favours me and even the worst excesses your Interrogator-Chaplains plan to inflict pale against the pain I have already endured. I'll bide my time, maybe scream occasionally, sob for mercy, look as if I'm playing along. Then, when the time is right, I'll disappear. One morning, you'll come down to my cell, torture implements all clean and ready for another day's work, and it'll be empty. And do you know what the *really* ironic thing is?'

All eyes were fixed coldly on the Plague Lord.

'If my escape fails the first time, the second time, the third, I'll get more chances. You'd rather die yourselves than let me die without a confession passing my lips.' The grin he wore was so large that necrotised flesh tore at the edges of his mouth. 'At this point I would hold out my hands so you could put them in irons but your whelp robbed me of that particular grand gesture.'

Azrael took a step towards Corpulax.

'Have you finished?' the Supreme Grand Master said, voice awash with disinterest.

The smile dropped from Corpulax's face. 'When you were speaking about the Rock just now, you said "us". Something about how "you make us try to repent". What did you mean by that?'

Corpulax bared his teeth again, half-smile, half-snarl. 'I meant that the only thing that matters to you is securing the atonement of us Fallen.'

It was the Dark Angel's turn to laugh now. Asmodai and Gabriel followed suit. Balthasar joined in, though he wasn't sure what was so funny.

'You used the word "us" again. "Us Fallen".' The laughter ceased. 'What makes you think that we consider you to have fallen?'

'Because I turned my back on both Emperor and Imperium. I swore fealty to the Plague God and took up arms against those I once fought alongside.' Corpulax spat at Azrael's feet. 'And I'd do it again in a heartbeat.'

'But why did you turn? Was it for power? Did your rotting deity promise you the means by which to attain all that you desired? Or was it in exchange for your life? Did you fear death so much that you sold both body and soul to prolong your life, no better than one of those plague zombies you commanded? Or were you forced to do it? Did a former master lead you down that path, constantly telling you that it was the right thing to do, all the while knowing that he was driving you towards damnation?'

It was Corpulax's turn to remain silent.

'I know that the Consecrators still remain loyal to the Lion and the Golden Throne so you cannot claim that you were led astray, that you believed you were carrying out the will of your master, blind to the truth.' Azrael moved closer to Corpulax and knelt down so that he could look him in the eyes. 'You turned to the Plague God for entirely selfish reasons, be it self-advancement or self-preservation. Those brothers of the Dark Angels Legion who betrayed us during the Great Heresy did so because of Luther. Some turned out of loyalty to him, others because they were told that it was the will of the Lion, Luther acting as his hand on Caliban while the primarch put down Horus's rebellion.'

Azrael got to his feet. 'Either way, Luther was the catalyst. Without him none of them would have fallen.' He walked away from the kneeling traitor. Asmodai and Gabriel followed him, leaving Balthasar as a lone sentinel over the prisoner.

'Though they fell, they were pushed and still have the chance to rise again in death, to denounce their dark masters and recognise the folly of treachery. You were not pushed, Corpulax, you jumped into the arms of your new god, and for that we do not grant you the honour of considering you among the Fallen.'

None of the three retreating Dark Angels looked back.

'End him, Balthasar,' Azrael said as casually as if he was asking him to check his chronometer.

Before any protest could pass Corpulax's lips, Balthasar's blade had parted the Plague Lord's head from his shoulders.

'THAT WAS QUITE some trick you pulled there, Draigo,' Azrael said as he approached the Supreme Grand Master of the Grey Knights. 'I'd ask you to teach it to my Librarians but I suspect I know what your answer would be.'

Apothecary Raguel finished suturing the wound to Draigo's calf and moved on to tend to the wounds of less seriously injured Grey Knights. Beside him, Tzula handed him back the greave of his armour while she too had her deepest cuts stitched by an Imperial Guard medic.

'I saw the way your Dark Angels fought, Azrael. Not a single one of them needs any tutelage from me.' Draigo clamped the leg piece of his Terminator armour in place and held a hand up to Azrael. The Dark Angel clasped it and lifted the Grey Knight to his feet. Their gauntlets remained locked in a warrior's salute. 'I believe our debts to each other are now paid.'

Azrael smiled. It was a few moments before he spoke. 'Indeed they are.'

'The Plague Lord, Corpulax? Is there any sign of him?' Draigo asked releasing his grip.

'One of my Deathwing has just executed him. Traitors like him cannot be allowed to live.'

Draigo nodded. 'A shame. I would have liked the chance to question him before he was killed. During the final battle he said... things, things about me, about my future.'

'I'm sure with the application of the correct techniques he would have said a great many things,' Azrael replied. 'Come now, Grand Master Draigo–'

'*Supreme* Grand Master Draigo.'

'Supreme Grand Master Draigo,' Azrael corrected. 'My Ravenwing have cleared a path to the Damnation Cache. The time has come for us to end this war.'

'Our part in this particular war is over, Azrael. It falls to another to seal the Damnation Cache.'

Both Space Marines looked down at Tzula. Her shredded bodyglove had been abandoned altogether and she was back wearing Catachan fatigues and a grubby vest which was tied off above her torso, allowing air to her freshly sealed wounds. She waved the medic away and sprang to her feet.

'What are we waiting for?' she said, pulling the athame from her waistband and cockily throwing it in the air, end over end. She caught it by the handle as it fell. 'Lead on.'

POSTLUDE

227961.M41 / The Rock. In orbit around Pythos, Pandorax System

AN ARMY OF Chapter serfs stood waiting at the foot of the embarkation ramp as the rear hatch of *Roar of Vengeance* ground open with a hiss of escaping pressure. Its massive engines spooled down from a growl to a whine, and the clang of Terminator armour rang out over the noise of activity on the hangar deck.

As Balthasar set foot on the Dark Angels spacebound fortress-monastery for the first time in months, five of the serfs approached him in obeisance. He removed his storm bolter and handed it to two of them, before unsheathing his sword and giving it to another pair. To the final serf, a bulky man with the Dark Angels winged sword icon tattooed below one eye, he passed his helm. Each of them bowed before carrying the items back to his chambers. All across the deck, other serfs were doing the same with their particular master's artefacts and equipment.

In honour of their valour and victory on Pythos, Lord Azrael had granted all of the surviving Dark Angels the honour of travelling back to the Rock on board his own personal transport. The ancient Thunderhawk had made fewer journeys than any of the Sons of the Lion would have liked, but Balthasar and his squad were the penultimate group – only

Lord Azrael himself along with an honour guard of Death-wing Knights still remained planetside.

Balthasar looked down at his suit of relic armour, worn into battle by two dozen former warriors of the Dark Angels First Company, and felt both pride and dismay at its sorry condition. Pride that he had lived up to the legacy of its former owners by helping win yet another campaign for his Chapter, dismay that he had allowed it to sustain so much damage in the process. With the vast majority of the Dark Angels already back onboard the Rock, the Techmarines and artificers were likely already inundated with orders for repair and replacement, but his place among the Chapter's elite would grant him preferential treatment. Instead of joining his battle-brothers and returning to quarters, Balthasar set off in the opposite direction towards the forge.

He had barely taken ten paces when two figures stepped out to bar his passage, one in black armour, the other ivory.

'And where do you think you are going, Brother Balthasar?' Gabriel said, the condition of his armour the mirror of the younger Space Marine's.

'I was on my way to visit Master Serpicus in the forge to petition him to repair my armour and wargear.' There was an uncertainty to Balthasar's voice, he was unsure of the two high-ranking Dark Angels' reasons for stopping him.

'There will be plenty of time for your plate to receive the attention it requires,' Asmodai said, his voice a gravelly whisper. 'Right now, there are things you must know. Secrets we must share with you.' The Interrogator-Chaplain nodded to the Master of the Deathwing and ran a finger across the cheek of his skull mask, just beneath his right eye.

Shepherded from the hangar deck by both Gabriel and Asmodai, Balthasar took another step closer to the centre of the circle.

227961.M41 / The Governor's Quarters. Atika, Pythos

THE STARK RAYS of Pythos's midday sun filtered in through the gaps in the shutters of the makeshift governor's quarters and reflected from every inch of Kaldor Draigo's silver armour. The suit had been cleaned and polished in the weeks since the victory on Pythos, but it still bore the dents and cracks of combat and would require many hours of work once the Grey Knights returned to Titan.

'And neither the Grey Knights nor the Dark Angels can spare even a single squad to garrison Pythos?' The new governor's tone was insistent rather than pleading. 'We have both witnessed the lengths the Archenemy will go to take this world and fill it with horrors. This time we were fortunate that Strike and his men were here and prepared for the assault and could hold out for reinforcements. Abaddon escaped. If he comes back again and with greater numbers, I fear the outcome will be very different. Not to mention the Chaos forces left behind who are already hampering our rebuilding efforts.'

Draigo grinned, impressed at how quickly and firmly the new governor had grasped the nettle of politics. 'Governor Digriiz, the Adeptus Astartes are not the personal armies of planetary rulers. Colonel Strike and the 183rd will remain here in defence of Pythos and another three Catachan regiments are being sent here to bolster his forces. Two Navy fighter wings will stay behind to patrol the skies and elements of Battlefleet Demeter are to be placed on permanent patrol in the Pandorax System. You know as well as I how dark it has got in the galaxy of late, how stretched our forces are. You should thank the Emperor for what you have.'

Tzula returned his smile. 'You can't blame me for trying.'

Strike had immediately ruled himself out of consideration for the role of governor the instant offensive operations had halted. When Tzula had pointed out – without going into too much detail – that she had prior experience of ruling over a world, Azrael immediately granted her the role with Draigo's full endorsement.

Though it was not unprecedented for a member of the Ordos to be granted governorship of an Imperial world, it was rare for a junior interrogator to be elevated to such a high post. She had already used her Inquisitorial sway to good effect and the first Departmento Munitorum vessels were even now en route to Pythos to begin the rebuilding process. Within months, new miners would arrive from Gaea and other outlying worlds and she was determined to have the planet back up to full operational capacity before the year was out.

'Perhaps at least one Grey Knight will remain behind regardless,' Tzula said, adjusting the lapel of her unfamiliar ceremonial gown with her augmented hand. Gone was the crude bionic fitted by the Catachan medical corps, in its place a sleek, silent limb crafted by one of Azrael's Techmarines and fitted by a Dark Angels Apothecary.

Draigo's aspect darkened. 'Epimetheus is no longer on Pythos. I know that he would rebuff any attempt for me to hail him telepathically, but since our communion I have no longer been able to detect his psychic spoor.'

'Do you think he has gone into the Maelstrom, as he told Shira?'

'It is possible, but I sense the hand of another in this. It is not my warp gifts telling me that but rather a feeling I have inside my gut.'

They remained in silence for a moment, Shira stood behind a jury-rigged desk made from an old ammunition crate, Draigo stooping in the enclosed confines of the temporary structure.

'My Grey Knights and I take our leave of Pythos tonight but before we return to Titan there are still a few loose ends I have to tie up,' Draigo said eventually.

Tzula knew exactly what one of those loose ends was and, though it made her feel uneasy, as a loyal servant of the Golden Throne she knew it had to be done. What Draigo said next caught her completely off-guard. 'You have something that is the property of the Ordo Malleus. I will see that it is returned to them in good order.'

'K'Cee? I thought–'

'I am not referring to the xenos, Governor Digriiz. I meant the knife.'

'Oh,' Tzula said, slightly embarrassed. She had almost forgotten about the knife, having barely given it a thought since… since… since she did *something* with it. She remembered using it to help kill the daemon in the Emerald Cave but what did she do with it after that? The Damnation Cache – how had she closed it? Draigo spoke again and the thought eluded her like smoke in the breeze.

'May I have it?' he held out a gauntleted palm.

Tzula pulled back the folds in her robe and slid the athame out from beneath. Gripping the point between the tips of her fingers she placed it in Draigo's hand. Somehow, impossibly, when she took her own hand away, the blade had grown, appearing to be a perfectly reasonable size in the Space Marine's enormous fist.

'And K'Cee? The jokaero?' she said with trepidation.

'What jokaero?' Draigo said, the corners of his mouth upturning slightly. Tzula mimicked his expression. 'And now to my last few bits of business on Pythos. May the Emperor watch over you and keep this world safe, Governor Digriiz.' Still dipping his head to prevent it from scraping on the low ceiling, he turned to exit the prefabricated structure.

'Lord Draigo?' Tzula said, causing the Grey Knight to stop and rotate to face her. 'There is just one more thing you could do for me. One last favour.'

'I have already turned a blind eye to the fact that you are harbouring a xenos – a xenos that should by rights be back under the custody of the Ordos. Please do not push your luck.'

'Perhaps I misspoke. This favour is not for me, it's for Colonel Strike and the Catachans.' She looked him dead in the eyes as she spoke. 'What they've endured, all they've been through. They deserve time to grieve properly, to honour their dead in the proper way. Is there any way you could delay mind-wiping the 183rd? They've earned that much at least.'

Draigo considered this for a moment. 'Very well, Governor Digriiz. I'll have Castellan Crowe commence with the other regiments. The Catachans' minds won't be wiped until sundown,' he said before stepping out into the noon heat of Pythos.

THE TEN-MAN SQUAD of Deathwing Knights flanked the approach to the *Roar of Vengeance*, maces held high to form a processional archway under which their lord and master could board the Thunderhawk.

As he neared the waiting craft, Azrael noticed the heads of some of his honour guard twitch, turning slightly to look back behind him. Usually, this sort of infraction would result in a stern rebuke at the very least, a writ of penitence at worst, but Azrael would have expected only a single battle-brother to show such indiscipline. This was a whole squad, of Deathwing Knights no less. Curious as to what had distracted such immaculately disciplined and well-drilled Space Marines, Azrael turned around to look.

Just in time to catch a silvered fist in his face.

The blow was controlled, not hard enough to render him unconscious or break any bones, but with enough force to knock him brusquely to his backside. In a blur his assailant was on top of him, gripping the collar of his cloak and snarling.

'What did you do with him, you bastard?' Draigo yelled, spittle trailing from his lips and teeth. 'Is he up there in those dungeons of yours, along with all those others you've collected down the centuries? What do you want with them? What is it that you do to them?'

The Deathwing honour guard surrounded the pair of Supreme Grand Masters, their weapons primed and aimed at Draigo's head. Azrael gestured for them to lower their arms.

'I don't know what you're talking about,' Azrael said, trying to remove the Grey Knight's hands from upon him.

Draigo slammed the Dark Angel against the ground again. 'Liar! You've taken him. I know you have. Were you in league with Abaddon all along? Did he deliver him up to you in exchange for his escape?'

The Deathwing's guns rose again. This time Azrael did not order them dropped. 'Are you accusing me of heresy, Grey Knight?' It was as much a warning as an accusation.

Draigo paused, fully aware of the implications of responding in the affirmative. He released his grip on Azrael and stood up. 'You figured out who he was, and what he was, and you had to have him to yourself. Pray that I never obtain the proof as the fury of the entire Grey Knights Chapter will make what you faced here on Pythos look like a training exercise.'

'As I said, Draigo,' Azrael said, hauling himself upright, 'I have no idea what you're talking about.'

As his Grey Knights counterpart marched off into the distance, Lord Azrael of the Dark Angels would have given anything in the universe for the opposite to be true.

COLONEL STRIKE SHIELDED his eyes from the sun and looked skywards as the *Roar of Vengeance* raced towards the heavens. As he watched the vapour trail lengthen and fade, he could not help but feel a pang of jealousy, that the Space Marines got to return home while he and his troops would live out their days light years from Catachan defending a world they should never have been on in the first place. The feeling soon passed when he realised that both the Dark Angels and the Grey Knights would live out their extended lifespans defending countless worlds that were not their own, destined to die at the point of an enemy's blade, at range by the gun of some unseen killer or in a heroic act of self-sacrifice. That thought also gave rise to envy.

With the Dark Angels gone and the Grey Knights due to leave Pythos come nightfall, the colonel was now back in overall command of the planet's defence. Most of the Chaos forces had fled the planet but pockets of invaders remained behind harrying the Imperial forces in a guerrilla campaign. Plague Marines still prowled the tunnels beneath Atika, a handful of Black Legionnaires had made a killing ground of a thousand square kilometres of jungle in the southern hemisphere and packs of cultists laid claim to abandoned delver-strongholds and were using them as bases of operation. There were corroborated rumours that a winged daemon engine had taken up home in the Olympax Mountains and was preying on both foot and air patrols.

Strike walked briskly through the city of tents and huts that the Imperial Guard regiments had erected on the Plain of Glass after the war had ended, the heavy kit bag over his shoulder clanking with the sound of metal on metal with each step he took. Soon the temporary shelters would be replaced with more permanent structures and a new hive city built to replace the one that had been destroyed in retaking the planet. In the meantime, tens of thousands of soldiers from dozens of different regiments were living on top of one another, and without a clear and present enemy to fight had begun to turn on each other. In the past week Strike had spent as much time dealing with indiscipline as he had organising troop movements and rotations.

Accepting salutes as he went, the colonel came to the end of the neat rows of tents and canvas gave way to open ground. Soon reaching his destination, Strike dropped his bag to the ground and opened it, revealing the cache of Catachan blades within.

The orbital bombardment of Atika had been brutal and absolute but one tract had avoided destruction in the firestorm. Whether by some error on the part of a Calculus Logi who determined the targeting pattern, a missile malfunctioning and detonating astray or the whim of the God-Emperor himself, the area used by the Catachans as a memorial prior to the invasion, and the land around it, had remained intact. In the weeks since the war ended, new markers had been added and the red of Catachan bandanas had been joined by Mordian blue, Cadian grey and many other colours as fellow Imperial Guard regiments tied the tunics of the fallen to bayonets and combat blades by way of remembrance.

Strike had just taken the first armful of knives from the bag when the sound of heavy boots crunching over the vitrified approach drew his attention. His vest and bandana drenched with sweat, Brigstone was following the route his commanding officer had taken.

'I thought I'd find you here,' Brigstone said drawing alongside Strike. 'We've received word from Lord Draigo and the Grey Knights. There's to be some kind of ceremony tonight before they leave the planet. Attendance is mandatory, all personnel. Do you think they're going to honour us in some way?'

Until a few months ago, Strike – like many Imperial Guard commanders – had never even heard of the Grey Knights, yet now they were the subject of hearsay and speculation among the various regiments stationed on Pythos. Some of those whispers and half-truths had a dark edge to them: the Grey Knights killed anybody who laid eyes on them – even Space Marines from other Chapters – to keep their existence secret; anybody fighting alongside them was turned into a servitor after the battle; any world on which they set foot was destroyed to cover their tracks. Strike had heard them all but believed none – if the Grey Knights were going to execute them it would have happened by now. But the fact remained that the Grey Knights obviously went to great lengths to keep their existence clandestine. He had harboured suspicions for a while as to how they maintained their secrecy and had a feeling these would be confirmed before the next morning.

'I think in their own way they are,' Strike said regretfully. He handed Brigstone the knives he was carrying and retrieved more from the bag. 'But for now, let us remember our dead while we still can.'

Strike started off across the memorial field, a sea of glinting blades and fluttering scraps of uniform as far as the eye could see.

* * *

OVERHEAD, A WING of Imperial Navy Thunderbolts flew in tight formation, nine craft forming a perfect V shape. As they reached the Imperial Guard memorial, eight of them peeled off leaving just the flight leader to continue flying true and straight. Traditionally only one of the craft would have broken ranks, but the losses incurred on Pythos were such that eight seemed a more appropriate salute.

Besides, the new wing commander of the Pythos Third Fighter Wing was anything but a traditionalist.

Epaulets gleaming under the high sun, Shira Hagen sat in the cockpit of her Thunderbolt gripping the controls to maintain her course. Her new ride was unfamiliar to her, but it had enough in common with the Kestrel that she had been cleared to fly one as soon as her ankle had healed. Rumour had it that the ejector mechanism actually worked on this pattern of Thunderbolt, which given the fates of the previous two craft she had flown, might be useful at some point.

Her new rank and fighter were not the only things that had changed. The instant she had left the medicae on a pair of proper crutches, she had started to ask questions around the Imperial Guard camp about obtaining certain items. The brushes had been the easiest to get hold of, the treadheads in the armoured battalions always keen on marking their kill tallies along their hulls. The paint was a little trickier to come by but after convincing a Cadian quartermaster to join her at the dice table she had walked away with the exact colours she had required.

The vox-link in her newly repainted helmet squawked into life, the tinny hiss of a ground controller. 'Wing Commander Hagen. Heldrake spotted over the Olympax Range. Second Wing are already engaged but require assistance.'

'Ragwing?' she replied hopefully. Her exploits against the daemon engine – along with a recommendation from the new planetary governor – had helped secure her promotion and the legend of the beast, along with the name she had given it, was the talk of the Navy mess halls.

'Affirmative, wing commander,' came the crackling reply.

'Back in formation, Third Wing,' she said, switching to an open channel.

She looked out of her cockpit to see all eight of her fellow pilots slotting in behind her. Another set of eyes watched on, large and reptilian where once was the image of a pair of hawk eyes, set above a fanged maw painted over the hooked beak. Gone too were the representations of grey feathers, replaced by the likeness of green scales.

'We have a dragon to slay.'

227961.M41 / The Emerald Cave. Atika, Pythos

IT MOVED ON all fours, bounding over the corpses yet to be removed from the killing field and darting between the scorched and mangled ruins of tanks and flyers. Occasionally it would stop to look more closely at one of the abandoned vehicles, sometimes scoring a strange mark into the hull, other times removing some component and placing it carefully into the pack it carried on its back. In the main it ignored them, intent on recovering what it had come down so deep to find.

Its inhuman eyes could see perfectly well in the darkness, but it wore a lamp fashioned from Pythosian crystal strapped to its forehead. To any onlooker it would have seemed as if a miner strayed too far from the pit tunnels, but the only eyes that looked upon it were dead ones and what it sought was far more important – to it, at least – than mere jewels or rocks.

The red beam of light refracted from the emeralds in the wall as it turned to look around, casting the entire chamber in a strange, dull hue. Spotting what it had come for, it emitted a loud exclamation of success and leapt from wreck to wreck, seemingly heedless to its own wellbeing as it slammed against the hard metal.

Halting atop the sheared hull of a super-heavy, it looked along its length, making certain that it had located its quarry. Jumping down, it ran the back of a hairy arm along an armoured fairing, wiping away the coating of soot and daemonic residues. Shining its lamp upon it, two words carefully scripted in High Gothic were revealed: *Traitor's Bane*.

With another screech of joy, K'Cee pulled a wrench from his backpack and set to work at the long task he had ahead of him.

??????.M?? / Somewhere in the Eye of Terror

THE HEAVY DOOR to the cell creaked open slowly, sending two of its occupants scurrying to the corners. If they could, the other two beings in the cell might have done likewise but, fused together and suspended from chains made from an unbreakable warpforged metal, that was beyond their current abilities.

Abaddon stepped into the darkened prison, the amber eyes of one of the xenos blanks regarding him with fear. On the other side of the cell, the female human blank, naked and caked in filth, snarled like a cornered beast. The Warmaster ignored them both, focused solely on who – or, more accurately what – was hanging in the centre of the cell.

His powerful arms bound at the wrists, Epimetheus's similarly shackled feet hung a metre above the cold stone floor of the dungeon. His skin was a ruin of scar tissue, his black carapace having been removed early in his captivity, and his eyes and mouth having been sewn shut with fibre hewn from the sinew of daemons. Behind his sealed lips sat the void where his tongue used to be, Abaddon making good on his promise at the time of capture, and a clean surgical wound ran along the side of his throat where his progenoids had been extracted.

The price in oaths and fealty that the Warmaster had received from Fabius Bile and his ilk in exchange for this particular genetic material was immeasurable. When next he launched a Black Crusade upon the Imperium Abaddon would not only reap the benefits of that loyalty but, with the blessing of the Four, have new and more powerful troops at his disposal.

And, if his ultimate plan should come to fruition... No, similar ventures had been attempted in the past and come to naught. The Warmaster dealt in practicalities and actualities, not what ifs.

Sensing a presence in the room, Epimetheus twisted on his chains, his enhanced physiology still granting him the strength to do so in spite of the unknowable amount of time he had been in captivity. As he spun above the ground, the true extent of the horrors wrought upon Epimetheus became apparent, driving a smirk to Abaddon's lips.

His limbs removed, the third blank was grafted to Epimetheus's back, one last failsafe should the emasculated Grey Knight slip his bonds and attempt to escape. The man was barely alive, the dull eyes set below a heavy brow barely open, and tubes protruded from holes bored in his torso through which flowed dark liquids, sustaining his hellish existence.

Abaddon drew close to his captive, causing both Epimetheus and the symbiotic blank to flinch. The Grey Knight's nostrils flared. Despite being deprived of most of his senses, he could tell that the Warmaster was near.

Leaning in close to his prisoner's ear, Abaddon whispered, 'Soon, Epimetheus. Soon.'

The breath being forced from Epimetheus's nose became grunts, and he pulled and twisted more forcefully at his bonds causing the blank joined to him to murmur a plaintive wail.

Exiting the cell, the Warmaster left the Grey Knight to struggle against his restraints, safe in the knowledge that he would never be able to break them no matter how long he hung there.

Abaddon had waited ten thousand years to depose the Corpse-Emperor and claim the Throne of Terra. To break one of the founding brothers of the Grey Knights, to have him bend his knee in unswerving allegiance, the Warmaster could wait for all eternity.

ACKNOWLEDGEMENTS

EDDIE ECCLES, ROB 'Cypher' White and Sarah Cawkwell were the best first readers a writer could hope for. Karen Miksza sadly isn't on that list but redeemed herself by commissioning some of the finest artwork ever to grace a Black Library product.

The author would like to thank Nick Kyme and the Black Library editorial team for their hard work, patience and dedication in helping me bring this novel from concept to print. Special mention must be made of Graeme Lyon for turning me on to ludes, especially the postlude.

I would also like to thank several of my fellow authors: L J Goulding for giving me a Grand Master to kill, Aaron Dembski-Bowden for not leaving too much saliva on the Grey Knights when he put them down, Mitchel Scanlon and Mike Lee for what I hope by now is obvious.

Much of this novel was written in various hotels and bed and breakfasts across the UK and France. I would like to express my gratitude to the staff at those fine establishments, especially the ones that leave little chocolates on the pillows.

ABOUT THE AUTHOR

Domiciled in the East Midlands, **C Z Dunn** is the author of the Space Marine Battles novel *Pandorax*, the Dark Angels novella *Dark Vengeance* and the audio dramas *Trials of Azrael*, *Ascension of Balthasar* and *Malediction*, as well as several short stories. Having spent many years in the publishing industry, with a strong leaning towards genre fiction, he is an expert in e-publication, audio production and zombies.

THE HERESY STARTS HERE...

Discover the truth behind the legendary conflict that shaped the Warhammer 40,000 universe. The *New York Times* bestselling novel series begins in Horus Rising by Dan Abnett.

Available from

blacklibrary.com and all good bookshops

READ IT FIRST

EXCLUSIVE PRODUCTS | EARLY RELEASES | FREE DELIVERY

blacklibrary.com